The Funn

Geoff H

Dave,

You never know you may appear in the sequel!

Best wishes

Geoff

For Vicky, Tom and Nel.

Chapter 1

"Well, ya know, well um, ya know. Ya know, like that, I don't care how long it takes. I just want a good job doing, ya know, a good job, ya know, like that. Well, ya know, I hate spending money, but I may as well, ya know, 'bite the bullet' and have the job done properly, ya know, like that."

My eyebrows perform a backward somersault, and I stifle a squeak in the back of my throat. Wayne and I exchange the briefest of glances. Frank Knight hates spending money? Have the job done properly? Everyone knows that Frank will readily spend ten-grand when the same effect can be achieved with two; he believes that every pound spent adds ten to the value of his pile. His pile should be worth billions.

"What do you mean have the job done properly, Frank? It's only about twelve months since we last did this bathroom; I thought we did a good job of reproducing the one you found in that interior design magazine," I say defensively.

"Oh I'm not saying you didn't do a good job Charles," squawks Frank, glancing from me to Wayne, then 'dosey-doing' to the opposite end of the bathroom to maintain his space.

"No. Hell no. I'm not saying that at all," he blurts, sweeping his Bobby Charlton into place with his left hand, "I think, ya know I think ya know, you both did a fantastic job. It's ya know, it's ya know, nearly more like two years, and it's looking like, ya know, looking like shit," he explains, apparently to a white spattered area of exposed floor boarding. One of only a few that hasn't been covered by the enormous Tracy Emmins style sculpture, which could easily be entitled, The Unwashed Mountain.

"I don't think it's shit Frank," I say, catching Wayne's dumbstruck expression, "I think it's toothpaste; unless you've been keeping chickens in here."

Wayne snorts.

"Eh? What? Oh that. No not chickens," Frank squawks, studying the toothpaste spatter as though seeing it for the first time. "Toothpaste? I don't know how that got there - it must be the girls."

"I thought they had their own bathroom," I say casually, knowing full well that Wayne and I had only finished the girl's bathroom about six months ago.

"Eh? Oh they do. But ya know ya know, they're always, ya know, using this one."

"I suppose they're responsible for those as well," I suggest, nodding at the suspiciously bleached floor-boards around the toilet bowl.

"Eh? What?" yelps Frank, following my gaze, "Oh yeah, definitely…"

Wayne stifles another snort, and sounds as though his Adam's-apple's stuck in his windpipe.

It's not surprising my hearing has deteriorated since I've been working here, with Frank squawking at over a hundred decibels, like a throttled parrot every time someone speaks to him.

"…Oh definitely, yeah definitely the girls," repeats Frank, as though trying to convince himself as well as us.

"And there's me thinking you'd got to the age when you needed to sit down to pee Frank," I joke.

"Eh? What? No that's not me. No I don't need to ya know, I don't need to ya know, sit down to pee…" he says, manfully puffing out his chest and displaying his 'man-boobs', "…it's definitely, ya know definitely, definitely…"

"The girls?" I suggest.

"Yeah, the girls."

"So what do you want us to do?" asks Wayne, at last recovering his powers of speech and scratching his head that resembles a tennis ball that has over-wintered in a hedge bottom.

Apart from fumigate the place, I think, and take a deliberate step in Frank's direction, with predictable consequences.

Not long after I was first commissioned by Frank several years ago, I became aware of one of his many idiosyncrasies. He seems very protective of his own space, and dislikes anyone from invading it; he appears alarmed and automatically backs away to maintain an acceptable distance. Being aware of this, we often manoeuvre him around; like schoolboys playing with magnets. When indoors, Frank will suddenly 'dosy- do' down to the opposite end of the room; as though encouraging us to take part in a ceilidh. I often wonder whether he'd had an uncomfortable experience in the school showers - Or was it just my B.O?

"Well ya know, ya know, I'd just like you to ya know…"
"Do a good job?" I suggest helpfully.
"Yeah, ya know," he pants, backing into the space between the bath and the hand-basin, "…Ya know, I'd just like a ya know, good job doing," he stutters, apparently addressing a discarded pair of pink 'apple-catchers' beside the bath… Lack of eye-contact is another of his many idiosyncrasies.

I'm surprised Frank isn't really fit from all the darting around the room that he does. He looks ten years older than his forty-two. He looks more like a composite cartoon character with every passing week. According to Frank, he's six foot two, but I'm a gnat's todger under five eleven, and taller than him by an inch or so. I would estimate his weight to be between sixteen and eighteen stone; with about half of it in the middle. I'm always surprised, and impressed at Frank's nimbleness around 'the dance-floor', considering his legs weren't designed for what is now expected of them. His tight trousers and flapping boot-straps give the impression of frog's legs; yet he pings about the room to maintain his personal space like a ball-bearing in a pinball machine.

The front door opens, immediately followed by a breathy, "Hi!" The house then shudders as though receiving a visit from an anti-terrorist squad, as Nisha throws the front door to behind her with the finesse of a Russian shot-putter. Wayne and I flinch and visibly start, despite the years of experience. Frank seems oblivious.

"Nisha back from the school run already?" I ask, stating the obvious.

Frank sighs and moves to glide out of his safe harbour, but then appears to think better of it. "Hi Ni. We're in the bathroom – our bathroom," he clarifies unnecessarily, fearing she could waste valuable life-saving seconds.

"Oh yes," she calls back, laughing suggestively.

Wayne and I laugh. Frank looks decidedly uncomfortable at the suggestion that his sexuality is being questioned. He unconsciously presses his backside firmly against the wall, and returns his wayward locks with a sweep of a stubby hand; patting it as if commanding a dog to sit.

I'm sure he'll still be maintaining a phantom sixties style, Bobby Charlton, long after he's completely lost it; producing a burnished dome.

Nisha's heavy tread can be heard ascending the stairs, together with her increasingly heavy breathing.

I wonder whether she moonlights on one of those adult phone lines.

Frank coughs, "Can you come and tell us what you want doing in here," he asks nervously.

"Ooh, I don't think I want to share my fantasies with these two," she wheezes, leaning on the door frame, smiling from Wayne to me. "'Morning boys…"

"Morning Nisha," we chorus.

"…What do you mean, what do I want doing in here? This is the first I've known about this – I didn't know anyone was going to be working in here," she says flatly, surveying the room as though seeing it for the first time. "God, how embarrassing."
"Oh, I've seen far worse," I lie gallantly.

I've seen farmyards more sterile.
"Eh? What? What's wrong with it?" asks a bewildered Frank, surveying the room.

Nisha's eyes and mouth widen, simultaneously. She slowly shakes her head in disbelief, causing her thick black mane to shift like a wilted Busby while closing her eyes and mouth, respectively.

"You're supposed to be the self-confessed picky bastard," she says, levelling her chocolate eyes on Frank, who seems to visibly inflate with pride. "… you pick the smallest faults with the men's work and yet…"

Yeah, I've screwed dado rails in more positions than a porn star.

Nisha's roving eyes sweep the mahogany effect window board spattered with dollops of toothpaste, interspersed with assorted mugs, and wine glasses containing ancient vestiges. Several mugs contain a dark suede skin covered with an assortment of yellow, white and dark green crop circles of culture; giving the impression of a liberal sprinkling of corn-plasters across their surface. Some of the mugs contain several razors, and associated his and hers shaving paraphernalia, and toothbrushes showing varying degrees of wear. The disturbed dust and fluff being the only indication of those in current use. A sprinkling of cotton wool buds and an open box of tampons, interspersed with a few strategically placed tea-lights for atmospheric effect completes this shrine to The Domestic Goddess. Nisha's gaze takes in the mountain of laundry, which has almost spread into a carpet, and the various stained floorboards, and eventually settles on the bath.

"... Frank you could have cleaned the bath after you'd used it this morning! It's a wonder you've got any hair left!" she blurts, nodding towards the plug-hole. "It looks like a grubby snowman - complete with pubes, or..."
"Snow-woman," I correct, and that's definitely not a 'Brazilian', I think, wondering whether she meant a snowman bending over.
"Eh? What?" shrieks Frank.
"There's no balls," I explain.
"Eh?" puzzles Frank.
"Okay, snow-woman then," Nisha concedes, suppressing a laugh.
"...I could have at least got rid of the pile of washing if I'd known..."

"I thought you'd be pleased..."
"Pleased? Why should I be pleased? None of these projects are to please me..."

I find it incredible to believe that the woman now standing in the doorway is the same, slim attractive woman captured in the various photos, scattered throughout the house.
Nisha is forty-two, about five foot three. Her features reflect her ancestry. She has lovely thick black shoulder length wavy hair, and permanently fading tan; the result of a couple of generations of mixed race unions which apparently included some Indian.

Her weight increase is divided equally between her stomach and her bottom. Mind you her breasts have grown from oranges, to melons. Her stomach resembles that of a heavily pregnant woman, which is very attractive, on a heavily pregnant woman; it's exactly the same shape as Frank's. It provides a useful perch for the ample breasts, like a pair of pigeons roosting on a window sill - I half expect them to coo.

However, Nisha still denies all the evidence, and appears to force herself into the same size eights. Very often, a carbuncle of coffee coloured flesh, marbled with stretch marks, like silverside beef, is revealed between an ascending top, and the ligature of a waistband.

Nisha permanently displays the symptoms of someone suffering the early symptoms of a summer cold. She habitually sniffs every twenty or thirty seconds, always up the right nostril, producing a mouse like twitch of the nose. However it is far more marked when prefacing speech, when her nose deflects considerably and her right eye appears to wink, and distorts her face.

Her size sixteen accessories are now jiggling with pent up emotion; like a couple of bald cyclists on a cobbled street. Nisha sniffs and winks at Frank.

"…this must be the first time you've ever consulted me on any of these, 'projects'…" she protests, making a rabbit's ears gesture, with two fingers either side of her head.

"What do you think I'm doing?" shrieks Frank, "I'm consulting you now!"

"Yes, *now*, being the operative word - as usual I'm presented with a fait accompli…"

You're lucky that's all you're presented with, I think glancing at the knicker mountain.

"…There's hardly been a week since we moved here that there hasn't been workmen in the house; I think I know them better than I know you," she states.

I resist the urge to say, 'You'd think you'd know how I like my coffee by now then'. Instead I try to conceal my embarrassment by feigning an interest in the plumbing. Frank feigns an interest in his wife's protestations, by assuming a stung expression.

Wayne doesn't bother to conceal his interest and enjoyment in someone else's 'domestic'. He's been following the exchanges between Frank and Nisha like a spectator at Wimbledon. A modified version of the Elvis Costello number springs to mind, 'Watching The Domestic'.

Frank's shrew like nose twitches with nervous tension. The turned up end, reddened from alcohol, gives the impression of already having recently met with an opposing force; the dark teabags below his two small sapphire blue eyes only reinforce this image. His red wattle cheeks and double chins all quiver like a trifle on a food-trolley with a sticky wheel.

"So are we going to be without a bathroom? - I don't want to be without a bathroom for as long as the girls were…"

Nisha catches my affronted expression, and checks Wayne's reaction, to see if she's about to be lynched. She needn't have worried; Wayne's more interested in her wobbly bits than the actual dialogue. However, sensing that he might have somehow unexpectedly become implicated in the proceedings, twitches his mouth in a nervous smile; like a pair of curtains being opened then instantly drawn.

"…sorry Charles, Wayne, I know it wasn't your fault- If his lordship wasn't such a picky bastard and changed his mind so many times, you could have had it done in a week - instead of a couple of months."

"Eh? What? I just want it ya know, I just want it ya know to look right…I like ya know, I like ya know beautiful things ya know, like that…. I want my ya know, I want my ya know home to be beautiful like that."

"Yeah, I realise that Frank," I say, resisting the urge to admire the current state of this bathroom, "It was real 'Homes and Gardens' when we finished last time."

Pity you didn't keep it like that.

"Oi, cheeky," Nisha laughs throatily, "…you mean, it's a pity we didn't keep it like that.

You're right about knowing me.

"Well, when are we going to choose the new suite Darling, or have you already done that?"
"No that's not my department; that's down to you and Frank," I say.
"Eh? What?" Frank looks bewildered.
"Oi cheeky, I wouldn't call you Darling," Nisha again laughs throatily, "Well shouldn't we have the new suite ready to put in before they take the old one out?" she argues.

Wayne and I nod sagely in the background.
"Yeah. Well we can go and have a look today- but they've got ya know loads to do, ya know loads to do before ya know, the new suite can ya know, the new suite can ya know go in like that."
"Like what?" asks Nisha.

Yeah. Like what?

Frank frantically castes about for inspiration, "Eh? Well like, yeah well like, after the old suite has been taken out ya know, after the old suite has been taken out like that, Wayne has got to retile the ya know, retile the shower like that..."
"Retile the shower? What's wrong with those?"
"They're shit quality..."
"What? They were really expensive."
"They're shit. I want it done ya know, I want it done ya know, properly I want some real quality tiles like that... Charles has got to ya know, Charles has got to ya know, change the floor, and ya know ya know, do things... like that."

That's nice to know.

"Sounds like you've already planned it. What was all that, come and tell me what you want in the bathroom, business? Am I allowed to choose the toilet roll holder?" she adds sarcastically, before flouncing for the door, where she stops and turns around, "If we're sharing the girls bathroom, you'd better improve your aim; or start sitting down... I'm not having their bathroom ruined as well, we've only just had it done," she adds, before stomping through their bedroom.

"Eh? What? That's not me that's the girls!"

Yeah, we believe you Frank.

"There are benefits to sitting down to pee Frank; especially in the wee hours, so to speak," I say encouragingly.

Frank and Wayne look at me as though I'm about to 'come out'.

"Yeah, at least you don't have to turn the light on and risk frying your eyeballs…

Perhaps that's been the trouble; maybe he doesn't.

"…The worst bit is when your todger touches the cold water," I add, trying to keep a straight-face.

Wayne takes a few seconds to compute this information before his tentative curtain twitching grin breaks across his face, into a full curtain raiser, "Oh yeah, braggin' again."

"Well I'll leave it with you, I'm sure you'll ya know, I'm sure you'll ya know, do a good job," Frank announces feebly, again addressing a distant undergarment, adding, "I'll see you both at lunch time."

Wayne and I take a leaf out of Frank's book by avoiding eye contact by studying the site of the latest Frank Knight project in an effort to contain our childish hysterics. Our ears strain. I hold a finger to my mouth, as we monitor Frank's progress down the stairs, listening for the opening and slamming of the front door, followed by the roaring Range Rover accelerating across the gravelled car park. Instead we hear raised voices.

"I thought he was going to take refuge in the shower cubicle," I hiss.

"Charles bloody Wilson! You'll get us in deep shit one of these days!" hisses Wayne, "…you'll be back in your fuckin' workshop, all alone; with no-one to have a laugh with," he whispers with mock concern.

The raised voices reach a crescendo; indicating the imminent departure of at least one protagonist.

"Hey-up. Stand by your beds," I whisper, "I bet Nisha heads this way."

The stomping and wheezing on the stairs is accompanied by the opening and slamming of the front door.

"That poor door," I mutter, "…replacing that'll be the next job."

Wayne wheezes.

I follow the laboured progress of Nisha as she crests the stairs, heaves herself onto the landing and heads in our direction. I'm also aware that I haven't heard the customary roar of Frank's Range Rover as he attempts to impersonate a rally driver spraying gravel across the car-park.

"Sorry boys, I didn't mean to embarrass you," Nisha wheezes apologetically, like a pair of moth-eaten bellows as she enters the bathroom, "…but Frank can be such a…"

"Oh, that's okay, there's nothing like a healthy exchange of views," I say in a theatrically loud manner…

And that was nothing like a healthy exchange I think, while surreptitiously positioning myself to afford a view of the dressing table mirror in the bedroom.

"…So where are you and Frank going to view bathrooms, Nisha?" I continue stage whispering to a bemused audience, while keeping a weather eye on the reflection in the mirror.

"Christ knows. We'll be lucky if it's done by Christmas…"

"Would you like it wrapping then?" I say dryly, observing Frank's reflection, hovering outside the bedroom door. I pray Nisha doesn't say anything flirtatious.

"That's not funny Charles."

"So, you're sick of the sight of us are you?" I feign affront.

"Wouldn't you be? It's been nearly ten years non-stop… It's so difficult to keep the house clean and tidy," she moans.

So I've noticed. I avoid eye contact with Wayne. I marvel at how quietly Frank had sneaked up the stairs. For a fat'n he can move like a cat; a fat cat in more ways than one. I have a horrible mental image of him doing what cats are best known for – and I don't mean slaughtering the wildlife.

"You'll be sorry when we've gone," I say, trying not to show my amusement at the sight of Frank attempting to avoid disclosing his presence by holding his breath.

"Oh yeah, of course I will – like haemorrhoids," she says facetiously. "Will you miss me?" she adds suggestively.

Like you say, like haemorrhoids.

"Well this isn't getting the bairns new shoes," I announce in a pretty suspect Scottish accent, then add, "…I'd best get some tools up here," as I disappear through the doorway.

"Oh Hi Frank, I thought you'd gone ages ago."

"Eh? What? Oh, Charles I couldn't ya know, I couldn't ya know find my, er car keys like that," he blurts, scrabbling like a terrier at a rabbit-hole, amongst the flotsam on top of the bookcase.

Frank's expression suggests he might also have lost control of his sphincter muscle.

"Or your boots," I observe, looking at his stockinged feet, before continuing, "…Aren't they on the hall table, I thought I saw them there when I came in? – Perhaps Nisha put her bag on top of them when she came back from the school run," I offer helpfully.

"Frank? I thought you'd gone…"

"Bye Ni, I'm going to be late. I'm expecting an important phone call at the office," he calls back while descending the stairs at a worrying speed, his padding feet sounding like a drum roll. Pausing to slip frantically into his leather soled ankle boots and snatch up his car keys by the front door, which is then also snatched and left wide open, allowing the tip-tap of leather soles retreating on the rustic looking block pathway to be heard by a bemused Nisha who has joined me on the landing.

"Sounds like he's wearing high-heels," I laugh at the image of Frank in drag.
Nisha ignores this comment and studies me for a few uncomfortable seconds before regarding the open front door and silently digesting events.

"Well, we'd better get on with it… Any chance of clearing the washing out while we prepare our tools?"
"Uuugh, what a revolting thought," she laughs.
"I'm sure the washing isn't that bad."
"Ha ha."
"Well a nice cup of coffee after will help us all get over it," I hint, scooting out of the door.

*****

"Uuugh!" Wayne grimaces, "Did ya have t' ask for coffee? Ya know it's disgustin'."
"I know," I cringe, "…but it makes her feel useful," I laugh.
"That is stretching the fuckin' 'magination," Wayne wheezes, watching me select tools from my van, "…it wouldn't be so bad if she boiled the fuckin' kettle."
"She does boil the kettle; there's just too long a delay between the kettle boiling and making the coffee," I laugh dryly.
"Yeah, by about half a fuckin' hour."
"Her tea is even worse."

I look pointedly at his empty hands.
"What?"
"Are you going to undo the plumbing with your bare hands?"
"I ain't got any fuckin' plumbing tools; I'm a fuckin' bricklayer," he protests, "…I thought I was goin' t' be workin' on the fuckin' patio; I'm never going t' finish the fucker at this rate."
"And I'm supposed to be a cabinet maker and furniture restorer – but I've been coming to this mad house for about eight years, so I

try to bring tools for every eventuality; 'cos I never know what I'm going to be doing 'cos Frank changes his mind more often than Jenson Button changes gear.

"You've been working here longer than me. When's the last time you did any brickwork here? I'm surprised you haven't built up a collection of tools – of your own."

I bet you've got a good collection of mine in your garage. "Why should I buy tools to fuckin' work here? I've got all the bricklaying tools I need; if he wants me to do plumbing and electrics and whatever, he should provide the fuckin' tools," he states emphatically.

He is a bricklayer by trade, a bloody good bricklayer I have to admit; a bit of a cowboy at everything else though. He's worked regularly for Frank for nearly ten years, evolving into something of a 'Jack of all trades'. He can turn his hand to basic plumbing, electrics, tiling and general building. However he avoids decorating, and is kept well away from woodwork; unless it's to be buried under plasterboard. Wayne only has to pick up a piece of timber, and it immediately looks as though it's received the attention of a frenzied beaver – with broken teeth.

"I bet you've got more tools for your metal detecting than for working here – or do you expect the farmers to provide you with a metal detector?"

"Actually I've just upgraded me machine," he says brightening at the prospect of discussing his real passion. "Are you interested in me old one; it's a good un?"

On cue Wayne's mobile warbles a theme tune that I half recognise. He retrieves it from his back pocket and answers it with a deftness usually reserved for his brick trowel.

"Hello. Wayne Hall? Yes speaking… sorry we seem to be breaking up…An Edward the Second hammered Gold Quarter Noble? Sorry could you bear with me while I try and find a better signal?"

Wayne lumbers bear like across the lawn and up the immaculately mown field, the steep gradient causing him to respond in breathless gulps.

"…Yes, very fine…best I've ever found…"

You have to admire the way he switches effortlessly from effin Wayne the brickie, to the articulate, knowledgeable and successful treasure hunter.

Wayne is thirty three years old, and about the same height as Frank; but his 'Bank's baby' beer belly is only half the size, however he probably weighs at least a stone more than me; about fifteen stone. Between his grubby tennis-ball haircut, and his round face, made matching by permanent brown stubble, are his small shiny brown eyes and nose; like conkers newly liberated from their padded shells…I've long had my suspicions on how he acquired one of his shiny brown features.

Wayne's great passion is his treasure hunting, which he probably holds above his wife Sally, and their three year old daughter; known by the sobriquets 'the missus' and 'the little un'. It's so long since I heard his daughter's name that I've forgotten what it is.

Returning to the bathroom, I'm confronted on the stairs by an enormous bundle of laundry, grunting its slow descent.

"I hope that's you in there Nisha, and it's not moving under its own steam – if you'll pardon the unfortunate choice of phrase."
"Oy, you cheeky bugger," grunts the muffled crusty bloomers, "…these aren't steaming – You won't get a coffee."

Is that supposed to be a threat or a promise, I wonder? I don't suppose that'll be steaming either.
"Do you need a hand?" I ask, praying she doesn't.
"No it's okay, this is the last lot," she grunts.

*****

"Here," wheezes Nisha, proffering a couple of mugs. "Where's Wayne?"

"Thanks," I say feigning delight as I take the congealing coffees from her, "…I'll just put them on the window sill to cool…"

I hope the finely balanced eco-system of the sceptic tank can tolerate two more caffeine injections, once Nisha has gone.

"…Wayne's up in his office – building his pension fund," I laugh, nodding through the now open window toward the figure reclining on the boundary fence halfway up the field, enjoying an animated conversation on his mobile.

Nisha raises her eyes, chews the right hand corner of her of her mouth and slowly shakes her head, "Well his coffee will be cold – I'm not making him another."

Why should he get away with it?

"So how are the girls getting on?"

Nisha brightens at her favourite subject; her second being food.

"Oh fine. They're doing really well," she beams, "Sophie is doing really well at sixth form; working really hard- and Alice is doing really well at school, really enjoying her GCSE's; she got top marks for her year in a recent maths exam."

"Oh well done - Sophie must be seventeen soon, is she going to start driving lessons?"

""Yes, fifteenth of April, how did you remember? I'm impressed."

"I only remembered it was sometime in April because it's the same month as Adam's; I can't remember any of your others."

"What? You mean you don't remember mine?"

"I have enough of a job to remember my own family's," I laugh.

"Hmmph," she feigns injury, before continuing, "…yes she's sent off for her provisional licence, and her granddad's, Frank's father

not mine," she laughs at the idea of her father being affluent or indulgent enough, "… buying her a brand new car – one of those little Toyota's."
"Lucky girl…

Spoilt sod.
"…Yeah I couldn't imagine your dad spoiling her like that - he's got more sense," I half joke. "So the business is obviously doing okay then."
"Yeah, Frank says they've picked up some really good orders recently," she answers guardedly.

I laugh. "Don't worry I wasn't thinking of hitting Frank with a rate rise - but now I think of it…"

Nisha laughs and glances out of the window as if checking Wayne's whereabouts; she needn't have worried, Wayne is still propping up a fence post. "You've only just increased your rate haven't you?"
"Yeah but the way fuel's going up…

"So what is it they actually do at the factory; Frank is always a bit vague when I ask him?
"Oh, something to do with plastic I think…"

God, talk about top secret.
"Really, that sounds interesting," I say somewhat insincerely.
"I don't think you'd find it particularly interesting…Frank never talks about it much."

"I just hope the tax-man never quizzes me about it - according to my invoices, I do a lot of maintenance at the factory; and I haven't a clue where it is or what they do there."
"Oh don't worry, your invoices are peanuts compared to all the other outgoings," she laughs dryly.
"I wondered why Frank treated me like a monkey," I laugh.

You mean, compared to all the company funds that gets spent on this place.

"It's not Frank that treats you like a monkey," she says pointedly looking at Wayne, "…how come you end up doing all the work?"
I shrug, "Saves me having to replace half my tools."
Nisha laughs, "Yeah I've noticed he never seems to have any – don't you get fed up lending him yours?"
"It's not the borrowing I mind; it's the state they come back in – if at all."
"How does he manage to break them – or lose them come to think of it?"
"Well let's just say he wouldn't get a long service award as a bomb disposal expert."
As for the 'lost' ones, it would take a search warrant to recover them.
"Are you saying he doesn't have a delicate touch?" she laughs.

He's light-fingered alright.

"I just wouldn't want him as my brain surgeon," I say dryly.

Nisha laughs briefly at the same time as watching Wayne lolling on the fence as though he were a boxer, desperate for the ref's intervention.

"So how's Alex getting on with her job, is she still enjoying being a Head?"
"Yeah I think so - she enjoys the challenge. It's the threats of school closures across the county that are getting her down at the moment; the axe is poised over hers – That, and one or two parents who seem to complain about the smallest things and then splatter it all over Facebook."
"What like?" she half laughs.
"Just petty stuff really - Like one of the kids seems to scuff her shoes regularly. You'd think the teachers dragged them around the playground, judging by the parent's reaction…

"Thing is I suppose, she has loads of other far more important things to do and worry about – planning and policies and other crap, that she can't get on with during the day at school; so ends up doing them at midnight at home."

"Ah ha, you mean she's too tired for a bit of nooky," she laughs.

I laugh dryly. "It's not just that – it affects everyone. I think Lizzie feels a bit neglected, Alex never has time to watch her playing sport; even at the weekends come to think of it."

"How is Lizzie getting on?"

"Well we never hear anything about her academic subjects, so we assume everything's okay– she's costing us a fortune in sports equipment though."

"Is she still playing netball?" laughs Nisha.

"What doesn't she play? Hockey, netball, rugby, cricket – if there's a ball involved she'll be there…

It's when two balls are involved that I'll be worried.

"… fortunately the rugby and hockey have almost finished until September; but now it's the athletics and cricket."

"Oh you poor thing," she coos, "…stop bloody moaning…

"How's Adam getting on, do you see much of him now he's left home?"

"No we only see him when he wants something; so no news is good news, as they say…He seems to be getting on okay at work – seems to be enjoying it anyway – maybe the novelty hasn't worn off yet," I laugh dryly.

"Maybe," Nisha laughs, "He's still doing landscape gardening then?"

"Yeah – They've left him to lay a patio for someone this week; very trusting of them."

"I hope he's quicker than Wayne," she snorts, "He's been working on this one for months," she says flatly, gesturing to the area below the bathroom window.

"Well I suppose to be fair; Frank does keep taking him off it for different projects – I've lost count of how many unfinished projects are on the go," I say lamely, knowing the real reason.
"Excuse me. You mean, to be fair, if Wayne got his fat carcase off the fence, he'd have less unfinished projects," Nisha bristles, challenging me to disagree.

I remain silent; I know she's right.

"See. You know I'm right," she triumphs, and turns to glare at the fat carcase hanging on the fence.
"In fact the only time I don't see him up there is when you, stop for a break, bait or whatever it is you call it."
"Well there's one way to test your theory," I say brightly, consulting my watch, "…it's about bait time."

Chapter 2

Lizzie holds the phone out to me with one hand covering, "For you, I think it's Frank."
"Oh ffflipin' 'eck!" I mouth. I take the phone and a deep breath and look skyward, "Hi Frank everything alright."
"Oh yeah hi. Hi Charles, sorry to ring you in the evening. Is it convenient?"
"Well I was about to…"
"Well ya know what I was thinking Charles… ya know what I was thinking was, ya know, ya know I was thinking…"
"I thought I'd pick up the floor-boards on the way in," I offer in an attempt to jolt the needle and move the record on, "… so that I can make a start replacing the floor- we've nearly finished removing all the fittings, only the shower…"

"Um yeah, well um, ya know…"

Oh fffor crying out loud; change of plan.
"…I was thinking ya know like that…"

Dangerous.
"… I was thinking ya know, Nisha hasn't decided what we're having on the floor."

Nisha hasn't decided? I manage to avoid spluttering.
"So I was ya know thinking,"
"Yes?"
"Yeah I was thinking ya know, I was thinking like that about replacing the worktops in the kitchen. I was thinking ya know, about granite."

I raise my eyes to the ceiling yet again. Yeah you'll be getting granite sooner than you think, in the form of a headstone; once Nisha hears this. I wonder why this conversation couldn't have waited until tomorrow, and whether I shall ever finish any of the dozens of jobs I've started.

"Granite, that's nice - When?" I wonder if he does anything at the office apart from trawl through interiors magazine.
"Yeah granite, I think it'll look really good. I was thinking ya know, I was thinking those tiles that are there now, they're a bastard to keep clean, and they're looking pretty crap now - I mean they were really good quality at the time, they've been down more than fifteen years and they were really expensive ya know like that…"

I risk laying the phone down on speaker mode to finish serving and eating dinner; I know from experience that he'll go for hours without expecting a response from me. I've been chasing my tail since rushing home from The Funny Farm. I've fed and walked the dog, seen to the chickens, put on a sausage casserole and prepared the veg., and then rushed over to Hereford to collect Lizzie from an inter school athletics.

I was just enjoying a nice relaxing merlot while waiting for the spuds to boil and wondering whether Alex would be back in time to sit down with us.

"…really expensive, I mean really expensive…"
"Not cheap then," I say.
"What! No. God no, not cheap, they were really expensive, really good quality, ya know but they're breaking up now…"

I wish this bloody phone-line would.
"…they look really scratched to shit. Ya know what I mean? Really crap…"

I wonder how he knows, they're usually hidden under a pile of dirty dishes; the last time he'd have seen them would have been the day they were laid. I prod the spuds and broccoli with a sharp pointed knife. Turning off the hob I mouth to Lizzie to drain the veg and serve. She laughs at my predicament; she's witnessed these calls before.

During the day I just say that a customer has turned up; but an evening visit is less plausible. I collect the butter-dish and plonk it down on the kitchen table.

"…so I was thinking granite ya know like that… and I thought we might as well change the oven unit while we're at it, and I thought the fridge unit like that ya know. The sink unit looks shit so we might as well change that as well while we're at it…"

I pour myself another glass and swirl it around then admire the legs while half listening to Frank.

The units don't need replacing; they just need a good clean. I take a large sip, Alex would call it a gulp, which has probably left me with tell-tale ruddy tusks, "Mmmm, just what I needed," I say appreciatively, raising my glass to the phone.

"Eh! What! Yeah exactly!" squawks Frank, "That's what I thought, they need changing so we may as well do it all at the same time…"

Lizzie and I exchange grins, she has almost collapsed into the spuds, tears running down her cheeks. I help her serve up, keeping one ear out for any change in Frank's tone that might indicate that he's expecting a response. I guess at random contributions whenever Frank pauses, "Really?" or, "Yeah, that sounds good," or just, "Mmm, possibly," he never actually takes advice or listens to opinions from anyone anyway.

I move the phone to the table, "I must go now Frank, Lizzie has just served up dinner," I know it won't have registered with him, so Lizzie and I just carry on with our meal at the opposite end of the table and discuss her day and taxi requirements for the next few days in lowered tones.

"Eh! Okay, I won't keep you … the brass socket fronts and switches are looking really crap now as well, they're looking reeeally scratched to shit so I'll get some more of those ordered…."

"Yeah, that sounds good."

"What have you got after school tomorrow?"

"What day's that? Oh yeah, Tuesday – rounders I think."
"What time does that finish?"
"I need picking up at six."

I raise my eyebrows expectantly.

"Pleeease can you pick me up at six o' clock?" she pleads with a false grin as wide as a piano keyboard.

"…. Nisha wants one of those white ceramic sinks, they look really good, reeeally stylish ya know like that, they're reeeally expensive like that…"

That's a laugh, the first Nisha will know about the new sink, as with any other project that Frank credits her with, is when it arrives.

"Have you got hockey on Saturday, or has the season finished?"

"Yeah, but I don't know what time yet, and there might be some matches that got cancelled in January," Lizzie replies in that tone that suggests that I'm being unreasonable.

"Can't you text Clare? It would be nice to plan my weekend you know…I know you think I just sit about with your private taxi all fuelled up, ready and waiting."

"Yees Daad," she sighs, with that 'change the record' tone.

To dissipate the tension I offer more casserole.

She tilts her head and considers, "Mmm, yes actually I think I will I'm starving. Are the new potatoes ours? D'you want some more?"

"No it's a bit early yet, I haven't even planted ours yet. No thanks, I'm stuffed …. Can you make sure you leave plenty for your mother?"

"You must give me the recipe sometime," she effects, while taking the plates. "…What do you call this little creation?"

I pause to consider an appropriate name, "Little Eric."

"Little Eric? I thought that was Frank's gardener's name?"

"Yeah, they're both well marinated."

She looks at me rather pointedly and inclines her head, “Pots and kettles…Think I’ll have a banana instead.”

“What? I don’t breakfast on whisky and need topping up all day …Put the kettle on for coffee while you’re up there… pleeease,” I plead.

I drain my glass and refill it, draining the bottle. “I’m sure they don’t make them as big as they used to,” I say holding the empty bottle to the light for inspection.

“Eh! What!”

“Christ I’d forgotten about him,” I mutter.

“The bottles are the same; they just make the glasses bigger,” says Lizzie, laughing at Frank’s participation in our evening meal. “Does that make you an optimist or a pessimist – thinking the bottle is only half the size?” she laughs.

“Ha. Ha, don’t give up your day job,” I say, secretly admiring her humour; not bad for fourteen

I quickly direct my raised voice at the phone, “I said they don’t make sinks as big as they used to Frank.”

“Eh! Oh no! This is really big, the biggest they do, fantastic quality like that, really expensive. They’re normally several hundred pounds ya know like that, ya know, but ya know I managed to do a deal ya know like that…”

Lizzie returns grinning and shaking her head, then suddenly remembers something, “Oh yeah, Katt’s having a party on Saturday night, can I go?”

“Haven’t you got netball or cricket on Sunday? … I don’t want to have to come and get you from Hereford first, if we’ve got to be in Walsall or wherever for nine…you know how useless you’ll be after being up all night.”

“What, so I can’t go?”

“….so I was thinking that tomorrow after ya know, after you ya know you’ve finished removing ya know the bathroom fittings like that, you could ya know, make a template of the worktops, ya know like that, the one with the sink and hob to start with like that, and have a measure up so that I can get some prices…And Barry can come in and start ya know decorating in the bathroom like that."

I stare irritably at the phone. Why do we always do everything arse-back'ards. I cock an ear to assess whether Frank requires a response, but he doesn't pause.

I return my attention to Lizzie, "I didn't say you couldn't go, I just don't think it's a good idea to stay over. I know you lot, you won't get any sleep… then you'll be crabby as hell for the rest of the weekend….and if you've got sport Sunday morning it'll be an early enough start without having to collect you from Hereford to start with…I'd rather collect you from Katt's on Saturday night."

"Not toooo early!" she wails.

"Eh! What!" yelps a distant Frank. Lizzie stifles a laugh with a hand, and Frank continues, "No no, normal time, I was thinking if you did it first thing, so that I'd have them for lunch time like that ya know, then I can …."

"Er where was I? Oh yeah. No, I think midnight is plenty late enough…actually I'm not sure whether your mum and I are out Saturday night."

"Talking of which," says Lizzie picking up the empty wine bottle, "…you've drunk a whole bottle, you'd better get rid of the evidence before mum comes home; unless you enjoy being nagged….she's right though, you *are* drinking too much."

"Don't you start," I respond with more than a hint if irritation; but I'm forced to think about Little Eric.

"And don't forget to get rid of your tusks," adds Lizzie.

I'm halfway to the backdoor with the empty bottle when I remember Frank is still babbling away on the phone. I remember the ploy Barry uses to get him off the phone.

I mouth to Lizzie to ring the doorbell then hold the phone near Ebony's bed where she's lying flat out with her legs in the air. As soon as the doorbell announces a new crotch to ram her nose into, with its urgent old-fashioned no nonsense alarm bell, Ebony unwinds herself in a blur and scrabbles to her feet in an uncharacteristic display of agility, usually only reserved for scavenging scraps of food, and goosing my elderly female customers. She releases a series of deep resonating barks; her legs and feet flail in a 'wheel spin' on the quarry tiles and flagstones while attempting to charge the front door.

"Christ! Shit! What the fuck was that?" shrieks Frank.
"Oh sorry Frank, that was the dog, somebody at the door. I'd better go; I'll see you in the morning okay."
"Eh! What! Oh okay. Yeah see you in the morning," Frank splutters.

Ebony slinks back to her bed wearing an embarrassed expression, with her twitching tail tucked between her legs, sensing that she is the butt of a practical joke and the source of Lizzie's hysteria; not realising she is a hero.

Lizzie leaves me to clear away the rest of the dinner things by disappearing to the office computer on the pretext of doing homework.

"Let's have less Facebook or whatever it's called, and more homework then!" I call after her.

Instinctively I glance at the old school wall clock as I make myself a coffee, and then automatically check it against my watch, which shows twenty-to-eight, the clock is set five minutes fast as it helps in the battle to catch the school bus.

******

I'm engrossed in the last few chapters of my latest Ian Rankin novel when a hundredweight or so of schoolbooks with familiar legs bursts through the front door. The books are unceremoniously dumped on the sofa and bounce a couple of times before settling; like a child suddenly remembering the lecture about respecting the furniture.

"Oh Christ! What a shit day I've had!"

I instinctively glance at my watch, quarter past eight. Lovely to see you too dear, I think, but instantly regret saying the equally inflammatory, "Do you ever have anything else?"

"What's that supposed to mean?" she snaps.

"What's what supposed to mean," I reply, knowing full well what *that's* supposed to mean and wishing I'd just kept my mouth shut; or mumbled an appropriate supplicant.

"What's, *do you ever have anything else*, supposed to mean?"

"Well you say the same thing every day."

"What?"

"That you've had a shit day."

"Well I have."

"I rest my case," I say with more than a hint of exasperation.

Alex whines, "I can't help it," as she stomps through to the kitchen,

You say that every day as well, I think.

Alex sniffs the air, "Have you two eaten? Where's Lizzie?"

"Yes thanks. Yours is in the oven, we couldn't wait any longer…you said you'd be back at six… She's on the computer. Ask her how she got on with the discus and javelin today."

"I couldn't help it," she predictably whines and I mouth the words.

I'll have that put on your gravestone.

"Has she had athletics today then?"

I raise my eyes, "The inter schools between Bishop's, St. Mary's and The Cathedral."

"You don't have to say it like that, I can't remember everything."

The tee hinges on the office door squeal as a scowling Lizzie emerges and breezes through the sitting room to the kitchen, "You two are like a pair of kids."

"It's not me, it's your father; he's the mardy one," Alex moans defensively, "…How did you get on today?"
Lizzie looks blank for a few seconds, "Oh the athletics, I came first in the javelin, and second in the discus," she says matter-o-factly. Then more brightly, "Mum… Katt's having a party on Saturday night… can I go? Can I stop over?"

My mouth drops open in disbelief.

"Yes, I should…"
"We've already had this discussion you cheeky madam, I said…"
"Oh it doesn't matter," Alex cuts in, "…she hasn't got school the next day."
"No but if she's got to be at Walsall for quarter past eight…"
"Oh I didn't know did I, you didn't say…"
"I shouldn't have to - When's the last time she didn't have something on a Sunday; or nearly every other day come to that. Perhaps if you could take your head out of the computer for five minutes you'd know what…"
"Oh that's right, blame me!" Alex shrieks, as I mentally mimic this stock response knowing the next part.
"I'll give up my job then!"
"I couldn't earn enough to cover the phone bills if you were home all day," I say, hinting at the monthly arguments.
"Well get a proper job then!"

"Oh shut up!" screams Lizzie

"Don't tell me to shut up, this is all your fault anyway - trying to get your mother to undermine me!"

Lizzie flounces through the door leading to the hall and stairs, "No wonder Adam left home as soon as possible, I bet he couldn't…"
"At this rate I'll be following," I cut in, "I'm fed up being treated like a piece of shit."

Alex storms off into the office slamming the door hard enough to cause an expensive if not time consuming splintering sound; and the eighteenth century two foot thick stone walls to tremble. Lizzie stares motionless at me apart from her bottom lip trembling, her eyes overflowing down her cheeks, her mascara turning into a snowman's puddles of coal eyes. She silently implores me to withdraw that last remark.

My head flashes through rapidly changing scenarios; for the sake of maintaining status quo, I regret my outburst. On the other hand I want to get everything into the open; tell Alex I'm sick of being in this lonely loveless marriage, tell her that I've only stayed because of Adam and Lizzie and now Adam has left.

Suddenly I'm drained of energy and emotion, I feel my head aching and my body deflate and crumple. Lizzie interprets this defeatist posture as a reluctance to deny my desire to leave. Her face folds like a foam doll's, and emits an unintelligible wail that seems to start deep inside and becomes momentarily strangled in her throat before bursting out and tearing at my chest.

I quickly step forward wrapping her in my arms and pulling her face into my chest; muffling the sobs and smearing my shirt with snot and mascara.

"No. I'm not going anywhere," I mumble, trying to comfort but failing to sound convincing.

I haven't the money or the guts to.

Chapter 3

Chris Rea sings, ‘this is the road to hell’, as I swing into the lane leading to The Grange. It could just as easily be, ‘The Road *From* Hell,’ thinking back to last night.

I’d lain awake, seemingly all-night, my mind running and rerunning the various scenarios and their implications and repercussions. Alex huffed and sighed to let me know that she wasn’t sleeping either, and to make sure there was absolutely no danger of me getting any she would regularly and violently toss and turn at seemingly calculated intervals. It was like sharing the bed with a crocodile performing a death-roll with the duvet.

A tentative tug to re-cover myself told me that she had it wound tight around her. The sense that she was daring me to retrieve my share and risk accusations of a cartoon style assault was palpable. I permitted myself a brief devilish smile in the dark, at the cartoon image of her spinning horizontally out of her side of the bed.

I’d simply put on my dressing gown and lain on my permitted strip of bed.

Pulling onto the car park I’m reminded of the first time I came here to look at some furniture; I can’t believe it’s nearly eight years. Obviously you don’t have to be enjoying yourself for time to fly.

Originally, Frank contacted me regarding restoring some furniture that he’d brought back from France. The first phone call lasted nearly an hour, during which time I’d changed ears and hands several times to massage the ‘pins and needles’ away, and restore the circulation to both hand and ear lobe. At the end of the phone call I was still none the wiser about whether he was a dealer, or serious collector. He kept going on about Louis XV this, and

Louis XVI that. He made several references to Napoleon trois, which I always felt was rather pretentious; after all we don't say Louis quinze or Louis seize.

Most people in the trade just refer to that distinctive neoclassical period of French furniture and architecture, which I assumed Frank was referring to, as French Empire, which only lasted from about 1790 to 1810. Whereas Napoleon *Trois*, ruled from 1852 to 1870

At the time I had about twelve months work in hand. I could afford to be choosy. I didn't want any more dealers, in fact, I was trying to get rid of them; they were a pain in the arse. They invariably paid too much for the piece at auction, expected to clutter my workshop by dropping it straight off on their way home from the saleroom, screw me down on the price, and have it done 'the day before yesterday'; if not sooner.

There had been a few dealers that knew the difference between Chippendale and Chipboard. They'd been really helpful in the early days, sharing their knowledge and genuine passion for antiques; but they'd gone 'tits up' in the early 90's recession - There was obviously a lesson there.

After being routinely pestered for about six months, by hour long calls, I thought it would be easier if I agreed to visit Frank at his home, and look at his, *absolutely fantastic collection of quality, French, period furniture; absolutely fantastic!* How could I refuse such a treat?

I'd pulled onto the car park at The Grange, and was greeted by someone obviously proud of his home. The customary hand shaking was like trying to guess the weight of a dead fish, while he appeared to check for dandruff on his left shoulder. Frank then led the way towards the house while repeating, "Lovely isn't it? Lovely isn't it?" and sweeping an arm towards the two and a half acre immaculately manicured lawn; as though feeding the brace of pheasants that appeared to vainly forage a billiard table.

Well I'm not exactly a diplomat, but I know better than to upset a prospective client; especially one that is obviously loaded. I agreed enthusiastically, and refrained from questioning the missed opportunity for a wonderful wildlife haven.

I was intrigued by the way we seemed to tack our way across the gravelled car park like a pair of drunks weaving through pub tables, for the toilet. I was also puzzled as to why Frank also appeared to be walking crablike, even as we climbed a short flight of simulated Portland-stone steps to take us up to the level of the house. I concluded it was in order to maintain a running dialogue with me, as I'd decided to hang back a couple of paces to avoid him suddenly cutting across my path; tripping him up wouldn't have been a good start.

I then realised that he was looking in the opposite direction to the house while gesturing toward it, "Lovely isn't it? Lovely! He was evidently inviting admiring comments. He was obviously proud of his 'pile'.

"Lovely," I hoped I sounded genuinely enthusiastic, as I wasn't sure what I was supposed to be admiring.

"What!" He yelped.

Christ. Had he seen through my poor attempt at sincerity? Did he think I was taking the piss?

"I said it's lovely," I repeated somewhat cautiously.

"Yes, it's lovely," he yelped, still appearing to look away from the house.

Suddenly his hand jerked towards his head as though remembering something important, at the same time as changing tack yet again. It dawned on me that all this zigzagging was just to keep his long strands that camouflaged his thinning locks, in position. I permitted myself a wry smile as I admired his 'Bobby Charlton', and thought that if the wind keeps changing direction we might never get to the house.

Again I opted for diplomacy and refrained from asking if he'd a hand in the design of the house. I feared he may have sought further adulation, and I knew the limits of my acting skills. A lot of money had obviously been spent transforming a picturesque Victorian cottage into a large characterless house. The type found on the vast housing estates that are slowly invading the countryside; like fungus around every town.

It seemed such a shame that the lovely isolated rural location of, I would guess six or seven acres, about a third being woodland, had been blighted by the combined efforts of unimaginative architects, and local planners.

I was soon to learn that yelping, "What!" and "Eh!" are just a couple of Frank Knight's many unnerving idiosyncrasies.

My first thought on seeing this *incredible collection* was, that the French dealers must have seen him coming; and were still dining out on their tales about a gullible Englishman. Frank was convinced that he'd acquired a tasteful collection of eighteenth century French bargains.

I hadn't the heart to tell him he was the proud owner of a pile of early twentieth century, mass-produced, and poorly constructed reproductions. Besides which, I was concerned that if he knew that the restoration costs were considerably greater than their value, he wouldn't have the work done. If the French could benefit from Frank Knight's naivety, then why not our local economy; or more particularly mine?

I noticed that there were also quite a few nice pieces of early eighteenth century English walnut, and some later Regency mahogany. I thought he obviously has a good eye for aesthetics; and an eagerness to part with his money.

Over the years I have allowed Frank to monopolise me, mainly out of convenience. I now allow Frank three days a week, either on furniture repairs, carried out in my workshop at home, or building related projects at The Grange.

I often wonder why I put up with him.

I always sense when it's Frank phoning but I don't like to risk losing new business; I'd like to be able to reduce the time here. On hearing his voice I mentally curse, and promise to invest in a caller ID phone system.

*****

"Frank and Nisha gone already?" pants Wayne, staggering into the bathroom.

"Yeah, they'd gone before I arrived – Frank must be trying to avoid us – It's usually Fridays that he makes himself scarce; 'specially if I've invoiced him."

"Invoices, what are they?" laughs Wayne, parking his fat arse on the toothpaste spattered window-board.

"I wouldn't sit there."

Wayne regards his perch for several seconds as though seeing it for the first time, before ejecting, "Aagh, shit!"

"No, toothpaste; we had this conversation yesterday," I laugh, "I'd love to be a fly on the wall when you explain to Sally how you got toothpaste all over your arse."

Wayne contorts himself to admire his expansive rear.

"Aaagh, shit," he groans this time, while searching in vain for something suitable to wipe himself.

"You could always grab a quick shower before I disconnect it."

"Ugh. I aint goin' near that hairy fucker," he squeals, sounding rather like the Guinea-pig that appears to be wedged in the outlet.

"Well you've got to sometime – I can't shift it on my own.

"What the hell are we supposed to be doing?" I implore no one in particular.

"I don't bloody know, I thought you knew" replies Wayne, ready as always to pass the buck.
"They haven't even decided what flooring they're having."
"I thought Frank must've already discussed it with you - when I wasn't 'ere," he adds almost as an afterthought, but I recognised that he was fishing. I hum 'Suspicious Minds' under my breath.

Wayne is suspicious of everyone that works for Frank. He suspects that I charge a higher daily rate, which I do, and work more days for Frank than he does, which I do. Well some weeks I do, but then some weeks Wayne is required more than me. It's 'swings and roundabouts', and to be quite honest it doesn't bother me. We're different trades, a bricklayer, and a cabinet-maker, so it's obvious that we're not necessarily required at the same time - Apparently it's only obvious to me.

"I wonder what 'Shanking' is?" I ask
" Eh? Shankin'?"
"Well according to this," I nod at the disconnected toilet-pan that I'd placed by the door ready to take downstairs, " Armitage does it," I say dryly, closing the lid.

Wayne's mouth twitches catlike, while he contemplates Armitage's personal habits.

"It makes you laugh dunnit?"
"What does?"
"The last time we ripped this bathroom out, remember? There were stains all over the bloody place… remember?"
"How could I forget?" I say wistfully.
"Well Frank blamed it all on the girls, remember? Well he didn't actually say, *the girls*, he said, *the others*, and as *the others* are all girls….well you just 'ave to laugh don't you?"
"Ha ha," I oblige.
"Oh fuck off."

"Have you got Alkazalzas? I'm sure we had that conversation yesterday with Frank. Or were you in your *open-air office*?"
"Yeah, must've been," he laughs.

Opposite the window and hand-basin is a large radiator painted in the same sage green as the embossed papered walls. This is also spattered in toothpaste.
"How the hell do they get toothpaste over here?"
"P'raps they have kinky toothpaste fights....might explain all those half empty bloody tubes that were lyin' 'bout the floor," offers Wayne.
I regard him quizzically, while trying to block out the image of Frank and Nisha cavorting like a couple of squealing Sumo wrestlers plastering each other in toothpaste.
"Something you and your missus practise?"
"Don't knock it 'til you've tried it," he laughs.

I look behind me into the bedroom at the antique pieces of furniture. Under the windows at opposite ends of the room are a pair of small early eighteenth century matching walnut chests of drawers, the tops protected by a sheet of toughened glass. Obviously 'his and hers'. Nisha's having a tri-section dressing table mirror, covered in make-up and jewellery boxes and a couple of photos of their two daughters, Sophie and Alice as toddlers on a beach somewhere.

Frank's has a photo of himself and one of Nisha both holding the girls as babies, and barely recognisable; an attractive couple in their youth. There is also a bowl with coins, a mixture of francs, euros and sterling. Laying scattered amongst the thick dust are a few golf tees, some broken; no doubt the contents of his pockets after playing a round.

"You wouldn't think that those photos are of Frank and Nisha," I laugh, nodding into the bedroom.

"That's what years of stuffing ya face and no exercise does t' ya! Wouldn't think Frank was at least ten years younger than you," responds Wayne scornfully, sounding almost jealous of the Knight's practise of eating out several times a week.
"I'll give you the name of my moisturiser if you're interested," I camp, waving a limp wrist in his direction and flicking my head back.

"Perhaps they've always been a couple of Sumos, and those photos have just been cut out of a catalogue," I joke, "…or they're the original pictures that come with the frames."
"Yeah, ya mean that's what they wished they looked like; a couple out of an eighties pop video," Wayne says, quickly warming to the theme.
"Perhaps they should do the same to the mirrors, then they would never be disappointed," I say dryly, but start to laugh aloud as I imagine the two porkers, posturing and posing this way and that, in front of cardboard cut-outs of bodies beautiful.
"Who should we have for Nisha?" cackles Wayne.
"How about Halle Berry, and Lawrence Dallaglio for Frank," I suggest. "You know how he goes on about twenty stone rugby players. I'm bloody sure Frank has an unhealthy interest in big blokes."
"Yeah, did ya notice how he could 'ardly keep his hands off Big Mac the plumber," agrees Wayne enthusiastically. " Kept patting 'im, and squeezin past 'im whenever 'ee bent over in the kitchen."

We both cringe in silence remembering Frank pawing the six-foot-three, twenty-seven stone Glaswegian plumber.

"Mind you he's a bit like that with Toby up at the office."
"Really?" I respond disbelieving. "Toby's not exactly in the same league as Big Mac…he may be a little tubby but he's not big."
"Tubby Toby," Wayne muses with the idea of a nickname.
"Not exactly subtle," I say discouragingly.

"Nah, we shouldn't be cruel," he laughs, "…but you should see the way Frank leans over 'im when he's working on the compooters up there ….He looks like a bloody Labrador trying to hump his leg."
"Toby always reckons he prefers a 'desk job' to working down here," I laugh. "…now I know what he means…

"That doesn't seem to square with the way he was trying to keep his back to the wall in here yesterday… p'raps he's saving himself for Mister Right," I laugh.

A sharp noise downstairs causes Wayne to freeze.

"Are you sure Nisha isn't here?" he whispers.
I laugh, "Blimey you're windy today; that was the milkman pushing the papers through the door."
Wayne sags like a deflated soufflé, "Bloody 'ell Charles, one of these days you'll drop us in it."
"'Scuse me," I bristle, "…you're the one who was casting nasturtiums about Frank giving Toby a stiff talking to.

"Well make yourself useful then, give me a hand to get this shower out; apparently we've got to get this lot out so Barry can start decorating," I say, shrugging in a 'don't ask me why', way.
"What? Surely we need to change the floor and tiles before Barry can start fuckin' papering…He phoned me last night to say I'd be working outside, on that bloody patio; I'm never gunna finish the fucker."

"Yeah? Well he phoned me as well to ask me to make templates for the kitchen worktops, apparently he wants to change them for granite – I'm not sure whether I'm supposed to do that at the same time as this or after – he wanted them both doing first thing."

"Christ. How many unfinished fuckin' jobs have we got?"
"Well if you're supposed to be on the patio, what are you doing in here then?"
"I just thought I'd come up and see what you were up to."

"I'm up to my neck in toothpaste and shit – thanks for your concern..." I nod at the loo waiting by the door, "...You could take that down."

"Me stomach aint that fuckin' strong," he snorts, admiring the piece of porcelain with the same dog's bum expression Henry Sandon might wear, if presented with an eighteenth century chamber pot complete with original contents.

Wayne picks up a flannel and wipes an area of the window-board. After inspection, he heaves his dainty rear back onto his perch, checks his mobile and places it beside him, and assumes the expectant manner of a spectator at the Coliseum.

"Aren't you going to take the pan down then..."

"Fuck off. I aint goin' anywhere near that shitty fuck..."

His squawk is cut short by the sound of one of the bedroom doors opening, followed by soft padding feet, the girl's bathroom door being firmly shut. In the tomb like silence on our side of the wall the bolt being rammed home sounds like a rifle report. Wayne and I exchange worried glances, and try to remember every last word since about half-eight, an impossible task considering that we frequently forgot what tools we went to our vans for in the time it took to reach them - apart from Wayne who doesn't have any in his van in the first place.

"Must be one of the girls – if it was Frank or Nisha it would have been a much bigger fart," whispers Wayne, attempting to constrain a wheezy laugh.

"It couldn't have been Frank; that sounded like someone with a good aim," I whisper.

The flushing loo is followed by the running of a tap, then the reverse of the original warning sounds.

"I wonder how much she could hear from her room?" I ask, once the reverberations produced by her bedroom door have subsided. "I wonder why they all feel the need to test their strength every time they close a door."

"I'll be doin' me patio when you need a lift," he says flatly, slipping off his perch and scooting out the door.

"Shi…!"

"Morning Wayne – morning Charles."

Christ, it must have been her we heard coming back and taking the paper out of the letterbox. She's taken lessons from Frank.

"Morning Nisha," I reply as casually as my thespian skills allow.

Nisha's imperceptible smirk, as she fills the doorframe, tells me I'll never get an Oscar.

"So what were you boys laughing at," she enquires casually.

"Oh nothing much – just something Charles said – Well I best get on with me patio – Don't forget to give me a shout when you need a lift," he says grinning broadly over Nisha's shoulder.

Yeah thanks for nothing you wanker.

Nisha looks at me expectantly, "Well – I like a good joke." Her smirk less disguised.

"Yeah you need a good sense of humour here," I laugh, playing for time. "I was just saying…"

Saved by the bell…or rather the ring-tone.

Nisha and I stare momentarily in the direction of the all too familiar, if not recognisable tune. 'Money Money Money' by Abba would be far more appropriate, either that or 'Gold' by Spandau Ballet. From my position I can see the caller ID informing, Sally, is calling.

Nisha is the first to react. With her face set with the determination to rugby tackle a charging rhino, she crosses the floor in a couple of strides, which wouldn't have been possible had the knicker-mountain still been in her path, and snatches up Wayne's phone. Her face suddenly softens as though she's had a change of heart.

"He-lloo," she purrs in an Eastern European accent.

I've never met Sally, I just hope she knows Nisha – I just hope *she* has a sense of humour.

"Wayne? I no sure. Who I say calling?"

She's bloody Chinese now.

"Sallee, his wife – I no sure, hold on I go see." Nisha holds the phone away slightly, "Hey big boy! Wake up. Are you Wayne? If so, wife on phone – Your time up en-way."

"You can say that again," I mumble in disbelief.

"Oh, phone dead."

"You sound surprised – It won't be the only thing."

Chapter 4

Wayne swaggers into the garage with a grin broad enough to park a two-man Canadian style canoe.

"Sorry about that – How did you manage to get out of that one?"

You won't be grinning like that with a frying pan wrapped around your head, as soon as you walk through the door tonight.

"I was saved by the phone," I say ambiguously.

"That reminds me," he says patting himself down and casting about, "I can't remember where I left my fucker…

"Was that Nisha I saw going out?"

"Yeah, 'parently she's gone shopping – must be at least a day since she last went, must be getting withdrawal symptoms.

"Did you signal that it was bait-time to Little Eric?" I say changing the subject.

"Yeah, he was turning the Kubota 'round at the top of the field."

"I'm surprised he can see you at that distance; I don't suppose his breakfast will have worn off yet," I laugh.

"Do you think he pours it on his cereals?" laughs Wayne.

"I don't suppose he spoils good malt with food…

"You should have seen your face when you walked into Nisha – You looked like Frank when his ol' man turns up here unannounced – He always looks as though his world has fallen out of his bottom as well."

"What do you mean, as well," squawks Wayne.

"Well you looked like you should have smelt like that loo up there."

"Ha. Ha….You've noticed then."

"What?"

"That Frank is fuckin' shit scared of Simon …. 'Practically fills his fuckin' pants every time he turns up 'ere."

"I thought that was because he was scared of his ol' man seeing how much he was pulling out of the business to spend on this place."
"Well that as well, but he's like that up at the office as well…How come you never work up there?"

"I'd rather not fall out with him; I've heard about the way he talks to people working up there and at the factory. He boasts about being a millionaire; and talks to everyone as though they're cretins. I'd end up telling him where to shove his millions; it might make it awkward for Frank to employ me down here. They've asked me, but I've always made excuses; like I've got too much work."

I'm already regretting confiding in Wayne, he's one of the biggest clackfarts I know; I wonder how long before my comments are relayed to Frank or directly to Simon. Wayne's shiny brown nose is second only to Little Eric's, the gardener.

"'Swonder you've got any customers left Charles - been in business long?" he laughs.
"Funny you should ask. Do you think that's my problem, not suffering fools gladly?"
"How long 'ave ya been doin' this?"
"This or furniture restoration? I quit teaching about twenty years ago to make and restore furniture."
"You were a teacher? I never knew that. Bloody 'ell! What did ya teach?" he asks as though I'm a registered kiddy fiddler.
" Little bastards most of the time. … No that's not true, it's funny how it only takes one to ruin your week… I taught Design and Technology in secondary. I enjoyed the teaching; it was the politics that got me so frustrated… Thatcher and her merry men….. I could never vote Tory after what she did to the teacher's morale back in the eighties …. Mind you this lot just bog you down with paperwork, but the pay's a lot better…leaving teaching now would be a harder decision; twenty years ago the money wasn't anything

to get excited about. … 'Specially after the Tories kept awarding two percent piddlin' pay rises each year."

"Ain't that what they get nowadays?" says Wayne, "In line with inflation?"

"Your joking, teachers haven't had a pay rise at all for at least two years…you can tell the Tories are back in…

"…But going back to the eighties, I wouldn't have minded so much if they had applied that across the public sector… but they awarded the Police and Fire-service and maybe the nurses, I can't rightly remember, double figures, several years running, because they have the public sympathy; but only awarded teachers about two or three. Then they reneged on their agreement to abide by arbitration if we ceased taking industrial action. When ACAS, I think it was, suggested that teachers should have about seventeen percent, Ken Baker the education minister at the time said that he didn't care, as if it had been a game and he'd had his fingers crossed behind his back when he'd made the promise. We only got the original two-and-a-half percent … That's when I decided to 'take my ball home'."

"I 'spect that's when the education system started goin' down the pan," laughs Wayne.

"Well the Education Secretary keeps begging me to come back," I reply. "…I had to report them for nuisance phone calls…Thought about going ex-directory."

"Not very good for business though Charles," he laughs.

"Ya get bugger all from Yellow Pages anyway…. Anyway one teacher in the family is enough. I think we'd have been divorced years ago if I hadn't got out of it.

"Are you sure Eric saw your signal?"

The garage was built by Wayne a couple of years ago; during the period that I was engaged by Frank purely in my capacity as an antique furniture restorer. I say built, it still requires a lot of work before it could be classed as finished. The garage has been added to the growing list of unfinished projects.

Wayne and I sit in the garage and shudder violently like a pair of Labradors emerging from a river.

"Brrr it's bloody colder in 'ere than outside," we say in unison, then laugh, amused by the coincidence.

"It is April isn't it?" I ask, "It feels like January in here."

"Yeah only just - I know what ya mean - soon be Crimbo again."

I wince. I hate that word.

"It's not the first is it? D'ya think this is Frank's idea of an April Fool's joke?"

Wayne laughs, "Bloody expensive fucker if it is."

"Little Eric must have got lost."

"He'll be here in a minute, he might have decided to empty the mower at the top before coming down - I signalled, and he waved back."

"I'm surprised he can mow such straight stripes." I say, pouring myself a disgusting looking, vaguely coffee scented liquid.

Little Eric the gardener is a retired garage owner and alcoholic. Unfortunately he has only retired from his garage; not from alcohol.

"Oh, Eric can recognise a drinking gesture from a couple of miles, even when he's paralytic. His salivary glands are probably working overtime as he careers down the hill thinking about his *top-up*."

"He'll probably be drenched when 'e gets 'ere then," laughs Wayne.

"'ow do? Cor bloody 'ell 's bloody cold in 'ere; 's bloody warmer ou'side."

Wayne and I both laugh.
"Y'alright Eric?... We were just sayin'more or less the same thing," responds Wayne.
"It raining out?" I ask.
"No...why?" replies Eric inspecting his jacket with a puzzled expression.
"Ya face looks a bit wet that's all," I say, giving Wayne an imperceptible wink.
Eric feels his face for moisture, and Wayne's face disappears behind a spray of coffee; fortunately he wasn't facing in my direction. Wayne leans forward, legs apart to avoid the coffee dripping onto his lap, and gives me a sideways look while quickly mouthing something like, 'runt', and grabbing a corner of the dust sheet that he's using as a cushion to wipe his face.

Eric pulls in one of the vacant green plastic garden chairs to complete the triangle, studying Wayne as he parks himself, "Y' okay Wayne.... go down the wrong 'ole did it?"

The Whisky fumes reach me and I shoot Wayne a quick glance to see whether he's enjoying them yet. He grins and does an impression of 'The Bisto Gravy kids' and then pretends to topple sideways off his chair.

"I'm surprised you feel the cold with that antifreeze," I suggest.
"Breakfast must be wearin' off," laughs Eric, "time for a top-up," he adds unscrewing the top from his red plastic flask. The grey steaming coffee fails to disguise the fresh wave of peaty fumes of his malt cough mixture. He leans back in his chair and announces extravagantly as though we're in some plush gentleman's club, and not freezing our balls off in a poxy garage, "Ahhh, just what the doctor ordered."

"Would your doctor's name be Shipman by any chance?" I quip, before sipping my own coffee and grimacing. I inspect it, as though I've mistakenly drunk creosote. "Talking of poison, why do

tea and coffee from a flask never taste like tea or coffee? It's disgusting"
"I know, it's shite… but it's warm," laughs Wayne.
"Why d'ya think I put this antifreeze, as ya call it in mine?" laughs Eric.
"I just thought it was because you were an alcoholic," I say dryly.
"That as well," replies Eric, and Wayne splutters out another mouthful, as he attempts to control his laughter.
"Oh fuck it! Look what you've made me do; I've bloody soaked meself now."
"Get a grip Wayne, you look like you've escaped from a geriatric ward," I say, adding with mock reproach, "…we'll have to give you a bib at this rate."

"Here, this should help dry ya out," laughs Eric, waving a fag packet at Wayne. They know I don't smoke so he doesn't offer me.
"Oh, go on then, I shouldn't, but as you insist," Wayne accepts his nicotine hit with feigned reluctance, carefully balancing his sandwich on his knee while he lights up. The black indented finger marks gently reflating, imitating phantom piano keys against the bleached white bread; the oozing pickle which drips down the leg of his jeans, resembling a leaky nappy.

The garage sounds and smells are soon replaced by those of a public house.

"The whisky may be 'just what the doctor ordered', but I bet the fags aren't Eric," I josh, "…I thought the consultants told you to pack up?"
"They bloody did," he pauses to light another off his dog-end, "…so I've bloody cut down….You want another Wayne?" He adds, offering the packet.

I'm amazed at the speed that Eric manages to smoke a cigarette considering his lung capacity probably wouldn't allow him to extinguish one candle on a birthday cake - let alone sixty odd.

"No thanks, I ain't finished this one yet.... I need to cut back as well... any way you're a bad influence.... I only smoke when you're 'ere...mind you it's cheaper to smoke yours."

I consider how Eric can regard chain-smoking as cutting back. "How did you manage to smoke more - two at a time?" I suggest.

"No, I only smoke when I'm awake now." cackles Eric, then bursts into a coughing fit that racks his body to the point of almost pitching him from his chair, creating a disgusting rattle of rising phlegm - or possibly whisky, that causes him to wretch and his face to turn the colour of over ripe damson. Throughout this charming solo performance Wayne and I grimace, yet stare as though hypnotised, unable to look away.

"Y' all right Eric?" enquires Wayne genuinely concerned.

"Can't you go outside and die? Or at least die quietly," I protest, when I see him returning to his usual pallor of old pastry, "... you're putting me off me bait!"

He eventually gurgles an impression of a female porn star.

"Aaaagh, ssshit ... Eric," Wayne and I cry in unison from shared revulsion, struggling to keep our half-digested sandwiches down; we press a free hand to our mouths. "Did you have to swallow it?" We again chorus.

"Sorry lads...it were a single malt ... couldn't waste it," he cackles and splutters, "...it's usually only the first bugger o' the day that bites."

I take one look at the half eaten sandwich that resembles a dental impression for a gum-shield in my hand, and then return it to my bait box.

"Wassup Charles?" laughs Wayne, "On a diet?"

"I suddenly lost my appetite," I say flatly; snapping the lid.

"Sorry lads," repeats Eric embarrassed, "I couldn't be bothered to walk ou'side," he croaks in a lame attempt to rally his humour.
"You won't have to worry about that next time Eric… next…"
"Next time we'll just bloody throw you out," interjects Wayne laughing.
"Yeah, you better just hope the bloody door's open," I add, laughing dryly while thinking that it must have seriously shaken Eric to have stemmed his swearing.

"What did you go into hospital for anyway; as if I needed to ask after that performance?" I enquire, attempting to change the subject.
"I've got problems with me bloody circulation ….. me bloody legs is the problem."
I study Eric's legs for a few seconds. "Mmm…I suppose they are a bit short, I thought they just affected your height; I suppose they must make circulating slower. Can't you just take quicker steps?"

"Ya bloody daft twat," rattles Eric, "The circulation *in* me bloody legs; the bloody blood ain't getting round bloody quick enough."

That's a lot of blood.
"What causes that then?" I ask.
"They reckon me bloody art'ries is blocked up."
"So what did they do in hospital?"
"They bloody opened me up across 'ere," he says, while slicing an imaginary scalpel across the vicinity of his nether regions. Wayne and I both suck on imaginary lemons, the tendons in our necks standing out like harp strings, and instinctively plait our legs and protect our tender regions with a free hand, while trying to avoid spilling the coffee held in the other.

"Ooooh, the bit between me balls and me arse just twitched," moans Wayne.
"I think you mean your perineum, my dear boy," I correct him in a Noel Coward voice while waving my free hand.

"Me what?" yelps Wayne.
"Your perineum," I repeat.
"I thought they was bloody mountains," cackles Wayne.
Eric rattles for a few seconds before adding, "I thought it was some kinda mountain rescue dog."

"Then what?" I ask reluctantly, unsure whether I could stomach the details.
"Yeah, then what?" asks Wayne.
"And then bloody nothing! They took one bloody look and decided it was too big a bloody mess; and bloody sewed me straight back up again!" Eric blurts incredulously.
"What do you mean, 'a mess', did they open you up with a chain saw?"
"Nah, they said me bloody arteries were in too bad a bloody condition to be able to bloody repair them… need too long a bloody section to bypass the fucked up stuff."

"So what are they going to do now?" I ask
"Fuck all! …. They say there's bugger all they can do. I have to keep goin' back for bloody check-ups… that's a bloody waste of time if they can't bloody do anything!"

"Wayne and I could soon run some copper piping round ya, we could do you a bypass… just charge you for the fittings, how about that."
"Couldn't do fairer than that!" adds Wayne.
"Fuck off! I've seen your plumbin'… I'll be leakin' every bloody where.!"

"So what's caused your arteries to block? I ask, I thought you had to eat loads of cholesterol, ya know, fatty foods … my brother's Action Man doll was bigger than you are." I say.
"Fuck off, I ain't that small!"
"I know, but you ain't exactly a Sumo wrestler, you're barely five foot..."

"Bloody am," squawks Eric, "I'm five foot two ya cheeky bugger!"
"And there's more fat in a fart." I continue. "You don't exactly eat much; I'd have the RSPCA on my case if I kept a mouse on your rations….'specially your liquid rations!"

Wayne wheezes uncontrollably.

"It's not what I bloody eat that's the bloody problem…. it's what I bloody do in between… bloody smokin' an drinkin'," he laughs rattling the crap in his throat again, and I fear a repeat performance.
"It's not what, but how much. That's the problem," suggests Wayne.
"Well yeah…. bloody obviously," rasps Eric.
"Not the brand then," I say dryly…… "sure there's nothing they can do?" I ask incredulously.

"Well they say if I stop bloody smokin' and really cut down the bloody drinkin'' for about twelve bloody months they'll bloody think 'bout it!" squawks Eric sounding surprised at the temerity of the surgeon.
"Twelve months…Christ, they might as well have said a year." I say.
"Pillock" cackles Eric.
"Ya'can never be serious Charles," sniggers Wayne…
"How many d' ya' smoke a day Eric?"
"About half of what he buys; thanks to you," I quip.
"Bloody right!" laughs Eric.
"I don't cadge that many!" protests Wayne.
"'bout eighty I guess," suggests Eric.
"'Much do you drink?" I ask.
"I dunno really; the missus just keeps buyin' it…."
"It's the little things ya' should notice," I say.
"Fuck off…she'll be sorry when I'm gone...."
"Not half as sorry as the landlord at the Black Swan," I respond.

"'S'bloodyright," he rasps…

"Let's see," he continues, " I 'as a couple o' tumblers when I ge's up, you know, for me breakfast like… a couple in me flask…. like ya do…"

"Like ya do," Wayne and I chorus.

"Yeah, like ya do… then I stops for a couple o' doubles - chasers of course, on me way 'ome at the 'op Pole on the square - then dependin' on who's in there I might move on up to the Queens for a couple more; before goin' ome for me tea."

"About what time is that - usually?" I ask casually.

"'Bout 'alf six, quart' t' seven…. Why?"

"Just makin' a mental note when to avoid the road, between Kingsford and Burley of an evenin'," I say facetiously…. "if ya' kill me I'd never speak to ya' again."

"Oh, don't get me wrong, I ain't pissed…"

"Course not, sober as a newt," I say.

"Na'...any case the car knows it's way 'ome…na' I ain't pissed - I'm jus' getting' warmed up"

"Not more?" asks Wayne incredulously.

"O' ar, like I sez ,I'm jus' gettin' warmed up…"

"Warmed up!" I splutter, "One o'these days you'll get warmed up… when you go to light-up, you'll really light-up… you'll have heartburn big time."

They both groan.

"Come to think of it," adds Wayne "How you've never fuckin' blown yourself up when you're filling the fuckin' mower with that fag in your kissa I'll never know."

"One of these bloody days you'll look like a bloody Christmas pudding running around the field," I say.

"Ahh, a lovely blue flame," adds Wayne.

"Ooh, my favourite colour," responds Eric.

"Yeah it'll match your eyes - and your lips come to think of it," I say.

Wayne and Eric laugh and splutter so violently their plastic chairs protest like tortured pigs.

"I wu'nt run roun' the bloody field," squeals Eric, "I'd run into Frank's bloody 'ouse, or in 'ere."

"Well we could certainly do with a clear up in here," I say dryly, surveying our surroundings, adding, "There's hardly room to swing a mouse let alone a 'cat'."

"We need to be scrunched up together to keep warm - know what I mean?" rasps Eric.

"Yeah, 's nice and cosy," agrees Wayne.

"Cosy!" I protest, "I can't even get this close to my wife nowadays.... I'm in danger of failing the breathalyser and having me lungs kippered just from your fumes."

"Just think of the bloody money you're saving," laughs Eric.

"Yeah, it's cost him a fortune to get in that state," wheezes Wayne.

Because Frank continually dreams up new projects there are always several 'in progress', and a garage full of building materials. Not to mention, ride on mowers, and other garden related machinery and equipment; enough to stock the average horticultural retailer.

Half of the latter category, has probably only been used once, when new. This being the result of Frank's impulse buying, without considering it's suitability, as he has no intention of operating it. By presenting the gardener with a new superfluous gadget, he was trying to appear the benevolent, considerate employer, 'making life easier for the old family retainer' - When really it was just another gleaming toy to reflect his wealth.

Then there is all the evidence of the family's various, brief flirtations with sporting activities. There are enough so called, 'mountain-bikes', and helmets, to start a hire business, the tyres no dirtier, than when they left the showroom. It's as if they bought new bikes, to colour coordinate with their ever changing wardrobe.

There are numerous racquets, with associated balls and shuttlecocks, horse riding hats and crops, rock-climbing paraphernalia, such as karabiners and fancy trainers, all in the same showroom condition as the bikes.

The overall effect is a cross between a builder's merchant, a garden centre, and a strange sports shop.

The timber materials are managed by yours truly, the painting and decorating materials, by Barry the semi-retired painter and decorator. Eric, the gardener attempts to organise the gardening equipment.

We attempt to maintain some order - a losing battle in the face of an army of lazy buggers, who seem to take one step inside the garage before jettisoning their load. Subsequently, building materials and domestic lumber are mixed together at the front of the garage. Not until you have penetrated a few feet into the garage by clambering over this 'tide line', can you find any semblance of order.

"So, what do you have once you've got *warmed up* Eric?" I ask curiously.

"Warmed up?"

"Yeah, so far you've only got *warmed up* between here and home for tea."

"O' ar….na don't get me wrong, I don't get pissed nor nothin'," protests Eric.

" Bloody ''ell, I weigh twice as much as you, if I'd sunk what you've *warmed up* on on an empty stomach, I'd think every girl in Kingsford was Miss World!" I blurt incredulously.

"Steady on," laughs Wayne, "I used to 'ang around Kingsford when I just started drivin', it didn't matter 'ow much I drank; I couldn't find no bloody Miss Worlds."

"If they were that grim why d'ya bother comin' over from Kenchester… did the cops stop ya lurkin' outside Hereford blind college," I joke.
"I never thought of tryin' there," responds Wayne with a chuckle.

"Do you 'ave anything with ya tea Eric?" asks Wayne.
"Or don't ya like to spoil a good meal by adding food?" I quip.
"Oh I 'as a bottle of wine wi' me tea," replies Eric, oblivious to the inference, "Well actually I shares one wi' the missus… but she only 'as one glass," he adds, leaning forward conspiratorially as though he's going to drop a cheek flapper.
"You mean she never gets a look in, the rate you throw it back," quips Wayne.
"'Can't 'elp it if she's slow can I?" chuckles Eric.
"In the uptake or the intake?" I say, instantly regretting opening my big mouth, but I'm relieved when I see Eric's blank expression; while he ponders the difference.

"Moving quickly on," I mutter, before adding, "I thought you went up the The Swan every night… don't you have to pace ya'self".
"Oh I bloody do…. I goes up the Swan every night…. But not 'til about ten… jus' for a couple ... or three."
"Just a couple – you lightweight!"
"O' ar, just a couple… a couple of doubles… well you have to be careful - drivin'."
"Drivin'! I squawk, "You only live a couple a hundred yards from the bleedin' pub!"
"Wot… walk when I got a car? That bloody road passed your place is bloody pitch dark….can't see fuck all…..you're on the bloody parish council… get some bloody street lightin' put in."

"I don't think street lightin' would improve your sight … after the best part of a bottle of malted cough mixture… I'm surprised you can even find the car."

"Don't get me wrong…I ain't pissed…car knows its way 'ome anyway," laughs Eric.
"So ya' keep sayin'," I say.

Wayne and I give one another a quick glance, and raise our eyes to the ceiling.
"Bloody 'ell if I'd had that lot I wouldn't know shit from custard," I groan.
"Oh no," rattles Eric, "I'm fine, I 'as a couple o' night caps 'fore I goes to bed, then I sleeps straight through to 'bout five…..then I starts all over again."

"You must be bloody pickled," groans Wayne.
"Your missus will give your body to Damian Hurst when you've gone…"
"Which won't be long," interjects Wayne.
"Yeah, Hurst won't even need any formaldehyde … If your missus cremates you though, there'll be an eternal' blue flame from the chimney…."
"Yeah… probably last a couple o' weeks!" chimes in Wayne.
"Eternal' that long is it?" I say.
"Fuck off!" retorts Wayne; forever the master of quick wit and repartee.

"Talking of crap art," I say, "I'd better get back to it - better have something to show for a morning's work." I say feigning enthusiasm. "I'm supposed to have everything out so Barry can start decorating," I laugh at the absurdity.

"Barry comin' in is 'e? When's he starting?"
"Your guess is as good as mine, Eric. Maybe tomorrow."

"You'll be a bit crowded in that bloody bathroom wunt ya Charles? How's Frank expect ya t' work?"
"Frank doesn't think about practicalities – In fact I often wonder if he thinks at all."

I also wonder how long it'll take Eric to relay that comment to Frank.

"S'pose I best get back to it as well," Wayne groans, stretches and scratches with his characteristic enthusiasm. "I wish I could remember where I'd left my fuckin' phone."
"I thought you were going to say, bollocks, the way you were stock taking," I say dryly.
"Lost ya phone 'ave ya Wayne?"

Such powers of deduction; I can see who Sherlock Holmes was modelled on.
"Yeah – I'm sure I had it when I came – I'm fucked without it."

You've been fucked with it mate.

"Yeah, it must be an essential tool for laying patios – I'm sure it'll turn up, there can't be many places to look as you probably haven't done much so far."

Pots and kettles, I don't seem to be getting on very fast either.
"I've been looking for me fuckin' phone, it's essential to me fuckin' business," squawks Wayne.
"I best get back t' bloody work," groans Eric, with the enthusiasm of a bee keeper in a naturist's colony.

They both pinch the ash from their fags, and with a well-practised move, secrete them on the RSJ above our heads; to be enjoyed like naughty schoolboys at their next playtime. Perhaps not so practised a move from Little Eric; he only succeeds on his third attempt after finally resorting to perching precariously on a couple of gallon tins of paint. Wayne and I laugh at the spectacle.

"Reminds me of the fuckarewee tribe," laughs Wayne, "Ya' know… that tribe o' short arsed pygmies… that jump up and down in the long grass."
"Shoutin', 'Where the fuck are we?'" I oblige.
"Fuck off…'s alright for you lanky fuckers."
"It won't be smokin' the fags that kills you," I laugh, "It'll be tryin' to hide the buggers."

It always amuses me that Eric and Wayne should think Frank and Nisha are unaware of the stench in the garage. It's probably the reason why Wayne has been putting off installing the smoke detectors that Frank bought nearly twelve months ago.

"Aah fuckin' 'ell, I just remembered where I might 'ave left me fuckin' phone.

Chapter 5

"Hey Wayne!" I call.
"You don't see many of those 'round 'ere," he calls from the bathroom.
"What?"
"Hay- wains," he laughs.
"One comedian 'round here's bad enough."
"I've been workin' with you too bloody long…Found me bloody phone," he triumphs, appearing in the doorway frantically checking for missed calls, "...anyway what did ya want?" he asks absently.
"Do you remember all that bullshit Frank gave us about this four-poster?"
"Ya mean how it was supposed to be twenty grand… but he knocked the dealer down to eight….like ya do."
"Yeah…like ya do….yeah, anyway ya know how he claims to be such a *picky bastard* when it comes to attention to detail…his words not mine…"
"I could think of better," mutters Wayne.
"Me too…anyway I've just noticed the two ends… the headboard and the footboard are from two different beds….
"A marriage-bed," he titters.

"How the fuck did ya spot the difference just walkin' through 'ere….or 'ave ya spent some time lying here studying it before?" he adds suggestively.
I cringe at the implied image…. "My eyes would have been screwed up so tight I wouldn't have been able to notice the details of the bed …Anyway it's my job, same as you'd spot dodgy brickwork a mile off – Actually I thought there was something not

quite right when I've walked past it before, but not had a chance to stop and examine it."

I survey the room for another example of something 'not right'

"D'ya think she's testing us?" I say nodding at Frank's walnut chest of drawers, adding, "I'm sure that wasn't open when we were up here earlier.

The top drawer has been left open to reveal passports and what, from a distance look like a sheaf of bank statements. More disconcertingly is an unmistakable bundle of twenty pound notes.

"Fuuuckin' 'ell!" exclaims Wayne stepping forward, and after fingering the bundle like a perve in a lingerie department, pushes the drawer firmly shut, "…there must be a few grand there," he drools, even more disconcertingly.

"Seeing that I'm already up here, I may as well give you a hand to get that shower out – but you'll have to lend me some tools."

"How could I refuse such an offer," I say, with as much enthusiasm as a snowman winning a tropical holiday.

"Well go and fetch 'em then if ya want a hand."

"Blimey, you're keen all of a sudden."

*****

"I just hope they realise that they'll all have to share the other bathroom for a couple of weeks."

"Probably be months - he ain't even ordered the new suite yet - probably ain't even got a clue what 'e's 'avin yet."

"Don't forget to allow for Frank to change his mind a couple of times a day about what he's having, and where it's going." I say dryly.

"Well at least that's dictated a certain amount by the shit pipe."

"I'm impressed by your technical vocabulary."
"Fuck off," snorts Wayne.

"All it needs now," I muse, "…is for Barry to turn up and start decorating - Frank usually arranges for Barry to come in and start papering the walls and ceiling, ages before we're ready - Perhaps he gets excited watching grown men playing 'Twister', that's what it felt like last time we were all crammed in the same room; trying to work around each other."

Wayne's wheezy laugh is cut short by the noise of the front door opening and closing.

"Best look busy; that sounds like Nisha," says Wayne endeavouring to crawl under the shower-tray, giving the impression of an alarmed toad trying to hide under a stone.
"Since when did it bother you what Nisha thought?" I say glancing at my watch, "Bit early…'s only just gone twelve – besides they didn't slam the door as though they were trying to knock the front of the house out."
"Sometimes ya have to make an effort," he grunts.

I listen to the laboured wheezing, punctuated by a delightful death- rattle, "'s only Little Eric - could take half hour or so - sounds a picture of rude health, scampering up the stairs like that."
"You're a cruel fucker you are; you'll be old one day," wheezes Wayne, reversing his scrabbling.

"Old! He's only just turned sixty; he sounds more like hundred and sixty. How can he expect sympathy with everything he does to his body?" I retort.
"SSSShh, he'll fuckin hear ya," he stage whispers.
"He's still only about half way up the stairs….'sides he couldn't hear a church bell above his own racket."

The wheezing had broken into another rattling coughing fit, like a Morris Minor struggling to start on a cold damp winter's morning.

"Glad he ain't bringing us a cuppa; be stone cold," I laugh.
"Be no different to Nisha's cold milky brew then," says Wayne.

Several minutes of tortured breathing follow before a ghostly apparition leans against the doorframe. I turn around and jump as though startled.
"Bloody 'ell Eric.. . Do you have to creep about like that? I never heard ya comin'. Did you Wayne?"
"Nah, nothin'," says Wayne, shaking his head and returning under the shower-tray to hide his face.
Eric interrupts his wheezing long enough to laugh, "I know…they don't call me The Bloody Phantom for nothin'," before breaking into a particularly violent rattle.

"It'll be for a different reason before long, looking at the state of you …you may as well spit that on the floor; looks like everyone else does," I say flatly.

Eric surveys the bathroom from a half bent position, hands supporting his wheezing body on his knees. "Fuuckiiin' 'ell….what the fuck…They been keepin' birds in 'ere?"
"We wondered that," laughs Wayne.
"I just popped..."
"Popped?" I spluttered. "A wet firework 'ad 'ave more ooomph"
"Well crawled then," laughs Eric, triggering a short rattling fit. "I just *crawled up* 'ere to see what you was doin'."

"Nothin' excitin' enough to die for," I say nodding at Eric as another coughing fit takes over, and his face takes on the appearance of one of the blackcurrant faces in the 'Robinsons' advert.
"You okay?" I ask casting about for something that Eric can perch on, "Here sit down on the loo."

"If the fags don't get ya', the bacteria will," says Wayne with a concerned expression.
"I'll be a'right in a minute…just need to get me breath back…sure those bloody stairs is gettin' steeper."

"Do you think it would be unreasonable to expect Frank to install one of those stair lifts for you," I say.
"Should shouldn't he," responds Eric returning to a marginally healthier shade of grey.

"What ya gotta do?" asks Eric inspecting the bathroom, with the expression, and come to think of it, the colour of a man that has slipped onto the crossbar of his bike.
"Fuck knows," retorts Wayne sourly.
"Fuck nose? Is that Frank?" cackles Eric, "….'E's got an 'elluva bloody 'ooter."

"Talkin' of which," I say, "It's only twenty minutes 'til bait-time Eric, if it takes you as long to get down the stairs as it did to get up 'em, you'd better set off now."
"Oh, I'm much quicker goin' down…"
"As the actress said to the bishop," I mutter.
"Yeah," cackles Eric,

"…Anyway I hopes ya di'nt mind me comin' up - I won't bein' nosey or nothin' - don't get me wrong Wayne - I was jus' in'erested - Know what I mean?"
"Nah we don't care," says Wayne, "…'s no skin off our nose, please ya'self."
"Ya' 'ad t' take all this lot out did ya'?
"Well were assumin' so…usual vague instructions," replies a muffled voice from under the tray, *"Well ya' know... I'd like a good job doing... ya' know like that..... I don't like spending money... but gotta bite the bullet.... well I'll leave it with you....I'm sure you'll do a good job,"* Wayne imitates Frank.

"I hope ya' don' mind me sayin', don' ge' me wrong - I ain' tryin' t' interfere or nothin'…."

Come on Uriah Heap, spit it out.
"…but shou'n ya' 'ave 'ad the new stuff ready t' put in 'fore ya' ripped this lot out? … I mean don' ge' me wrong or nothin'."

"Ideally, but this is Frank Knight were talking about; we do everything arse-about-face here remember," I say.

"Oh ar…the usual bloody instructions - then whatever ya' do 'e changes."

"You' got it," says Wayne.

"Eric, did you ever meet a guy called Charles Dickens?" I ask.

Eric looks puzzled for a few seconds. "Where's 'e live…. the only fucker I've heard of with that name used to write bloody books - before my bloody time - Why?"

"That's the one…I just wondered whether you were at school together."

"I ain' tha' bloody old! …I may feel it," laughs Eric.

"And look it," I say laughing.

"Charmin'," says Wayne.

"I s'pose I best ge'rout ya bloody way then…see ya' at lunchtime…ta rah."

"Yeah, ta rah," comes a ghostly voice from the shower-tray's waste-hole.

Eric's laboured breathing recedes through the bedroom. I consider pouring a cup of water into the tray, but think better of it.

"I've heard of Thomas the Tank Engine…but never one called Eric before," I say

Wayne's wheezy laugh hisses from the waste-hole.

"I thought for a minute…"

"That must be a record," I say

"Ha bloody ha…I thought for a second…"

"That's more like it; I knew you must have been exaggerating,"

"Are you gonna let me bloody finish?" laughs Wayne, "I thought for a minute…."

"Is that it?"

"I was expecting you to bloody interrupt."

"Who? Me?"

"Thought we were gonna 'ave to use this shower-tray as a bloody stretcher."
"Must admit he had me worried for a while," I confess.
"Oh your all heart after all; I didn't think ya' cared," croons the waste-hole.
"I don't…I was worried about how to get to the phone first - so's you'd have to give him the kiss-of-life."
"I'd sooner kiss that shitty bog!" laughs Wayne.
"Now who's all heart?"

Wayne's laughter is momentarily interrupted by the "boing" of two empty vessels colliding. "Agh!… Don't make me bloody laugh under 'ere," he laughs, " ya' made me bang me 'ead."

Eric's laborious progress can be heard down in the hall. Eventually the front door opens and shuts and the house is plunged into an unaccustomed silence as Wayne and I listen for confirmation that the door shutting was Eric's departure; and not Frank or Nisha returning. Silence, save for Wayne shuffling as he changes position.
"Don't get too comfy."
"Thought I'd grab forty winks before lunch…

"Did you say we've gotta have everything out today?"
"S'posed to get it all out by bait time; his lordship wanted me to make those templates for the kitchen worktops after…Judgin' by the floor neither the basin nor the bog will be missed anyway."
"That's the trouble…" laughs Wayne, "…they usually were…Templates for the kitchen worktops? – Does he ever let us finish a fuckin' job?"

"I think he's afraid we might actually finish a job and clear off – this way he keeps us here forever," I say glumly.
"What a thought…Good job we fitted isolators to everythin' last time, it's been a lot easier gettin' the stuff out this time."

Well it seems to be taking you long enough to disconnect that waste pipe.

"Yeah, when was that - last week - or the week before?"
"Not quite, it's only been about twelve months though… imagine the mess if it'd been longer - say five or six years."
"Five or six years."
"Eh! Oh very funny…one o' these days you'll cut ya' bloody self," he chuckles.

Wayne's laughter is once again cut short as the front door slams. Immediately followed by Nisha's customary shout, "Hi, s' only me!"

This is usually treated as an announcement of her return, and not requiring a reply. The sound of shopping being dumped unceremoniously on the kitchen worktop is followed by the sound of water being drawn, and other noises associated with the filling of a kettle. The sound of cupboard doors banging, followed by the clatter of mugs on the tiled worktop heralds the imminent arrival of yet another disgusting brew.

Wayne and I look at each other, grimace and mime, "Yuuuk," in unison.

"Can't even pour it down a plughole…don't forget you can't pour it down the loo," I whisper, all too aware that Nisha is only a couple of feet directly below us.

We busy ourselves as Nisha's laboured footsteps climb the stairs. "Hiiii… hooow's it going?" she enquires again, her voice straining with exertion.
"Fine!" I shout. "God, listen to her…. Not exactly surrounded by fitness freaks," I whisper.
" Shurrup!" Hisses Wayne… "Ohaay!" comes a muffled reply, from the face pressed hard against the underside of the tray, sounding like someone with a broken nose.

Like a hill walker cresting the summit, Nisha's breathing and footsteps become lighter as she passes through her bedroom. "**Oh… my… god**," she drags out and emphasizes each word, standing in the doorway to the bathroom.

Wayne muffles an appropriate expletive as he bangs his head yet again on the underside of the tray, retreating like a terrier from a sett, when confronted by an unwelcoming badger. "Wha's the matter?" he asks, still massaging his crown.

"I thought somethin' serious had 'appened, thought I'd caused a flood or somethin'," he complains, disappointed that his stinging scalp had been earned in vain.

"It looks huge now!"

Yeah it's amazing what a good tidy up does.

Nisha then adds with a laugh, "I mean the room, before you say anything. Honestly, you men, I have to watch everything I say."

"Did I say anything?" I say with an exaggerated look of innocence.

"You didn't have to; I know that look," she laughs.

It's a good job you can't always read my mind.

"I never said nothin'," squawks Wayne.

"So, have you decided what you're going to do in here?" Nisha eventually asks, sniffing and winking at me.

"Well, we're not really sure." I confess, "All we know is that, *he wants a good job doing."*

"Oy! I'll tell him you've been taking the, you know what," she laughs.

"Well you know what he's like…"

"You don't have to tell me! I've been married to him for more than twenty years… and it seems like you lot have been here just as long - in fact I see more of you two than my husband."

I'd have thought there was more to see of Frank if we're talking stomachs.

"I think I've been seeing more of Wayne than I've seen of Alex lately," I laugh, nodding at Wayne's hairy, spotty cleavage as he resumes his prostrate position alongside the shower-tray. Nisha pulls a sucked lemon face and quickly averts her gaze.

"So – anyway, we thought we would rip everything out, and just hope he gives us more specific instructions after lunch." I

decide it wise to reduce the sarcasm, “I hope he doesn’t turn up with just the new toilet roll holder.”
“He’d better not that’s about the only thing I’ve got any say in.”

I consult my watch with an exaggerated display, “Well we should have time to get this lot out before bait time.
“Then you can bugger off and give me some peace,” she gestures as though defending a prize vegetable patch against a couple of marauding sheep.

Chapter 6

"Bloody 'ell Charles…you were getting' a bit near the knuckle there..."
"'s only a bit of harmless fun," I reply
"She bin flirtin' wi' ya again 'as she?" asks Eric.
"If I 'ad blokes workin' in the 'ouse I wun't want my missus talkin' to 'em like that," complains Wayne.
"You sound jealous," I say.
"I ain't fuckin jealous….I'm jus' sayin', that's all."
"You can't compare what we say, to complete strangers; I've been working here for god knows how many years."
"You might think it's harmless; but Nisha's practically leavin' snail trails 'round the 'ouse," continues Wayne.

Eric and Wayne have retrieved their dog-ends from above the RSJ, and are busy puffing away when Frank's Range Rover swoops into the car park, subjecting us to a drive by shooting as he crunches and sprays gravel across the front of the garage.

"Fuckin' 'ell," they chorus, and swing the evidence out of sight behind their backs, while frantically attempting to waft the smoke away with their free hands.
"Didn't hear 'im comin'," says Wayne.
"Nah, 'e usually sounds his bloody' 'orn on the bends," chirps Eric.
"Fat lot of good that does at ninety miles an hour," says Wayne, "be better if 'e just bloody slowed down."

Fortunately Frank exits his car and immediately heads for the house with the determination usually associated with someone with a certain stomach pain that not even the All Blacks defence could prevent touching down on the nearest porcelain. We watch amused, as he negotiates the steps crablike in order that the breeze he generates keeps his 'Bobby Charlton' in place.

"You must think he's completely blind… Or stupid," I laugh as Frank enters the house, slamming the door behind him, "Anyone who doesn't smoke can smell fags a mile off…well I can anyway… anyway I wouldn't have thought he would mind you smoking outside - inside yeah."
"Yeah but 'es a funny fucker… ya never know with Frank," says Eric.

I pour an alleged coffee from my allegedly indestructible, yet dented stainless steel flask, and then after cautiously sniffing my hands for evidence of bathroom contamination, I check a salami sandwich for pebble-dashing before attacking it. Wayne and I acknowledge the whisky fumes wafting from Eric's direction with simultaneous grins and raised eyes.

"So…are you detecting this weekend Wayne?" I ask.
"Yeah we're off to Suffolk …four of us …. stayin' in a pub…leavin' Friday and back Sunday night….should be a laugh… freeze our tits off all day, then stuff ourselves and get rat-arsed at night….great," Wayne manages to inform us between mouthfuls.
"It shouldn't be cold this time of year, I thought you said Suffolk, not South Pole…"

"You was goin' detectin' last bloody weekend wunt ya Wayne?" interjects Eric.
"Um yeah," he responds cautiously, "I didn't want to say anything in front of Frank," Wayne glances uncertainly at Eric, "…. found meself a hoard … early Roman…. Over a hundred silver stater and a dozen gold ones - worth a few hundred quid apiece… the gold ones 'specially"

"Bloody hell! Brilliant! That's like winning the bloody lottery," I say enthusiastically.
"What ya done with it?" asks Eric, almost too casually.
"Nothin' yet…it's at home …tryin' to find out exactly how much it's worth."
"Have you declared it?...

Talk about a stupid question.
"... Must be a really important find....historically as well as financially."
"Fuck off!" snorts Wayne. "Ya mean treasure trove...they fuckin' nick it off ya....they'll have the site crawlin' with archeologists so that ya can't find any more....and they'll give me fuck all for the find."

"I thought they gave you market value..."
"Do they bollocks Charles! They rip you off!" he snarls.
"I watched a programme not long ago," I say, "a detectorist had found a gold cup... bent to buggery but otherwise identical to one found somewhere on the continent. Anyway a panel of boffins - archeologists, art historians and museum curators decided how much it was worth - about three hundred thousand I think it was."
"And is that what the bloke that found it got?" asks Eric.
"Yeah, well fifty-fifty with the landowner..."

"Did 'e bollocks" interjects Wayne sourly.
"Who's got diddy bollocks?" I enquire.
"Fuck off! .... Certainly not Barry."
"Ooo that's cruel," Eric and I chime.

"He could earn a fortune as a porn star," I laugh. "It's one helluva hernia....I bet he's got merry widows queuing up to hold the step ladder while they have their bedrooms redecorated."
"'That what 'es got is it...an 'ernia?" asks Eric, looking from me to Wayne to see if he was the only one ignorant of Barry's embarrassing problem. Wayne shrugs and they both look to me for enlightenment.

"You didn't really think he naturally had balls the size of melons ...did you? He's got a testicular hernia...I think it's when the hernia in the groin pushes down into the scrotum."
"I knew he had an 'ernia," says Wayne, wincing.
"Yeah an' I did" chirps Eric.
"But I never knew it was in his bollocks," says Wayne.

"No, nor me, I never had a clue," says Eric genuinely surprised.

I shake my head in disbelief, "The poor bloke practically needs a wheelbarrow to cart his balls around to avoid tripping over them, and you two think it's natural....He's probably so pissed off with store detectives pouncing on him, that he wears a tee shirt when he goes shopping that declares, 'I'M NOT SHOPLIFTING, I'VE GOT A HERNIA IN MY FAMILY JEWELS!'."

"Why's 'e not done anything about it," asks Eric, still laughing at the image of the grumpy shopper. "I mean, it must be bloody uncomfortable."

"'Praps his missus likes them slapping against her arse," laughs Wayne.

"I get the impression his wife shut up shop years ago," I say.

"Join the club!" laughs Eric. "An' I'm nearly ten years younger than Barry."

"You've probably got permanent brewer's droop anyway," I quip. "Or should that be distiller's dick...

"Anyway," I say, "moving quickly on, I think he's scared of going into hospital - I've tried to encourage him to have it sorted, but he knows someone who had it done, and the surgeon made a bit of a balls up; so to speak."

"You had a hernia didn't ya Charles?" asks Wayne, "Is that okay now?"

"Mine was only in the groin, but I've had more discomfort since the op., than before; but I haven't told Barry. I know several people that've had successful ops. with the same surgeon as me; so I don't want to put him off."

"Did you say you're ten years younger than Barry, Eric...I always thought you were about the same age..." asks Wayne, realizing only too late that he has also just dropped a bollock.

"Fuck off! Barry's seventy-five. I'm only sixty three, ya cheeky bugger!"

I see from Wayne's expression that we both would have thought their ages should be reversed, but we decide not to pursue the subject.

"So does the landowner know you found this hoard Wayne?" I ask, again already knowing the answer.

"'Think I'm stupid? He'd only want to tell the whole world, get all the glory, not to mention the money."

"Surely he's entitled to half," I say, trying not to sound judgmental.

"Yeah, I'da thought so Wayne, know what I mean? Don't get me wrong." chimes Eric.

"Why? I bloody found it, it would still be in the bloody ground if it weren't for me!" snaps Wayne.

"It would still be in the bloody ground as you put it, if the farmer hadn't let you go detecting on his land in the first place. Neither of you would have found it; so that's got to be fifty-fifty." I say sounding like a smarmy ambassador.

"Sounds fair enough to me Wayne, don't get me wrong, know what I mean?" grovels Eric.

I wink at Eric, "Or maybe sooner or later his cultivator would have turned it up anyway; so 'praps the farmer should get seventy five per…"

"Piss off!" explodes Wayne before I can finish. "If it weren't for my bloody experience… being able to recognise the signs; I wouldn't have wanted to detect that bloody land in the first place."

"That's true, quite right Wayne. Don't get me wrong Charles, Wayne has got a bloody good point there. Know what I mean?"

Bugger off and grease your bloody mower Uriah. I immediately wonder whether I've actually expressed my thoughts because Eric jerks his head in my direction. Fortunately, as he opens his mouth so does the pedestrian door to the garage. All heads swivel as though linked, to watch a stomach glide into view, like a silent drummer leading a procession, closely followed by Frank.

"Oh, hi guys," he greets us while his snout scents the air like a pygmy shrew, and his beady eye searches vainly for the source of the cigarette smoke.

These two must have had lessons from Merlin himself, I think, while joining in the chorus, "Hi Frank."

"Yeah, hi. God the bathroom looks different doesn't it?

Yeah, I bet you haven't seen the floor since we put it down.

"You did want it all out didn't you?" Wayne asks anxiously.

"Eh! What! Oh yes! Everything! Yes everything! I've been over to Kidderminster and ordered everything. New bath, shower unit, toilet, hand basin, everything. I've ordered two baths; we've decided to do the other bathroom as well."

We? I wonder, whether Nisha has heard of this; she frequently despairs that the house is a permanent building site.

"We only finished the other one about six months ago," I say incredulously.

"Yeah but ya know, we saw these bathroom suites – absolutely fabulous quality ya know like that, absolutely fabulous quality – and I managed to do, ya know, I managed to do an amazing deal like that ya know."

"Why didn't you duplicate the other stuff as well then… while you were at it?" I ask.

Frank seems flustered and tries to pace around the garage while playing for time, but finds himself confined to the small space we've cleared amongst the lumber. Wayne, Eric and I steal knowing glances as we prepare for another of Frank's fantasy tales.

"Well ya know… um …ya know… they were doing a deal … ya know like that… I got a good deal if I bought two baths like that ….ya know….I got, I got, ya know fifty percent knocked off them like that! … Nearly half price! …Amazing ya know!" Frank becomes more animated as he starts believing himself; and as he believes we believe him.

I thought fifty percent was exactly, not nearly half.

"BOGOFF, as they say in the trade," I say.
"Eh! What! No it's true!" yelps Frank, "I got it nearly half price, I really did."
"Buy one get one free, BOGOFF in the retail trade," I explain.
"Eh. Whatever … anyway they're really good quality. Really good quality like that, fantastic quality. I mean they should have been, they should have been, ya know…"

We exchange 'Wait for it' glances.
"Ya know ... they should have been nine … um nine hundred ya know nine hundred pounds each … I got them down to ya know … I got them down to fifteen hundred like that."
"Each?" I ask, trying not to make eye contact with Wayne or Eric.
"Oh no!" he squawks, "For both!" he beams at each of us like a thespian delivering the last line, inviting applause.
"Reeeeally!" we croon, in feigned admiration; while I quickly double check the maths; and come to the conclusion that accountants are only programmed to calculate VAT.

"Wouldn't they do the same deal on the rest?" I asked.
"Well um, ya know I thought we'd have a problem storing them like that, ya know."
"Seemed too good a deal to miss … two for one … that's like freebies," I pressed.

Frank looks at his watch and makes a bee-line for the door saying, "I must get back to the office; I'm expecting an important phone call." Then adding without stopping or turning, "Oh I phoned Barry… he's coming in tomorrow - he's going to start papering the bathroom…Bye! See you in the morning."

Wayne and I can only impersonate a couple of suffocating fish.

Chapter 7

The Animals are declaring we gotta get out of this place. I couldn't agree more; I still didn't get around to making his bloody templates.

I can't believe it's only Thursday; this week is really dragging. I'm glad the hockey season has almost finished, last match this Saturday; otherwise Liz would have county training tonight. Good job she's only got athletics after school; I've only got to pick her up off the late bus in Kingsford at six. I don't know how I'd have managed if Adam had been sports mad as well; I'm already running around like a blue arsed fly.

I don't know why I'm complaining; I dread to think what life's going to be like when Liz leaves home. I'm too old and knackered to get back into any sport. I'd better find myself a sedate hobby; I don't fancy staring at the walls waiting for Alex to come home - Even when she's home she's got her face in the computer doing school-work 'til gone midnight.

'S funny that … thinking about it, I'd always thought she came to bed really late just so I'd be asleep; to avoid any amorous athletics… But then why the heck does she throw herself into bed, as though the chimney stack has just fallen through the roof and miraculously landed beside me; almost catapulting me out through the window? Is it her subtle way of letting me know how hard she works compared to me? It's certainly not a gentle hint that she's ready for a spot of 'how's-your-father?' Being woken abruptly from a deep sleep in that manner, isn't my idea of foreplay.

Meat Loaf is now complaining that, 'he'll do anything for love; but he won't do that.' I've never worked out what, *that* might be. The mind boggles. Don't knock it 'til you've tried it I say… I wonder what I'm supposed to be doing for dinner tonight.

Passing The Hop Pole on the square in Kingsford, I notice Eric's Escort van, recognisable by its highly appropriate personalised registration, PI55 EAD. Apparently, unbelievably, Eric Arthur Davies had not recognised the visual inference of the prefix when his wife had splashed out for his sixtieth birthday present.

He'd had the registration for a week before I saw it at The Grange. "Oh, PISS 'EAD, I like it. Where did you get that from?" I'd said. Eric had looked nonplussed at the registration for at least twenty seconds, which seemed like hours before the penny dropped.

"Bugger me! I thought she'd bought it for my fuckin' initials," he'd squawked.

I've never known him refer to his wife by any other title than, 'She'. Occasionally 'She' gets elevated to, 'The Missus.' I still haven't a clue as to her Christian name.

*****

Going up Kings Way I'm held up by the monthly ritual of Welsh Water digging up the road; I'm sure the site is a permanent training venue. Perhaps the location offers every condition that the trainee pipe layer or fitter is ever likely to encounter in his career. I'd soon realised after coming to Kingsford more than twenty years earlier, that the pipe work was a colander in desperate need of wholesale replacement. Within a week water will erupt within a few yards of this latest repair.

Arriving home about five minutes later, I find Adam's car parked on the drive.

I'm met by the whiff of stale cigarette on opening the front door. Going through the front room into the kitchen I see that he's made himself at home. The worktop is covered in breadcrumbs; a jammy knife lies beside the breadboard leaving a sticky smear.

There's a milk puddle near the kettle, and a trail of sugar leads from the sugar container, halfway across the worktop to a circular white shadow; presumably of a mug. Why he can never take the container to the mug or vice-versa I'll never know I wonder, admiring the snow scene.

"He must have bloody Parkinsons," I mutter, adding, "…at least he's put the milk back in the fridge," shaking my head despairingly.

I check the pot, stone cold; he must have made it in the cup. "Yuk." I flick the kettle on, place a couple of bags by the teapot and get a mug from the cupboard below. Opening the fridge for the milk, I find that the only milk-bottle barely contains enough to wet a gnats eye. I could have sworn there was enough to last until the milkman came tomorrow. Looking again at the worktop I notice that there's a much larger but feinter shadow in the 'snow drift' of sugar, next to the mug shadow. I guess at cereal bowl, and a look in the sink confirms it. I flick the kettle off and return the tea bags to the caddy.

I follow the smell of 'Au de Ashtray' to find Adam spread over the sofa in the back room, like a roman emperor, watching some Australian soap. Hmm, not sure about Romans and tellys.

"Hi. Is this 'Nymphos, or 'Have it away'?"

"Eh, do you mean 'Neighbours', and 'Home and Away'? I don't think they have those anymore; but this is about everyone copping off with each other's girlfriends or boyfriends ... or any other permutation of partner, they have to be so PC nowadays."

"I don't see many examples of the aesthetically challenged, or are they represented by that café owner," I say nodding at the potato face filling the screen…I don't suppose you'll have long to wait before something cultural like 'The Simpsons'" I say dryly.

"I thought you liked that."

"I do actually, but I can't remember the last time I had time to sit and watch it…

"Which reminds me," I quickly check my watch, "I've got to feed and walk Ebony and the chickens before collecting Liz from the bus."
"I didn't know you walked the chickens, I thought that was the idea of free-range."
"Ha ha. One comedian in the family is bad enough," I retort.
"I thought Liz had inherited the Wilson humour as well," he laughs.
"She's turning into her mother … one crabby women's bad enough; two's hell," I mumble turning to leave.

"I'll walk the dog with you," he says, nonchalantly as though it was routine, and not the first time since Ebony had been bought for him as a puppy, thirteen years ago. I turn back but try not to show my surprise and avoid any sarcasm. I ponder what he wants as I watch him casually aim the remote control and silence the telly.

How come I have to study the damn thing for ages, as though it's a fancy restaurant menu, before I can even identify the off button; even then I have to press the damn thing so hard I resemble someone trying to throttle a highly venomous snake at arms-length.

"Slowly but surely."
"Slowly but surely what?" asks Adam.
"Well you're slowly but surely getting house trained," I say over my shoulder, "…not so long ago you'd have just left the room leaving the telly talking to itself; not to mention leaving all the lights on."

I pointedly look at the sugared worktop as we pass through the kitchen, "Mmm, perhaps that should be, 'very slowly and not so surely'."
"I was going to clear that mess up before I go…"
"Are you going to make that your family motto," I interject "… you feed the dog, while I feed the chickens and collect the eggs.

Do you want to take some back with you?… Silly question I know; you must need a conveyor belt to keep you stoked up with food…Are you taking milk-shakes or whatever it is body-builders take; you seem to be filling out really fast? One minute you're a puny sapling, the next you're a ruddy tree."

Adam laughs, "I think you mean protein shakes. No I wouldn't touch them; I think it's just the hard work…"
"You make me feel like a midget. Even Liz's going to be taller than me, I'm beginning to question your parentage – I'm considering requesting a DNA test."

I slip the lead on Ebony, and we head off across the field full of sheep next to our house.
"You don't usually put her on a lead, she's never taken any interest in the sheep before," observes Adam.
"It's not the sheep she wants to eat, it's what they produce; she Hoovers it up as though it's a great delicacy; I was thinking about hiring her out to Sludge gulpers."
"'That the company that empties the sceptic tank?"
"Yeah…. Trouble is, after stuffing her face on sheep muck she then unloads it in the house…. I'll let her off in the next field.
Adam grimaces at the thought as he picks his way through the turds. He mumbles, "Gives a new meaning to, 'taking the dog out for a shit.'"

As if on cue, Ebony gets a whiff of a particularly succulent clutch just off to the right of the footpath and nearly dislocates my shoulder.
"I bet if you gave her a bowlful for dinner she'd turn her nose up," laughs Adam.
"I wouldn't bet on it," I reply.

Adam is still wearing his work clothes and boots. Or rather, almost wearing his work clothes, due to the fact that his jeans are the wrong side of his buttocks and are only prevented from dropping to his ankles by an awkward, stiff legged gait; giving the unfortunate appearance of someone who's had an 'accident'.

I wonder how he can possibly perform the manual tasks associated with landscape gardening.

"So, you've come straight from work then," I say, rather stating the obvious.

"Nussing escapes those leetle grey cells," he mimmicks Hercule Poirot.

"Okay Columbo," I tease.

"God, that dates you."

"Well you know what they say; the old uns are the best," I say, heaving on the lead and almost choking Ebony, causing her to bite fresh air inches from another savoury morsel, "Come here you disgusting creature!" I snap, pulling her through the gate into the next field, like a child that doesn't want to go to school. Slipping the lead off, she looks back at the first field longingly, like the same spoilt brat being dragged from a sweetshop. Adam and I walk on and ignore her.

"So, how's the landscaping going?" I ask, wondering what we've done to deserve the pleasure of his company, especially midweek.

"Oh, 's alright, I've been laying a patio this week…"

"Alright." I repeat, "You've been raving about the job since you started. How long have you been there, about six weeks? And now it's only 'alright'."

I can feel a, 'It's boring,' or 'I think I'm gonna start looking for another job,' coming.

What I don't expect is for Adam to blurt, "Is everything okay with mum and you?"

I look at him quizzically, wondering where that came from and he takes a sudden interest in Ebony, realising that his question was rather more direct than he'd planned. Probably because I'll be rushing off to collect Lizzie and he senses urgency.

It dawns on me that Lizzie must have phoned him after last night's little episode. Funny, she's never got enough credit on her phone to save me wasted journeys. I've met loads of buses that she hasn't been on.

"Why'd you ask that?" I feign surprise.

"No reason. Just wondered," he lied, uncomfortably. "Just that …"

I raise my eyebrows quizzically, "Yes?"

"Well I was talking to Lizzie, and … well she said that you and mum have been rowing a lot lately … and last night you more or less threatened to leave."

"Oh that, just empty words … you know… people often say things they don't mean in the heat of the moment… deliberately say hurtful things during an argument then immediately regret it".

"So, you're not leaving then? Lizzie really thinks you are; she's really upset."

I couldn't afford to even if I wanted to.

"No. Don't worry, we'll be celebrating silver at least; if not ruby…. If I can find a ruby small enough," I laugh.

"How long's silver?" he asks laughing.

"Twenty-five - six years to save up."

"How long's ruby then?" he asks.

"Oh blimey, I don't know if I want to think about that … forty I think. I might be through my midlife crisis by then," I say dryly.

I stop and turn to check on Ebony who'd been following as though she's wearing lead boots, and a sulky expression. She's now crouching in the long grass, hunched up with her back to us, and looking at us over her shoulder with a, 'Do you mind not watching, is there no privacy?' expression. She suddenly lurches forward as if shedding her load has unbalanced her, and breaks seamlessly into a trot resembling a rocking horse, and heads back towards her field of goodies.

"Who's taking who for a walk?" I say watching her bounce away. I automatically glance at my watch, "My life's being governed by bus time tables, training sessions and matches; not to mention Liz's social taxi service".
"What social taxi service?"
"I said not to mention the taxi service."
"Ha ha," says Adam, humouring me. "So everything's okay with you and mum then?" I sense his directness and persistence is borne of urgency. I suspect he's promised to report back to Lizzie.

"Are you staying for dinner?" I ask.
"No. I've got to get back… I'm going down The Barrels."
"Oh yeah? Who are you meeting?"
"No one…. just see who's there," he replies unconvincingly.
"New girlfriend?" I probe, already knowing the response.
"No….Why does there always have to be a new girlfriend?" he protests.

Thou protesteth too much.

"Does Lizzie know you were coming over? She'll be sorry to have missed you."
"I said I might pop over."
A sudden thought occurs to me. "Does your mum know that you've 'popped' over, and if so, why?"
"Eh, oh no. I haven't spoken to her for ages."

Join the club.

"Well I'll have to mention that you've been over. Shall I tell her you're training as an agony aunt?"
"Actually, I need to use the computer to do a C.V… just in case I see any jobs that I want to apply for in the future."

"Just in case," I repeat, "I hope one of them isn't for a secret agent; a greenhouse is less transparent."
"Eh. What do you mean? I'm not leaving this job, it's going well. I just realised I haven't got an up-to-date C.V. … just in case."

"Well, just in case, of course you can, I'm surprised you didn't do it instead of watching that crap on the telly….

"Which reminds me, better put this shit tanker back on the lead." Ebony is eagerly waiting at the gate as if she were first in the queue at the Harrods sale, determined not to allow anyone to get past her; her nose is jammed between the gate and post, while swinging her backside wildly from side to side with her tail, like a giant beached tadpole.

She tests my patience, by repeatedly ducking her head, avoiding the choker chain from being slipped on. This infuriating little game only serves to make her realise how it got its name when I finally manage to slip it over her head.

She trots obediently alongside me determined to keep the chain slack, as Adam and I march purposefully for home through the field of sheep. She occasionally coughs and contorts her head and neck, like someone wearing too tight a shirt collar, and looks up at me as if asking, 'Where's your sense of humour? Haven't you heard of the RSPCA?'

"That's one way of taking her mind off the sheep shit," comments Adam, "…half throttling her."

"Yeah, I must remember that."

I wonder wistfully if a little throttling makes people more amenable.

"Can you tidy up your mess before you get on the computer?" I ask, although he knows there isn't a choice, and simply nods.

"I'm going to have a quick shower before starting dinner and fetching Liz."

The sounds of clearing up lasts for at least twenty seconds, and I wonder how much I'll have to re-do when I get downstairs. I also wonder whether Adam has already lost his latest job, landscaping, or whether he's just getting bored with it already. I expect we'll find out eventually; we usually do. I can't really comment; I've lost count of the number of career changes I had before settling on this.

*****

I open the fridge. "Mmmm. Looks like another casserole coming up," I mumble to myself, "…well they say variety is the spice of life."

"Somebody in the fridge or have you started talking to food?" asks Adam, who judging by the couple of sheets of paper in his hand, has completed, and printed off his C.V.

"I can't resist auditioning when the fridge light comes on…actually I was talking to myself. I don't know if that's worse."

"Probably get more sense from those loin chops," he says, nodding at the worktop above the fridge, where I've been assembling the ingredients for yet another piece de resistance.

"Are you staying - there'll be plenty, Liz and your mum will be sorry to have missed you?"

"No thanks. Like I said, I've already arranged to meet down at The Barrels."

I thought you said you were just going to see who was down there, but decide against pursuing the matter.

*****

"Adam was over earlier," I say to Lizzie, on the way home after collecting her from the school bus.

She becomes more alert as though suddenly remembering a forgotten task.

"Oh really, is he still here?" She asks, sounding as though she already knows the answer.

"No, reckons he's meeting someone at the Barrels."

"Oh," she says, staring straight ahead.

"I thought you'd be disappointed to have missed him," I say, endeavouring to sound nonchalant.
"What do you mean? I am," she responds defensively, looking intently at me, while I stare ahead trying to keep a straight face.

We finish the drive home wrapped in our own thoughts.

"So have you met his new girlfriend?" I ask casually, as we reverse into the driveway.
"No. What new girlfriend? Did he have a new girlfriend with him?" Lizzie asks grinning, with genuine interest.
"No… But there's usually a new girlfriend involved when Adam is cagey about who he's meeting."

Lizzie's grin and enthusiasm dissolves faster than ice-cream on hot tarmac. She raises her eyes, and tuts, to suggest my evidence is rather flimsy.

"Mmmm, smells nice. How long's dinner Rumpole?" she asks, dumping her bags on the first armchair she passes.
I hold my hands about a foot apart, and pull a guess 'the one that got away expression'. She raises her eyes in a 'you're so predictable, not to mention infuriating' expression.
"About an hour… Rumpole? I suppose that's preferable to Columbo." I say, opening my arms to invite appreciation of my sartorial elegance.
"He the scruffy one with the raincoat?"
"Yeah. They don't still run that old series?"
"No, but I saw it years ago. It always seemed to be on when I was off school ill."
"I bet that made you feel better…. Probably a government ploy to make skivers get back to school – or work."
"Ha ha. Anyway, he's smarter than you."
I wait expectantly for the punch line.
She obliges, "In more ways than one," she laughs, looking me up and down.

"Well if you don't want to end up as thick as me, you'd better get on with your homework."

"I wondered how you were going to work that one in," she sighs, grabbing her bags and struggling to avoid demolishing the furniture and doorways on her way through the kitchen towards the stairs; pausing only to harvest a packet of crisps.

"I may as well check my emails," I mutter to myself, "…you never know, there might be an enquiry for an interesting commission." Although I'd be very surprised if there is; most of my work comes from personal recommendation. Advertising seems a waste of money; but you feel obliged to do it. It would be an even bigger waste of money if I missed an enquiry due to not checking the emails at least daily.

God. I thought I had something to block all this so called spam and pop-ups. Bloody penis enlargers and viagra! They'd be more useful in a monastery…be like a blind man winning a Ferrari…. I suppose it'd provide a useful place to hang the shower-gel. In fact I wonder whether it would stop Alex winding the duvet off me.

I go down the list, deleting without opening; resisting the opportunity to be hung like a donkey with a permanent hard-on. I've never been a fan of Speedos, but I'd like to think I could have the choice of wearing them without being arrested.

Well no work enquiries. There's a surprise.

Suddenly I'm aware of a moving image on the right hand side of the screen. The silhouette of an apparently naked woman writhes, provocatively; reminiscent of the James Bond opening credits. Bold pulsating letters proclaim Illicit Encounters.

I hover the curser over a, 'Join Now' button that winks invitingly.

I resist the temptation. Talking of temptation, I wonder how Wayne has managed to explain the eloquent young lady answering his phone. Perhaps I should email him.

I suddenly remember that I haven't got his email address in my contacts. I haven't emailed him for ages; and I've set up this Hotmail account since then. I'd set up an account to keep my business separate to the home and Alex's school emails; she has so many forwarded from school that I was missing the odd one for me.

I bring up the main account to access the address book. I notice that Alex is still hopeless at deleting unnecessary emails and spam; eight hundred and forty five messages, three hundred and twenty unopened messages and spam. I wonder if there are any for me, and scroll down noting that Alex also gets as many offers for penis enlargement and viagra; the difference being, I delete my offers.

I scroll toward the date I opened my own account, through all the forwarded school's correspondence, offers from Boots, Dorothy Perkins, airport-parking, penis enlargement and viagra, mostly unopened. I wonder why they bother to forward the stuff from school if she doesn't open it.

My subconscious becomes increasingly aware of a recurring name. Because they have all been opened, they are made prominent by the bold type of the surrounding unopened messages.

My curiosity is aroused. Why does Simon Gatley send Alex so many emails? The name rings a bell, I think he's another Head, but I can't really place him, Alex hasn't mentioned him for ages.

The emails start not long after I'd opened my own account. Coincidence or what? With an uneasy feeling I click on one.

Chapter 8

I clamber from my van with as much enthusiasm as King Charles I skipping up to the block. I arch backwards to relieve the ache in my lower back. No one else has arrived yet and there doesn't seem much sign of life from the Knight's household. Both Frank's and Nisha's Range Rovers are misted with overnight condensation, so Nisha has yet to do the school run. Although as Sophie is at Sixth Form, technically speaking as she has been quick to correct me, *hers is the college run.*

The tranquillity is broken by the sudden cacophony of several female voices trying to compete as they spew from the front door, producing a sound reminiscent of a fox in the chicken pen. Sophie scuttles hermit-crab like at the head of the procession, her little spindly legs going ninety to the dozen. Nisha brings up the rear, in every sense, zapping the key-fob vainly as she bundles Alice along in front of her like flotsam caught on a ship's bow. Alice would otherwise prefer to proceed in a more languid style.

"Morning!"

"Morning Charles!" chorus Nisha and Alice.

"Morning Sophie," I address her pointedly. "Birthday soon. Are you going to start driving lessons?"

She ignores me, and scuttles up to the car and tugs on the handle.

As if commanding the door to magically open she commands, "Mum! Hurry up and open the doors will you!"

"Whatever happened to OPENSESAME?" I ask.

"God, I'm trying!" Nisha snaps, jerking her extended arm around Alice at the car, which eventually produces a strangled bleep and a couple of winks from the indicators.

Alice's face suddenly breaks into a great beaming smile, " Oh Charles!" she calls out, and breaks away from her mother's bow and bounds towards me, " I've got a good joke for you…"
"Not nowww Alice!" Nisha's shriek redirects Alice towards the car as though she'd been Tazored, "We're running late! We'll miss the bus!"
Then apologetically, "Sorry Charles we're running late, here're the keys," she says bowling another set underarm. I have to leap skyward full stretch just to get a finger to them. "Oops. Sorry," she laughs guiltily as I shake my sore fingers and check for blood before retrieving the keys from the gravel behind me.
"Plenty of power, just need to work on the direction," I laugh.
"Sorry…Alice! Hurry up! We'll be late, you can tell Charles later," she shrieks.

Alice raises her eyes as she turns around and yanks the heavy door open, "I'll have forgotten it by then."
"Never mind I'll try and think of one for you," I call out before the door crumps shut.
Nisha winds down the electric window of the front passenger door that frames the stony faced 'Miss Moneybags', "You're not telling my daughter any of your filthy jokes," she laughs while manoeuvring the car.
"As if I'd know any," I call back
"I don't mind…"

"Can't we just go!" snaps Miss Moneybags, interrupting Alice, "We're going to be late…"
"Ooooh!" we three chorus.

The things ya see when you haven't got the gun.
"Why do you *always* start a conversation with *the staff* when we're in a *hurry?"*

Such a charmer.
"Sorry Maam," I mock, touching my forelock and inclining my head towards Sophie, and then address a wide-eyed and equally

wide mouthed Alice, "You should know better than to fraternise with the servants my lady."

As the car retreats slowly down the drive Nisha chastises Sophie, "That was rather rude young lady, I think you'd better apologise next time you see Charles."

Alice adds astoundedly,"I can't believe you just said that, you're just sooo rude!"

"He only works for us, he's only like staff… You should hear the way Granpappy talks to the men at the factory."

The car drives off down the lane with Sophie sitting bolt upright in the front passenger seat, staring straight ahead like a chauffeur driven Nazi SS officer. Her cold piercing eyes ready to vaporise any oncoming traffic that has the temerity to share her stretch of private highway, and hinder her progress.

A couple of minutes later Wayne's battered old grey Transit, still showing the shadow of the old BT logo, swoops onto the car park. He clambers out ritualistically checking his phone messages with one hand and his family jewels with the other; with such vigour I fear he might be trying to remove them for inspection.

Well there's not usually any danger in him *working* them off.

I casually check him for signs of physical abuse. No black eyes, broken nose or split lips. No dents or lumps from rolling-pins, or frying pans.

"Fuckin' 'ell what's the matter with 'The Fuhrer' this mornin'?" Wayne asks sullenly.

"Princess Sophie? Just her normal charismatic self. Why?"

"If looks could kill," he grunts, "I'm glad she won't drivin', I reckon she'd 'ave driven straight through me!"

"Better make the most of it then. She'll be able to start driving next week."

"Really? Is she gonna be seventeen? You'd think Alice were the older one, wunt ya?"
"Normally I'd say we should make allowances for her age, but she seems to get snootier as she gets older."

Nothing a good slap wouldn't cure, I think, but keep it to myself. Frank has a funny habit of letting slip remarks that could only have come from the workmen, but I know he hasn't heard from me; and I'm certain Barry is the soul of discretion.

"Anyway, what are you on today?"

Apart from the phone.
"I think I'm on the bloody patio, laying those bleedin' setts," he replies, with the enthusiasm of a prisoner of war on the Burma railway. "What about you? What you on?"
"Oh ripping out the bathroom floor - Gawd knows what Barry's going to stand on."
Wayne laughs,"'Ee's definitely comin' in today then? That sounds typical Frank organisation."
"Yeah. If we were building a house for him we'd probably have to start with Barry trying to put up wallpaper."

Wayne laughs at the image, " Yeah prob'ly. … Has 'ee come out yet?"
"You really think he's gay? I know you've got this thing about him and Toby."
"Not *come out* like that ya pillock, I mean out of the 'ouse?"
"Not yet. Which means he's probably going to come rushing out and jump into the car and bugger off before you can ask him anything awkward, like, 'What do you want me on today?' He's probably cowering behind the curtains like he's under siege… mind you, it's usually the cowboys inside."
"Ya reckon?" laughs Wayne.
"Haven't you noticed before? Well I don't particularly need or want to see him so let's go 'round the back and discuss your patio, bet you a fiver he does a runner."

We trudge around to the back of the house where Wayne has been laying a patio for god knows how long, in between juggling other projects for Frank and operating his telesales from his open air office half way up the field.
"Have you got enough materials? I ask.
"I think so."
"Sharp sand? Setts?"
"Yeah, yeah I think…"

Wayne is interrupted by the sound of the front door slamming. We listen to the tapping of leather soles on the paving stones across the front of the house and down the steps to the car park.
"Sounds like he's got his stilettos on again," I say.
"'Praps he 'as come out, that's why he didn't want us to see him," laughs Wayne half-heartedly.

"Don't knock it…" I pause for him to finish the expression, but he simply surveys the unfinished patio with a distinct lack of enthusiasm – even less than usual; which I didn't think possible
"…'till you've tried it," I mutter, not liking to leave things unfinished.

A short pause is followed by the opening and slamming of a car door. The Range Rover immediately roars and spits gravel as Frank accelerates across the car park and down the drive.

I hold my hand out to Wayne.
He looks blank, "What?"
"I think you owe me a fiver," I say.
"I hope he doesn't meet Barry in the lane, he can't have had time to clear that misted up screen," he says flatly, quickly changing the subject.

"You been on the beer again, got a hangover? You look a bit rough, don't seem your usual chipper self old boy."
"Nah – Just didn't sleep very well…"

Join the club.

"You don't look so fuckin' good ya self… Ya got the fuckin' lurgy or what, or is it just this fuckin' place?" he laughs a little more brightly.
"Yeah, something like that."
"Told ya t' keep ya jabs up to date," he laughs, "Well fuckin' keep it t'ya self," he adds over his shoulder as he ambles in the direction of his van, while enjoying a vigorous game of pocket billiards.
"You'll be pretty safe up in your office," I shout after him.

I stare at the half finished patio without seeing it. The words, his fucking words, to my wife go through my mind like the news headlines at the bottom of the TV screen. The feeling returns to my stomach like a brick has just dropped into it, and half way towards my backside. I feel cold and empty.

Now I know what her first husband must have felt like.

*****

Barry Roberts' immaculate eight year old cream coloured VW camper van, which he's had from new, crawls to a halt beside my ten year old blue Transit. According to the garage where I bought mine from, it had been 'cherished'. I just thought it was used. Its gold sign-writing proclaims me, Charles Wilson, to be an Antique Furniture Restorer and Fine Furniture Maker. I look at the lump-hammer in one hand and the jemmy in the other.

Ha bloody ha. What the hell am I doing here? It's a good job my other customers can't see me now; with these precision tools in my hand.

Weighing the jemmy in my right hand, I think about where I'd like to shove it. That would cramp the smarmy Simon fuckin' Gatley's style.

Barry and I acknowledge each other with a smile and a two-fingered wave. He exercises the same meticulous routine. After much deliberation over the precise parking spot; he applies the handbrake and switches off the engine. He then removes his tweed cap and best specs and places them carefully on the dashboard shelf, replacing them with an ancient paint spattered pair, which he hangs around his neck ready for work. The lenses appear to have been polished with wire wool, making looking through a pot of Vaseline seem crystal by comparison. He opens the driver's door and slides out, closing the door with a careful yet firm push. He walks around his van; his movements never hurried.

Not exactly the flying squad, it's difficult to imagine Barry ever having been an exponent of the ancient art of Aikido. Mind you I don't suppose I'd be leaping around like a Meercat if I'd got the equivalent of a leg of pork stuffed down my trouser leg.

We shake hands firmly and Barry produces an exaggerated wince, "Crikey Charles. I could see you had an evil look in your eye when I pulled up, you trying to break my hand? How are things at The Funny Farm?"

"Oh mad as usual." I laugh, "How's things with you?"

"I don't know what the hell I'm supposed to be doing here," he says lowering his voice conspiratorially, "…I bet you're not even ready for me yet are you?"

I look around in an exaggerated manner to see who's likely to overhear.

Barry laughs, "Ya never know 'round here."

"How do like playing Twister?"

Barry nods towards the battered and rusting grey Transit, "Are we all in the bathroom?"

"'S'okay, we finished taking everything out yesterday, 'part from the floor; so Wayne's back on the patio 'til we're ready for him."

"Blimey how long's 'e been on that?" Barry laughs, "Seems years." Then nodding at the jemmy and lump-hammer, "That for the flooring?" he moans despairingly, "How the hell am I supposed to work in there with no ruddy floor?"

"'Praps he thinks you're Lionel Ritchie."

"You've lost me."
I give a brief rendition of Dancin' on the Ceilin'. Mercifully brief. Barry slowly shakes his old head, "Your talents are wasted here dear-boy," he laughs.
"…Frank must think I was born in the bloomin' circus?"
"Oooh language Barry, go wash your mouth out with soap".
"I know 's awful, I don't like to swear … but this place…"
"I know what ya mean …You'd think we'd be used to it by now, we do everything arse about face."

"I see their cars are gone. Frank and Nisha at the office?"
"Yeah. Frank always makes himself scarce when he's dropped a bollock."
"Getting me to start papering the room before you've even got the floor down you mean?
"Haven't even got the old one up yet!" I laugh "At least you don't have to worry about laying dust sheets."
"Well there is that. … Although it could be interesting if we lay some over the open joists before we go tonight…
"Well I'd better get my overalls on, then come and see what's what."

"I'll see you in the bathroom," I say, I know it'll take him a while to struggle into his paint encrusted bib-and-braces. I head toward the house still chuckling at the image of Frank, wedged by his stomach between a couple of joists; his legs dangling through the kitchen ceiling like a misdirected parachutist.

Barry Roberts has recently turned seventy-five. He's been forced out of retirement due to the disastrous performance of pension funds, relying on the 'black economy' like so many others to supplement his state pension.

He's about five feet eleven, and about thirteen stone. His evidently once powerful body is now beginning to hang on his frame like too large a coat. However he never ceases to amaze me with his strength, often moving large pieces of furniture unaided.

I've witnessed Wayne literally huffing and puffing as he struggles on occasion to assist Barry.

The once thick black hair is now styled on that enduring Friar Tuck look. The drum tight skin over the crown bears badges of honour from recent and historic conflicts with low unyielding obstacles, turning to ripples, reminiscent of a solidified lava flow over his forehead, and also down to the nape of the neck. In fact he looks more like my image of Friar tuck than any screen version I've seen so far.

However Barry's one un-friar like feature, as far as I know, not having attended a school run by Franciscan monks, so not over familiar with either friars, or Barry come to that, is a humungous melon sized right testicle; courtesy of a hernia. I've often wondered if he has his trousers custom made to include a tent flap, and an extra wide thigh.

I set about removing the wooden pellets to access the screws securing the deep Taurus skirting boards. The dark mahogany stain hides the pellets rather too well. I regret making such a good job; if I'd known the skirting board was only going to be in temporarily I'd have used Velcro.

The clatter of Barry's aluminium stepladders announces his arrival.

"Christ, Barry are you trying to give me a heart attack, I didn't hear you coming."

"Oh they don't call me 'The Cat' for nothin'," he laughs while taking in the spattered and pee stained floor, and shakes his head.

"I thought that was 'cos you can reach your parts others would rather not, or words to that effect, as they say in the advert."

He throws his head back in a wheezy laugh that is cut short. He sniffs the air, then shuffles over to the window and pushes both casements that I'd half opened, to the full extent of their stays.

While Barry increases the ventilation I say, “I wish cats had to drag a bollock like that around, they wouldn’t be such successful bloody murderers; they’d think twice about rushing through the thistles after the local wildlife.”
“Ooooh!” Barry winces as though attempting to suck the air out of a room through a keyhole.

“Any news on your op.?” I ask, nodding in the direction of his nether regions hidden behind the empty, yet still bulging front pocket of his overall.”
“No. Still on the waiting list, they said it would be at least six months; and it’s only been about four,” he replies awkwardly.

I get the impression that it’s a generation thing, not discussing personal problems, possibly even with a doctor until it’s too late. Although I suppose to be fair, it is quite an embarrassing subject. I suddenly have a worrying thought, “Don’t worry I’m not going to ask to see it.”

Barry throws his head back and laughs, displaying his shiny metallic fillings in his top teeth; a legacy of all the sugar he’d drunk before conceding to sweeteners.

“I just can’t get over the fact that your doctor reckoned that it wasn’t much of a problem, and that you should just learn to live with it.”
“Well to be honest, it isn’t much of a problem to me…. I don’t have too much discomfort… unless I cross me legs without thinking,” he laughs.
“I can’t say I’ve noticed you doing the splits lately either,” I laugh
“I only do that to paint the skirting,” he laughs, “and I’ve had to pack up ballet…
“…It’s Irene that finds it…”
“Finds it! How could you lose that!” I interject.
“Ooh you are a one,” Barry responds with a camp Larry Grayson impression. “I was going to say, It’s Irene that finds it… how shall I say…. *off-putting*.”

"I'm not surprised, I should think most women would find the prospect of that bloody great demolition ball quite daunting…. They would probably expect to be shunted through the headboard and into the neighbours."

Again Barry throws his head back and displays his teeth in an almost silent roar, his convulsing body being the only indication that he is indeed laughing.

"We don't do that sort of thing anymore," he wheezes. "It's like I remember you saying once…. They trap you under false pretences, making out they're nymphomaniacs until you've married them and had the kids… then they shut up shop."

I never even got a Closing-Down Sale.

I receive a tepid shower as Barry liberally soaks the walls and ceiling to facilitate the paper stripping. No such concessions as to modern steam strippers.

"Sorry Charles, am I in your way?"

"Don't worry about it; I got my fifty meter swimming certificate at school….If I'd known I'd have borrowed Alex's shower-cap… We'll just have to work around each other."

"Just say if you want me to move."

"I'll try not to knock you off your steps, out the window," I say laughing at the Laurel and Hardy image as I manoeuvre a length of skirting board through the window.

"That would have been another fine mess you got me into Stanley," he mimics, instantly tuning in.

Knowing Wayne is supposed to be laying the patio beneath the window, I call out, "Oi! Wayne are you there?"

"He was up the field trying to get a signal when I came in; just for a change," he says with uncharacteristic sarcasm.

"He's always on that bloody phone; spends more time on that than working," I say, scanning the field.

Wayne is hanging on the fence about a hundred yards up the sloping field.

"Hey! Wayne!" I call, waving my free arm hoping to attract his attention. He waves back and points at his ear. "I can see you're on the bloody phone ya wanker! I'm not blind," I hiss.
"You won't get him off his phone; 'specially if he's flogging his detecting finds," says Barry disapprovingly, now standing at my shoulder watching Wayne.
"Well I can't just drop this out the window; with my luck it'll bounce back'ards through the bloody kitchen window," I complain.
"I'll go down and take it off you," says Barry.
"No, your all right, I'll take all the others up first, makes more sense.... Probably be bait time by then; and maybe Doris up there will have finished his secretarial duties," "Doris," Chuckles Barry, "...that's a good one."

"So... if you hadn't got taken into hospital with .... Was it your kidneys?"
"Yeah."
"You wouldn't be on a waiting list for your hernia?"
"Well that's right. The surgeon couldn't believe I hadn't had anything done about it."
"I'm not surprised".
"He went mad when I told him my GP reckoned I should live with it."
"Live with it," I repeat laughing, "... makes it sound like a lodger sharing your house."
"According to Irene, it feels like three in a bed."
"I never had you down as a swinger, in that sense," I laugh.

The noise of blocks being moved below the window signals activity.
"Better late than never," mutters Barry.
"Are you two stoppin' for bait? Wayne shouts from outside.
"D'ya work up an appetite walking up the field? I call back, checking my watch. "Bloody hell, it's ten," I say to Barry. Then

louder for Wayne's benefit, "… doesn't time fly when you're working hard."

"Fuck off, I 'eard that ….. I was selling some of me coins," shouts Wayne.

Fortunately for Wayne, Frank doesn't inspect our work in terms of quantity; just quality.

"Wayne must be trying to stretch that patio project out to his retirement," Barry mutters as we head downstairs.

"The rate he's flogging the nation's inheritance, that won't be long."

Chapter 9

"Just sold another three coins this mornin', a rare gold Quarter Stater of Vosenos…"
"'Avuseenus," I interject, "…sounds like that dinosaur that they've discovered, Dyathinkeesawrus."
Barry guffaws, but Wayne appears to have his serious detectorist head on. He sulkily pours himself a coffee, yanks the lid off his bait box and snatches a sandwich as though avoiding a poisonous snake bite. Barry looks at me over imaginary spectacles, and mouths a silent 'Ooooh', while pouring his tea.
"We're all ears," says Barry.
"Speak for yourself Wing-Nut… Sorry couldn't resist that," I add smirking like an admonished schoolboy. Barry suppresses his laughter, convulsing silently. I cough to relax my facial muscles.
"So prof., apart from Avuseenus, what were the other two?" I ask, in what I hope is my sincere voice
"Oh fuck off. You'll only take the piss," he snaps, skewing his body to turn away from us. Barry and I exchange looks, raising our eyes heavenward and shaking our heads.
"Kids. …Who'd 'ave 'em," says Barry solemnly.
"You can shut up an' all," snaps Wayne.
Barry sits bolt upright, stunned.
"Steady on prof. we…"
"See! You're just takin' the piss ... don't fuckin' call me prof."
"I wasn't taking the fuckin' piss, as you so eloquently phrase it…"
"Language Charles," Barry cuts in with mock reproach.
"Sorry Sir."
"Ya don't care about me swearing," says Wayne.
"You're beyond salvation," says Barry ministerially.
"Ya mean, I'm just a thick twat," growls Wayne.

"No one thinks you're thick. Calling you 'prof' is a way of recognising your superior intellect, in areas pertaining to archaeological finds," I attempt a plumy Etonian. "The rest of the time you're a thick twat," I add laughing.
"See! You can't be serious for five minutes," snarls Wayne.
"Life's too short…Anyway who said I was joking?"
I can't stand sulking. I resent being manipulated or made to feel at fault by someone sulking; I get enough at home I don't want it at work.

My tolerance is exhausted, "You want me to be serious? When you take your work seriously, then maybe I'll be serious." I snap.
"Wha' d'ya mean?" he asks warily.
"Well Frank's paying you god knows what, or should that be, 'god knows why?...'"
"I can earn twice as bloody much on the sites!" cuts in Wayne.

I ignore this remark as we all know Wayne wouldn't last five minutes on a site. "…And all you've done for the last two hours is conduct your own bloody business…"
" Like ya say that's my bloody business. What the fuck's it got t'do with you?"
"Your bloody conscience is nothing to do with me. But when you use me as an excuse for bugger all to show for a mornings work, then it's my business."
"Wha' d'ya mean?" he responds defensively.
"I bet when Frank comes back at lunchtime, you'll say," '*Charles asked me to give him a hand*'. …It wouldn't be the first time either," I add, just to make him aware that Frank is not as discreet or diplomatic as he might be.

I'm already regretting this confrontation; after all we've still got to work together. But as they say, 'hung for a lamb', "If you want me to be serious, you could also try being a bit more professional, and bring your own tools; 'stead of knackering mine."

"I ain't never..." Wayne's mouth snaps shut, like a drowning fish, as a conveyor carrying the catalogue of my broken tools goes through his mind. As though on a TV game show, Wayne attempts to list them.

"That lump hammer weren't my fault ... nor that 'lectric drill... or that wodumacallit that..."

"Auger bit?" I prompt.

"Yeah. That weren't my fault neither... nor that wassaname..."

"Electric screwdriver?"

"Eh! Oh Yeah. I'd forgotten about that. No I meant that other thing... wha's it called?"

"Hacksaw?"

"Oh yeah, no I meant that other thing..."

"Safety specs?"

"Oh yeah. No that other thing."

"Adjustable spanner?"

"Oh yeah," he says as though remembering a rather enthusiastic ex-girlfriend, "I'd forgotten about that... No I meant that thingy thing ya know..."

"Angle grinder - burnt out? Hand saw - bent at right angles? Spirit level - minus bubbles? Jemmy - snapped in two?"

Wayne has continued his drowning fish impression, while Barry has looked on in silent disbelief. His eyes growing wider with every item; 'til he looks like an owl that's perched on a thorn.

"Well yeah. No I was thinking of that other thing ya know....Putty Knife! He declares triumphantly, as though he's just won the whole lot; not fucked them all up.

"That was mine!" declares Barry, suddenly regaining the power of speech. "...You got any tools left Charles?"

"Well, I haven't got any old tools; they're nearly all brand new. On the other hand," I say, pointedly looking at Wayne, "…my bank account's non too healthy."

Wayne's phone warbles into life. He whips it out, flips it open with the slickness of a gunslinger in a spaghetti western, and looks at the caller ID uncharacteristically longer. He looks visibly disappointed.

"Hello…. Roman silver denarii…yes mate… Hang on you're breakin' up let me get a better signal..."

He sprints out of the garage with an alacrity and energy reserved only for his tax free enterprises, and jogs panting up the field; trying to maintain dialogue. "'Ello….'ello, you still there? 'ello?…."

"I notice he forgot to put on his posh telephone voice," Barry says flatly.

Chapter 10

"Do you get a set of wings with that halo of yours?" I ask Barry.
"No, just a chitty…"
"Well you're in the right place for a chitty," I cut in, nodding at the space vacated by the loo, "'cept you're a bit late as we've taken out the facilities."
Barry looks at the floor and then back at me with eyebrows raised, "Would it make any difference? …. I was going to say, I've got a ch, sorry, a note to say I can collect them at The Pearly Gates. Why?"
"Just wondering how you're going to cope when the floor's gone… I can't see you being able to get a foot on opposite walls."
Barry laughs, "You mean, like climbing a well."
"I think the best thing for you, would be, if I just remove the nails; and leave the loose boards for you to stand on…. I've got something I can carry on with in the kitchen."
Barry flutters his eyebrows, "Oooh. Is Nisha here then?"
"Don't you start; I get enough comments from Wayne and Eric."
Barry looks over his shoulder at me, "They're just jealous…'cos they've been here longer than you, and she doesn't flirt with them… or me come to think of it," he adds with mock disappointment.
"We're not flirtin'; we're just having a laugh," I say, wondering what the difference is.
"If you say so."
"I'd rather be shot than poisoned," I say defensively.
"She's smartened herself up since I was here last; I bumped into her in Kenchester last week. I hardly recognized her. Don't tell me you haven't noticed? …I wonder why?"

"Mmmm. ….I had noticed, but hadn't suspected an ulterior motive thought….'praps she just saw herself in a mirror."

I think back to the conversation I'd had with Nisha last week, before she left for the office. "Going somewhere nice?" I'd asked.

"No, just to the office…Why?" she'd asked.

"You look smart today, I mean smarter than usual," I'd hastily added.

She'd preened, "Thankyou," turning sideways so I couldn't miss the weight loss.

"You mean I usually look a right slut?" she'd joked, but fishing for more compliments.

"No." I'd lied. "You've lost weight as well," I'd said genuinely.

"Or are they those Magic Knickers, from M&S," I'd half joked.

"No they're not! You cheeky bugger! I've lost seven pounds!" she'd squawked.

"Well done," I'd said. Only another five stone to go, I'd thought.

She'd laughed, "Magic knickers… huh' don't know why I bother…I've gone off you… Anyway, how come you're such an expert? You one of those perves that hangs about the lingerie section? ".

"Well one has to keep a-breast, of developments in that department."

With a throaty laugh she'd asked suggestively, "Oh yes. You a breast man?" and raised her eyebrows and heaved her doughy baps for consideration; which had only reminded me of a Les Dawson character.

Barry coughs theatrically, "You wouldn't like to turn them over as well?"

"Eh!" Startled, and thinking I'd been thinking aloud; I turned to find Barry looking at the floor.

" I wish I'd brought my wellies." He said glumly.

"Eh. Oh yeah, no problem.... You're lucky you're only standing on it, look at the state of me," I complain, looking down at my jeans. ".... I've had to crawl about in it.... looks as if I've slept in a pigeon loft."

"Penny for them?"

"What?"

"You were miles away."

"I wish I was...I was thinking about Magic Knickers... Do you think Nisha wears them?"

Barry laughs, "What on earth are magic knickers? Are they self-cleaning?"

Thinking back to the pile of bloomers that were recently evicted, "That would be a good idea; perhaps we should patent the idea... No, they're knickers that squidge everything in so that you look about half the size.... I wonder if they have a warning label, like they have on tipper lorry tailgates, 'Warning Stand Well-Back When Unloading!'.... Imagine being buried alive when you release it all."

Barry grimaces, "What a way to go."

"Gives a new meaning to the expression, 'passion killer'."

"'Glad girls never wore them in my day," says Barry.

"Yeah, you'd have come out from behind the bike shed with a hand looking like you'd fallen asleep in the bath," I say laughing at the image.

"You had to marry a girl if you got that far," he laughs, "...anyway we never had bikes when I was at school,"

"Maybe not the wheeled variety," I say.

"Oy! 'You casting nasturtiums about my wife," he says convulsing; almost losing his footing on his stepladder, "Whoa! Nearly. You'll be the death of me Charles."

"Well as I'm such a health hazard, you'll be glad to know, I'll be out of your way in about... ten minutes."

Barry tilts his head at me, "You're too kind old boy."

"Any time old thing."

"What you got to do in the kitchen?" he asks.

"Oh, Frank wants the kicker-boards replacing, although it was so long ago that he asked, he's probably forgotten… probably take all afternoon to find the new ones; I put them in the garage months ago. They'll be buried under mounds of rubbish by now," adding with more than a hint of exasperation, "There's nothing wrong with the old ones."

We continue working absorbed in our own thoughts, accompanied by the noise of our work. Barry sounding like a high performance car with wide tyres on a wet road, as he removes the paper from the walls in long rhythmic arcs. While I produce tormented screams from the reluctant nails securing the floorboards; conjuring up images of a certain person impaled on the same jemmy

"So… does that mean you and Irene were at school together then?"

"Eh. Oh yeah. But we weren't courting then; not 'til we met at a dance a couple of years later."

"So was she your first girlfriend then?"

"First - and last I suppose."

I look at Barry, "What? D'ya mean you've never been out with anyone else?" I try to mask my astonishment; obviously unsuccessfully.

"It was quite normal in those days. People didn't, how do you call it, 'Play the field', like your generation.

"So how old were you when you got married?" I asked.

"Twenty," adding wistfully, "…Yes, happily married for five years."

I laugh, recognizing an old joke coming.

"Yes, we've been married fifty five years," Barry says laughing, "…the first five were happy."

Remembering what Barry had said earlier, "So, if you two got together a couple of years after school, and you *had* to get married at twenty," I said mischievously, "It must've taken you a heck of a long time to get past the old knicker elastic."
"There was such a thing as a women's honour in those days," he says laughing. Then suddenly realising exactly what I'd said, "We didn't *have* to get married, we…"
"Just couldn't wait any longer to get your leg over."
"Irene couldn't," he laughs.
"I suppose you're still holding-out now; still a virgin."
"Vergin' on the insane…I wondered why our two looked like the milkman."

Barry looks at me, "How about you? Where did you meet Alex?"

I wonder whether I should lie. Barry is obviously pretty straight laced underneath all the joking. It wasn't a period of my life to boast about. Besides it appears as though things have come full circle, and now I'm on the receiving end.

Barry senses my hesitation, "Tell me to mind my own business…"
"No. Fair's fair, I started it; I'm the nosey bugger…

"…Alex was originally a neighbour when I lived with someone else. She was married." To avoid Barry feeling the need to say anything, I enlarged, "It's not a period of my life that I am particularly proud of. … I was only about twenty…. I don't even know how it started… But when you realise that you're in love with someone, the feelings of their partner don't enter the equation."

Not that I'll be so understanding if I get my hands on Slyman bloody Gatley.

I'd been watching Barry out of the corner of my eye. I was aware that his scraping action was less determined or directed; it was now confined to short strokes in one place. He was looking at me, attentively, his expression displaying neither disapproval nor encouragement, merely interest; with no indication that he intended to interrupt me. I wondered with some amusement whether Barry might unwittingly scrape a hole through the plasterboard wall.

I continued, "You can't imagine how painful it is to know that the person you love, is sharing a bed with someone else every night. And if her husband's unaware of her infidelity, probably expects a normal physical relationship. And even if he is, he may be trying to hold their marriage together by pretending things are normal; avoiding a confrontation …'praps hoping the affair would fizzle out…

It obviously didn't work. So is there a lesson there?

"Christmas' and holidays were a nightmare. Christmas' were spent with our own families; and obviously I didn't go on holiday with them."

I looked at Barry who had by now thankfully stopped scraping and avoided falling through the wall. I wasn't sure whether he was uncomfortable by my confession, or surprised by my serious tone; not a particularly common event. He appeared to be cogitating.

"Well Father Barry, what are the chances o' me gettin' one o' them there halos like yours?"

"Better than they are of an Oscar for that Welsh accent," he laughs.

"Welsh? It wasn't that bad was it?"

"Well put it like this, these are probably the only boards you'll tread….. It was obviously not your acting skills that attracted Alex." He picked at a loose piece of wallpaper that had caught his attention; like an irresistible scab.

"Hmmm," he continues, while tearing the shard like piece of wallpaper up to the ceiling in one satisfying piece; momentarily looking like a stalactite before fluttering like a wounded bird to the floor.

"…I suppose you can't help who you fall in love with," he muses, "…if the chemistry is there, and I suppose you have been together for twenty years or so… so it wasn't exactly a feckless fling…

"What was his name?"

"Alex's first husband?" I had to think for a second, over the years he'd become a vague memory, maybe a subconscious act. I'd been trying to remember it since last night; I expect he'll have a good laugh when he hears; if he hasn't already. Maybe I really am the last to know.

"Gwyn." His name just popped into my head.

"Is he Welsh?"

"Most of Kenchester, in fact, most of Herefordshire seems to have Welsh blood…'s wonder there are any left in Wales."

"Did he marry again?"

"Yeah. He found someone quite quickly, didn't hang about, got a couple of kids just a bit older than ours. I'm really pleased… worked out well for him. Though I don't suppose he feels he owes me a drink…. a barrel or two maybe… of a shotgun."

"He didn't ask you to be his best man then?" laughs Barry.

"I've never forgiven him for that," I say dryly.

Barry squints at his paint-spattered watch, through paint-spattered spectacles, and more by instinct, declares, "It's nearly bait-time; time to make my flask. Do you want me to make yours, or have you got plenty?"

"No thanks. I've got plenty left, thanks to the Perky Professor; I didn't feel much like drinking at morning bait...I'll just finish lifting these last couple of boards, then I can have a clean start in the kitchen after."

Barry laughs, "Did you say, 'clean start'?

"I was trying not to think about that before I'd eaten," I say, "…let's see if we can cheer the prof up."

"Well you could start by not calling him, Prof."

“Yes dad.

Chapter 11

Wayne is half way up the field; in his open plan office. I make a drinking gesture, which he acknowledges with a thumbs-up, I cross the car park to the garage and plonk myself down on one of the plastic garden chairs opposite Barry. I'd called in at the kitchen to wash my hands and nearly walked straight back out again.

"How the hell did you manage to make your flask?" I ask incredulously, "…I could hardly get my hands under the tap, let alone a kettle…"

"Why would you want to put your hands under a kettle?" laughs Barry.

"Eh, oh very quick."

"I've been working with you too long, pay-back time."

"…I'm surprised you could even find the kettle….that can't just be last night's washing up, looks like a week's. Considering they eat out so often, they seem to generate a lot of washing up; especially as they have a dishwasher."

Barry shakes his head, I'm not sure whether it's in amazement or disgust.

"Maybe they haven't worked out how to use it…I thought I might have to come and prise you off the floor," he says, "…my feet kept sticking."

"I know….It reminded me of those sucker things that we kept the soap on the side of the bath with, when we were kids. Shhlup, shhlup," I try to impersonate the sound of feet being peeled off sticky quarry tiles, "It reminded me of the one and only time I did a shift behind the bar as a student….It's a good job I do my laces tight, otherwise my boots would still be in the middle of the floor now."

Wayne enters the garage looking extremely pleased with himself, but then remembers that he is supposed to be mardy with us. He flops into the other vacant chair, alongside me, ignoring us. He attends to his bait box and flask with an exaggerated air, acting the specialist on the Antiques Roadshow; presented with a rare find. I half expect him to turn the box over and have orgasms on discovering the Tupperware sign. Or have a dead faint when realising he's been using a flask for daily use from the Thermos Dynasty.

I look at Barry to find him shaking his head, and grinning at me over his mug. I hadn't realised before just how much head shaking Barry does. I'd read an article recently about sportsmen and headbangers having strokes. Could he give himself brain damage I wonder?

I consider simply ignoring Wayne; hoping that he will soon come out of his sulk. I would normally have asked about his morning's progress, but as I hadn't heard much activity below the bathroom window, I'm sure he would have quite rightly misinterpreted my interest as stirring; likewise any references to his detecting.

The awkward silence is unbearable.

"How come you didn't bring that collie of yours, Midge, as you're working outside today, Wayne?" I ask out of inspiration. Barry gives me a thumbs up, down by his side away from Wayne, and mouths, 'Good one'.

Wayne seems a little startled by the shattered silence, and nearly chokes on an entire steak and kidney pie. His usual impression of a cement mixer, is replaced by one of a large reptile trying to swallow its prey whole. I'm just grateful not to have Barry's frontal view of this spectacle. I glance at him, and notice he's trying to conceal his discomfort; yet appears to be mesmerised. His face is a picture of revulsion, and to avoid Wayne's wrath, I turn away from them to hide my amusement.

I've almost forgotten my question by the time Wayne stops 'slapping his chops', and noisily sluices his gullet with an enormous slurp of coffee.
"Haaah!" He gasps, "I never bloody well knew that I was gonna be outside … I thought I was gonna be in the bloody bathroom with you two."
"Doing what?
Nothing, the same as outside.
"…. I've finished up there for the time being, I'll be in the kitchen this afternoon." I see Wayne's grey cells working overtime, "I thought I'd bake us a cake for tea," I quickly add.
"Oooh, I'll look forward to that," jokes Barry.
"I bloody don't," snaps Wayne, " I wunt eat anythin' from that kitchen; 'ave you seen it today," he half laughs. He checks his phone for the time, "They're late back … do you think they're comin' 'ome or eatin' out?"
"I've no idea, they didn't say, maybe they've run out of crockery. Come to think of it, I think Nisha said she'd see us at lunchtime," I say.
As if on cue, a loud blast of car horn signals Frank's rapid approach.
"Look out! Here comes Stirling Moss," says Barry.
Wayne and I both laugh, "Blimey, you're showing your age," we chorus.
Frank's Range Rover sweeps onto the car park, scattering gravel, and abruptly stops as though abandoned in the middle. Frank heaves himself out using the roof handle and door pillar for leverage, then swings his legs out and slides earthwards. In the process, his trousers are pulled up so tight that it looks as though he's been suspended, rather uncomfortably from the waistband; leaving little to the imagination. His trouser legs halfway up his calves, reveal pasty white hairless flesh and bright green socks He looks as though he's auditioning for the circus.

"Hi. How's it going?" he asks in a slightly higher than normal pitch.
He walks round in a circle; like a dog before lying down. His left hand frantically attempts to hoick his trousers from between his buttocks, while the other attempts to salvage his family tree before the lack of blood supply does irreparable damage, at the same time flinging alternate legs in a jig in an effort to reunite his trousers and flapping boot straps..

"Nice moves Frank, you look a real disco diva," I laugh, joined by Barry and Wayne, much to Frank's embarrassment.
"He's still auditioning for Legs and Co.," I mutter.
"God, now who's showing their age?" hisses Wayne, stifling a laugh.
"Eh! What!" yelps Frank, "What's that about Sebastian Coe?"

I wonder what Frank actually hears when he's eaves-dropping; it's probably more interesting than the truth.

"We were discussing Seb Coe, I said, I bet you'd know him… you moving in all those sporting circles years ago." Realising the unintentional pun I add, "I didn't mean the circles you were moving in just now."
"Eh! Oh, I thought I'd dropped something," Frank responds, embarrassed as he realises he hadn't exactly looked Mister Cool.
"It looked like you were trying to *get* a couple of things to drop," I laugh.
Barry shakes his head, before appearing to be myopic by hiding his face in his bait-box. Wayne wheezes.

"Well ya know um, ya know. When I was at school ya know like that, I used to run for the county," Frank said, looking at each of us, as though expecting adulation.

Here we go, Frank's Fantasy World.
"Really!" I say, trying to sound genuinely impressed. I make a winding–up motion on Frank's blind side for Barry's benefit; who closes his eyes to avoid smirking.

"Oh yeah, I was as fast, I was as fast ya know like that, as Seb Coe when I was at school; faster probably. Yeah faster. I could have run for England, mmm definitely, yeah definitely."

"I ran for England once," I interjected.

"Yeah? Really?" Frank sounding genuinely impressed.

"Yeah from about two hundred yards inside Scotland."

"Closely followed by a couple of million midges," laughs Barry.

"I thought you were going to say husbands," I say, giving Barry a conspiratorial look whose expression gives nothing away. He could have been a poker player…For all I knew he was one.

"Yeah, anyway," continues a baffled Frank, "I reckon I could have run for England. Yeah, easily."

I can't imagine Frank running for a bus; let alone for England. He'd just about manage twenty yards providing there was a 'Take-Away' waiting at the end. As for anything resembling a run, well that was stretching the imagination. I have a vision of Frank chasing a pie on a piece of string; like dog racing.

All I manage to say with a straight face is, "Really! Wow! That takes some believing I mean doing."

"Yeah I could definitely have run for England," he repeats more confidently; believing we believe him.

"What happened?" I ask.

"Eh! What d' ya mean?"

I don't want him to feel cornered; or to think that we don't believe him. Which we don't, but, "Well why did you just stop, when you were obviously so talented?"

"Well ya know um, well ya know…"

I try to help, "'Cos didn't you used to play cricket for England…and rugby… and football…and…"

"Jump tall buildings," interjects Barry.

"Stop speeding trains and bullets," I add trying to keep a straight face, but my stomach gives an impression of a couple of ferrets fighting inside my sweatshirt.

"Oh yeah!…Well ya know, they wanted me to, ya know like that… I could've done…mmmm definitely, definitely. Ya know ya know I was in all the school teams, all the county teams… everything ya know, everything."
I try to sound solicitous, "So what happened… to this dream?"
Apart from waking up.
I continue quickly, "…I mean it must be every schoolboy's dream to play for their country; let alone at nearly every sport. Did you have a terrible life transforming accident that ruined your sporting career?"

Frank looks decidedly uncomfortable, and attempts to pace around the small clearing we have excavated amongst the flotsam and jetsam. "Well ya know, ya know, it was like ya know, I left school, like that. Yeah I left school…"
"Like ya do," I say encouragingly.
"Eh! Yeah, course ya do. What I mean is, I left school, I left school like that…"

At this point I'm dying to see Barry and Wayne's expression, but daren't look at them; I sense that they're bursting.

"….ya know, I left school…"

I was beginning to wonder how many schools Frank had attended.
"….Oh that's right!" he exclaims as though experiencing a sudden return of memory; instead of a flash of inspiration. "…I left school to do my A levels," he declares triumphantly.

Several expectant seconds pass, waiting for Frank to enlarge. Talk about a pregnant pause.
"So you gave up the chance to fulfil your dreams of running out onto the turf at Wembley, Twickenham, Lords and god knows where else….For A levels?" I ask, with just a hint of cynicism.

"…I thought most sportsmen manage both, perhaps you should have dropped a few… ya know concentrated on just a couple of national teams." I hold the inside of my cheeks between my teeth to keep a straight face.

"Oh no, no, no not just A levels. No, course not, course not…" he stammers.

He has the air of someone who has discovered that the lifeboat that he has just jumped into, doesn't just have a hole in the bottom, it doesn't even have a bottom.

"…. ya know, not just A levels, ya know…. I discovered girls," he declares beaming salaciously and attempts to puff his chest out, like a strutting cockerel.

Unfortunately he can't pull his stomach in enough to make any discernable difference, and his pervy grin just makes him look demented. I think, the poor sod's lifejacket has turned out to be made of lead into the bargain. Wayne perks up at the prospect of sexual revelations; even Frank's.

"So did ya put it about a bit then Frank… before ya met Nisha?" asks Wayne enthusiastically.

Frank looks noticeably relieved. At last! A seaworthy lifeboat. Although he must be the first man to throw away the chance of making sporting history, to get his leg over; I assume most athletes manage both.

I'm not sure if the broad grin he is directing at Wayne is out of gratitude for saving him, or he recognises a gullible victim, and is relishing the prospect of more tales from Frank's Fantasy World. Barry and I exchange knowing glances and prepare to be entertained.

"Well ya know what it's like lads," he says, grinning at each of us conspiratorially.

I sense Barry glance in my direction and remember our earlier conversation.

"I can't remember that far back," I laugh.

"Nor me," laughs Barry.

Frank's 'Cheshire' smile momentarily fades as he suspects that we're not going to accommodate him.

Wayne again to the rescue, "How many did ya have?" he asks eagerly, his curtain grin twitching in anticipation of some titillating details.

"Well ya know ya know," Frank says, his eyes quickly sweep each of us, trying to gauge our gullibility, while avoiding eye contact. He looks at the floor, shrugs his shoulders and pulls a face to suggest nonchalance, but laughs nervously, "… hundreds," he coughs.

"Oh is that all? I thought you were going to say thousands," I say mischievously, giving Barry an imperceptible wink to return his eyeballs to their rightful place.

"Eh! What! Yeah well it could've been thousands... yeah thousands...it could easily have been thousands. Well ya know what it's like, you lose track, I wasn't counting… different one every night, ya know," he laughs, unsure whether he has convinced us.

"Well in that case I suppose it could have been tens of thousands," I say encouragingly.

Barry snorts and Wayne looks wistful. Frank looks up at the garage ceiling as though doing a mental calculation, "No I don't think it was that many; could've been I suppose," he says seriously.

A few seconds lapse in stunned silence as we mull over the absurdity of Frank's latest fantasy, while trying to keep a straight face.

"Your dick must have been a blur," I say. "So how old were you when you met Nisha? You both look to be in your early twenties in your wedding photos."

Recognising my line of questioning, Frank realises the need for a sharp exit; as they say in the adverts. He pointedly consults his watch, "Oh, I need to make a phone call…see you in a bit."

Frank attempts a manly swagger across the car park, which is difficult while trying to keep his 'Bobby Charlton' in place.

I do a poor rendition under my breath of, "I must have been through a million girls…"

"Elvin Bishop , I Fooled Around In Love, 1975."

"Ooh, I'm impressed Wayne."

"You missed your vocation there Rumpole," chuckles Barry.

"I presume you're referring to my cross-examination of Frank, and not my singing."

Nisha's Range Rover, by contrast to Frank's, cruises sedately onto the car park and manoeuvres around his recently abandoned one. Unlike Frank, Nisha maintains her modesty while alighting, by the simple fact of being obscured by her car as she slithers out. But her body movements betray the hurried rearranging of clothing; like a hen shaking down its feathery petticoats after the cockerel's given her the best three seconds of her life. She walks round to the back of the car to collect her shopping and greets us with a wave, "Hi. Alright?" she calls brightly.

"Nice hair-do," I call back.

"Oh, you noticed," she calls back, "I'm impressed…. Do you notice when Alex has her hair
done?

"'Course. I wonder how many bottles of wine it cost," I shout back.

She laughs throatily and shakes her new hair, "You men!" and does her best to skip as lightly up the steps to the house as is possible, when burdened like a pack-mule. Carrier bags bounce off her knees with each step, and the straining handles look in danger of giving out.

"'Hope they like scrambled eggs," I say.

Barry laughs, "I was just going to say, I hope they like broken biscuits."

I wait for Wayne to remark on my flirting.
Instead he eventually surfaces from his reverie and says dreamily, "Thousands."

Chapter 12

I return to the house, and walk straight into the kitchen where Frank is hunched protectively over a mountain of chicken drumsticks. I can't help staring, I'm mesmerised. Gripping a drumstick in each fist a few inches from his face, smeared with a reddish sauce. His arms swing rapidly on small arcs, elbows at shoulder height, allowing him to snatch a bite from alternate drumsticks. He reminds me of a crab, stuffing its mandibles with rapidly moving stubby pincers. Each stripped drumstick is discarded, and replaced by sleight of hand.

While gorging, he continues to discuss my morning's progress and plans for the afternoon. I was just glad to be out of range of the spray of barely masticated chicken and spicy sauce.
"Mmmmm, owd dya ge on iss ornin?
"Fine, I was …"
"Dy ink yull ge fished safnoon?
"I've done as much as I can 'til Barry finishes stripping…" I try to sound relaxed and conversational, but find myself swaying like a boxer, ready to take evasive action in the event of any long-range discharge, although I was rather a sitting-duck as I was having great difficulty peeling my feet off the sticky floor.

"…I thought I'd replace the kicker-boards in here the s'afternoon while I've got the chance…. if I'm not in Nisha's way."
Frank swallows hard and frantically, "Mmm, yeah, good idea."
I nod at the drumsticks awaiting his attention, "I'll come back when you've finished your lunch."

Fortunately his mouth is otherwise engaged, and I interpret the contented growl that follows me to the front door as gratitude.

I return to the van to collect a few tools and dustsheets, and notice Wayne lurking awkwardly with a carrier bag.

"Been shopping?" I say.
"Eh. Oh yeah, very funny. I er..I heard the front door and thought you were Frank going back to the office."
"So you got him a present?"
Wayne's curtain grin flashes, "No I've got a load of receipts for Frank... he claims the VAT back for me...I reckon there's about eight hundred quid here."
"Of VAT?"
"Yeah."

"How do you both put the same receipts through your books? .... Doesn't your accountant want to see them?"

Wayne laughs as though he were a tutor at finishing school and I had committed a breach of etiquette common amongst undergraduates from the lower classes.
"What accountant?...You should ask Frank to claim the VAT back for ya, I got 'undreds last year."
"I wish my accountant wasn't quite such a picky bastard," I say pinching Frank's line, adding, "P'raps he's worried about my lack of beauty sleep."
"Oh no! There aint no risk, they can't prove nothin'."

"I'll think about it," I lie. I have no intention of getting involved in anything remotely dodgy with Frank, especially if Wayne knows about it; neither of them could be described as discreet. No one likes paying tax, and all self-employed stretch the imagination in terms of creative accountancy, or so I'd thought; but you try not to wave too many red flags. If you've not even got the receipts to back up your expenditure claims then you're inviting trouble. You could get the same response by addressing the tax inspector as, Mike Hunt.

The front door slams, immediately followed by Frank shouting, "Oh fuck off!" at nobody apparent, as he marches determinedly towards his car with an expression that defies anyone to stop him.

Unfortunately Wayne is not very perceptive when it comes to body language and trots off, clutching his carrier bag of receipts as though catching a bus; hoping to intercept Frank before he gets to his car and races off to the office. Judging by Wayne's reaction he must have been about halfway across the car park, and starting to hail Frank, before realising Frank's impersonation of a man trying to hold a wasp in his mouth, meant that now was not the time to discuss dodgy VAT receipts.

"FRAaa.." It was now Wayne's turn for an impression, one of a pheasant running to and fro to avoid oncoming traffic. He nearly falls flat on his face as he changes direction half a dozen times in half as many seconds.

"Eh! What!" barks Frank.

Wayne almost collides with him, "I've brought those receipts," he blurts proffering the scrunched up carrier bag as though he were clutching a chicken by the neck. "I…"
Frank looks blankly at Wayne, "What receipts!" and then for a split second at the bag before grabbing it… "Oh yeah I'll see what I can do!" he barks.

Frank's attempt at a dramatic departure falls rather flat and only heightens his embarrassment, as he wrestles the roaring Range Rover to perform a twenty-five-point turn. Wayne is left standing as though he's the victim of a bag snatcher.

"Teach him to park properly," I laugh.
"Fuuckiiin' 'ell," Wayne drags out, "What's got into 'im?"
"I don't know, but I'm not looking forward to working inside; it's not exactly going to be, 'The House of Fun'"

I return to the now empty kitchen. The remains of Frank's lunch, a plateful of stripped chicken legs, sit at the far end of the table along with an opened can of diet coke; probably Frank's only concession to calorie control intake. Well at least there's no blood, so at least they hadn't come to blows; not in the kitchen at any rate.

Come to think of it, the house is unusually quite considering Barry is supposed to be working upstairs. I stick my head round the door into the living room on my way to the stairs. No sign of Nisha.

I glide stealthily up the stairs and through the master bedroom and enter the ensuite bathroom. Barry has his back to the door and is engrossed in his own thoughts while trying to remove the old tiles from the wall silently. It's strange how the embarrassing domestic scene has transformed the usual buzz, into the atmosphere of an empty church.

I tap the door lightly and as Barry lumbers around inquisitively in a clockwise direction, rather like an ageing bear, I shadow his movement and then lean nonchalantly against the wall that he'd been working on.

Shrugging his shoulders at the empty doorway he gives a puzzled, "Hmm…" before taking a step forward to peer into the bedroom, "…Hmmm, must be going mad."

"Well you know what they say about talking to yourself."

Barry jumps so high his head nearly hits the doorframe, "Uugh!" he grabs the doorframe for support as his knees momentarily buckle on landing. He turns around trembling, "Where the bloody hell did you come from? Are you trying to give me a bloomin' heart attack?

"Sorry," I say genuinely shocked at Barry's reaction, and feeling rather stupid, "I didn't expect to startle you as much as that; I forget how old you are."

Fortunately Barry sees the funny side, "You'll be the death of me creeping around like that…. I still don't know how you got in here," he says laughing. Then, as though struck by guilt for a lack of reverence, he almost mimes, "I take it you weren't downstairs when they were having their little spat?" Some of his words are almost lost; I attempt to lip-read and strain my ears.

I reply in hushed tones, our murmurings probably travelling further than normal conversation, and betraying our gossiping. "No. That's why I've come up to see you; get the goss. You should have seen Frank's face, talk about, 'if looks could kill'. Poor old Wayne, I don't think it was the best time to discuss reclaiming VAT on receipts, I thought Frank was gonna chew his head off; Wayne nearly filled his pants....Where's Nisha? She's not downstairs."

"She came storming into the bedroom, slamming the door behind her...between the two of you I've probably aged about twenty years in the last ten minutes, then she must have remembered I was in here 'cos she stormed out again, I think she went to the girl's bedroom. It sounded as though she was crying."

"Blimey, what was it about, did you hear?"

"Well I didn't really catch it all... they started in the kitchen... I heard him shouting at her from the hall before he slammed out though." Barry chewed his bottom lip and looked at me as though reluctant to betray a confidence.

I pretend to study the empty bathroom now that it's a blank canvas for potential layout ideas; not that Frank will listen to anyone else's ideas.

"Well. I haven't got all afternoon; I've got kickers to replace, I'd better have something to show for this afternoon."

"Mmm, like I said, I didn't hear it all, but it sounded as though Nisha was having a go at him for not noticing her new hairdo, reckons she might as well wear a bag on her head for all he'd notice."

"'s not her head that needs covering up, it's the middle ....short of permanently advertising Michelin tyres I don't know what to suggest."

He gives a dry laugh, "You are cruel; you'll be fat one day... Anyway, she reckons that he spots the smallest mistake in our work but never takes any notice what she looks like."

"Maybe she wants to be screwed in as many positions as the dado rails get around here," I laugh, but sense that Barry is holding back on a crucial piece. "Mmm, but that wouldn't be enough to send him schizo…surely."

"She reckons that it's only the men that notice when she makes an effort."

"Well you'd have to be blind not to notice when she's had her hair done, she usually leaves it until she looks like Whoopie Goldberg in 'Sister Act'; ya know like the proverbial black sheep, only electrified. Then she's like a freshly shorn one when she gets back.

"Well, from what I heard, Frank reckons I'm blind, and Wayne's a sheep shagger; so apparently we hardly qualify as Miss World judges."

"'Praps the black sheep analogy was rather unfortunate," I laugh, "anyway you're not blind - well not completely, and Wayne probably wouldn't shag just any old sheep…he's too racist to shag black ones…

"… And on what grounds did he invalidate my opinion?"

"He didn't…. that's when the shit hit the fan."

Suddenly bathroom design no longer held any interest.

"What d'ya mean?" I ask, feeling my eyebrows pole-vault into my hairline.

Barry looks awkward and probably wished that he could claim deafness to add to his growing list of failing faculties.

"Well I'm not sure I heard her right…she was screaming from the kitchen," he flicked his eyes to me and then back to the floor, "I…. Well I thought she said something like, 'Well Charles isn't! And he always notices anything new about me!"

"Shit! That's all I need…What did Frank say to that?"

"Nothing. Well not about that…Then he slammed out the door."

"Mmm. Maybe he's jealous 'cos his only alternative to his Bobby Charlton, is a French polished job," I say almost distractedly.

"Oh you are aweful… you'll be bald one day," he camps distractedly.

I puzzle over Barry's even greater apathetic demeanour. I rerun everything Barry has just relayed to me. Surely it should be me that has cause for concern.

"Hang on. What do you mean, *nothing well not about that?* What was his parting shot before storming off, that's got you behaving like a condemned man?"

Barry studies me awkwardly as though we're complete strangers, and not sure whether I can be trusted. I feel decidedly uncomfortable. I wonder what the hell Frank could possibly have said that seems to have dissolved nearly ten years of friendship, together with the trust and respect. My awkwardness probably only reinforces any suspicions of guilt that Barry is harbouring.

"I don't know whether I should repeat this, or even how…it's not easy…"

"I can see that. It looks as though Frank has accused me of something and you believe him, so perhaps you should…"

"Oh no, that's just it. He accused Nisha of taking a load of money from his dressing table to pay for all these fancy gym sessions - clothes and hairdo's. That's the problem, she denied it. She reckons that she hasn't touched a penny of the tight fucker's - her words not mine."

I'm stunned. I'm pretty sure I know who has had his fingers in the till; the image of Wayne fondling that bundle of notes yesterday springs to mind. But pointing the finger may appear that I'm trying to deflect suspicion, and just incriminate myself further…especially as it was only Wayne and myself present.

"Did he say how much has gone missing?"

"Frank reckons he put two thousand in the drawer last Friday, and now it's gone…"

Again the image of Wayne in front of the drawer fondling the wad springs to mind.

"Trouble is... If Nisha didn't take it, who did? We're all under suspicion, and I know I never had it," Barry says adamantly, holding my stare.

I feel as though I'm in front of the headmaster again at school.

"I think I know who had it, but I expect you'll think that's rather convenient... "

Barry maintains eye contact, "I'm all ears."

I resist my usual impulsive *wing-nut* quip, even I realise the seriousness of the situation.

"The drawer was open yesterday displaying a great wad of twenties and Wayne shut the drawer, but not before giving it a good feel...judging by the look on his face it was the best sex ever."

"I can't believe it," Barry sighs.

I'm not exactly sure what he doesn't believe.

"Trouble is if I tell Nisha what I suspect, she'll wonder how we know the money's missing...and suspect I'm laying a false trail..."

"I'm surprised you and Wayne couldn't hear them outside - I bet half the village could hear them."

"I wonder whether we should wait for her or Frank to raise the subject...

As if my life wasn't complicated enough at the moment.

"...Oh well, I'd better get on replacing those kicker-boards."

"So Wayne's still bringing receipts for Frank to reclaim the VAT is he? I don't know how they get away with half their scams," says Barry in an attempt to change the subject. But I'm preoccupied with the various scenarios generated by Barry's eaves droppings.

"I'll see you later," then retreat downstairs whistling, 'Wish me luck as you wave me goodbye.'

*****

Apart from the sound of tools clinking, clanking and scraping on the quarry tiles, and the peeling of dust sheets off the sticky quarry tiles when they require repositioning, I work in silence; feeling like an intruder. Judging by the lack of noise from the bathroom above me Barry obviously feels the same; aware that Nisha definitely wishes the house was free of workmen this afternoon.

The sound of a door opening upstairs at the far end of the house, followed by watery noises in the girl's bathroom above my head, tells me Nisha must be on the move.

Probably getting ready for the school run.

A few moments later I look up as she enters the kitchen looking like a child that's just woken up after crying herself to sleep. One side of her face needs a good steam iron to remove the deep creases, and her eyes look puffy and red. She works her tongue around the inside of her lips and around teeth, and flexes her mouth attempting to generate saliva.

Obviously gasping for a drink she heads straight for the kettle, "Cup of tea." It sounds more of a statement than a question, but I answer anyway. It seems rude not to, "Great. I'd love one."

Leaning forward to fill the kettle, her stomach envelops the worktop edge in front of the sink. She arches backwards as though to counter balance and avoid being pulled in.

She stifles a yawn, "Ohhhh god. …I never sleep in the afternoon; I always feel terrible when I wake up."
"I know… You won't be able to sleep tonight," I say suggestively, and instantly regret; recognising the direction this will lead.
"Pah! He can forget about that, the bastard!" and puts the kettle down harder than intended, forcing it to ejaculate. "Oh bollocks," she says flatly, and sets about mopping up.

"Lan-guage!" I reproach.

"Sorry," she says. "You know I don't usually swear.... It's all your fault anyway."
"Oh it usually is," I say.
"What do you mean?" she asks defensively.
"Well at home if anything goes wrong, it's my fault; so why should it be any different here?"
"Ah, you poor boy," she coos.
"So why's it my fault today?" I ask.
"Oh it doesn't matter," she sighs, "...it's not really your fault."

The kettle climaxes with a noisy click. I hope Nisha preoccupies herself with tea making; offering the chance for a change of topic. I should have known better; Nisha ignores a boiling kettle in normal circumstances. I mentally grimace at the prospect of another tepid cuppa.

Nisha pretends to find something of interest outside the window; eventually she gives an enormous sigh. She gives the impression of an inflatable Father Christmas that pops-up annually in certain front gardens to accompany the perennial garden gnomes, but has just received the attentions of an air rifle.

Then she remembers the kettle, as if tea made using tepid water wasn't bad enough, made with tea bags in the mug is decidedly disgusting.

I attempt to change the subject, "Have you got the school run in a bit, or are they staying for clubs?" I ask knowing full well that although Alice is quite sporty, the most energetic thing Sophie does is brush her teeth.
"Well Alice has rounders, but Sophie needs picking up at the normal time after sixth form, and she needs a new jacket; so we'll go straight on into Hereford," she says, sounding a little more enthusiastic.

"A little retail therapy for you," I suggest, then noticing the rapidly chilling mugs of tea, "Is one of those for Barry, shall I take his up?"

"Would you mind? They're both the same ..."

Yeah they're both probably disgusting.

"...Barry has sweeteners."

"No, it's okay, I need to ask him about tomorrow anyway," I say, thinking, it'll take more than sweeteners to make this palatable.

"Oh, in case I forget to ask before I go, can you two lock up and set the alarm when you go?"

"Yeah okay. It'll probably be Barry. Wayne and I finish before him.... as we're supposed to start earlier ..."

" Oh crikey! I've forgotten to make Wayne a cuppa."

"I noticed you were only making two, I thought you were only making it for the workers."

Nisha laughs while proceeding to make Wayne's tea from a tepid kettle.

Why should Barry and I be the only ones to suffer I think, looking at the two congealing mugs in my right hand.

"Two sugars in Wayne's?"

"How many years have you been making drinks for us?" I laugh.

She laughs, "I know, I don't know why I asked; I do know really..."

"...Course I've noticed. Do you think I'm blind ...and deaf? Eric gets here really early, sometimes about seven if the weather's really nice, but usually about eight; the same as you. Wayne gets here about half past... see nothing gets past me...

"Talking of which, what's he supposed to be doing today?"

"Wayne? I didn't know he was a witch," I laugh, "...the patio."

"Well he's certainly not a wizard, at laying patios, every time I look out the window he's halfway up the field on his damn phone."

"Really? I hadn't noticed."

Nisha laughs, and looks pointedly at me, "I thought *you* noticed everything."

"I'm selective....I'd better get this cuppa up to Barry."

At least it won't scald him, the skin might choke him though.
"Here, eat this," I say to Barry, offering a mug, "…a present from Nisha."
"Oooh tea! Thankyou, you are kind," he dramatizes, hauling himself to his feet from a kneeling position where he's been removing the bottom course of tiles, accompanied by groans and cracking knee joints.

Because Barry has never received anything other than tepid tea in all the years he's worked at The Funny Farm, he's learnt not to let it hang about to get any worse. He takes the offered mug, and without removing his spattered specs, takes a huge gulp. I watch expectantly.

He doubles up hoping to siphon the brew back into the mug, "AAAAGH!" he splutters through a fluttering curtain hanging from his top lip. "Uuugh! One minute you're trying to give me a heart attack…" he spits back into the mug and wipes the tea skin from his face, with a rag produced from his overall pocket, "…the next you're trying to poison me!"

"Sorry," I laugh, "I'll make us a decent cuppa in a few minutes when Nisha does the school run…. We could pour them down the soil-pipe," I say eyeing the pan connector that resembles the communications pipe between a ships bridge and the engine room.
"Good thinking," he says, taking our mugs and disposing of their rusty brown contents, while continuing to evict stubborn traces of rubberised tea from in and around his mouth, by alternately spitting and wiping with the back of his free hand.

"While you're there ask Scotty for max factor five."
"Eh. Oh Star Trek. Shouldn't that be warp factor? … I think the Enterprise had a better communications system than a smelly soil pipe," he laughs.

"Simple but effective," I say. "Oh while I remember, can you lock up and set the alarm, Nisha's not coming straight back; apparently Sophie needs a new coat or jacket."
"Probably find several new ones in amongst the piles of clothing …Have you noticed how many have still got the price tags on?"
"I know 's'ridiculous, they've been lying around for months," I say.

"You here tomorrow?" asks Barry.
"I'm not sure. Will I be able to get in here to put the floor down?"
"Well I should be finished stripping and ready for redecorating by the end of today…
"Is Nisha still here?"
"Why, do you want a cuppa?"
"Yeah that as well, but the phone's ringing."
"Blimey I can't hear it," I say leaning towards the doorway, straining to hear.
"That's because I'm only blind…'s you that's deaf," says Barry.

Our laughter is interrupted by Nisha calling up the stairwell, "Charles! The Bastard's on the phone, can he have a word?"

"The course of true love and all that," I mutter. Then another thought occurs to me, "Yippee! He's probably going to tell me not to bother coming back."
"You should be so lucky," laughs Barry.

I clamber down the stairs and take the receiver from Nisha who is busy mouthing obscenities at her beloved.

"Hi Frank. Everything okay?"
"Oh yeah, hi Charles. Yeah everything's fine. How are you getting on, you replacing the kickers in the kitchen?"
"Yeah I should get the long run, ya know…" I cringe, realising I've just adopted another of his catch phrases, "…with the sink units, dishwasher, fridge, hob and oven replaced this afternoon. I won't get the units on the other side of the kitchen done today

though, it'll take a while to move all the stuff in the garage to find all the new kicker-boards."
" How much more has Barry got to do before you can do the floor? I mean can you come in tomorrow if possible?"

"Er…" I try to think of a reason not to, but several days in succession are better for the cash flow, "… yes I should think so, I…"
"I mean, I'm not sure when the bathroom suite and shower are coming, but we may as well be ready ya know… ya know, so we can put the bathroom back together as soon as possible. The sooner we have our own bathroom back the better. It's a fuckin' nightmare having to share with the girls like that…"

I expect they'll get used to wearing wellies in the bathroom.
"Yeah I can imagine," I say sympathetically.

I imagine the poor girls are probably more fed up paddling in misdirected piddle and toothpaste though.

Chapter 13

Do I confront Alex? If I do, I know it will only lead to a blazing row. Especially as I know Alex will deny everything, despite the evidence, and I'll probably throw her out; that's if she doesn't flounce out first.

I can't believe she'd put everyone through this again.

"Dad, what's for dinner? ….Helloo."

"Eh. Oh what? Sorry, what did you say?"

"You've been working at the Knight's too long; you even sound like him now," Liz laughs. "I asked what was for dinner, I'm starving."

"Oh Christ knows, I haven't thought about it," I say checking my watch. "I suppose I'd better make a start… Be just my luck for your mum to come home early."

"Early? You mean before about nine," she huffs.

"Apparently she works flat out," I say dryly, feeling my stomach tightening.

I sense Liz regarding me cautiously as I rummage and inspect the contents of the fridge, with the enthusiasm of a vegetarian in an abattoir.

"Oh ff…" I slam the fridge door, "…I can't be bothered, we'll just have to have pizza and chips," I snap, reaching for the knob on the oven.

Returning from the freezer, my mood not helped by the bloody drawer fronts falling off, I try to bring the conversation back to less stressful topics.

"So, what time's hockey on Saturday?"

"I need to be in Kenchester for nine thirty," she replies listlessly.

"So you're not playing away then?"

Unlike some people I could mention.

"…Who are you playing?"

Liz shrugs, "Don't know…What time's mum home?"
I snort and shrug.

Her expression betrays her thoughts. I don't want her to know the truth, if Lizzie knew she'd been betrayed as well, it would make reconciliation almost impossible. I wonder what Adam' reaction would be?
"What's the matter?"
"Nothing. Why?" I try to sound surprised.
"Nothing? You've hardly said anything since you picked me up."
"Hmmph. I can't win – you and your mother always want me to be more serious – so now you've got serious," I shrug.
"There's serious and there's miserable – So what's wrong?"
"Oh nothing – not what you're thinking anyway – Can you make a salad, and keep an eye on the pizza and chips; I want to do something on the computer?" I say testily.

"Right you bastard. Let's see how much you really care for my wife. Is it love or lust?" My instinct was to find the bastard and bankrupt the tooth fairy. With a bit of luck I'd hit him in the pocket first.

In less than ten minutes I'd opened a new Hotmail account in Alex's name, and sent Slimey Simon an invitation I hoped he couldn't refuse.

"Are you on drugs or something?"
"What do you mean?"
"Well one minute you're a right mardy arse, the next you're grinning to yourself like someone that's escaped from the loony-bin."
"I thought your generation was supposed to be so PC - Oh, I was just remembering a joke that Barry told me today," I lied, frantically trying to think of one.
"So let's hear it then."

God, she sounds like a bloody teacher as well; as if one in the house wasn't bad enough.

"You won't like it."
"Try me."
"You asked for it…A white horse goes into a bar, and the barman says, 'We've got a whiskey named after you.' 'Really? Eric?' says the horse."

Liz raises her eyes and groans, "You telling me that's responsible for that idiotic grin since you came off the computer? Do you lot spend all day pulling crackers at Frank's?"
"No, just going crackers."
"Is it a coincidence that the name Eric features in a joke about whiskey?"
"Must be my subconscience."
"I thought you said it was Barry's joke."
"Now who fancies herself as Rumpole?"
"I suppose I should be flattered that you didn't say Columbo," Liz smirks.
"He may have been scruffy, but to the best of my knowledge he never appeared as a cross-dresser, 'specially girl's school uniforms…Not that Rumpole did either, maybe I should have said Miss Marple."

*****

"Spose we'd better put your mum's pizza in the oven to keep warm," I say, clearing our plates away. "Have you got much homework?"
"I wondered when you'd say that."
"I bet the suspense was killing you."
"Ha, ha, don't give up your day job," she laughs dryly, heading for the comfort of her lair, equipped with homework essentials, like TV and laptop.

The way things are going I definitely won't be able to afford to – I might even have to find another as well.

*****

The squeal of the front door hinges, followed by grunting and door slamming announces the return of the prodigal wife. Ebony unravels herself from her bed.

That was good timing; the washing up's done.

"God I'm starving, I've had nothing all day," she states, sniffing the air, and self-consciously pushes Ebony's nose away. Ebony seems more persistent than usual.

"Hi. Had a good day?"

Alex looks at me for signs of sarcasm.

"Not too bad," then brightens, "Our kids won a tag rugby match at Hampton Green Primary today."

"Day-night match was it?"

"I can't just come straight home, I left my classroom in a right mess; I had to go back and get it all ready for tomorrow, I haven't stopped all day," she wails.

"Your dinner's in the oven."

"Thanks," she says ungraciously.

I hope Slymon wasn't with her this evening otherwise he'll know the email can't have come from her. At least they'll know I know – That should be interesting.

"Is this it?" she asks.

"That's all we had; although it wasn't so shrivelled when we had ours."

Alex places her plate on the table with enough force to bounce the leathery repast nearly a foot above the plate.

"Do you want some water with that?" I ask calmly.

"No thanks, I'm not thirsty," she says, regarding her plate sullenly.

"I didn't mean to drink – I thought you might like to soak that," I say dryly.

"Thanks, you're all heart."

Alex tentatively attempts to chew on a triangle, resembling the skin of a Congolese leper.
"Oh, I heard a good bit of goss today. You remember that Head, what's-his-name, you mentioned him a few times, what was it… Gatley…Simon Gately…"

Alex stops chewing; even the slice of leper wilts symbolically in front of her gaping mouth.
"Well I heard today that he's been playing away from home… with some slapper he met on one of those Heads conferences…"

Alex chokes and splutters, "Really? I can't believe that…
"Sure you won't have a glass of water….

"…Apparently…" I continue nonchalantly, "…these conferences are real shag fests."

Chapter 14

Little Erics' gleaming white Ford Escort van is parked parallel with the front of the garage, as I park alongside I can hear him strimming nearby; but out of sight. I glance at my watch, five past eight. Eric likes to arrive about seven providing it's light enough, and he always starts under Frank and Nishas' bedroom window; reasoning, *"Why should they bloody sleep when I'm workin'?"*

The shrieking strimmer coughs, splutters and farts into silence as I get out of my van, the welcome silence announces that he's run out of petrol. Little Eric rolls into view, and approaches like an ancient mariner; or maybe that should be an ancient marinated. I always assumed his gait was the result of knackered knees, due to years of kneeling on cold concrete floors in his days as a garage mechanic - but now I'm not so sure.

He beams at me, "That was bloody good timing, I needs a refill."

Sniffing the whisky fumes I wonder whether he's referring to himself or the strimmer but I'm not in the mood to joke about his alcoholism so I just say, "I see you've been giving them their early morning call … are you going to take them tea in bed?"

Eric's laugh stimulates a phlegm shifting coughing fit. Backing into the garage so's to be out of sight from the house, he reaches into his pocket, "'Bout time for a quickie," he rasps.
"Best offer today," I mutter in as camp a way as I can muster.

In fact the only offer for ages.

But Eric is preoccupied with lighting up. He inhales deeply, his head momentarily thrown back in ecstasy, before the smoke triggers such violent coughing that I fear his false choppers may hurtle towards me at any moment. I wonder how I explain a 'love bite' to Alex – I wonder if she'd care.

Eventually the coughing slows to the sound of a badly running old grey Fergie tractor and he takes another long drag, followed by an equally long release, with the fumes appearing to escape from every orifice and shroud his head in a cloud. He closes his eyes and with an orgasmic facial expression exclaims, "Aaaah! That's better!"

"If that's better, I dread to think how you were feeling before."

Eric ignores the remark and asks, "What you on today? Ain't ya finished that bathroom yet?" he laughs, knowing full well that no job is ever allowed to progress smoothly here at The Grange; Frank wouldn't enjoy the project unless he has managed to complicate it.

Frank believes there is a direct relationship between expense and value. In other words, the more complicated and therefore more time consuming a project, equals more expense, therefore more added value to the property.

"I'm not sure… I should really be putting the floor down, but Barry's in there decorating…

"…Are they up and about yet?" I ask jerking my head towards the house.

"Well they won't be asleep even if they're not up," cackles Eric. "Which reminds me," he wheezes, kneeling down by the strimmer and unscrewing the filler, "I'd best get on."

"I don't know about getting *on*, you'll be getting *off* this planet if you don't take that fag out of your kisser," I say, courageously retreating a couple of hasty steps.

"Oh I've not blown meself up yet," he splutters dislodging half inch of ash, which narrowly avoids a direct hit into the petrol filler; which he's oblivious to because the wisps of smoke are causing him to close one eye and squint with the other.

Before I can say anything the front door opens and slams with such force Eric and I feel like we left the ground by half a foot, believing my warning had tempted fate. Eric's start caused the remains of his fag to drop from his lips and lodge somewhere between the fuel tank and the engine.

I look expectantly towards the house, but there's no Frank waddling along the path, only the best part of a loaf of white bread and what looks like a large cow-pat rolling across the lawn, but which is in fact a chocolate cake.

I laugh as I watch the still pale Eric frantically trying to retrieve his fag.

"You'll warm yourself up in a minute, shaking it like that with the cap off," I say.

"Fuck off, I can't waste it, there's a few drags left in it yet! Squawks Eric.

"You'll be well and truly smokin' in a minute," I laugh. "Have you seen what they've put out for the birds?"

My question falls on deaf ears, Erics' frantic poking with his pocket knife has produced a lacerated 'dog end' with shreds of tobacco sprouting out in all directions; like a scarecrow that's had both barrels of a sawn-off shot gun at close range. He cups it in his leathery, oil ingrained hand; as a child might a deceased pet mouse or budgie. By the look on his face I fear he's going to cry. I wonder whether he'd need counselling if it had been a whole cigarette; or heaven forbid a whole packet.

"Well that's one way to cut down," I suggest brightly. "Shall we have a burial, or would cremation be more fitting?"

"Eh," he responds absently as though contemplating the possibilities of resurrecting his mangled mate.

"Never mind…. I'd better go and see if I can get in the house without getting a face-full of bird food, or should that be rat food?"

Eric notices for the first time the *healthy options* for the birds on *his* otherwise immaculate lawn. His weather-beaten face displays the gradual range of emotions, from grief, through to incandescent anger, as his pickled brain registers, then computes the image of desecration. As though a photograph of another face was being unfurled downward over his - firstly the eyes, which could have been watery due to smoke, widen, bulge and then recede under a furrowing brow to resemble a couple of shiny marbles sinking slowly into a bucket of cow muck. His mouth and jaw initially slacken, but immediately tighten into an impression of a cats' bum.

"Fuckin' 'ell! he screams, "I don't knows why I fuckin' bother… they're just a load of fuckin' pigs! I don't know why they don't just shit on the fuckin' lawn as well!"

"Who's shat on the lawn?" asks a bewildered Frank, whose exit from the house was concealed by Erics' ranting, "Have the badgers been digging up the lawn and crapping everywhere again?"

Eric splutters, then recognises the lifeline, "Y-y-yeah!" he stammers, then, as though aware of his unconvincing tone, "I mean yeah, the dirty little bastards!"

"Some nights we get, ya know, some nights we get about twenty on the lawn, yeah twenty," says Frank, beaming at each of us in turn and nodding his head like a salesman eliciting agreement.

"Badgers or rats?" I ask, glancing at the chocolate cake and the newly created patio of randomly placed white polystyrene bread tiles.

"Eh? No, badgers - oh actually we've seen a few rats the last few nights. I don't know where they're coming from or what they're doing 'round here."

"'Snot as though there's anything for them to eat," I say dryly, looking at the wildlife buffet.

"Eh? What? No! No there isn't- *and* they're coming into the house."

"Really?" I say with a genuine grimace. "Rats give me the willies outside - The thought of them inside - Uuuugh," I shudder violently. "Where are they getting in?"

"I dunno! Actually that's what I was going to ask you to do this morning, ya know, find out where the little buggers are getting in. They've made a fuckin' mess of the vegetable rack again last night," he squawks.

"I thought I was supposed to be more Thomas Chippendale than Davy Crockett - Do I get to sell the skins?" I joke and glance at Eric, but his vacant expression tells me he's lost the plot; probably still grieving for his fag buddy.

"Eh? What?" squawks Frank again.

Someone shoot that parrot.

"If you can find out where they're coming in and block up any holes. Barry can carry on in the bathroom; it'll give him a chance to get ahead."

"What's wrong with the one he's got, I've got used to seeing the threadbare one."

"Eh, what?

As if on cue, a pristine camper van scrunches sedately over the gravel to berth alongside my Transit. If mine were a child it would be taken into care; it looks woefully neglected by comparison. Fortunately Wayne spares my blushes by careering his typically abused builders Transit alongside. Now mine looks mint condition.

Wayne yanks the handbrake on and slides from his van, slamming the door behind him. He rearranges his family jewels and walks as though extricating his feet from glutinous mud. He stops and flexes his arms so that his fists are almost touching either ear, while arching his back in a twisting motion emulating a body builder's pose, and yawning a stifled lion's roar of a greeting, "Maawwnin."

"Beer and curry night was it Wayne?" cackles Eric. Wayne just nods while performing another enormous yawn.

He looks like I feel.

Meanwhile Barry is still ceremoniously swapping his 'best' glasses for his opaque work ones; as though he were an ancient martial artist preparing for combat.

"Good curry was it Wayne?" enquires Frank.
Still yawning, "Yeaahh- brilliant," he manages, but at least now his gait resembles a homo-sapien's.

There is a soft click followed several seconds later by another as Barry exits his van with the stealth of a chameleon.
"Yeah? Where dya go?" asks Frank.
"That place in Kenchester - just up from the roundabout."
"Oh that's supposed to be good in there," says Barry.

Despite his apparently deliberated movements, Barry covers the ground with remarkable speed, and has now joined our little ensemble near the front door to the house. And despite now wearing spectacles with the opacity of welding goggles, he doesn't miss much and does a double-take on seeing today's offerings to our feathered friends; or possibly furry ones. He catches my eye, then raises his imperceptibly and ruminates to avoid grinning.

"Yeah? Have you been there then Barry?" asks Frank.
Barry shakes his head as though trying to watch a bullet ricocheting down an alley, "Oh no. Irene doesn't much like curry, but I've heard good reports about it. Give me a gooood steak any day," he says licking his lips and patting his stomach cartoon style.

"Yeah, we used to go there quite a lot. Two or three times a week, they do really good takeaways. Yeah really good takeaways," Frank boasts as if he feared once a week would not be regarded decadent enough.

Then as though he has read our minds he subconsciously caresses his enormous stomach and smacks his lips Billy Bunter style.

So, it's not a Banks' baby after all; it's a Delhi Belly. Judging by their smirks, I can see Wayne and Barry are thinking along the same lines.

"Well I'll see you at lunchtime," Frank declares before scuttling off towards his Range Rover.
"What…"

Frank anticipating, cuts Wayne short, "Charles knows what you're doing," he shouts over his shoulder, instinctively slapping a hand to his forehead, keeping his 'Bobby Charlton' in place.

"It'd be a first if I knew what *I* was supposed to be doing here half of the time," I mutter. "I suppose Barry is carrying on in the bathroom and you with the patio," I say addressing Wayne.
"Sure there's nothin' I can do inside?" Wayne asks, sounding and looking like a puppy that's being tied up outside the butchers.

"Not unless you fancy a few weeks housework," I say looking up at the blue cloudless sky, "We'd swap places any day…. Just think, you don't have to worry about your tetanus jabs being up to date working outside. *And* you don't get any phone signal in the house," I say giving Barry an imperceptible wink.
"Actually I get a good signal if I put the phone out on the bathroom window sill," he says almost begging, and missing the point.

Pity you don't have it set to vibrate, then it could toss itself off to smithereens.

"So were you celebrating last night?" asks Barry.
"Sort of…" Wayne sounds cagey, "…oy Charles – ya know when I left me fuckin' phone in the bathroom the other fuckin' day, did you answer it?"
"No. Why?" I reply dead-pan.
"Some fuckin' joker answered it a couple of days ago, and that was the only time I can think that I never had the fuckin' thing with me – The fuckin' missus nearly fuckin' left me for good."
"If it was for good, why are you complaining?"

Barry wheezes.
"It won't fuckin' funny Charles. She went to her fuckin' mums and took the littlun with 'er…I 'ad an elluva fuckin' job convincing 'er that I 'ad no fuckin' idea who answered me phone."

"What did they say to Sally then? I say feigning ignorance.
"Yeah, she'd have recognised Charles voice, and known it was a joke," suggests Barry.

I don't think we've actually met, or even spoken on the phone.

Ignoring the question Wayne chews his bottom lip, seemingly deep in thought.
"There was one other fucker in the 'ouse - *and* she was upstairs…"

As if on cue Wayne's phone warbles a tune that I still can't place, and his arm is the usual blur as the phone is retrieved from back pocket and swept up to his ear, with only a nano seconds pause to glimpse caller ID.

"Hellooo! …A Henry Seventh groat? …Mint?" he repeats in a surprised tone, " It's been in the ground a helluva time, but it's very fine, very fine, could you bear with me a minute your breaking up, let me move to a better position,"

I nod toward the field, "Yeah, better take it in your office," I say dryly to the back of a rapidly departing Wayne. "You'd think he'd be a lot fitter, all that running up and down the field," I say, as we watch him attempt to jog up the field, his 'love handles' bouncing over the top of his jeans, like an overflowing cake mix.
"You'd think it would keep the weight off him at any rate," says Barry shaking his head. "I can see now why they refer to that as 'a muffin top'."

I enter the kitchen to do a recce of project 'splat-the-rat', and find Nisha alternately snatching mouthfuls of her breakfast; toast and jam and gulps of weak looking coffee.
"Oh hi Charles," she splutters brightly. Then as though remembering my unsavoury mission, she grimaces, "Has Frank told you about our rodent problem?" She then tilts her head heavenward in the direction of the girl's bedroom and shrieks, "Sophie! Alice! We're going to be late!"

"Yeah, thought I'd better refresh my memory, I can't remember how to get behind these units. It's a good job Frank wanted me to replace the kickers anyway, I replaced those on that side yesterday," I say nodding at the units under the window.

"You'll probably want a long screwdriver," she offers sagely.

"You could liven up an evening by saying *that* the next time you get in a taxi," I reply.

Her throaty laugh jettisons crumbs in an arch that fall just short of me, adding to the detritus of sweet wrappers, tea bags and bits of potato peel. The result of well- intentioned but half-hearted shots at the rubbish bag.

"I might get a free ride," she laughs.

"In more ways than one," I say.

She cackles, "I can't remember the last time we used a taxi."

"I can't remember the last time I had a long …" I tail off, thinking better of it.

Unfortunately Nisha really does know me too well.

"Oh you poor boy…" her face switching mid-sentence from crooner to alarmist as something, possibly lateral thinking relating to taxi drivers, reminds her of the time. "Alice! Sophie! We've got to go!" She rushes from the kitchen into the hall, "We'll miss the bus - oh there you are Sophie. Where's Alice?

"I've been waiting ages," declares an impatient Sophie, just as Alice's nimble footsteps thrum down the carpeted stairs, like driving over a level-crossing at speed. "Hi Charles! Bye!" she calls brightly from the hall.

"Yeah, bye Charles. I'll be back in a mo!" shouts Nisha.

"Okay. *Bye Sophie,"* I call pointedly.

The front door opens and they almost collide with Barry trying to enter with his stepladder.

"Sophie! Manners! Don't push past Barry," protests Nisha.

"We're late!" whines Sophie.

"It's okay, your need's greater than mine," says Barry mildly.
"You'll have to *excuse* my sister," says Alice apologetically.

The receding cacophony of squabbling high-pitched voices, and the staccato clicking of heels clipping paving stones is silenced by the closing front door. It's replaced by the sound of a modern day Ghost of Christmas Past, as Barry shuffles across the hall carpet; accompanied by a clanking stepladder.

"Little madam," he grunts "they should get a refund from that finishing school," he jokes as he enters the kitchen and leans the stepladder against his body, wrapping a protective arm around it.
"Who's your girlfriend?" I laugh, nodding at the stepladder.
Barry laughs but then appears to suddenly remember something, "Oh are these yours? I found them in the garage, I thought they were Frank's, I took mine home to do a job last night and forgot to bring them today," he says apologetically.

"It's okay, you're welcome to them- my real ladders died when I was quite young."
"Eh. Oh very funny," he laughs, "step ladders," he repeats, "I'll have to remember that one," he says shaking his head. "That's a good one, especially for this time in the morning… even for you."

He looks at me for a few seconds as though considering the most diplomatic way of raising a question.
"Don't tell me you were out on the curry as well last night?"
"No. Why? If it smells in here it's the rats not me."
He gives a restrained laugh, "I know it's none of my business, but well, you look as rough as Wayne. Sleepless night?" he asks suggestively, in order to avoid any suggestion of sounding too much like an interfering social worker.
"You could say that, *awake* all night unfortunately, not, *up* all night."

“Oooooh, those were the days… and nights,” he coos, sounding like a randy dove. He continues, “Nowadays ‘up all night’ for me usually means half a dozen trips to the loo.”
“Now you know why it’s called, ‘the wee hours’.”

Laughing, Barry picks up the stepladders one handed like a double-bass player leaving a gig. Surveying the kitchen, he declares with the air of an executioner, “Don’t envy you today.”
“You mean, you usually do?”
“I mean just no more than usual; I hate rats. I hope they’re not nesting under there,” he nods at the cupboards that I’m kneeling in front of, “ …wouldn’t want to come face-to-face with one *or two*,” he adds with a mischievous grin.

“Hmmm, nice thought. Come to think of it, rats aren’t exactly notorious for their celibacy, or for their hermit habits.” I lower my nose towards the base of the units and inhale tentatively, “It does smell rather rodenty.” I pull a sucked lemon face.

“Think I’ll wash my hands, then get some gloves on, I don’t fancy weils disease… I’m surprised they’ve not had trouble with mice before let alone rats with all this food on offer,” I say, gesturing at the opened packets of biscuits and boxes of chocolates that are spewing their contents onto the worktops.

Barry raises his eyes to the ceiling and then shakes his head briefly before nodding at the table, which is still strewn with the remains of last night’s dinner, “They may be partial to Indian takeaway; plenty of that on offer as well.”
“It never looks quite so delicious the next morning does it?” I say.
“Could be the way it’s so nicely presented,” he says dryly.
“Mmm, it does look rather like a scavenging horde has fought over it…

“… Bloody hell look at the state of the table. I only French polished it last year, and he was such a picky bastard over it. I’d dread to think what that curry does to your insides! There’s hardly any polish left, and the wine stains and cup rings; it's like it's been attacked with paint stripper."

"It's too posh a table for a kitchen," says Barry, "…it's more for a proper dining room."

"It looks like one of those forensic descriptions of a blood-spattered frenzied attack. But no you're right, French polished mahogany isn't very practical, and those spindly tapered legs with spade feet aren't anywhere near robust enough for a kitchen table, a stripped pine farmhouse style job would be better…or a trough."

Barry throws his head back and guffaws, displaying a set of gleaming metallic fillings and bashing the fridge with the stepladders, "Oops! Oooh you are rude," he camps, "…well best leave you to your furry friends before I do some real damage," he says inspecting the fridge door.

No sooner has Barry left, than the sounds of a key fumbling in the front door lock announce Nisha's return. I glance at my watch. Blimey, that was quick, I'd got bugger all done while she was on the school run. I'd best look lively and get some tools. I slip silently out of the back door.

Well it would have been silently if I hadn't almost fallen over Wayne sitting on the step composing a text message.

"Bloody 'ell," I curse, as I just about avoid going arse-over-tit but still manage to knock his precious phone out of his hand.

"Aagh me phone! Steady! What's the rush is it bait time?" he shouts after me.

"Sorry Wayne!" I shout back.

That was a stupid place to sit.

"Is your phone okay?" I ask, wondering but for the cost of replacing it, if there is a god.

Honestly, I think, this place gets more like a farce every day - She usually stops at the phone in the hall to check for messages, and ring Frank at the office; so I could be back in the kitchen looking busy by the time she gets in there. Not that Nisha would give a damn. Apart from the odd comment lately about Wayne's excessive phone habits, she's never in all my years working for them given the impression that she notices or even cares that we are industrious or otherwise. In fact when Nisha's around we tend to be even less productive, she seems to contrive to be in the same room and distract us with her general chat and flirting; I'm sure she misses our company when we're not here.

While I'm frantically grabbing a few tools from the van, I have this image of working in the dusty, cobwebby loft, and Nisha dragging an ironing-board up a ladder behind us, and then complaining about workmen getting under her feet. Remembering the mountains of washing around the house I wonder if the ironing scenario wasn't an unrealistic choice.

Fortunately Wayne has sauntered up the field to get enough signal to send his text, and Little Eric is nowhere to be seen so I can make my return unhindered. I slip in through the back door and scamper over a pile of laundry in the utility room. I can hear Nisha on the phone; the tone suggests she's in full flow.

I'm just about to kneel down in front of the units to pop the kicker-board off, when to my horror, I realise that I have a pair of ruddy great pink apple-catchers hooked on one foot. They make my boxers look like thongs.

Why do their wash piles seem only to consist of knickers? Hopping quickly back into the utility room, I flick my foot to shake off the offending article. Finally and with relief, after half a dozen or more attempts, the desperation and vigour increasing, as though I'm performing the Cancan, the pink cloud hurtles towards the wall and sticks to the tiles above the washing machine.

Yuk! Isn't that supposed to be the sign of a good night. I quickly check that Wayne isn't gawping through the back door witnessing my antics. I needn't have worried; he's still in his 'office'. That must be the first time I was glad to get Nisha's knickers off… and the last. I wonder whether Brian Rix did his apprenticeship here.

The first kicker-board eases off, just as the general hum of Nisha's voice rises to indicate the termination of the phone conversation. The wafting movement of the board blasts the distinctive pungent, sickly-sweet aroma, of rotting flesh, overlaid with the ammonia of rodent pee into my face.

"Phaaw! Fuck me!" I gag, just as Nisha enters the kitchen. "Charming. Do I look that ba...Jesus Christ!" she wretches, slapping both hands over her nose and mouth. "Wads thad sdink? Where thit comin' fwom?"
"Udder dare," I say through clenched teeth, pointing at the bottom of the kitchen units, while trying not to breathe. "Led's dry und keep da thmell oud of da rest of da owse," I say, like a bad ventriloquist. I dodge past Nisha to close the door between the kitchen and hallway. Then while vainly fanning my green face with one hand, I again dodge around her to open the door to the utility and then the outside door. I rush out and gulp fresh air like a floundering fish, pursued by Nisha.

Turning to check behind me in case I'd done a Pied Piper impression, and Nisha wasn't my only pursuer, I catch sight of the pair of pink bloomers dropping off the wall onto the worktop; like a giant canary succumbing to the fumes and falling off its perch. I briefly consider what the collective noun for knickers might be.

"Oh my god! That's disgusting."

Not for the first time, I wonder whether I'd been thinking aloud. Turning to Nisha I see her tentatively take her hands away from her face to sample the fresh air. Barry leans out of the bathroom window directly above the back door, "Is everything alright? Crikey what's that smell? Phaw! Smells like someone's died, have you found a body?" he asks grimacing and wafting his hand in front of his face, the colour draining from his face, producing the complexion of old mashed potato that's been overlooked in the back of the fridge for a week or so. He ducks back inside.

"There seems to be a helluva stink for just one dead rat. Have you been putting poison down?"
"We put loads down under the vegetable rack last week, we thought it was mice chewing the spuds; we put several lots down because it kept on disappearing along with the spuds and carrots."
"I'd say the whole nest has been poisoned, the adults and young, judging by the stink," I say. "I'll give it a few minutes for the air to freshen and then take a look under there. Have you got a torch?"
"Yeah there's one in the cupboard."

The sound of the front door opening and closing means Barry is fleeing the fumes.
"When did you first notice the vegetables being attacked?" I ask.
Nisha considers the question for a couple of seconds, "I'm not sure, maybe two or three weeks?" she replies.
"Those Aussie TV soaps have got a lot to answer for."
"Why, what d'you mean?"
"That way of speaking; making statements sound like questions."
After a few seconds reflection she laughs, "Sorry, I hadn't realised."

Barry lumbers around the side of the house and joins us, "It's a wonder we couldn't smell it before. What did you do to stir that stink up?" he asks.
"Just took the kicker-board off; it must have been a good seal..." I reply non-too convinced. "...In which case how did the little buggers get behind there?" I speculate.

I take a few steps towards the doorway sniffing tentatively as I approach, suspecting a good lungful might provoke retching. Behind me I hear the approaching thudding of a flat-footed runner, gasping as though completing a marathon, and not the fifty yards downhill from his 'office'. Wayne has obviously been attracted by the evacuation from the house. "Bloody 'ell what's wrong?" he asks breathlessly of no one in particular. Then seeing that Nisha is rather green around the gills, "Bloody 'ell are you all right Nisha?" he asks with genuine concern.

"Yeah. It's just the smell nearly made me sick," she replies rather feebly.

"They're used to working in the same room as me; you'll get used to it Nisha," I laugh, adding, "…you're lucky I wasn't on the Bank's Mild last night; mind you Wye Valley's Butty Bach is almost as lethal."

Nisha joins in the laughter, which brings her colour back.

"Well I best check under the units for the source of this fragrant aroma," I say with as much enthusiasm as though I was volunteering for 'the snip'.

"I'll find you that torch," Nisha offers with equal enthusiasm.

All three follow me back into the kitchen. Wayne and Barry chorus, " Phaw!" and retreat to the utility room fanning their faces. Barry realising he's standing on a pile of washing shakes his head and returns to the great outdoors.

Kneeling in front of the units trying not to breathe, I peer underneath. All I can see is the vague shape of what appears to be a large hoard of potatoes and what I can only assume are carrots.

"Well I can't see any rats; it's a bit dark right at the back."

"Here try this," suggests Nisha, who is standing as close as she dare, leaning forward proffering a torch. She presents the image of someone offering a stick to a drowning man.

I thank her and resume my impression of an Indian tracker listening for the sound of approaching horses. The torch now illuminates the space under the units. It's not the Apache Nation I'm confronted with.

It seems like several seconds for my brain to switch from the comic image of Nisha, to registering the not so comic image less than two feet from my delicate features.

"Shit!" I shriek, which galvanises the owners of several pairs of irradescent eyes into escape mode.

I'm not quite fully on my feet, when a blur of fur explodes from the cover of the kitchen unit causing Nisha, who was temporarily paralysed by my momentary lapse of machismo, to regain the use of her faculties.

"Chaaarles!" she screams diving forward and wrapping her arms around me as though I were some flotsam to cling to for dear life.

Unfortunately, because I was not fully upright at the point of contact, her flabby yet surprisingly strong arms wrap around my head, and I find myself suffocating between her spongy breasts. In fact, with my hearing cut off, not to mention my oxygen supply, her vibrating breasts were the only contact with the outside world, and the only indication that she was still screaming.

I'm just wondering whether I'll ever see Alex and the kids again, and hoping I can be a fly on the wall at the inquest, when suddenly I'm released. The daylight seems brighter than before, and as I gulp air it seems to have a stronger smell of urine than before - human urine.

In what was probably only a few seconds, I seem to have completely lost the plot. Nisha is prancing around the kitchen like a Lipizzan horse from Vienna performing an unnatural looking dressage, while frantically searching around her and shrieking, " Where'd they go! Oh where the fuck are they!"

Bewildered, I reply, "I don't know," adding, "I couldn't see a fat lot."

I could feel a lot of it though, I think, scanning the room for any signs of our furry friends.

Looking towards the utility room and the backdoor, I see Wayne scrambling to his feet, frantically searching around himself, wearing a petrified expression as he exits the back door like a cork from a bottle of bubbly. He must have stumbled over the washing as he hastily retreated. I hope in advance of the equally hasty and petrified escapees.

"Did they come your way Wayne? Did they go out the backdoor?" I shout after him.

"I'm not sure," he shrieks, continuing hysterically, "I think a couple went behind me into that pile of washing."

"One came out here, and ran across into the flowerbed," shouts Barry calmly.

Nisha is still prancing in a tight circle, and producing a terrified mewing, while looking over her shoulder, as if fearing an imminent attack on her ample rear. Fortunately she has her back to the utility room when a pair of striped boxer shorts, that resemble Siamese twins in striped shortie nighties, twitches. I wonder whether the oxygen deprivation has caused me to hallucinate. Then a beady eye blinks at me from a pair of flesh coloured apple-catchers.

Nisha catches my intense stare at the wash pile. "What!" she shrieks. "What have you seen? Have you seen one?"

"I think I've just seen something stirring in Frank's boxers," I say, "and er – something winked at me in your knickers." Through the window I catch sight of Barry guffawing.

"It's not funny Charles!" she screams, "This isn't the time for jokes!"

"I'm not joking," I say. I notice the puddle where we had 'embraced', and the shiny trail marking her circuits, "Look Nisha," I say gently, "…perhaps you should go upstairs while we sort this out."

And clean yourself up.

"Okay. But what if they haven't all gone outside?"

"Well they won't have gone upstairs," I say trying to reassure her.

Unfortunately, just as Nisha turns around to walk past the utility room for the door to the hallway, a sodding great rat's head pokes out of the knicker leg.

"Aaagh shit," she screams, spinning around, and again wrapping her arms around me.

At least I haven't got my head between your tits this time, at least I can breathe… and see.

Over her shoulder I notice the rat duck back into the safety of the pile of clothing. I waltz Nisha towards the utility door. Realizing the direction we are headed, and summoning the strength of a woman possessed, she clings tighter, trapping my arms by my side and screaming, "No Charles! I'm not going in there! Not with that fucking rat!"

"It's okay I just want to shut the door so that it can't come back in here," I wheeze, trying to reassure her. I sense an almost imperceptible relaxing of her grip, which I take as permission to continue. I don't think we would have won any ballroom competitions, but at least we got within striking distance of the door and I manage to hook my foot under the handle and flick the door shut.

I manage to extricate myself from a trembling Nisha, who looks to be on the verge of howling. I feel inept. I realise she needs comforting, but I'm worried about how she might react; after all she has just clung to me like a limpet twice in almost as many minutes. I place my arm across her shoulders and usher her from the room, "We'll give you a shout when we've got rid of them, and cleaned up under the cupboard."

With her eyes darting everywhere she just nods. Then as I'm about to shut the door behind her, she blurts over her shoulder, "I think I'll go up to the office after I've changed."

"Good idea," I say. "Are you okay to drive?"

But she is already scurrying like a Japanese geisha towards the stairs and a hot bath.

I hope her drawers go straight in the bin.

I close the door, and cross to the window to confer with Barry. I can see that Wayne is almost as useless as Nisha. He has positioned himself on the lawn, about thirty yards from the house, with a clear view of the backdoor. Opening the window I become aware for the first time of the sound of strimming coming from the wood.

"Could do with a little terrier in here," I say, nodding in the direction of the distant whining.

"It's okay," says Barry laughing, "I think the last two have just made a break for it, well two more have just come out of that pile of washing, whether they're the last I don't know… maybe they couldn't stand the smell any longer," he laughs.

"I don't suppose you fancy jumping about on the wash-pile to either crush 'em or flush 'em do you Wayne?" I call.

"Fuck off!" he squawks, then continues hysterically, "I reckon I put me 'and on one when I tripped over! Then a couple of the fuckers ran over me legs before I could get up!

Wayne's high pitched Pythonesque squealing almost prompts me to ask, 'Are there any, women here?' I don't think he'd appreciate the inference.

Instead I say, "In that case you might find a marginally cleaner pair of boxers in the pile," I joke.

"Thanks," he laughs dryly, "…but they might already be occupied by something furry, but with sharp teeth."

Barry laughs, and says, "Have you seen the size of them? He could get in one leg and wear it like a mini skirt."

Wayne again laughs and is beginning to look a little more relaxed even though he maintains a healthy distance.

"Anyway, while I was rolling about in that rat infested pile of knickers, you were shovin' ya face in Nisha's knockers!" he shouts.

I wince. Nisha's bedroom and ensuite which is out of commission, and the second bathroom is directly above the kitchen; and the noise of the bath filling is as clear as if it were down here. I fear that she must surely have heard that last comment. Did I imagine a pause in the activity up there? I just prayed as I place a finger to my lips and then point to the ceiling, that the noise of the running water masked our conversation…Well, it always works in Bond films to avoid being overheard by bugs.

Wayne's complexion has returned to the old pastry that he had only a few moments ago. For the sake of Nisha's feelings I refrain from saying, 'It was a shit job, but someone had to do it.'

The sound of water sloshing above my head brings me back to the job in hand.

"Well, we need to make sure there are no more lodgers in their drawers before opening this door, we don't want the buggers back in here," I say hoping for volunteers. "I've got to check under the units to make sure there aren't any more, and I was planning on having the doors open to give them an escape route."

"Well I'm not exactly what you'd call agile at the best of times," says Barry. "I don't fancy my chances of fancy footwork on that pile of bloomers; I'll probably go arse-over-tit and break my neck," he adds, only half joking.

"Okay. I'll come through…Is there a broom handy?"

Wayne visibly inflates with relief. Barry visibly shrinks with embarrassment. I feel guilty for making him feel guilty.

"Don't worry about it Barry," I say brightly, or as brightly as I can at the prospect of another close encounter with my least favourite animal.

"I don't know what it is about rats," I say once I've closed the utility door behind me, leaving the open backdoor as their only escape, "…they really give me the willies."

"Yeah me too," they chorus.

I notice that Barry has taken his position next to Wayne on the lawn, with a direct view into the utility room. Both have the manner of spectators at an execution; mesmerised yet ready to flinch and avert their eyes. I laugh at the drama created by a few rodents.

Picking up a mop, I quarter the pile of washing like a Springer Spaniel scenting rabbits. Gradually working my way towards the open door, tamping and stamping, hoping to drive out, or kill any unwanted squatters. Praying that there aren't any.

"Well there was no squealing or scrunching, so I guess there weren't any more," I say as I get to the door. The scene resembles an orgy that has been hit by a runaway steamroller; the original mountain of underwear is now compacted to a mere six inches or so.

"I dread to think what I've done to any underwired bras."

As if on cue, a padded cup pops up, slowly followed by another, reminding me of the Sydney Harbour Opera House.

"Excitement over then," says Barry, "best get back up to the bathroom," he adds with an all too familiar enthusiasm.

"That might be a bit difficult at the moment; Nisha's probably going to be in the bedroom changing," I say.

"That's alright," pipes up Wayne, having recovered his composure, "Why should you have all the fun?" he laughs.

"Being practically suffocated wasn't exactly fun," I say dryly. Then laughing as I remember, "My whole life flashed before me, it was like drowning in a warm blancmange…Even when she relaxed her grip, the aroma of dead rats and their pee, not to mention the fact that I think Nisha's world fell out of her bottom, didn't exactly enhance the romantic situation."

"Oh you are awful," camps Barry.

"Well, I suppose I'd better make sure there are no more lurking under the unit," I say glumly, "then it must be about bait time…give it a chance for the air to freshen," I say brightly. Wayne nods as enthusiastically at the suggestion of food, as a Labrador's tail wags at the sight or smell of it.

I pick up the soft broom that Wayne's been using to work the fine kiln-dried sand in between the paving setts, and return to the fray, or hopefully not.

Unfortunately the torch that had been unceremoniously abandoned has lost its charge; producing about as much illumination as a glow-worm in a Marmite jar. This time I don't prostrate myself before the units. But kneel as though to be knighted, and bend forwards while holding onto the worktop, 'til my head's at ground level. I reason that, if there are any sharp teeth under there, whose owner is not decomposing, I can retreat with more alacrity.

The gentle and infrequent splishing of water above tells me that Nisha is enjoying a long soak, and is in no hurry to go to the office.

After gingerly prodding the pile of rotting vegetables, it soon becomes evident that there are no more rats. Not living ones anyway. The prodding reveals a few corpses and creates a fresh, (if that's not a contradiction of terms), stomach-churning wave of fumes.

Gagging, I scramble to my feet. Clenching my teeth to avoid decorating the cupboard fronts and quarry tiles, I stagger to the sink and empty my mouth, then run the cold tap.

Unfortunately the taps are those lever types, and the water pressure is so fierce that you only have to move the lever slightly, to avoid splashing. In my haste however, I fling the lever to its full extent. A serving spoon lying directly below the jet produces a spectacular effect; making Great Witley fountains look like the pathetic dribble of a prostate sufferer.

"OH BOLLOCKS!" I yell, snatching at the tap. The spluttering from the open window tells me I'm not the only victim. Barry and Wayne are circling the unfinished patio, wiping their faces while laughing hysterically. I quickly survey the kitchen. Water appears to be dripping off everything and running down even the farthest kitchen units. In fact the whole kitchen resembles the inside of a car wash.

"Oh bugger this for a game of soldiers!" I stomp out of the backdoor pulling my shirt away from my body, my jeans away from my legs, and shaking water from my face and hair. I feel as though I'm contaminated, I just want to bugger off home and have a long hot shower; but I know I can't leave until… well until the kitchen has been returned to its normal mess.

"I'm glad it was only me fuckin' face at the window," laughs Wayne, who is now perched on a pile of setts mopping his face.

"What do you usually poke through the window then?" I ask suggestively. Then assessing the damage more closely, "Look at me I'm bloody drenched!"

Barry finishes mopping his face with what appears to be the remnant of an old tee shirt, "Ah well, I suppose we'd better set to and help you mop up before Nisha comes down," he chuckles, ambling towards the backdoor tucking his 'flannel' into the front pocket of his painter's overalls.

Wayne looks alarmed at the mention of 'We'. "I thought it was bait time," he scowls.

"Well you two can, but I can't leave all that water on the furniture, it'll mark it…make a right mess of the polish," I argue.

"Wunt be able to tell with all the other fuckin' stains," he scoffs.

"Please yourself, I need to get these wet clothes off first though, I'm freezing my tits off," then calling out, "Barry I'm just going to change, I've got spare clothes in the van…for a rainy day. I'll be back in a mo."

"Okay," replys Barry from inside the kitchen.

I see Little Eric emerging from the woods, rolling with his usual mariner's gait.

Nodding towards him, "You can tell Eric all about your heroics," I say before turning and waddling briskly for my van.

I round the corner of the house trying to pull my obstinate, soaking shirt over my head, and cursing.

"Oh my god! What's happened to you?"
Momentarily startled, I reply, "Jeez, where did you spring from, I thought you were still luxuriating like the Queen of Sheba. Are you popping out for more asses milk?"
"Yeah," she laughs throatily, "…the milkman's late today, always the same whenever I feel like a bath."

I finally emerge from my shirt to find Nisha surveying my wet crotch with a mixture of amusement and embarrassing interest, after all I don't suppose he's looking his best wrapped in cold wet denim.
I grunt, "Don't ask, it's a long story, involving decomposing rats, vomit and high water pressure. Lucky I carry a change of clothes. Good job I was in the scouts, ya know, 'Be Prepared'."

Noticing that Nisha looks more her usual self, I ask, "You feeling better?"
"I am now," she says with an exaggerated suggestiveness as she checks me over.
"Oy! Keep your eyes off my 'man boobs'," I laugh, covering my chest.
"Your 'man boobs'?" she laughs.
"That's what Lizzie calls them, anyway I can see you've recovered, that must be the quickest bath ever. You off to the office?"
"Yeah and I'm not coming back 'til you've got the kitchen back to normal."
"Have you packed a case then?" I say, wondering how to replicate normality in there.
"It shouldn't take you that long should it?" she laughs.
"Did you go into the kitchen just now?" I ask cautiously.
"No thanks. The smell was turning my stomach over enough without going in there. Why?"

I automatically glanced at her carbuncle straining the fabric of her top, and tried not to imagine it turning over.

"No reason, just wondered," I lied. "I'm getting cold, I need to get changed and back in there, else Barry'll think I'm skiving."

The sound of Wayne's excited voice, presumably relating events to Eric, causes Nisha to glance uncomfortably past me. Their voices are far enough away to indicate that they are still near the backdoor and out of sight.

She puts a firm hand on my arm to stop me moving away. Chewing her lip she looks at me with an expression to suggest she might be trying to silently release trapped wind, "Charles I…"

"Yes?" I prompt, aware that her hand is still gently gripping my arm and feels noticeably hot and damp; reminding me of those steaming flannels they provide in Indian restaurants.

Wayne's hysterical squealing, accompanied by Eric's customary phlegm rattle, causes Nisha to furtively glance once again past me, but they don't sound any nearer. I wonder if Wayne has got to the finale, with the water feature.

I notice Nisha's face and neck are colouring. "I just wanted to apologise for how I acted, and to say thanks… for what you did in there… or rather what you didn't do," she says, "…you're a real gentleman," she adds, leaning quickly forward and lightly pecking me on the cheek with the speed of a striking Cobra, before withdrawing her hand, but not before an imperceptible squeeze.

Feeling my own face warming, "Oh you're welcome, anytime," I say awkwardly. Then realising what I'd just said, we both laugh.

"I don't think I'll make a habit of examining your chest that closely," I say, "…Most customers feel the odd cup of tea is quite sufficient hospitality."

"Really," she laughs throatily, adding, "…they obviously don't appreciate you as much as I do."

She immediately appears embarrassed, as though she'd lost the battle to control that wind.

Approaching voices break the awkward silence. We ping further apart, resembling a pair of boxers breaking apart....By the time Wayne and Little Eric round the corner of the house, Nisha and I are at our respective vehicles. As she roars her Range Rover across the car park and disappears down the drive in a cloud of dust, I'm left wondering why I should be feeling guilty.

It's not as though we were nearly caught in a compromising situation. Is it? Nisha was just trying to apologise for her hysterics. Wasn't she?

Wayne and Eric reach me as I'm hopping around trying to pull my wet jeans off.

"Oh ar!" cackles Eric, "What you two been up to then?" he laughs suggestively.

"Did she take one look at it, and then run screaming up to the office?" says Wayne forcing a laugh.

"Yeah she was screaming something about a monster...Talking of which, "I'd best get back or Barry'll think I've abandoned him."

Chapter 15

Meat Loaf blasts out 'Bat out of Hell', as I head for home along the narrow lanes as fast as I dare, and reflect on the day's events.

Had I read too much into Nisha's actions? I know it was purely accidental; the bosom diving, and the hugging was due to genuine fear. But had I imagined it, or was I reading too much into it? I'm sure she held my arm just a little too long, and that squeeze just before she let go? Perhaps I'll have a chat with Barry tomorrow, he's known Nisha longer than I have; it's probably quite innocent. I bloody hope so. Life's complicated enough at the moment.

Although, I can't help wondering whether it might not have been me straining a few seams if she were a few stone lighter.

*****

I wrack my brains trying to remember the exact name and password of the new email account, while the laptop boots up. "Oh come on! Why are you so slow!" I curse…It's a good job I've got a couple of hours before I have to go and pick up Lizzie from netball training.

At last.

Hesitantly, I type in Alex's new Hotmail account details. I feel guilty while I wait for the computer to admit or deny me access; as though hacking into someone else's bank account.

Three new messages. The first two welcoming, and confirming my details. As if I could read them if I didn't know the login details and password.

The third sender is identified as Simon Gatley. I wonder whether he was with Alex when I sent the email to him last night. Apprehensively I click to open.

"My darling, you are clever, why didn't I think of Hotmail accounts before.

I must say it's taken you long enough.

I knew you fancied me all along, I bet you've just been playing hard to get, ignoring all my suggestions, even ignoring me altogether at that last Heads meeting last week.

I must say, you do have expensive taste. Do you know how much a room at Alveston Manor costs; let alone Dom Perignon 1996?

Couldn't we just have a room at a Travel Lodge and a bottle of Asti?

This weekend is a bit awkward as we've got the inlaws coming but I've managed to book a room, the following Saturday, and theatre tickets as you suggested, or should that be requested!

I'll be there at 3 I've got to take Fred to football in the morning.

I hope you're worth it!!

Si x x"

Oh shit! What have I started? Hmm. Who's setting who up here? Alex could have been in touch, I wish I'd just kept my mouth shut last night… until after the weekend at least.

Oh well, here goes. I quickly check her previous emails to see how she starts. It's quite interesting that she doesn't call him

Darling, or anything else that indicates affection of any degree. No, *Bunnykins, Biggus-dickus,* or even *Si.* I note too that she signs off simply, *Alex.* I click reply.

"I'll be there about half 3, get the bubbly chilled. Don't forget some of those little blue tablets, shame not to make the most of the room – apparently for best results you need to take them half an hour before so if you're getting there at three that should be perfect!!! Not that I need to tell you I expect you use them all the time!
In fact why not take 2?!!
I think Charles is suspicious, so don't use my mobile, I think he checks it. Only use this Hotmail address – I can pick up emails on my phone and he can't read them – he's only just mastered texting – he still thinks a Blackberry is something you have with apple!
Asti!!? Don't you dare!! You'll be suggesting cider next!
Can't wait.
Alex x

A thought occurs as I hover the cursor over SEND. I quickly locate the phone number for the Alveston Hotel, courtesy of Aunty Google.

"Macdonald Alveston Hotel. How may I help you?"

For a split second the Macdonald bit throws me, and I think I've misdialled; I refrain from ordering burger and chips.
"Oh good evening," I say trying to guage the right level, "This is Mister Gatley, Simon Gatley – I believe I made an online reservation for Saturday 19th, and my computer is playing up – could you just confirm that I have managed to make the booking?"

"Let's see sir – these computers are marvellous when they are working aren't they sir?... Mister Gatley – Ah yes, Saturday 19th of April, a double room for one night, bed and breakfast. Is that correct sir?"

"That's lovely thankyou, I just wanted to make sure as it's a birthday treat for my wife."

"That's no problem sir. Is there anything else I can help you with?"

"Oh, would it be possible to make that a champagne breakfast in the room?"

"Certainly sir. Is that in addition to the Dom Perignon '96, in the room on arrival sir?"

"Oh definitely, my wife loves her champagne," I say, barely able to disguise my enjoyment.

"Very good sir – May I compliment your wife's taste in champagne sir – Will your wife be requiring the Dom Perignon '96 with the breakfast also sir?"

"Oh why not? It is her birthday after all."

"Very good sir. Is it a special one sir?"

"Aren't they all?"

"I'm sure you'll both have a lovely stay sir."

"Oh – incidentally, what is your cancellation policy? With my business you never know what's going to turn up."

"Of course sir, normally it's twenty-four hours, but I see you are on a specially negotiated rate for the room; in which case I'm afraid you will be charged sir."

"Oh goody. Oh sorry, I was talking to my son Freddy, I mean, that's quite understandable."

The bloody cheapskate; *specially negotiated rate,* indeed - He'll be welcoming the bloody tooth-fairy with open arms, to get some cash back.

"Can I help you with anything else sir."

"No I don't think so thankyou - you've been most helpful – I look forward to seeing you on Saturday. Thankyou, goodbye."

Let's see how his flexible friend feels on Sunday. It won't just be his credit card that's feeling worse for wear by Sunday if he takes two viagra – his other flexible friend will be feeling a bit mangled as well – not to mention a chronic case of repetitive strain injury.

All I need to do now is keep Alex occupied and prevent her from contacting the wanker.

Chapter 16

I pull up at The Funny Farm. Turning off the engine, the exhaust produces a death rattle.
"More bloody expense," I curse. I'd better check that out later, make sure it'll get me back to Kingsford without falling off.

The senile DJ has tittered and wheezed at his own jokes for the whole journey without playing a single record. Sounds like he's regressed to the infantile stage… 'bout time they pensioned the silly old bugger off… They should send *him* to The Funny Farm.

Talking of silly old buggers, it doesn't look as though Eric's here. Condensation on Frank and Nisha's cars resemble the opaque second eyelid that slides over cold reptilian eyes. Well Nisha hasn't done the school run yet, and Frank's probably still in bed; unless he wants to avoid discussing work to be done.

As if on cue, the front door opens and Frank emerges while calling "Bye!" back into the house, before slamming the door. He walks with the determination of someone fleeing the scene, head down avoiding imaginary security cameras; a hoody is the only thing missing.

"Morning Frank," I call out as he is about to descend the steps. His head jerks up and his leg freezes as though momentarily forgetting how to perform the intricacies of the Hokey-Cokey. Fortunately his hand shoots out and grabs the balustrade, preventing an embarrassing, if not uncomfortable descent.
"Oh. Hi," he forces a smile, "I didn't hear you come Charles. Are you early?"

His eyes say, 'Fuck! Too late!'

"No, 'bout the same as usual," I say casually, resisting the compulsion to lean against his Range Rover, sheathed in early morning condensation. "So is it the bathroom floor…?"

"Eh! What!" Frank looks at me as though I'd propositioned him in a public toilet.
"I presume you want me to do the bathroom floor or…"
"Oh, I haven't got time now, I'm er, I'm er, I'm ya know, I'm expecting an important phone call at the office – I'll er leave it to you," he stammers, and waves his key fob frantically at the Range Rover.

Snatching the door open, he seeks refuge with the dignity and air of a randy tortoise pursuing a female over rocky terrain. Lowering the side windows to remove the condensation, he looks agitated as though he's exposed himself to an assassin; casting his eyes rapidly in all directions, but mine.

"Are you sitting comfortably?" I ask, removing a neatly folded invoice from my back pocket, and offering it through the open window, "This is for the last couple of weeks, up to tonight."

I turn and walk determinedly back to my van to demonstrate a sense of purpose; I slide the side door and make a show of selecting tools. Frank pulls his Range Rover alongside; looking marginally more relaxed now that he doesn't have to make a decision.
"I'll er, I'll er talk to you about it at lunchtime okay?"
"Yeah, fine."

Whatever I do this morning will be wrong. Frank can't make a decision, but he wants to feel in control. I just wish he'd give me a list of projects that he wants doing, and let me get on with it. Realising Frank's still idling alongside, I turn and give him an enquiring look. Like the snooty shop assistant that asks, 'Can I help you?' But their tone suggests that they rather doubt that you can afford anything. Frank's eyes nervously scan the van's interior, like someone trying to watch a squash-ball.

"Well er, well er, what are you er going to do?"

What happened to the important phone call I wonder? Whatever I decide, Frank will impose his authority by changing my plans, so it's best to suggest the opposite of what I want to do.
"Well I thought I'd do those templates that I didn't get around to doing the other day."
"Well I was thinking ya know …"

That's dangerous.
"… I was thinking that perhaps you should do the bathroom floor ya know like that."
"Yeah good idea, wish I'd thought of that."
"And Barry can carry on decorating."
"Depends on how good he is on the parallel-bars."
Frank looks blank.
"All he's got to stand on at the moment are the joists."

Frank's eyes are still chasing the imaginary squash ball

"….Any news on the sanitary ware yet? We could really do with it soon."
He appears to swallow a boiled sweet, "Eh. Er. Well. Ooh I'd better get up to the office," he chokes and splutters.
"Important phone call?"
"Eh. Oh yeah," he agrees sheepishly, and disappears in a hail of gravel and a cloud of dust.

I kneel beside the van and peer underneath. The exhaust pipe has parted company from the first box, it needs supporting; I wouldn't want to drive back to Kingsford with it like that. I'll sort it out at bait time, some thick wire should sort it out; I'd seen a carrier bag full of wire coat-hangers dumped near the front of the garage.

The front door opens again, and Nisha strides out purposefully, shrieking, "Alice, Sophie. We're going to be late!"

Alice and Sophie appear to be sucked out of the house in her wake, caused by the vacuum of their mother's whirlwind exit. They soon overtake her and witness me grovelling beside my van.

"What's the matter Charles?" Alice asks, beaming.
"Oh, nothing really, part of the exhaust broken that's all."
"You should get a new van, then it wouldn't fall apart," sneers Sophie. "Granpappy's buying me a brand new car for my birthday."
"Oh yeah. Lucky girl," I feign enthusiasm. "Next week isn't it? What sort?" I feign interest.
"You mean 'spoilt cow'," Alice interjects caustically.

Nisha laughs throatily, while zapping the remote at her Range Rover. "That's not nice Alice. Granpappy spoils her, yes, but she's not a cow."
"I'm not spoilt!" declares Sophie. "I wanted one of those Audi TT's … not a poxy Vauxhall Viagra!"

"Vauxhall Viagra!" we chorus hysterically.
Sophie glares at her mum, "That's what you called it," she says defensively.
"Is it blue?" I ask, trying to keep a straight face.
"Charles!" splutters Nisha in an attempt at token admonishment.
"No, it's red actually," says a bemused Sophie.
"Can it go for ages?" Alice splutters.
"Alice!" shrieks Nisha rolling her eyes heavenward.
"I'm not sure, Grandpappy just said it was a reliable and economical little car," says Sophie cautiously, seemingly puzzled.
"Are you sure it's not called a *Renault Rabbit*?" splutters Alice, collapsing against the side of the car.
"Alice! What do you know about Viagra and Rabbits!" shrieks Nisha.
"Muuum. We do Sex Ed. … *Remember?*"

"Mum, do you think Eric would clean my new car for me when he does yours and dad's?" says Sophie seemingly oblivious. Nisha opens and closes her mouth like a baby bird; words fail her. Which can't be said of Alice, always the master, or rather, mistress of wit and repartee, "Wash your own you spoilt cow!" she snaps.

Probably can't even wipe her own.

"Oh get in!" Nisha commands. "We're going to be late," she adds wearily, slamming her door shut and firing up the engine almost simultaneously.

Thank god it's Friday.

No sooner has the dust from Nisha's rapid departure settled, than Wayne's rusty steed gallops into the car park and kicks it all up again. I half expect the doors to fall off, culminating in an enormous backfire from the exhaust.

As if telepathic, he disembarks and slams the door, and lets rip with an enormous cheek flapper.

"Fuckin' 'ell! That's better!" he exclaims, with a satisfied expression.

"Who for you, or the environment? I think you've just blown a hole in the ozone …if not your pants…Been on the curry again?"

"Mornin'…" he laughs, continuing with the clown theme, striding as though wearing oversized shoes, due to the vigorous scratching of his balls as though frantically computing a complex mathematical problem on an abacus.

"…Nah, just the Banks'"

"Did you meet Nisha in the lane?" I ask

"Yeah she nearly fuckin' 'ad me…"

"In her dreams I'm sure."

"Eh!" Wayne puzzles that one for a few seconds before giving up and continuing. "Yeah she nearly 'ad me, her bloody windows was all steamed up. Neither of 'em clear their windows before driving off. I've seen Frank drive off with his screen frozen over and just an 'ole like a letter box to see through….One of these days they'll 'ave someone."

"Maybe he always wanted to be a tank driver."

"What driving with his 'ead out the sunroof?"

"That's a tank commander – the driver looks through a slot ya pillock."

"I suppose I'm on the bloody patio… as usual," he grumbles.
"S'pose so; you've been on it so long they must be able to see it from outer space…You never know you might be on Google Earth."
"What you on then?" he asks, in a tone that suggests I always get the best jobs.

I'm tempted to say that I'm cleaning the toilets with a toothbrush; just to cheer him up. But I'm saved by the warble of his phone.

Wayne scurries up the field to his 'office'; alternately clamping his mobile to his ear and shouting, "Hello," and studying the phone's screen for signal strength and shouting, "Bloody useless phones!"

I decide to crack on with the bathroom floor before Wayne comes back, and to get ahead of Barry before he arrives.

******

Occupying Alex was easier than I'd anticipated. In fact she seemed to be making a great effort to be friendly. It didn't take long for her to get the conversation around to trying to find the source of the gossip I'd heard about Slymon.

I managed to deflect the conversation by informing her that I'd booked a table at The Jolly Friar for Saturday at seven-thirty. It was really booked for eight-thirty, but I thought it would make her get her arse into gear; we're always late for everything. I need to think of something to occupy her during the day to prevent contact with shit-face. Trouble with mobiles is that it's so easy.

The other problem with mobiles is that we store all the contacts on them, but never need to learn them – so we're stuffed if we lose it. So I made a big show of playing with her phone, apparently not really looking at anything. Alex is still under the impression that I don't know how to use her bloody Blackberry anyway. What a stupid name for a phone. I suspected that she'd be as bad with her phone as the computer, so wouldn't have deleted any texts.

By the time I'd finished 'playing' I'd forwarded Slyman's contact details to my mobile for future reference and changed the last digit in her Blackberry's address-book to render the number useless to her

I'd also had a quick look through her inbox - I can't remember the last time I'd had a rummage in her 'inbox'. I then checked the sent items.

I hear the front door open, and also feel it slam shut in the inimitable Knight style, followed by Nisha's call sign, "Hi, 'sonly me."

I check the time. She must have missed the bus and had to take Alice to school, then Sophie to college. I butt up the next floorboard. The sounds of a kettle being filled and mugs clattering on the tiled worktop produce a Pavlovian response at the prospect of weak tepid tea.

By the time I hear Nisha's laboured breathing approaching, I've cramped and nailed half a dozen more boards. Nisha slumps against the doorframe with an enormous sigh. "Hi. Cuppa tea?" She manages to make it sound like a question, then groans as though it were to be her last words.

I laugh, taking the proffered brew as though it were a poisoned chalice, "You sound like that roman soldier who ran the original marathon to deliver an important message, and then dropped dead…or was he Greek? Anyway, I don't think the message would have been, 'Tea up!"

"I know. Those stairs seem to get steeper. Don't suppose you'd give me the kiss-of-life if I dropped down dead."

It sounded rhetorical, but I thought it would seem rude to ignore it.
"I'd drink my tea first. Wouldn't want it to get cold," I laugh, wondering whether it was possible for it to get any colder.
"Anyway if you'd dropped down dead, the kiss-of-life would be rather futile, unless I was a necrophile."
"Ugh, charming. You know what I mean. Don't be so pedantic."
"Besides, you should be fit with all the running up and down stairs you do," I say, attempting to change the subject.

She laughs throatily for a few seconds before her expression transforms. I turn to follow her stare. The open window provides a splendid view of the immaculately mown field, and of Wayne leaning on a fence post about halfway up the slope; talking animatedly into his phone. He gesticulates pointlessly for the benefit of his listener, presumably a punter, his thumb and index finger forming a circle; I hope it's to indicate the item's size and shape, and not his opinion of the client.

I immediately wonder whether he's been up there all this time. I can't remember hearing any activity on the patio below this window.
"I really would be fit if I took his tea up there to him every time," she says flatly. "Has he done any work yet? What's he supposed to be on today?"
"Question one, I honestly don't know… Question two, if you mean work – the patio. If you mean drugs, I don't know."
"The way he leans on that fence all day you'd think he *was* spaced out," she scoffs.

Nisha considers the expanse of exposed floor joists between her and the window for a nano second. Dismissing that option she strides purposefully to her bedroom window that shares the same view as the bathroom. Even she realises she's no longer built like a gymnast. I watch her fling open one of the casements and lean out. At least she wouldn't have fallen between them, at least not all the way through; not with those 'pushin' cushions'.

Nisha surveys the scene below for a few seconds, long enough to realise that Wayne has done diddly squat since he got here, which was presumably within minutes of passing her in the lane. Wayne is still leaning on the fence with his back to the house, oblivious to Nisha's surveillance.

She pulls herself abruptly back into the room, chewing her bottom lip in contemplation. Before I can react she catches me checking out her rear, "Oy. Stop looking at my bottom," she laughs, "I know I've got a fat arse, I can't help it," she complains.
"I was just thinking, all that running up and down stairs is doing wonders for your glutes," I lie.
"My what? Do you mean my arse?

"Is he taking the bloody piss or what?" She spits vehemently with such obvious resentment that I'm stunned into an awkward silence. Again it sounds rhetorical anyway so I don't respond.

I realise that I don't exactly work my balls off here anymore; so I can't criticise anyone else. We all used to graft, and take pride in our work, and worry about having something to show for a day's labour; but we all eventually lost heart.

Undoing painstakingly executed workmanship, several times, on the whim of a psychologists dream, eventually ceases to be viewed as character building.

I wonder whether Nisha's broadside is intended for the benefit of all of us, Barry, Eric and myself and not just Wayne; and that she hopes I'll be the messenger.
I try to humour her, "Oooh, language. I should get your money back from that finishing school."
"Sorry Charles. Everyone else usually has something to show for a day's work; but Wayne's just taking the Michael. Especially when

he's doing it in front of me, it's like saying, 'Frank pays me, you're a nobody'." She looks at me for confirmation.

I know she's right, but before I can formulate a diplomatic reply, she continues.

"It's not just today, for months he's been spending more time flogging his bloody treasure than what he's supposed to be paid to do here…"

I open my mouth but she continues.

"…It's Frank's fault. He's too soft, he wouldn't know a day's work if it slapped him in the face…"

Probably because he's never done one.

"…He thinks that a handful of bricks or whatever they're called…"

"Setts," I provide.

"God. Is that all you think about?"

"I said *SETTS*. Actually they might be called paviors. Setts might be cobblestones." I realise I'm in danger of becoming a little nerdy. A look at Nisha's expression confirms it.

"I think I'd have preferred it if you had said sex," she says dryly…. "He hasn't even got his tools out yet," she complains.

"You should be thankful for small mercies," I laugh. "Maybe that's why he's making that gesture; we're lucky he's got his back to us."

Nisha laughs. "Charles, you get worse… Anyway, it strikes me that the only tools he's in danger of wearing out, are his metal detector, and his mobile phone."

I had to agree, but I didn't want my views being used in a confrontation with Wayne. Nisha looks as though she's getting herself worked up enough to go stomping up the field to do just that.

"I bet the tax man would be interested in his tax free income…at my expense," she says sourly.

I look at Nisha to gauge whether she's being serious; I hadn't expected that approach I must admit.

"They're probably already aware of it," I say, "I've heard the Inland Revenue have software to monitor sites like ebay... I think it's a shame that some of the things he's found haven't been declared, purely for their historical importance. I mean the sites must be of significant importance to have held the treasures that he's found."

"Like what?" Nisha asks, endeavouring to restrain her interest.

"Well he recently found a hoard of gold coins, Quarter Staters I think he called them; worth a few hundred quid each apparently. He showed me a gold pendant once that he reckons was Anglo-Saxon, gold with garnets, it was Y shaped with what looked like the toggle off a duffle coat on the end of the stem. He reckoned it was about fifteen hundred years old....Amazing to think something can be in the ground for over a thousand years, and still be in such good condition."

"How much was that worth?" She asks, almost salivating.

"I've no idea, he didn't say....Another time he showed me a Roman brooch; I thought it looked like a small door knocker. But the point is that the sites were obviously important; the average peasant or roman soldier didn't run around dripping in gold; I think Chavs took another couple of thousand years to come on the scene..."

Nisha snorts.

"...So they should be recorded...apart from the fact he's ripping off the landowner who presumably gave him permission to go gallivanting about on his land."

Nisha appeares to be mulling this over while watching Wayne prop the fence up. "So where are these sites?" she asks absently.

I laugh, "No idea. Wayne maybe stupid enough to brag about his finds, but if he's greedy enough to cut out the landowner, he's not going to risk anyone else finding out about the site 'til he's milked it dry.

"I'm sure with your womanly wiles you could find out quite easily though. Especially as he's secretly got the hots for you," I add mischievously.

Nisha shoots me a look, equivalent to grabbing my throat and slamming me against the wall. "Uugh! Don't even joke about it. I'd rather be shot than poisoned!" she spits.

My embarrassment is literally saved by the bell; well the phone. Nisha exits rather more rapidly than she arrived. Even so, I doubt she'll make it to the phone in the hall before it goes to ansa-phone. An impression of a rabid dog growling on the stairs confirms my prediction.

I check my watch. Blimey, quarter past ten already. I wonder what's happened to Barry. I feel guilty for stopping for bait after Nisha's whinge about Wayne. Perhaps I'll put a few more boards down first. I notice he's no longer hanging on the fence; I don't suppose he'll have any qualms about stopping for his well-earned bait.

*****

Fifteen minutes later as I reach the bottom of the stairs, I'm intercepted by Nisha scuttling from the kitchen, like a spider aware of something on its web. Judging by her thoughtful expression it's obviously no coincidence.

"Um Charles…Look. … I'm sorry I snapped up there…I know you meant it as a joke, but, it's just that… well Frank's been making comments. I don't mean about Wayne in particular," she adds with a meaningful look. "So I'd appreciate it if you didn't make jokes like that in front of Frank. In fact I'd appreciate it if you didn't make jokes like that at all; especially concerning Wayne."

"Yeah fine. Sorry if I touched a nerve," I say reaching for the door handle, "...your secret's safe with me," I laugh, scooting out the door. I catch a glimpse of Nisha shaking her head as I quickly close the door behind me.

What was more important though, she was smiling. At least she knows my humour well enough, even if it's not always appreciated.

Chapter 17

"Bloody 'ell, I thought you was never stoppin'," splutters Wayne through a mouthful of what looks like cheese and pickle sandwich.
"That's what the wife always says," I say, plonking myself into an empty chair opposite him. I take one look at his masticating orifice and move to the chair on his right. "I was just finishing off a couple of boards; otherwise I might forget to fix them after bait…

"So how's the patio going?" I ask, feigning ignorance of his progress; or lack of it. I'm not sure whether to mention that Nisha is on his case. Wayne will probably assume that I've been stirring it; perhaps even drawing Nisha's attention to him.
"Mmm, okay I suppose. I've had a couple of phone calls about me sales to sort out," he says blithely. "I'll crack on after bait."

I instinctively check my watch without actually registering the time.
"What is the time?" he asks.
I check again, "Just gone twenty to eleven. Did you stop at ten?" I try to sound casual.
"Yeah but whose watching?" he laughs conspiratorially.

I open my mouth to tell him, but then I think, fuck him, he deserves everything he gets. Instead I use my open mouth to take a bite from an egg and tomato sandwich.

"Good job I'm on my todd in the bathroom," I say, waving the sandwich at him. Wayne looks blank, but while I contemplate whether I can be bothered to explain the causal effect of boiled eggs on my digestive system Wayne responds.
"I'd better keep you company while you have yours," he says considerately.
"You're too kind dear boy, but don't let me keep you from your work; I bet you can't wait to get started."

"Nah. So long as I've got a few down before Frank comes back at lunchtime. He'll be none the wiser."

"You do realise Nisha's here, and not up at the office don't you?"

"Oh yeah, but she don't care. I saw her come back from the school run. She was gone longer than usual … I was beginning to think she'd gone straight to the office."

"Good vantage point in your executive suite," I suggest.

Wayne looks puzzled, his eyes follow the last of my sandwich to my mouth like Ebony.

"What office? Oh right, very funny," he laughs theatrically, "My office, ha ha," he repeats, grinning broadly as though his peers have just voted him, 'Bricklayer of The Year'.

"Anyway, she can't talk… she's never done a day's work in her life."

"Nisha?"

"Yeah… According to Frank She draws fifty grand a year out the business … and she only works a couple of mornin's a week, for a couple of hours."

"I bet you'd do the same in their position… you seem to use all the tax dodges you can get away with…. We all do to some extent.

"So what have you sold this morning Walker?

"Walker?"

"Yeah, don't you remember Walker in 'Dads Army', the wheeler dealer spiv?"

He laughs, showing glutinous white bread stuck to the roof of his mouth, resembling a dental impression, "Oh yeah....blimey, that dates ya'…

"No I wasn't sellin'…. Some stupid Yank that I'd sold an Edward the third Half Noble to, reckons it's a fake, and wants his money back."

"Why does he think it's a fake?"

"Christ knows… Cos he knows jack shit about coins but got plenty of money I 'spect. Reckons it looks too good to have been in the ground for nearly seven hundred years… I told him gold's like that, and it was described as very fine…very fine… that's why it's worth eight hundred quid."

"So how have you left it?"

"Told him it was genuine and that he couldn't have his money back… told him to take it to a half decent museum and they'd verify it."

"What did he say to that?"

"Reckons he's gonna complain to ebay," he says thoughtfully, "Ignorant fucker aint got a leg to stand on."

But by his tone Wayne is obviously wondering whether a complaint, valid or not, if investigated could open up a can of worms; possibly attract unwelcome interest and spoil his nice little earner.

"So what was the other call?"

"Uh? What other call?

"You said you had a couple of phone calls."

Wayne's face flickers, like the little light on my computer that indicates that it's thinking.

Talk about care in the community.

Eventually the flickering stops, and I wonder if he's 'crashed'. I stifle a laugh as the computer analogy extends into the vision of Nisha rebooting him up the arse; so to speak.

"Oh yeah," he says brightly. "It was an enquiry about my Roman bronze figure…"

"I wouldn't have described you as that," I interject, looking him up and down, "ruddy or weathered maybe; but not bronzed. What dodgy sites are you advertising on, male escorts?"

"Ha fuckin' ha. A little first century Roman bronze figure of Fortuna…"

"Aptly named I'm sure."

"Yeah, I reckon I should get about a thousand quid for it," he says smugly.
"Five hundred each for you and the landowner then," I say mischievously.
"Ha fuckin' ha!" he scowls.

"I thought the idea of selling on ebay was that it was all done on the internet, you know, emails."
"It is."
"So why do you spend so much time on the phone?" I say pointedly, flicking the dregs from my mug out through the garage door and screwing it back onto the flask. If that fancy phone of yours has internet can't you just email?...

"…I wonder what's happened to Barry," I say, announcing the end of bait time by rising from the chair which responds with a tortured squeal.
"His missus has probably got him doing something, like taking her shoppin'; he's under the thumb," Wayne says sourly… "I don't take my missus shoppin'."
"Well Irene doesn't drive, and your missus has got a car….What's she need a Chelsea tractor for anyway?"
"I need the Freelander for going across the fields detecting…"

Freeloader more like.

"Best get on; some of us don't get an hour for bait," I say, instinctively checking my watch, conscious that Nisha may have turned into a clock-watcher and wondering how long I'd been one.

"S'pose I should make a start," Wayne says with the enthusiasm of a fat kid being forced to do a five mile cross-country run. "Are you gonna try and shove your face in her tits today?" he shouts loudly after me.

I stop mid stride, close my eyes, and look to the heavens. I turn back to Wayne and glare, "Jeees Wayne I'm sure there must be someone at the other end of the village who didn't quite hear that," I hiss, "…I hope Nisha wasn't in the garden hanging out washing."

Or hanging out the window spying on you again.
"Fuck 'er – I still owe her one for nearly fuckin' up my marriage."

"Charles…" Nisha summons from the kitchen as I close the front door.

"Yeees," I answer, approaching the kitchen in that suspicious tone, reserved for when you suspect the kids either want something that involves money, or they're going to confess to breaking one of your prized possessions.

I enter the kitchen to find Nisha leaning over the sink, surveying the half paved patio through the window. Or more accurately, I suspect she's hoping for a rare glimpse of Wayne actually working. She resembles a twitcher in a hide. I wonder how long before she sets up a camera.

Nisha turns, "Hi. That was Barry trying to phone earlier, he won't be in today, he's got to take Irene for a hospital appointment, he forgot to tell us yesterday … That's not holding you up is it?"
"God no. Bit of a relief really, there's not much for him to stand on."

I wonder whether Irene really has got a hospital appointment, or if Barry has decided he's too old for the circus; and decided to let me get ahead. Good ol' Barry. He can ill afford to miss a day's pay though; it's a Funny-Farm not a Health-Farm.

"Did he say what's the matter with her?"
"No, he was a bit cagey… his generation don't like to talk about that sort of thing."
I laugh, "That sort of thing," I mime with a rubberised face, and crossing my arms, hoisting imaginary breasts.
She laughs, "You look like Les Dawson."
"Hooray. I got one right at last."

"You know what I mean," she laughs, "…you know, they like to keep personal things private."

"Either that or you can't shut them up," I say, then continue with my Les Dawson impression, "I'm ninety-three, don't you know. I've had two hip replacements, triple heart by-pass, a hysterectomy, lobotomy, mastectomy and a colostomy. You wouldn't know it looking at me, would you? I put it down to three pints of stout a day, and weekly colonic irrigation."

Nisha laughs throatily, "You'll be old one day. Go on, bugger off and get some work done…Talking of which," her expression transforming to despair, "Has he started work yet? He must have had nearly an hour for his breakfast, bait or whatever you lot call it."

Nisha sounds as though she'd like to march outside, and tell Wayne to go away in jerky movements.

"I don't know how much longer I can sit on my tongue," she snaps.

"Eh?" I laugh.

You could sit on mine if you lost a few stone first.

"Strange mental image there Nisha. They'll be calling you Cat Woman if you can do that. Talk about My Flexible Friend," I laugh loudly at the imagery.

Nisha looks puzzled, "What? What did I say?"

"I think you were mixing you're metaphors," I laugh. "I've heard of, BITING YOUR TONGUE, and SITTING ON YOUR HANDS, but never SITTING ON YOUR TONGUE," I laugh ungenerously.

Nisha absorbs this information, "Oh my god," she throws her hands up and covers her face, muffling hysterical laughter.

As though telepathic, the sobering rhythmic thud of a rubber mallet announces the resumption of normal service outside….Such as it is.

"Hooray," we both cheer spontaneously, as though welcoming the return of the water or electricity, after several days interruption.

"At fucking last!" mouths Nisha, clenching her fists, arching backwards and looking skyward, imitating the modern day footballer, celebrating the fact that he's managed to score a goal; after the last twenty shots have disappeared out of the stadium - I often wonder whether these multimillion-pound players could even hit a barn if they were standing inside it- I half expect Nisha to run, then slide the length of the kitchen on her knees. I just hope she doesn't expect me to complete the ritual; throwing myself on top of her and smothering her in kisses. It would be just my luck for Wayne to peer through the window and witness the simulated orgy.

Wayne's industry is short lived. The dull thud of rubber mallet is interrupted by the muffled warble of his phone, followed by muffled cursing. Wayne rises from below the kitchen window into view like an inflatable doll, turns and lumbers up the field. One hand clamping the phone to the side of his head as though staunching a head wound, the other struggling to return his jeans to his waist, and cover his pasty, hairy, spotty cleavage; resembling a couple of lumps of raw pastry that have rolled around Ebony's bed.

"Uuugh! Not a pretty sight," I grimace.

Nisha stands transfixed; her mouth gaping. I wonder whether the dull thud of mallet is going to be replaced by the dull thud of head on wall.

"It's a good job Frank hadn't arrived, I dread to think what conclusion he would have jumped to, seeing Wayne running away from the house with his pants round his knees," I laugh.

"I don't bloody well believe it!" Nisha explodes. "I just don't believe it!" she repeats, watching Wayne retreating in disbelief.

"Steady on Victor Meldrew, you'll give yourself a heart attack."

"It's not funny Charles. He's just taking the fuckin' piss! Look at him, I don't know why he doesn't put a chair up there."

"I'll suggest it, can't be doing him any good leaning on the fence like that, or the fence. What about a desk? Phone line?"

"Charles. You're not helping."

"Sorry, but what can I say? I know what I'd say to him if I were employing him, but I'm not. It's down to you or Frank I'm afraid…Well actually… it'll probably be down to you," I mutter.

Nisha's eyes continue to burn into Wayne, as though trying to will spontaneous combustion. I silently release my held breath with relief, thinking that my last remark went unnoticed. I should be so lucky; it'd just taken a few seconds to register. Suddenly, owl like, she blinks and swivels her gaze towards me.

"What did you mean by that?" she asks, sniffing and blinking again.

Me and my big mouth.

"Oh nothing, ya know me, hear, see and speak no evil, as my granny used to say."

"Bollocks Charles. You probably know more about what goes on here than anyone."

"You do have a delightful turn of phrase…I loves it when you talk dirty," I say, playing for time.

"Stop stalling. Now cough," she demands.

"Ooh matron, aren't you supposed to be holding something delicate of mine when you say that?" I say, attempting a Kenneth Williams impression.

"…Actually I think it's Wayne who has Frank by the proverbial."

Nisha tilts her head attentively, encouraging elaboration.

"Look, I know it's none of my business but I expect you're aware of all the dodgy goings on…I know everyone pushes the limits and tries it on with the old tax man; part and parcel of being self-employed, we all do it…"

"But…" Nisha encourages.

"…Well… Oh shit. I'm beginning to wonder how much you're aware of. Do you think that if I tell you something you don't already know, you can keep it between us… or at least be diplomatic?"

Nisha considers this for a couple of seconds, "…What if I had you by the proverbial as you put it?"
"Oooh, that might just stiffen my resolve," I say suggestively.
"I've never heard it called that before," she laughs. "Seriously I wouldn't drop you in it …but what could Wayne have over Frank?"

"Aagh, horrible mental image - Seriously? Well they probably sound pretty petty on the face of it, but it's been going on for years, so it probably adds up to quite a bit… and Frank's probably got enough on Wayne to create a stalemate."
"Like what?" Nisha asks, with growing frustration.
"Well, for one thing Frank knows a lot about his detecting finds…"

Apart from his latest hoard…unless Eric has already informed him.
"…and for years Frank's been claiming the VAT back for Wayne on his carrier-bags full of receipts. I mean that puts Frank in a strong position, because Wayne obviously doesn't produce proper accounts."

"How do you know that?"
"'Cos if he's given the receipts to Frank, he won't have any for his accountant…and the fact that he just files them in a carrier-bag, suggests that he doesn't keep proper books in the first place…

"How often do you fill your Range Rover up with diesel at a garage?"
Nisha looks puzzled, wondering what the connection is; she shrugs, "Well, never. We've got a tank up at the office."
"How many tanks have you got?"
"Only one. It's not exactly Milford Haven," she laughs, "…we've only got…" Nisha looks to the ceiling as she counts them off, "four diesel cars; we have an account at Hardings for the petrol ones."

"Plus a tractor and Kubota mower. Do they fill up from the same tank?" I prompt.
"Yeah, of course; they're diesel."

"Well that tank is red diesel. It's illegal to run a non-agricultural vehicle on red…probably why Frank encourages Wayne to fill up his van as well whenever he's working up there."
Nisha looks worried, "I didn't know it was red diesel…I didn't know it was illegal…. Why would he encourage Wayne to use it?"
"So if they ever fall out he's got something on Wayne. That way they've both got something on each other…. trouble is neither can resist boasting about their little scams.

"And another thing," I say, "…everyone knows that all the work we do here, or lack of it from a certain person, comes out of the business… Eric and Barry are cash in hand; probably down as casual labour at the factory."

"Huh, casual labour. A certain person is so casual you'd think this was a holiday camp," she scoffs.
I shrug to indicate acquiescence, "Anyway, my invoices are for repairs and maintenance up at the factory; I wouldn't have a clue how to find the factory.

"I'm not sure what Wayne does, I've never seen or even heard of him actually give an invoice, but Frank reckons he has occasionally asked for cheques to be made out to his daughter; I don't know whether that's just another one of Frank's fairy stories," I say, but immediately remember who I'm talking about, and to whom, "Whoops. Sorry I…"
Nisha laughs, "'s okay. We all know Frank never lets the truth get in the way of a good story…. Anyway doesn't that make you a naughty boy as well?"
"I suppose so. But I'm not sure how much….I've always declared the invoices from here; so it's not like I'm avoiding any tax. I suppose technically I'm assisting Frank in avoiding tax; by providing him with tax allowable expenses."

"Aren't we the model citizen?" she laughs dryly in disbelief.

"Someone has to support the NHS," I laugh, "… make up for all you cheating buggers. It's no good complaining about the service if you don't help finance it."
Nisha feigns affront, "Ooh, you cheeky sod, we pay thousands in income tax, and corporation tax or whatever it's called…. You telling me you declare everything? You must be a mug."
"Of course," I lie, "I like to sleep at night. I know some friends that were investigated; it was a nightmare for them."

I wouldn't tell you anyway. Frank and Wayne are the mugs for boasting about their fiddles, especially to each other; they're both about as discreet as a Town Crier with a megaphone.

Nisha chews her lip, and sniffs up her right nostril so hard that it almost pulls her nose flat against her cheek during an otherwise silent contemplation of Wayne's rear view.

"The point is," I say, "I don't think Frank is likely to send Wayne off down the road, for fear of what he knows. The most you can hope for is a half-hearted inference from Frank, that he doesn't think Wayne has made much progress… Talk about people in glass houses," I say, glancing at my watch, "…at this rate, he'll be suspecting me of skiving as well."

Nisha looks momentarily deflated, her breasts sinking down to rest on top of her stomach, like a pair of plumped up broody hens settling over their precious clutch.
"There must be something we can do," she says, inflating, "I'm not going to let him get away with being paid for doing bugger all; while he runs his own little antiques trade," she says determinedly.

"Well just be aware of the repercussions, it could backfire if Her Majesty's Missionaries get involved; Customs and Excise make The Spanish Inquisition as fearsome as Brownies doing trick or treat…And the Inland Revenue aren't far behind.

"….I mean it pisses me, and probably the others off as well… seeing him doing bugger all, presumably, for the same money…Tell you what I'll have a quiet word with him at bait time.

I've already tried subtle hints; maybe it's time for unsubtle. Remember, be diplomatic if you talk to Frank…I think you should, but don't mention me; he's not exactly discreet and Wayne and I have still got to work together."

Nisha brightens at the prospect of an ally, "Thanks, I won't…By the way…"

I raise my eyes encouragingly.

"Wayne doesn't get paid us much as you; he just thinks he does."

"It's because I'm worth it," I say, tossing imaginary tresses as I head for the door; strutting like a super model.

"Ooooh, get you," she swoons.

A thought occurs, and I turn in the doorway, "You could always tell Frank, that you think I'm pissed off with Wayne being paid the same as me for spending all his time on the phone; so I'm considering increasing my rate…That might focus Frank's mind on the problem."

Nisha laughs until she realises that I'm not joking, "But I've just told you, he doesn't earn as much as you."

"But Frank doesn't know that I know that," I say mischievously.

Nisha turns, slowly nodding, with the trace of a smirk to confirm Wayne's activities before going to the office to confront Frank.

*****

"Hi, how have you got on up there?" Wayne asks, "You've been banging away like a fuckin' mental woodpecker."

I flop unceremoniously into a vacant chair and exhale noisily to exaggerate how knackered I am, "Aaah."

I hadn't given another thought to how I was going to confront Wayne. I hadn't heard much activity from the patio; but he must have been close enough if he'd heard me working in the bathroom.

"Not too bad a morning's work…" I say.

Considering the earlier interruption.

"…I didn't think I was going to get the floor down as quickly as that… good job I picked up the skirting and architrave on my way in this morning… Pity we haven't got the loo and stuff yet… mind you if the new stuff's going in the same place, we shouldn't have to mess with the plumbing too much… I could make a start on the skirting this afty… I might check with Frank when he comes back for lunch. Then again, it's probably better if I just get on and do it; don't give him the chance to start another project."

If he comes back, I think, if Nisha's had her four-penny worth this morning, he'll be avoiding us.

"Bet he don't come back today, it's pay day," Wayne says sourly, "…and he usually goes to the factory Friday afternoons remember?"

"Shit…."

I wish I hadn't suggested that Nisha uses me as a foil today of all days.

"I could do with being paid today," I say. "When did you give him your invoice then? You missed him this morning. Or are you on piece work nowadays, in which case you won't have much coming?"

"Ha ha! What d'ya mean? I've done loads this mornin'," he splutters, showering me in gloopy lumps of half masticated bread, "Oops sorry," he splutters again, belatedly putting a hand over his mouth.

"Thanks. That's another fine mess you've got me into. I look as though I've slept under a tree of roosting starlings." I stand, take hold of the bottom of my sweatshirt and give it a sharp downward jerk, catapulting the globules through the open garage door.

"You didn't start 'til gone eleven, and that was short lived." I say, more abruptly than intended.

Well Charles, don't apply for the diplomatic corps.

"You checkin' up on me, or what?" he laughs cautiously.
"Or what. …Actually someone else is," I say, knowingly.
"Who? There's no other fucker here," he asks. His eyes show that he knows the answer.

I ceremoniously unscrew the cup from my flask and pour a disgusting coffee and take a tentative sip. It may have said coffee on the jar, but I reckon this was definitely a case of trade description. I grimace, but still take another sip.

"Yuk," I say, straining my neck ligaments into harp strings.
"Was it Nisha? She were here 'til about eleven. She spyin' on me was she? Cheeky fucker. She wouldn't know a day's work if it slapped her in the face," he scorns.
I puzzle over that last metaphor. With infuriatingly deliberate movements I open my bait box, aware of Wayne's expectant gaze, and withdraw another egg sandwich.
His eyes flick between the sandwich and my face; I half expect him to pant and loll his tongue.
"Well? What did she say then?" he asks with slightly more anxiety in his voice, but still lounging indifferently.

I study my sandwich, as an art dealer might when presented with a suspicious forgery.
"Are you gonna eat that fuckin' sandwich or play it?" Wayne snaps. "What the fuck did Nisha say about me?"
I take a bite and savour it, "Mmmm. Home-grown, free-range boiled eggs, you can't beat them."
"Oh for fuck's sake! You can't fuckin' hatch them either. What did she bloody say?"
"Mmm." I say smacking my chops. "Do you really want to know?" I ask, taking another bite.

Wayne suddenly relaxes, visibly slumping in his seat, "You bastard. You nearly had me there. She ain't said nothin' has she?"
I finish my sandwich under Wayne's watchful gaze, and then attempt to dislodge the bread from between my capped tooth with a

generous, if not repulsive, gulp of tepid imitation coffee. "Fair Trade my arse, we've been done." I cough.

I notice Wayne's not eating, "Have you finished your bait already, what time did you stop?"
"I ate mine at mornin' bait," he says brightly, "so I went and got a pie from the garage.... and ate it on the way back," he says sheepishly as he realises the implication.

I consider him in silence as I slide the outer paper sheath from a chocolate biscuit, screw it up and toss it nonchalantly into my lunchbox. Wayne squirms uncomfortably; silently debating his position. With equal deliberation I peel the foil wrapper to expose the dark brown chocolate. Unfortunately my hunger overtakes me, and I devour it in two bites.
"What's it gotta do with you anyway?" he blurts defensively.
I probe the gaps between my teeth with the tip of my tongue to dislodge any remnants of food; Wayne could be forgiven for thinking I was participating in a gurney competition.

I casually scrunch the foil wrapper to pea size and attempt to flick it with equal nonchalance into the lunchbox. It imitates a premier league footballer's shot, and instead of a graceful downward trajectory to its intended target, it arcs steeply skyward, and ricochets off the garage ceiling, then the bonnet of the Kubota. The Tom and Gerry sound effects do nothing for the Clint Eastwood image that I've just spent the last couple of minutes cultivating.

"What's it gotta do with me?" I repeat, holding eye contact, "Well quite frankly, the fact that you've done sod all for several weeks, if not months, and you're paid the same as me, rather pisses me off." I say bluntly.
"I could earn twice as much on the sites in Worcester as I get here!" Wayne retorts defiantly.
"Maybe. Maybe I could too. So what's keeping you here; apart from my scintillating charm?"

"Ha, fuckin' ha. I could ask you the same; you're always bloody moanin'."
"I've often asked myself that," I half-laugh dryly, "But so far haven't come up with a convincing answer…anyway, that's no excuse to down tools… if you're getting reasonable money you should do a reasonable days work…Anyway, you'd have to work twice as hard on a site… You wouldn't be able to sit on a pile of bricks all day with a phone sticking out your ear, selling the nation's treasures…To earn good money you'd have to lay bricks faster than an aphid lays eggs, otherwise you'd soon be off down the road…And you'd have to pay for the labourer …And you wouldn't be able to fiddle your tax anything like you do now, the shock of declaring your income would kill you… the tax inspector too," I laugh. "Probably make him look more closely at all those previous years," I tease.

"I'd still be earnin' better, money than 'ere," he snaps. "You been promoted to foreman or sommut?" he growls, grasping for defence.

"Look, I'm pissed off, but Nisha's spitting nails. She's noticed you spend more time on your telesales; they've taken precedence for quite a while… She's worried you're gonna build an office half way up the field and ruin her view; 's bad enough seeing your spotty arse every time she looks out of the kitchen window….She was banging on about having a go at Frank…make him talk to you… after all…"
"Huh! Frank," Wayne says derisorily, "…he won't do nothin', he knows I've got too much on 'im," he laughs dismissively.

"…Look I'm not expecting you to bust a gut here, nobody does, there's not much incentive I know, when you know the silly fucker will wake up with another idea, and make us rip out what we've already done. But I'd be more afraid of what Nisha might do if I were you, if you keep taking the piss….cos she doesn't know what you and probably everyone else knows about Frank's little scams…

At least, she didn't until about quarter of an hour ago.

"…She just might open up a right can of worms."

*****

I return to the bathroom, leaving Wayne muttering about Nisha not being able to do anything either, and by the time he'd finished, she'd have too much to worry about to think about how much he got done in a day.

"Bugger!" I just remembered I'd not wired up the exhaust. Better not do it now, be just my luck for Frank to come back and assume I spend all day working on foreigners too. He'll think we all regard this place as a holiday camp - not an asylum.

I switch my radio on in the bathroom, Madness are chanting, 'Welcome To The House Of Fun'.

Chapter 18

'Why do you work here?' I'd been trying all afternoon and not for the first time over the years, to answer Wayne's question, and still not found a convincing answer. Good job it wasn't an interview.

I'm scrabbling around under the van securing the exhaust with a coat hanger, when Nisha's Range Rover returns, she crosses to my van, and carefully, opens and immediately closes the passenger door. I assume she hasn't spotted me, but she walks quickly around the van and pauses, only long enough, to inform my protruding legs that she's just put a cheque from Frank on the seat, and that she'll speak to me next week, before her shapely legs retreat purposefully to the house. Allo, Allo springs to mind, 'I vill zay zis only vonce', I muse, as the front door slams.

The slow rhythmic thudding from Wayne that had ceased, presumably to determine Nisha's arrival, resumes.

Almost before the door, and possibly the whole house, stops reverberating, it reopens, but this time closes with a prolonged, agonising click, in an attempt at stealth. No tippety-tap of tell-tale heels on the setts, I notice. Withdrawing my head from under the van like a tortoise, I see why. Nisha is tip-toeing briskly along the lawn towards her car. Seeing my amused, comprehending expression, she realises she must be cutting quite a comical figure, and stifles a laugh. On hearing Wayne grunt and scrabble laboriously to his feet, Nisha shoots a frantic glance in the direction of the patio, and then mimes for me to set the alarm, as she dives into her Range Rover.

Wayne comes lumbering into view in time to admire the back of it disappearing in a cloud of dust down the drive.

"Where's the fire?" he asks, "Why's she in such a tear-arsing hurry?"
I shrug, "Perhaps she's just imitating us lot leaving here," I laugh, "… maybe she's late for the school run."

Wayne laughs unconvincingly and eyes me suspiciously.
"Honestly, I don't' know…" I profess.

I've got a good idea though.
"…She just came back, went in and out of the house like a flamin' cuckoo-clock, and then left without speaking," I say, trying to imagine the Oscar ceremony. I decide that an edited version would be less inflammatory; Wayne surely knew he was in the wrong, but I appreciated he needed to save face.

Wayne continues to look unconvinced. A sudden thought occurs to me, he might have seen Nisha cross to my van when he'd obviously checked to see whose car had arrived.

"Oh, actually!" I say, as though just remembering, "I think she put something in the van while I was underneath sorting out the exhaust." I was already mentally composing my acceptance speech.

Wayne's suspicious eyes swivel cartoon like to the van seat. I watch, amused as his eyes scan the width of the front seat and stop; like a couple of cherries coming up on a fruit machine. Wayne tries to read the contents of the crisp, plain white envelope, bearing Frank's scrawl; which could only be imitated, and deciphered by a doctor. I presumed it was my name, based solely on the assumption that it had been given to me, and that all previous envelopes from Frank had borne the same infantile attempt at a flourish; characteristic of cheap biros and resembling the printout from a heart monitor.

Eventually Wayne abandons his attempt at x-ray vision and blinks his gaze back on me, "What's that?"

Nosey sod.
"An envelope?"

"Ha. Ha. I knew you were gonna say that," he laughs dryly.
"What's in it?" he asks, unashamedly.

Mind your own business.

"I don't know, I haven't got x-ray eyes like you."
"I ain't got x-ray eyes," he says confused.
"Sorry, I thought you were reading it, you were staring at it so hard."
He ignores this last remark. "Has he sent your money down? He ain't sent mine," he says, disgruntled.

"I don't know; I'll open it when I get home. Considering it's April, it's either a late fiftieth birthday card, or an Easter card, either way it'll be too depressing for a public display of emotion," I say dryly.
"Or a late Christmas card… or a cheque," he says flatly.
"Ooh. That would be nice," I say, then think, sod it, "Well I have invoiced him; he does owe me. It's not exactly a backhander, a bribe, a bung, or whatever euphemism you use."

My name's not Wayne Hall

*****

Stuck behind a slow moving cattle truck on my way home, the van may sound sporty, but it only sounds it. The sight of all those hairy, shitty arses pressed to the ventilation slots, as the wagon takes the bends, somehow reminds me of Wayne leaning on the fence; not that he's got a particularly shitty one come to that.

He was definitely on a go-slow this afternoon, a hundred per cent improvement on the morning, but definitely a statement of defiance.

*****

"You're late," says Lizzie sullenly, "and why's the van sound like a boy racer?"
"Sorry ma Lady," I say touching my forelock, "…that's why I'm late; the exhaust nearly fell off, so I had to wire it up."
"Sounds real beasty," she grins.
"Glad you like it…'cos I won't have time to get it fixed before netball training…I'll get it done tomorrow, after hockey in Kenchester."
"Can't you get it done here now, at Kingsford Tyres?" she moans.
"There isn't time, it's nearly five, they'll be shutting now," I say testily, "and anyway, I've got to sort the animals out before taking you to netball training, we've only got about half an hour before we have to leave… I know you're embarrassed being seen in the van, but if you don't like it…"

"I'm not usually embarrassed about being seen in the van," she protests, "but it does sound embarrassing like this, everyone's looking," she laughs, holding her chin on her chest.
"Is that your ostrich approach… think no one recognises you? The name on all four sides is a bit of a giveaway," I laugh.
"All the other parents, s'pecially at county hockey have Beamers and Mercs and big four wheelers."

"This's got four big wheels," I laugh.
Lizzie looks puzzled for a few seconds, rerunning her last comment. "Oh you know what I mean," she says, determined not to laugh, "I meant, four-by-fours, off-roaders."
"'Cept the only off-roading they do is when they pull onto their drives," I say cynically, reversing into ours, "…anyway, I wouldn't get many dining tables or chests of drawers into a Beamer… even if I could afford one," I add.

"Right. Grab yourself a sandwich and get changed while I do the animals, shower and change... we need to leave at half past…"

"Sure you don't want to synchronise watches?" she says dryly.
I take her wrist and pretend to simultaneously listen to our watches, "They're not synchronised; yours is tocking while mine's ticking."
"Ha! Ha!"

*****

"Have you got the theme tune for The A Team?" asks Lizzie, as we exit the drive spitting gravel.
"I'm sure it can be downloaded if you're sad enough," I reply, realising her inference.
"That must be the quickest turn around yet.... Poor Ebony... she's been shut in all day, then no sooner is she let out, she's shut up again. She's hardly had time for a sh.. poo, let alone check out the sheep sh..muck."
"Your language has got worse," admonishes Lizzie.
"I think it's because of the language up at The Funny Farm..."
"The where?"
"The Funny Farm, that's what Barry and I call The Grange, ya know, Frank and Nisha's....Trouble is Wayne and Eric eff and blind every other word, so you get desensitised, ya know, immune to it."
Come to think of it, Nisha seems to be catching up with them lately.
"Oooh that sounds painful - actually it sounds like a toothpaste," she laughs.

*****

"That the last training session for county netball, wasn't it? Is it the last match this Sunday?"

"Yeah. But it's supposed to be the first county cricket match as well, and they're not pleased."
"Well at least it's the last, and then you'll be available for the cricket… Will it be every Sunday?"
"I think so," she answers absently.
"No one's forcing you to… if you don't want to play then don't," I say, "I just thought you enjoyed cricket."
"I do...well I enjoy batting and bowling…"
"But?" I encourage.
"Nothing," she says unconvincingly.

We sit in silence for several minutes. I know if I push it Lizzie will clam up. I press the button on top of the ipod, Marvin Gaye is wittering on most inappropriately about sexual healing.

After listening to the lyrics for a minute or so she asks curiously, "Who sings this?"
"Marvin Gaye. Why?"
"Just wondered."
"Well don't listen to the lyrics too closely, you're only fourteen, don't want you getting any ideas," I say, only half joking.
"Is he still around?"

"No, he died in the eighties…about eighty-four… He was originally with Motown Records. But I think this was his first with Columbia Records…I think his father shot him with a gun that Marvin had bought him… "
"I didn't want his life story for god's sake!"
"You asked."
"A simple yes or no would have done …
"Why did he shoot him?"
"I can't remember. Probably seemed a good idea at the time. Maybe he wasn't a big fan of his music, some critics take their work seriously…

I note Liz's unimpressed expression.

"…His father was a strict bible bashing preacher who often beat the stuffing out of his kids when they were young…. I think Marvin got into drugs, I don't know if that had anything to do with it."
"So his dad shot him?" she says incredulously, more a statement than a question.
"Yeah. We're too soft on kids nowadays. No wonder we have discipline problems in schools."
"That why you gave up teaching?" she laughs.
"Yeah. No fun in teaching when they stopped us shooting the little cherubs…Actually I think he attacked his father for abusing his mother."
"Oh, that's alright then," she says dryly.

We spend the remainder of the journey hearing only the intro to several tracks, either one or both of us stabbing a finger out to skip the track, like the tongues of chameleon. Lizzie justifying her action with, "I don't like this one," without considering that I might. So I just skip the ones I'm not in the mood for, without explanation; pay-back time.

It's a constant source of irritation; the kids assuming control of the channel changer. Walking into a room, or getting into the car and automatically changing the channel on the radio or television; the fact that they invariably walked straight back out of the room is even more annoying. It's like having my listening or viewing censored by my kids; strict parents are one thing but…

The silence is punctuated by, "Oh, I like that one."
"Tough. I liked the one you just skipped," I say.
I sense that Lizzie had put on hold whatever had been gnawing at her, until after training; which suggests it could be time to buy shares in Kleenex.

Not until we are nearly home do I get a hint.
"Do you think mum will be home by now?" she asks casually.

"Your guess is as good as mine," I reply flatly.
"She's never home…. What does she do all the time? Do all teachers live at school?"
"It's only since she's been a Head…" I say, trying unconvincingly to defend Alex.
"No it's not. She was never at home when she was a psycho either!" she snaps.
"I think you mean SENCO…" I laugh "…psycho is what she is now," I think aloud.

We laugh at her Freudian slip, and I wonder where her line of thought is going.
"What's a SENCO?" she eventually asks.
I have to think for few seconds, after years of hearing Alex talk a foreign language; I'd almost forgotten what the jargon actually meant.
"Er, Special Education Needs Coordinator. It's just the politically correct way of saying she was responsible for organising the teaching of the slow learners throughout the school."

Lizzie huffs loudly at the sight of the empty drive, "What time is it?"
Opening the van door I glance at my watch in the fading light, "Nearly half-eight," I reply, puzzled as to Lizzie's unusual level of concern. "I suppose I'd better crack on with the dinner while you grab a shower," I say, in an attempt at diffusion.
"Can't we just have pizza and chips," Lizzie groans, dumping her bags on the sofa.
"Ohh." I groan in mock disappointment, "I was going to produce my…"
"I know, sorry to cramp your culinary skills, but I'm starving, I just want something quick."

"I don't think we have much choice anyway," I sigh, "there's a limit to my creative skills, I'd need to be a member of the magic circle to make anything with the contents of that." I say shutting the fridge door more firmly than intended. The sound of clonking milk bottles triggers a Pavlovian response; I could murder a drink, I think, turning the oven on.

"Do you want to choose a pizza from the freezer, assuming there is a choice, and get the chips?"

"Oh do I have to, I was going to have a shower," she protests.

"I thought you were starving, you're younger and more nimble than me; so you'll be quicker…Anyone would think the freezer was down the garden, not in the office - you can shower while it's cooking."

Ebony has uncharacteristically remained on her bed instead of greeting us with the energetic tail wagging of a beached tadpole. "What's the matter Ebony?" I ask, instinctively sniffing and casting about for evidence of an 'accident'. She follows me with her eyes, her front paws hooked over the side of her bed, I can't decide if she looks guilty or whether she's sulking. Well she hasn't left any surprise presents that I can see or smell.

The clatter from the office, is followed by muffled expletives, followed by, "This bloody freezer! It's crap!"

It's a ritual followed by everyone who visits the freezer. Within a week of having the bloody thing, the plastic lugs that hold the drawer fronts on started snapping off. This meant that only someone with an octopus in their family tree could snatch the door open and place a hand on all the drawer fronts to prevent them from cascading to the floor, while opening and checking each drawer to find the desired item, then slamming the door quick enough to hold them in position. No one has mastered it yet. It's the only time swearing is tolerated.

I stick my head into the cupboard under the stairs, and cogitate for a few seconds. Sod it. I don't care what you're supposed to have with pizza, I can't wait for a red to warm up anyway; I'll have a Sauvignon blanc…Actually I feel like a beer first, so I take a bottle of Butty Bach as well.

Back in the kitchen Lizzie is doing her best to empty the remainder of a bag of chips onto an oven tray.

"Blimey, you are hungry," I say.

"Well I'm not taking any back to that bloody freezer," she snaps. "Anyway, I presume mum will want something when she gets back."

"When," I mutter.

They both watch me put the wine in the fridge, then set about opening the beer. I take an old pint pot from the cupboard above the dresser base and start to ceremoniously pour the amber liquid down the side of the tilted glass.

"Can I do that?" asks Lizzie, "I like doing that."

"I could get used to waitress service," I say, handing her the bottle and glass.

I pull out the terracotta floor tile that we use for baking things like pizzas and garlic bread, and remove the packaging from the frozen pizza; salami with mozzarella with a liberal sprinkling of mushrooms.

"Strange choice," I say.

"It was the first one that fell out, I lost the will to bother," she half laughs.

"I thought so. I didn't think you liked mushrooms," I inspect the topping again, "You might be in luck, I think they're dried slugs," I say.

"Aren't I the lucky one…here, perfect," she says, handing me, as advertised, a perfectly poured pint… "I'm off for a shower."

Ebony continues to sulk. Her eyes watch me, but find something fascinating in her bed, about three inches from her nose, when I look in her direction. I wonder whether she's been taking lessons from Alex.

I half expect Ebony to toss her head and say, "Huh. Well don't ask me how my day's been then. Well I've had a shit day, thanks for asking, shut in here all day… there's a limit to how long I can play 'eye-spy' on my own, not that you care."

Seeing the thermostat light go out on the oven, I sling the chips in like a professional; Jamie Oliver would be impressed. I pick up my beer and drink thirstily, then admire the remaining half before setting it down temporarily on the dresser.

"So Ebony, how's your day been then?" I ask, collecting plates to warm in the top oven that conveniently acts as a warming drawer. Ebony initially pricks her ears, on hearing her name; puzzled she looks around the kitchen for whoever I must surely be talking to.

"Yes. I'm talking to you stupid," I say, staring directly.

She repeats her stranded tadpole impression, writhing in her bed. I take another mouthful of beer, and study Ebony as if for the first time. I realise she's looking old, her muzzle and eyebrows look as though she's dipped her face in a bag of flour, and her eyes are no longer bright liquid pools of chocolate; more like stale ones with a bloom to them. I crouch down beside her bed and rub the side of her head behind the ear, "What's the matter girl, you getting old?" She responds as usual by squirming onto her back with all four legs in the air, inviting a tummy rub, "You slapper, you just like your tits fondled" I say, vigorously rubbing her belly, then neck.

Footsteps padding along the landing from the bathroom, remind me of the pizza. Fortunately I notice my hands have taken on the appearance of a werewolf, and quickly wash them before loading the pizza into the oven; I don't think I need 'the hair of the dog' yet.

"You seem to be permanently moulting," I say to Ebony, "it's a wonder you're not bald," I say, setting the table.

I drain the last of the pint just as Lizzie enters the kitchen wearing her pyjamas, which are several years old and now stop halfway down her calves. Her wet hair is swathed in a towel. The overall effect is that of a school production of Aladdin.

"How many's that?" she asks.

"Bloody hell, you're as bad as your mother," I answer testily. "If you must know, that was the one you poured."

"I was only joking," she protests, eying the table and noting that it's set for three.

"Are you being optimistic, or has mum rung?"

I raise my eyebrows appreciatively, "My, they do teach you big words at school nowadays… bet you can't spell it."

"I.T." she recites, with a smirk.

"Your brain is obviously deprived of energy, you'd better eat before you get too delirious; you're starting to think you're a comedian."

"Comedienne," she corrects.

"Okay smarty-pants, just check tonight's gastronomic delight, and serve up if it's ready."

"Please," Lizzie again corrects.

"PLEASE," I oblige, retrieving the wine from the fridge… "Ever thought about being a teacher?"

"Now who's joking. I think mums put me off that."

I wince involuntarily at the radiant heat on my bare forearm from the tile bearing the pizza as Lizzie sails briskly past.

"Smells good."

"Better than it looked earlier," she says.

I pour the straw coloured wine quickly, with satisfying glugs, before returning the bottle to the fridge.

I wait to fall in behind Lizzie on her return trip to the table with the chips,

"Well at least you're mum has helped eliminate one profession," I laugh.

"What's that?" she asks, "Cooking?"
"No, if I remember rightly your mum's a good cook – no, I've put you off that one, that makes two - No, actually, I was thinking about teaching …knowing what you don't want to do is pretty helpful."

Lizzie glances at the old school clock on the wall and moans, "It's nearly nine o'clock; where is she?"

Elvis singing 'Suspicious Minds' springs to mind.
I shrug, "I've no idea… Do you want to put a CD on?"
"Not really. Do you?"
"Not really. Well I do but I can't think of anything we've got that I'm in the mood for…I wish we'd got some classical stuff; that's what I feel like right now."

Lizzie looks at me as though I've suddenly declared myself homosexual. She considers this statement for several seconds.
"You mean there's *not one* CD - from Abba to…Zepplin, that *you* want to listen to?… I don't believe it. You must be getting old," she says.

It's the only thing I am getting lately.
We finish the meal in silence. Lizzie even refrains from commenting as I pour another glass.

"I never see mum nowadays. She never comes to watch me play anything," she says, sniffing loudly, and swallowing.

I can tell by the tightness of her voice it's Kleenex time. Scrapping my chair back on the tiles, I round the table as the dam bursts; washing a sludge of mascara down over both her cheeks.

"You should get your money back on that waterproof mascara," I say, pulling her face into my shoulder.
I feel the hot steamy mixture of laughter and sobbing through my shirt.
"Shud up dad, your nod fuddy."

I wonder why Lizzie has chosen this evening to air her feelings. She must have noticed her mother's absence from the side of the various pitches before. I wonder whether any of her teammates have commented, perhaps they've asked if she even has a mother. After all, I'm usually the only father amongst all the mothers. Not that I'm complaining.

"Look, your mother really regrets missing your games. She's so proud of you; we both are. She loves watching you play, especially netball; hockey pitches are too draughty for your mum… but it's a sacrifice she has to make to do her job - you know what she's like, she's so conscientious, she does everything thoroughly; probably because she can't take criticism."

Lizzie snuffles and clears her throat, "So are you, but you manage to take me to training and matches… some of the girls have asked if you and mum are divorced… they ask why it's always you that brings me, and watches me play."

"Do you tell them that I'm just a sad pervert, and that I can't wait for you to play in the adult leagues? Mind you, I've seen some of the butch hockey players," I joke.

"S'not funny," she laughs.

"Talking of which," I say, extricating myself and reaching for the box of tissues on the corner of the worktop. Peeling off a wad, I wipe Lizzie's face with half and give her the rest to blow her nose, while I check the damage to my shirtfront.

Lizzie grimaces at the shiny wet patch on the left side of my chest, that resembles the venue for a snail's ceilidh and laughs, "Ugh, sorry," and then snuggles her face into the right side.

"Because of the nature of my work and because I'm self-employed, I'm more flexible than your mother."

I can remember when she was very flexible, but quickly erase the images.

"Your mother has staff-meetings, governors-meetings, finance meetings. Ha! That's a laugh, your mum never even opens her own bank statements and yet she's responsible for a school's budget of over a million pounds…"

Lizzie snorts.

"… parents meetings, lesson planning, school policies, staff mentoring…"

"What's meantoring?"

"That's when you *meant* to be home five hours before you actually are," I say dryly.

Lizzie raises her eyes and tilts her head in that, 'can you be serious for one minute.'

"Okay. Mentoring, is when a senior, more qualified member of staff looks after a trainee, or in the case of teachers, a newly qualified - makes sure they are being professional, employing best practice; not getting into any bad habits, like working ridiculously long hours," I say facetiously..

"What! Mum's supposed to tell her staff not to work long hours?" she asks incredulously.

"I was only joking," I laugh. "Ha Ha….The thing is, if it wasn't for your mother, we wouldn't be able to afford all the things you - and Adam seem to take for granted… she earns nearly twice as much as I do."

"Really…What do you mean, *Adam takes for granted*? He doesn't live at home anymore."

"I know but we still have to subsidise him - help run his car, and help him out when we can; he's not really earning enough to live independently… Anyway, this is about your mum not Adam. You should be proud of her, not many people could do what she does."

Not many would want to I think.

"Not many would want to," Lizzie echoes my thoughts, "…not if it does this to their families."

"Does what to their families?"

"Well you and mum are always rowing; and she's always crabby with me."
"We're always rowing 'cos she's always crabby – She's crabby because she's stressed – and she's crabby with me because I'm never serious enough; it obviously irritates her… sometimes it's the things that attracted you to someone that can become irritating…I notice she still laughs like an old slapper when someone else tells, er let's say, an adult joke, but I'm being crude or vulgar if I'm a bit risqué."
"It's the way you tell 'em," Lizzie laughs.
"You can never be serious!" I mock.

"Just remember, your mum is extremely proud of you and Adam, and it really upsets her to miss out on watching you play - perhaps she'll come and watch you play hockey tomorrow.

"I know you're not going to like this, but have you got much schoolwork to do this weekend, because you're not going to get much time, what with hockey and netball and Katt's party?" I ask tentatively. "Perhaps you could do an hour before bed…while you're Facebooking or whatever you call that chat site,"

Lizzie visibly sags and groans, "Just when I thought my evening couldn't possibly get any better."
"I know, you must be the envy of all your friends - your life's just one long roller coaster of excitement," I say.
Lizzie regards me with mock compassion, "Was the roller coaster you rode, broken down?"
"I could never face anything faster than The Teacups…I was really upset when they banned me - the only reason I agreed to have kids was because I hoped I'd be able to accompany you on it."

"I don't remember you coming on the rides with us," she laughs.
"I wasn't allowed - you nearly found yourselves in the orphanage."
"Thanks. As if I wasn't already feeling unwanted enough," she states flatly, heading for the office.

I suppose I'd better clear the table before checking my emails. I put the remaining chips onto the tile with the remains of the pizza, and put it into the top oven to keep warm for Alex.

I've a feeling that I needn't have bothered. I don't know why we don't just wheel the shopping trolley down to the compost heap and throw half of it out and not bother with refrigerating it. There seem to be a lot of meals lately that get split between the dog, the chickens and the compost heap… Mind you, the other half of the fruit and veg seems to rot before you can use it; bags of salad turn to slime, bananas go from green to brown without bothering to go through yellow, tomatoes are tasteless…

My Victor Meldrew moment is interrupted by Lizzie wailing in the office, "God! Why's this computer so slow?" "Because of all the rubbish programs you've installed," I answer, assuming The Almighty might be tied up with more pressing problems like tsunamis and world famine; and anyway he's probably even less computer literate than me.

Booting up my laptop I'm intrigued to see that I've got ten new messages. Opening up the inbox I'm disappointed and even more intrigued, I wonder why the whole world seems to think I need viagra and penis enlargement. I scan the list of email titles but they're all along the theme of, 'Be like wood all night,' and 'Fill your woman', from names that look like anagrams.

A man could get a complex, I think, highlighting and systematically deleting – I'm sure there must be a quicker way to delete all these - I wonder who Alex has been talking to.

Almost at the bottom of the list I automatically press to delete the highlighted email, entitled, 'Large bow-fronted chest'…, which I'd assumed was an advert for breast implants and had thought for a second about forwarding to Alex's computer; I thought we could both get a complex about our anatomies. Before disappearing to the deleted box, my mind registered the word, Regency.

Aaagh! That looks like work. Going into the deleted files, I retrieve the details of a lady that does indeed want me to give her large chest some TLC; unfortunately it's of the Regency mahogany type.

Phew. That was close; I nearly lost that. I wonder how many work related enquiries I'd accidentally deleted from 'strippers' and people with veneer problems.

As if the computer were telepathic, the right hand side of the screen reserved for the ubiquitous adverts, the downside of Hotmail accounts, is suddenly occupied by the silhouette of the scantily clad writhing dancer, that appeared the other evening; asking if I'd like a hot sizzling date. Yes pleeease. I hover the cursor over the YES button, which responds by pulsing bright red, like an aroused blood enriched labia.

I feel the same hot flush of adrenalin that I felt as a twelve year old, psyching myself up to steal a sheath knife from a hardware shop, after coveting it through the window for weeks.

Worried about the consequences if I was caught, I must have looked guilty as hell just looking at the bright polished blade, with its leather and brass handle; let alone walking stiffly out of the shop with about ten inches of Sheffield Steel perilously close to the guardian of our family tree. I was thankful it was in a stout leather sheath. It made Crocodile Dundee's weapon look like part of a manicure set.

Mind you, if I felt guilty that day, it was nothing compared to a few days later when I accompanied three other friends to the same shop to witness one of them actually buy a similar knife. I had failed to mention that mine was on permanent loan when they'd admired it, and asked how much it cost.

When my friends expressed disappointment to the shop assistant about the gap in the display, which according to the progression in the graduations meant that the biggest was missing, I began to feel uncomfortably hot. I was half expecting one of them to ask if it was the one I'd bought, my stomach felt as though I had those ferrets in my shirt again.

But then salvation of sorts came from the assistant in his brown coverall, who apologised for not having a full display on account of someone stealing the missing one a few days earlier.

I felt as conspicuous as if I'd dropped a real cheek flapper in church after the vicar has said, 'Let us Pray', as three pairs of eyes swivelled in my direction….I have never found aluminium saucepans so fascinating; you could have cooked a pan of spuds off my red face. It's ironic that they all ended up in and out of prison, and I end up as a pillock of the local community.

Now as I watch the figure writhe alluringly, words and phrases seem to leap from the text on the screen, acting like the devil sitting on my shoulder, encouraging. 'Illicit encounters - consenting adults - no strings - rejuvenate stale relationships.' Phrases designed to condone and to salve the conscience. I swallow hard to suppress the adrenalin and consider the consequences.

An illicit bit of no strings attached rumpy-pumpy, with a bored red-hot nymphomaniac housewife, would be the end of my marriage…Two wrongs don't make a right, so I'm told … Or maybe not, it couldn't hurt just to have a look.

The pulsing red labia look like winning, when I wonder whether Simple Slyman has emailed. Was it lateral thinking?

I quickly bring up Alex's new account.

Christ, it doesn't take them long to start bombarding this new address with spam email.

I delete all except one marked from Simon Gatley, which I open with some trepidation; after all if he and Alex are together this evening, he must know about the bogus emails.

Darling, is everything okay for next Saturday? If you've changed your mind I need to know, the

hotel and bubbly is costing me a fortune and I can't cancel.
Why did you have to mention that 'problem'?
Come to think about it how did you know, have you been talking to that money grabbing bitch of a wife?
But just to be sure I've managed to get some 'insurance' like you suggested. Extremely embarrassing, I'm sure the bitch behind the counter deliberately played deaf just to make me shout.
I can't wait, don't be late!!
SI xx

Oh you're such an old romantic – you bastard. I wonder who he's got lined up if Alex does pull-out? Is it a bluff, does he know it's me sending these emails and not Alex?

I click reply.

Sorry I haven't replied sooner, but been up to my eyes at school.
Yes of course, everything's fine for next weekend, can't wait either.
I think Charles was checking my text messages last night so don't text me.

You say you need to know if I've changed my mind because it's costing you a fortune, so who have you got lined up if I couldn't make it??
I'm sure the embarrassment will be worth it, you know what they say, 'A hard man is good to find'!! Hope 'it's' not as flexible as your credit card.
See you about three-thirty.
A x

The front door shudders under the weight of someone walking into it. Presumably Alex had assumed it would be unlocked, and she would only have to turn the handle. I couldn't help but laugh at the Buster Keaton image as I hurriedly click 'SEND'.

Keys scrape around the keyhole for a few seconds, but I get to the door and pull it open, feeling as guilty as if I'd been the one caught with my trousers down.

"Hi. You alright? That's a long day. You must be knackered. You hungry? There's some pizza and chips in the top oven."

Again.

"I'm not hungry. I told you I was meeting the NQH's in Hereford for a meal, I told you weeks ago," she says defensively.

"What the hell's the NQH? It's not in the diary; you can't expect me to remember what you said weeks ago. I can't remember what I'm told this morning, that's what we've got a bloody great desk diary for," I say, attempting to stay calm, aware of the conversation I'd had with Lizzie.

"The Newly Qualified Heads, you know that. You know we meet every month."
"How long can you keep calling yourselves Newly Qualified; you've been a Head for years? Perhaps we should call ourselves something then; then we might meet at least once a month,"

The Nearly Separated Parents.

"Oh, piss off. Why are you having a go at me the moment I walk in?"
"Because I've just spent the last few hours consoling Lizzie, and explaining that the reason her mother doesn't watch her play, is because her mother works such long hours…not because her mother's having a jolly time with her friends."

Or shagging Simple Slyman.

"Oh piss off!"
"Ever thought of joining a debating society?"
"Oh sod off. I work bloody hard all the time, I deserve to go out and have a relaxing time with my friends, once in a while," she snaps.
"So you don't miss your family all the time you're working hard. You don't feel like some 'quality time' with us? It's your friends you miss, well thanks… Perhaps I should go out once in a while and meet some *friends,*" I say, thinking about Illicit Encounters.

Lizzie emerges from the office, her calm voice belying her watery eyes as she addresses her mother, "Are you coming to watch me play hockey tomorrow, it's the last one?"
"Oh what time are you playing?"
"Ten-thirty."
"Oh I'm sorry, we've got a netball tournament at school in the morning," Alex replies apologetically.

Tears burst from Lizzie's eyes as her face crumples, like a yoghurt pot on a bonfire.

I see the pain and helplessness in Alex's eyes as Lizzie turns from her, and instinctively heads for the safety of her room; like an animal to its nest.

I catch her in the crook of my arm, and am surprised at the force. I do a quick-step to regain my balance and avoid the indignity of going arse-over-tit. Once again Lizzie howls into my shirtfront.

I'm going to have to start wearing a bib.

"Look Liz, your mum can't help having the netball tournament tomorrow; that's part of the job…Perhaps she'll come and watch the netball on Sunday," I add, hopefully. But looking at Alex over Lizzie's head I see that I've just produced another nail to complete the crucifixion.

"I can't come on Sunday. I've got a report to the governors to finish; they've got a meeting on Monday" she almost wails.

I know what's coming next, and I chorus it mentally, "Oh I'll give up my fucking job, then you'll all be happy," she screams, storming from the room.

"Don't slam the…"

Too late. The slamming door causes a minor tremor, accompanied by the metallic clatter as the keeper for the Suffolk latch pings off the door-frame, skitters across the flagstone floor, and disappears under the armchair. I raise my eyes.

As if I haven't got enough jobs to do around here.

Alex's progress to our bedroom is monitored by the ripple effect through the house, as successive doors are wrenched open then slammed behind her; each tremor is noticeably less than the preceding one.

"Thank god she spent all her energy on the first one," I mutter, "…never could pace herself."

Lizzie thumps me on the chest and carries on sobbing.

Chapter 19

"Have you seen my phone, I haven't seen it since you were playing with it on Thursday night?"
"No, I thought I put it in your handbag."
"Oh shit, I hope I haven't lost it; there's so much on it that I need – I'm lost without it."
"Well it can't be far away, I'll have a good look for it when I get back."
"I could do with it this morning," Alex whines.
"Is there someone particular you need to phone, do you want to borrow mine?" I offer helpfully, knowing the numbers on mine will be as helpful as a Chinese directory.
"Not unless you happen to have the numbers of all the parents of my team, and the numbers of the netball umpires – just in case," she replies testily.

"Dad can we go, I need to be there for half past?"
"Yeah okay, coming. Here put your stuff in the van," I say tossing Liz the van keys, "… have you got yourself a drinks bottle?"
"Yeees."
"Gumshield?"
"Yeeees?"
"Hockey stick?"
"Yeeeees. Dad, I'm not stupiiid."
"Course not – Got your Astro's and shin pads?"
"Oh sh…!" she drops her bag and dashes upstairs.

"Where have you looked for your phone?"
"Everywhere," Alex wails.

You can't have looked everywhere otherwise you'd have found it. I recite the response mentally, that we usually give the kids in the same situation, but decide it's an unhealthy option right now.

"Well your handbag, was on that chair,"
"I've already checked the cushions," she informs me irritably, checking her watch, "…Oh I've got to go; I'm going to be late. I just hope none of the kids has an accident."

******

I drop Lizzie off at Kenchester Sports Centre as usual an hour before the match is due to start. God, in my day you were lucky if the whole team was there before push-back.

"I'm off to get the exhaust fixed, I should be back before the match starts, Kenchester Tyres is only just around the corner."
"Okay – have you got three pounds match fee?"
"Bet that's something you won't hear Rooney ask his wife before he trots off on a Saturday," I say rummaging for my wallet, "…here I've only got a fiver, have a drink after…"
"I bet you won't hear Rooney's wife say that," she grins, adding, "…You sure know how to wine and dine a lady, I can see how you swept mum off her feet."
"Just goes to show there's no truth in the saying, 'Treat em mean to keep em keen' then," I say dryly.

While I wait for the exhaust to be repaired I think back to the text messages on Alex's phone the other night. There was nothing to suggest that they had rumbled me; not even in their tone.

Nothing in the recent few days would suggest that they are aware of my interference. In fact, looking at the 'Sent' folder, Alex hasn't contacted him at all in the last few weeks. In fact the tone of Alex's texts are quite benign; mostly school related business, with the odd enquiry as to his wife and family's health and well-being. A vast contrast to the number and content received from him in the 'Inbox'; Slymon sounds like a dog on-heat.

Christ, I hope I haven't started something between them, instead of trying to finish it.
Surely Alex can't be using the schools computer; all the staff must have access to that. I wonder whether his wife would like to see all his texts and emails?

I wonder whether she should turn up at Alveston Manor… after Slymon's wanked himself senseless.

*****

"…I hated that; I always seem to play rubbish compared to school or county."
"You did okay – don't forget these are more experienced adults – You could do with getting down lower when you're defending – I know it's difficult when you're tall…"
"Don't you start…"
"You did really well – you only lost by one goal – You'd have won by miles if you'd converted more of your short corners; you had at least six compared to their two, and they made theirs count…

"…Are you off to change and have some food?"
"Yeah, are you coming up for a drink?"
"Nice of you to offer, I suppose I could force one down."
"Ha ha – Can I have three pounds match fee?"
"Ha ha, nice try Mister Rooney."

*****

"So what time have you got to be at Katt's tonight?" I ask as I reverse into the drive, noting that Alex isn't back yet.
"Anytime really after about seven."
"Hmm," I check my watch, two-thirty. "…Is anyone else going from Kingsford? Only I've told your mum we're supposed to be at The Jolly Friar for seven-thirty; which is going to be a bit tight, timing wise…I was thinking we could do the picking up after."

"I don't think anyone else is going from round here - you could take me earlier if it makes it easier."
"Your all heart…

"…Did your mum say what time her tournament finishes, or even what time she'll be home?"
"No, but she's probably doing a shop on the way home…What time are you picking me up from Katt's? – Not too early."
"I thought we'd agreed, about midnight – What time have you got to be in Walsall?"
"Not until twelve-thirty."
"That's a relief, if it had been nine you'd have been worse than useless – so would I come to that…Are you sure that's when you have to be there, and not when the match starts?
"Daad, I know you think I'm an idiot; the match starts at one-thirty."

I check the time again and compare it to the kitchen clock. Just after quarter-to-three.
"I'm going to have a shower."
"I don't know why you didn't have one after the match," I say absently, checking the clock again. Still just after quarter-to-three. I check my watch to see if the clock has stopped.

My stomach is churning worse than a first date.

"I'm taking Ebony for a walk," I call up the stairs.

*****

Cresting the brow of the hill, I'm bombarded by a cacophony emanating from my jacket pocket. I instinctively check my watch. Blimey, Twenty past four. Have I been gone that long? It was lovely being without a phone signal. Withdrawing my mobile I see I have a voice message.

I wonder what Lizzie wants? I'm surprised when I hear Alex's voice.

"Charles, I've been trying to ring you – Lizzie wants me to take her over to Katt's now – Apparently she's worried that if we wait 'til seven it'll make us late getting to The Friar – I shan't be long, it's about quarter past four now so I should be back just after five – love you – By the way, I still haven't found my phone, I'm really worried about it – Do you think I should contact Orange and cancel it in case someone's using it and running up a huge bill?"

I switch the kettle on for a cuppa. While I'm waiting for it to boil I phone Alex's mobile to see if I can hear it ringing anywhere in the house. I wander in vain from room to room until Alex informs me she is unavailable but I'm welcome to leave a message and she'll get back to me.

I'm just about to go upstairs to repeat the process when my phone rings. Caller display informs me it's Alex.

"Hi."

"Hi dad, did you just ring? I found mum's phone under my seat, it must have fallen out of her handbag."

"It's okay I was just trying to find it here. Have a good time – be careful, see you at twelve…"

I wonder whether Alex had actually lost it – or was she hiding it from my prying eyes?

Chapter 20

Ebony greets my return from dropping Lizzie off in Kingsford for the school bus with such enthusiasm that I fear she may dislocate her tail again; she did it a few years ago and her tail looked like an old starting handle. She obviously realises, and appreciates that she's not going to be shut up all day.

I've decided to spend a couple of days in the workshop and make a start at catching up on the backlog. It should also give Barry some room to work at The Funny Farm, without us tripping over each other.

I check my watch, almost ten to eight; I wonder if it's too early to phone the lady about her chest of drawers. Most of my customers are of pensionable age; some not much younger than the family heirlooms that they've decided need restoring before the encircling family vultures swoop in. Most of them still get up with the sun; I suppose it's difficult to break the habit of a lifetime.

The fact it was an email rather than a phone call indicates a younger age group. You either have to catch them before the school run and work, or early evening. Some are young mothers with pre-school children, some just work from home… there are so many permutations I decide to stop trying to play detective, and just bloody ring.

The phone is eventually answered by a young sounding female voice, in the manner of an answering machine, "Hello, Rachel Foxley…"

I clear my throat and prepare to leave a message after the usual electronic beep. Instead of the anticipated beep, I hear, "Hello?"

"Oh, I'm sorry," I say, "I thought I'd got an answer phone."

Flattery will get you everywhere.

"This is Charles Wilson, returning your call, or rather replying to your email."
"Charles, Wilson," she repeats slowly, obviously searching her memory.
"Charles Wilson, furniture restorer? …" I prompt.
"Oh yes," she says brightly as the penny drops, "I emailed you about my chest, thanks for phoning back so soon. I inherited it from my grandmother…"

Mmm. Definitely younger than my average customer. I have to suppress the urge to respond to her *double entendre;* I've been working at The Funny Farm too long. I hope she hasn't inherited her grandmother's droopy chest.

"…My grandmother says it could do with a little TLC; so I've left it in one of the empty stables until it can be restored."

My alarm bell starts ringing. Stables… horses, are usually associated with money; they require a lot of money. I remember a salesman telling me, if he ever turned into a farm drive and saw pony paddocks, he turned around. I have a feeling that this could all be a waste of time.

"Your email mentioned that you have a regency bow fronted chest of drawers…"
"Yes that's right," she confirms cheerily.
"When you say it needs some TLC, what exactly is wrong with it?" I ask, poising my pencil below her name, address and phone number, ready to make notes.
"Well, like I said it's in the stable, but from memory, there are pieces of carving broken off the front edges, or whatever you call them… some of the drawers don't run very well, they stick a bit…"

TLC?

"…there are some bits of moulding missing from some of the drawer fronts… and some veneer missing from between the drawers; I don't know what you'd call that part," she says, making it sound like a question.

"Drawer rails," I oblige, "It sounds like the drawer linings, which are the drawer sides, and probably the drawer runners, which are the bearers attached to the inside of the carcase, that the drawers run on, have worn causing the drawer to wear the drawer rail and catch the veneer, pulling it off," I explain, wondering whether I have confused her. Actually I'm a little confused myself; her reference to carving on the front edges doesn't match my image of a typical Regency bow front.

"Oh right," she laughs, "I wasn't sure what TLC meant, but it obviously sounds like a lot of work - can you do it? I mean is it something that you could do?"

"Oh yes, although it sounds like, *a little tender loving care*, is rather an understatement," I say nonchalantly, I don't want to sound too eager; she sounds like a customer who's expecting to have to pay. I continue, "It's probably best if I come over and have a look, when it's convenient for you, then I can give you an idea of the cost and when I can do it."

"That would be great," she says enthusiastically, "I'm here most of the time as I work from home, so to suit you really."

"Well how about this time next week?" I consult the desk diary…

"Say nine o'clock Monday the fifth of May?" I suggest.

"Oh, according to my diary, next week is the twenty-first of April," she puzzles.

I examine the diary again and realise the marker ribbon is a couple of weeks back. "Sorry my fault, you're quite right – someone has entered something in the diary but not returned it to this week – I'm always being caught out like that, I have a job to remember what day it is let alone the date."

Rachel laughs, "I know what you mean, I'm the same," then seemingly pointedly, "…at least I don't have anyone else messing with my diary…

"Anyway next *Monday the twenty-first*…" she stresses, laughing, "…should be fine - Do you know where I am?"
"I think so, the address you give in your email sounds familiar, but I must confess the surname doesn't ring any bells. Is yours the barn conversion on the road into Clifton, from the Kingsford to Bowley road- the one down the long drive? I've done some work for the people at the farm house next to it a few years ago before the barn was converted. You sound a lot younger though."

Oh you smooth bastard.

"That's right. That must have been my grandparents - sadly they no longer live there… Oh, I just remembered, one of the brass handles is missing, they're quite ornate, it's such a pity. I don't suppose you can you get replacements?"
"Like you say, it's a pity, because it's unlikely we can get an exact match off the shelf. I have had copies made in the past for… er how can I put it?..."
She laughs, "You mean if the furniture is worth it. It's okay, I think I know what you mean, you must get a lot of people that think their family heirlooms are priceless, just because it's been in the family for years," she says candidly.

I laugh, but my alarm bell is tinkling again, "What shape are the handles?"
"Oh crikey. I don't know how to describe them, especially as it's not in front of me."
"Well are the back plates oval, and are the handles the shape of a capital D, or do they resemble the silhouette of a couple of swans facing away from each other?"
"Oh crikey, now you describe them like that; I suppose they do look like a couple of swans," she says enthusiastically, like a helpful witness on a TV police drama.

"Why do you ask?"
"Well they sound like swan neck drop handles, which…"

"Really, does that make a difference?" she asks, sensing an important significance.

I laugh, "The swan necks are generally associated with earlier furniture than Regency, actually the original handles could have been wooden knobs, so those brass handles may not be original anyway," I say cautiously, trying not to offend.

" Another thing, there's a very thin drawer that I can't open, well I think it's a drawer; it's only about an inch thick. It's between the top and the top drawer; it doesn't have any handles."

I ignore the Carry On script, my alarm bell is tinkling like an impatient master of the house summoning the maid.

"That sounds like a brushing slide," I say, thinking aloud. "Are you sure it's Regency? Come to think of it, are you sure it's bow fronted?"

"Well it's what my grandmother always called it. Why?"

"If you imagine looking down on the top, is it like a capital D, or is it wavy… like a double U?" I ask.

"Ooh, umm, I think it might be wavy- like a double U… What does that mean?"

"It means it's not a Regency Bow front," I half laugh, " but I can't tell you whether it's an earlier Georgian serpentine front, or a twentieth century reproduction without looking at it."

"What's the difference?" she asks.

"Maybe a few noughts," I chuckle. "Um, do you mind me asking whether you've arranged for anyone else to look at it?"

I sense her hesitation. For some people, asking for more than one quote implies distrust, so I continue quickly, "Only I'd be very wary if I were you of anyone that tries to buy it without you inviting offe..."

"Oh I would never sell it; it has such sentimental value."

"Well you sound like you know your mind."

Even if you know diddly squat about furniture.

"Well, I look forward to seeing you next Monday, Mrs. Foxley."
"It's Miss, but please call me Rachel…I don't know if I can wait that long," she says excitedly.
"It's a long time since a young lady's said that to me," I laugh.
"Oh sorry," she laughs, "I meant, I can't wait to find out…"
"S'okay, just my warped sense of humour," I say.
"Makes a nice change from some of the tradesmen I've had lately," she says warmly.

You might want to rephrase that, you might get a reputation.
"Did you organise the barn conversion then, sort out the builders etc?"
"Yes it's been a nightmare, getting people to come when they're supposed to; you've no idea," she groans.

"Well I suppose I was lucky, I did most of the work here myself," I say quickly, it never hurts to let people know what you can do; there might be some work. "…This is a stone cottage that we extended and renovated - I had a couple of good local builders to put up the shell of the extension and roof it, but I did most of the rest. I can imagine what it's like though, trying to orchestrate different tradesmen to keep the project going smoothly."

"That's interesting, that's worth knowing, I've still got loads of stuff to do here, I'll show you when you come - That's if you're interested?" she says brightly.
"Oh yes, you know what they say about variety," I say rather too eagerly.

Anything to get me away from The Funny Farm for a while.

"I don't suppose you make furniture as well as restore it do you? Only I need some built in cupboards, and bookcases and various other things," she explains.

"Oh yes. It's amazing how many people see my advert but only register that I'm a restorer, even though the advert says that I also make furniture."
"Oooh that told me didn't it?" she laughs.
"Sorry, I didn't mean it to sound quite like that."
"I know, only joking," she says, "I'll look forward to seeing you next week, thanks for phoning so promptly…Don't forget to bring your sketch pad and pencil… and tape measure."
"Yes I'm looking forward to it Rachel - your chest sounds intriguing - I can't wait to see it," I say, trying not to sound too much like Leslie Phillips.
She laughs, "I hope you're not too disappointed."

We hang up, and as well as the rather unprofessional thoughts that I try to suppress, I make a mental note to check on Georgian serpentine fronted chests, complete with a brushing-slide. I'm pretty sure they didn't appear until the second half of the eighteenth century. It sounds as though this one has canted corners with carved pilasters; should make a nice change from all the damn chairs I've been getting lately.

Chapter 21

This could have been written for Frank; the contrary bastard. Mick Jagger is bemoaning the fact that he saw a red door and wants it painted black, as I pull up at The Funny Farm.

I'm going to have to stop calling it that; one of these days I'm going to put my foot in it with Frank or Nisha. Nisha would probably see the funny side; I don't think Frank would appreciate his little empire being slighted.

I immediately sense something not quite right. Sophie's new car has obviously been parked for all to admire; seemingly abandoned in the middle of the car park. I laugh remembering the Vauxhall Viagra conversation; even my dodgy hearing wouldn't have turned Agila, into Viagra.

I suddenly realise, it's the quiet that's not right, the absolute silence. No dawn chorus courtesy of Little Eric and The Strimmers – perhaps he should start a jazz band. Perhaps it's not his day, he'd be here by now, Waking Up The Neighbours, as the song goes. I'm sure he was doing more days now that the grass is growing like smoke.

As if I'd been rubbing Eric's oil-can, the Genie screeches to a halt beside my van, throwing up a cloud of dust for him to emerge from, just to add to the illusion; albeit with more of a hobble - In any case the whisky fumes are usually enough of a screen.

"What's up Eric, did you oversleep?" I ask, before registering that he's not dressed in his usual work attire of tight oily overalls, and steel toe capped boots that make him look like a Subuteo model.

"Oh, you not working today," I state the obvious.

"I've come to tell 'im that I ain't fuckin' working for 'im anymore," he says flatly.

"Bloody 'ell! Why not? I thought you'd be here 'til you dropped. Thought I'd get the job of digging a hole for you at the top of the hill," I laugh.
"You ain't far off the fuckin' mark," he again replies with uncharacteristic flatness.
"What's happened?" I ask; realising it must be serious.
"I got stopped and breathalysed on Sat'dy night- coming 'ome from The Queens in Kingsford - 'pparently I was three times over the fuckin' limit."
"You were having an early night then," I say dryly.
"Yeah, any other night…"
"Or day," I interject.

Eric cackles, dislodging a wad of phlegm, which he propels across the lawn in a graceful arc, landing with a stomach churning plop, resembling a small jelly-fish that has mysteriously dropped from the sky.
I wonder how he has the nerve to complain about the Knights desecrating his sacred lawn.

"…Yeah," he finally spits out, "any other time I'd've been at least five times over…" he cackles, "…so I'll lose me licence…"
"I suppose it would make coming over from Burley difficult - 'specially with all the kit you cart about," I say sympathetically.

Well it was bound to happen sooner or later. I'm just glad it happened before he killed someone.

"Then on Monday I had me hospital appointment… and they tells me I've got fuckin' cancer," he says somberly.
"Oh shit." I say, not knowing what else to say. "I didn't know you could get cancer from fucking."

Eric's face creases up as he cackles, "You are a stupid twat, I should have known I could rely on you to make me laugh at a time like this - I've been dreading telling people, 'cos I know how uncomfortable it'll make people - 'specially men - we don't like to show our feelings - should've known you wouldn't be serious," he cackles.

"So, bummer of a week then - things can only get better, unless you believe in things happening in threes," I say, attempting to keep him humoured; while at the same time the enormity of his news slowly overtakes me. It feels as though a large rock was slowly sinking through my chest towards my stomach.

"Is it your lungs?" I ask.

"Yeah," he coughs, "How'd you guess?" he asks.

"Just an educated guess," I say, "How long they given you?"

"A year at the most- probably only a few months," he says flatly.

I don't know what to say. My kids spend all their time hugging their friends. I was brought up to shake hands with men, and you only kissed women as a prelude to getting your leg-over. It hardly seemed appropriate to shake Eric's hand and say, 'Ah well, nice knowing you, take care now.'

Eric broke the awkward silence, "I can't blame any other fucker, it were the fags - you always think it'll be some other poor fucker."

"And I thought I'd had a bad enough weekend shelling out for a new exhaust – I thought I'd bought a new van when they gave me the bill...

"How's your wife taken it?" I ask, realising I still didn't know her name.

Eric looks blank for a second as though not realising that *wife* was a slightly more respectful name for *the missus.*

"Oh ya mean the missus - I dunno really, she just said, I've been telling ya t' quit for years..."

"Smoking or living?" I couldn't help quip.

"Both!" Eric squawks, his face briefly creased with a great beaming grin as he starts to laugh throatily, his leathery face resembling his old work-boots with a split; before shifting phlegm causes him to cough uncontrollably with hands supported on the fronts of his thighs.

I can only watch and hope it takes its usual course. When the spluttering eventually subsides, he straightens up and turns his wizened damson face to me,

"Fuckin' ell Charles, you'll be the death of me," he grins.

"Christ, for a moment there I thought maybe you'd said minutes not months."

"It'll be fuckin' minutes if I you don't stop makin' me fuckin' laugh," he laughs tentatively, "I don't want another of those fuckin' coughin' fits," he grins.

"Did you say coughin' or coffin?" I ask.

Eric puzzles over that one. I fear that explaining it will make it even more tasteless.

"I expect your missus must be worried about being stuck in Burley, and not being able to drive," I say, before hastily adding, "…as well as being upset at losing the love of her life."

"Yeah, well we're gonna sell up and move back to West Brom., at least the public transport is reglar."

"It's reglar in Burley," I say unwittingly imitating him, "I see a DRM bus go by towards Kenchester every weekday morning- and then come back towards Kingsford every afternoon - reglar."

"Ya fuckin' daft twat," he cackles, I think she'd like it a bit more reglar than once a day."

"Oooh. You didn't tell me she was so insatiable," I laugh.

"Insufferable more like," he cackles.

"Long suffering you mean," I say, grinning.

The familiar goose like honk of a VW Camper van horn, alerts us to Barry's approach.

Eric's grin retreats, like the poked horns of a snail.

"Fuckin' 'ell, I ain't looking forward to telling Barry, he won't make it easy - like you."

"You mean he's not such an insensitive bastard," I say.

"Nah, I know it's only your fuckin' way - I'd rather that than people fuckin' pretending to get upset."
"What do you mean, *pretending?* People will be upset - Wayne relies on you for his fags - and Frank won't know how to mow his grass," I laugh, "… not to mention the landlord at The Black Swan; he may as well sell up."

Barry cruises past us with a magisterial two-fingered wave, negotiates Sophie's abandoned pride and joy, and berths alongside Frank's Range Rover.

"I reckon I'm just gonna tell 'im that I'm givin' up 'cos I've lost me licence - same with the others…Do you mind tellin' 'em the other reason - when I've gone?"
I shoot Eric a puzzled look, raising my eyebrows questioningly. He gives a short cackle, "I mean, when I've fuckin' left 'ere…

"…after all I would've 'ad to 'ave left - I'll be fuckin' fucked without me fuckin' car," he reasons, so eloquently.
"Of course I will…. You know how I like a good goss. – best bit of gossip for ages," I laugh, wondering how various people will react. Nisha and Alice will be quite emotional I reckon, the others will feel they have to be stoic, apart from Princess Sophie; she'll probably just say, '*Oh well he shouldn't have smoked'* or, *' Who's going to wash my car now?*

Before Barry can clamber out of his van, with his usual chameleon speed, the front door of the house opens and discharges Nisha, closely followed by Alice slamming the door behind her.

"Bloody hell. Where's she going?" I mutter to Eric, nodding towards Nisha, "Morning Nisha, morning Alice," I say brightly, adding, "No Sophie this morning?"
"Hi boys," replies Nisha cheerfully, "No, Sophie's studying at home today, she's actually still in bed …"
"Thanks for the warning, we'd better watch what we say," I laugh
"Yes you better had," says Nisha, laughing, and echoed by Alice.

"Do you like Sophie's birthday present then, she only got it yesterday?" asks Nisha, gesturing towards the gleaming, bright red little bog hopper.
"You mean the Vauxhall Viagra," I laugh.
Alice's face lights up, "Oh yeah, Viagra," she repeats.
"Don't you two start all that again," laughs Nisha throatily.

"So where're you off to then?" I ask Nisha, nodding at her iridescent two-tone blue sporting attire, making her look like a bulbous fishing float. I quickly dismiss the image of her bobbing in a canal.
"Don't laugh, but I'm going to an aerobics class after the school run," she says, pausing for applause.
"Well done," I say, echoed by Barry.
"Mum's on a fitness regime, she reckons she's gonna lose at least three stone by the summer hols...."
"Cor blimey, go for it," I say encouragingly, to the accompaniment of approving murmurs from Barry.
Alice continues, "Dad reckons she's got a fancy man."
"No he doesn't," snaps Nisha, blushing. Then in order to divert attention, "Are you not working today Eric?" she asks, realising that he's wearing his civvies.

Eric who has been happy to listen to the banter, probably preoccupied with his own thoughts, is momentarily taken by surprise, "Eh. Oh, er, no. Is um, er Frank about? I just called by to 'ave a word with 'im."

"Oh right. He should be down shortly..."
"No need to call Little Eric, *Shortly,*" I quip.
"Oh god, it's been lovely the last couple of days without you here," groans Nisha. "I'll see you later boys, we must get on or we'll be late."
"Okay see you later," we chorus.

I glance at my watch, "Is Wayne in today?" I ask Nisha.

"As far as I know," she says, flitting her eyes over us, as if considering adding something, but then thinks better of it, "I'll see you later," she says hurriedly, clambering into her Range Rover.

Barry sidles over to me as we watch her swing out into the lane, while Eric has wandered into the garage, apparently to collect any of his own tools, and maybe a few secreted fag ends off the steel beams.

"Strange," Barry muses.

"She's that all right - don't tell me you've only just noticed," I laugh, but I think I know what he's thinking.

"I reckon she wanted to tell you something about Work-aholic-Wayne," he says, inclining his head knowingly, "You mark my words - just wait till she gets back."

"Do you know something I don't Sherlock? Has something happened since I was here last? Wayne would normally be here by now….

"…How have you got on anyway? Have you managed to get the papering done without me in the way…Has the suite of all suites arrived yet?"

Before Barry can respond to my interrogation, the front door opens and immediately slams to behind Frank, as he does his Butch Cassidy and the Sundance Kid suicidal run impression; albeit a solo performance.

I touch Barry's arm, "Hang on a minute, Eric's got something he needs to tell Frank," I mutter.

"Oooh, sounds intrigueing - now who's got secrets."

"Morning Frank," we chorus, but refrain from moving nearer, to allow Eric who is emerging from the garage like a hermit crab, scurrying as fast as his little legs will allow.

"Mornin' Frank, can I 'ave a word?" Eric hails Frank, before he can burrow into his car for sanctuary.

"Eh! What! Oh yeah. Mornin' guys - I er haven't got time now. I'm expecting an urgent phone call at the um office, I'll see you all

at lunchtime. Bye," he shouts before slamming the Range Rover door and firing up the engine.
"But it's important, I won't be here at lunchtime," Eric shouts vainly, attempting to be heard above the revving engine, before realising the futility and shouting, "Ignorant fucker!"
"This could be interesting," I say to Barry, "…I wonder if he's seen the Sophiemobile behind him?"

Half a second later my question is answered by an enormous bang. Instantly followed by the clatter of cascading plastic shards onto the gravel, and a flash of red, as the little car canons across the car park like a snooker ball, miraculously missing my van, and crossing about four yards of lawn; before being heroically stopped by an apple tree.

"Whoops- a- daisy," I say, adding, "My van has got more of a charmed life than her Viagra…so much for the prolonged performance; that must be the shortest on record."
Frank scrabbles out of his Range Rover, looking utterly confused, not to mention agitated, "What the fuckin' ell was that? What happened?" he shrieks, puzzled at the apparent absence of an offending obstacle.

"You just pocketed the red in the apple tree," I casually inform him.
"Eh! What!" he stammers, casting about wildly, for an apple tree, and something red, apparently already having forgotten the colour of his daughter's day old car.

Eric helps him out, "You've just rammed Sophies brand new fuckin' car into the fuckin' tree over there, you stupid fucker," he screams, before skulking back into the garage to finish collecting his tools for the last time.

Frank's mouth flaps about, emitting even more unintelligible noises than usual, while his eyes flick back and forth between the back of his apparently unscathed Range Rover, and the wreck that is wrapped around the apple tree about twenty yards away. The only evidence to link the two vehicles are two parallel lines across the gravel and grass, indicating that the handbrake hadn't been fully applied.

"Good job Eric parked the other side of me - good job the steering lock was on, otherwise it could have gone anywhere," I say.

But nobody seemed to be listening. Eric was slamming around in the garage, tossing lumbar aside to collect his stuff. Barry was spellbound watching Frank, waiting for him to grasp the situation.

"Oh my god! Oh my god!!…Oh my god!!!" he shrieks with increasing fervour.

"Either his god's out - or just not picking up," I mutter.

"That'll teach him to put washers in the collection plate," Barry replies from the corner of his mouth.

"Oh my god. What am I gonna do… Sophie'll kill me - Nisha'll kill me - Oh my god, dad'll definitely kill me," he shrieks.

"You'll be Alice's hero though," I mutter.

"If there's any consolation Frank, you can only be killed once," I say.

Frank looks at me blankly for a few seconds before continuing to beseech the almighty.

Barry and I walk over to the mangled wreck. It was pretty short before, but it was definitely compact now. The fragile car had moulded its rear around the apple tree. The tree now appeared to grow out of the car directly behind the back seat. The front hadn't put up much of a fight with the Range Rover either.

"You wouldn't want to be in an accident in one of these would you," I mutter.

"Specially if you're in the habit of rallying around orchards," mutters Barry.

"It must be something of a record as far as insurance claims are concerned…Although I have heard of cases where someone has driven off the garage forecourt into the path of another vehicle," I say.

Frank has joined us. He looks as though he's just received a death threat from the mafia.

"Oh my god. What the hell am I gonna do?" he asks hysterically.

"Well I suppose you'll just have to phone the insurance company - tell them what you've done - at least no one was hurt," I say, hoping to calm him.

I should have known better.

Frank looks stunned, "Dad only bought it yesterday, I haven't sorted the insurance out yet," he almost cries.

"Your dad must have sorted something out, otherwise the garage wouldn't have been able to tax it – they'd need a cover note from the insurance company," I say.

"But it wasn't my fault!" he squawks. "Who parked the fuckin' thing behind me? What a stupid fuckin' place to park it!" he rants.

"I must admit, parking anywhere near you - knowing the way you leave in the mornings, is asking for trouble," I say dryly.

Frank regards me with astonishment, "Why should I claim off my insurance?" he protests.

Suddenly he brightens, as if he's just received guidance from above - at last, "Can't you say it was you?" he says excitedly, regarding me expectantly, with an expression that suggests, problem solved, I'm off the hook, why didn't I think of it sooner?

Barry and \I both look at him as though he were stark naked, painted blue and with a yellow ribbon tied to his todger. We both splutter in disbelief. Words are unnecessary.

Panic returns to his eyes, "What am I gonna say to my dad, he'll kill me…"

"Mmm. Well they say every cloud…" I say

Barry snorts.

"What?" puzzles Frank.

"Well," I say tongue in cheek, giving Barry an imperceptible wink, "… you could tell him that someone tried to steal Sophie's car in the night… and that they ran into the back of your Range Rover - eventually found reverse - and rocketed backwards out of control into the apple tree - you rush out brandishing your baseball bat - in time to see someone legging it into the night."

Barry slowly nods, pretending to consider its plausibility, and finding no faults.

Frank's face lights up, "Yeah…"

"I was only joking Frank," I laugh.

But Frank sees a lifeline, "No. I reckon he'd believe that ..."

Only one fuckin' thing wrong with that story Charles," interjects Eric, who has joined us, having finished loading up his blower, strimmer, hedge-trimmer and most of the garden maintenance tools and machinery.

"What's that!" squawks Frank.

"Well ya dad would never fuckin' believe that ya came rushin' out, waving a fuckin' baseball bat… He'd know you were lying …" he pauses for Frank to ask the obvious.

He obliges, "Why? How?"

"'Cos he'd know it would be Nisha that would fuckin' rush out- while you hid under the bed," Eric says bluntly.

"Well it might need a little tweaking," I say dryly, still not believing Frank could even consider lying about the accident.

Frank is stunned, "Wha…"

Eric interrupts, "Well I'm off then Charles, ta-rah…" he says, offering me his leathery paw, "… look after ya self – Ya daft fucker - maybe see you up The Black Swan."

"Yeah I'll meet you up there for a few - take care," I reply lamely, but shake his gnarled hand firmly.

Ignoring the dumbfounded Frank, Eric offers a puzzled Barry his outstretched hand,

"Well ta-rah Barry, look after ya self ya big lump – try and get some sense into this fuckin' idiot," he says jerking his head in my direction.

"Ta-rah, Frank …" he says, pausing to consider an appropriate nugget of advice; but after years of being servile he probably decided against it. I imagine Eric's probably regretting his earlier, uncharacteristic outburst.

"Eh. Oh. You going are you?" responds Frank with bewildering perceptiveness

"Yeah well I tried to fuckin' tell ya earlier…" snaps Eric.

Three pairs of eyes widen. I think perhaps I was wrong.

"…If you'd fuckin' stopped to listen when I fuckin' asked this wouldn' 'ave fuckin' 'appened…" he rants, waving an arthritic leathery paw at the still gleaming wreck.

"…Charles can fill you in - I'm fuckin'off."

You most definitely are.

"But I…But I was in a hurry…" Frank floundered.

"Well you've missed your important phone call now," I say mischievously, winking at Barry.

"Eh. What phone call?"

"Exactly," I say, as Barry and I accompany Eric to his pristine van.

"I wouldn't have wanted to get between you and Frank, if Sophie's car had touched this," I say, patting the roof.

"Say ta-rah to Wayne for me."

"Yeah, will do," I promise.

Watching Eric drive away for presumably the last time, I think the world would be pretty boring without characters like him. Almost symbolically one of the local ravens flies overhead and gives an enormous honk, and simultaneously jettisons its load.

I have a feeling The Funny Farm isn't going to be quite so funny anymore.

I stand staring at the empty driveway, wondering what the next few months are going to be like for Eric. I hope he doesn't suffer too much.

Despite it being a warm April day, I suddenly become aware of feeling cold and lethargic, as though a heavy wet blanket has been draped over me. I shiver involuntarily, like Ebony emerging from a swim. I certainly don't have any enthusiasm for working here today.

I'm brought out of my reverie by a cough beside me.
"You okay?" asks Barry.
"Eh?" I croak. "Sorry," I cough to clear my throat. Barry sees something interesting by his feet while I quickly wipe the back of my hand across my eyes.

"Where's he gone? I didn't have time to stop and talk to him, I was in a hurry ya know, I had an important phone call," Frank protests pathetically.
I can't be bothered to respond.
"I don't know," says Barry.
"Is Eric coming back?" asks Frank.

"No… Eric's not coming back - he's probably going to lose his licence - he was caught, at long last, three times over the limit I think he said," I say flatly.
Frank digests this revelation for several seconds before responding incredulously, "What three times over the speed limit?"
Barry and I look at each other in disbelief, and burst out laughing.
"Alcohol limit!" I say, still laughing at the image of Little Eric batting along at possibly over two hundred miles an hour in his Escort van.
"Well he does drive fast," says Frank lamely.
"Not for much longer," I say.

"Bloody hell…" says Barry, sounding relieved.
"Seems like a day for uncharacteristic language."

"Yeah I know - But I thought by the way you were behaving, you were going to tell us Eric had cancer or something - that's a relief - at least the roads around Kingsford will be a little safer," he sighs.

"Ah … Well he's got that as well - may only have a few months – a year at the most," I say sombrely.

"Oh heck…" groans Barry, "…the poor bugger."

"What? Eric's got cancer?" yelps Frank, "Why didn't he say?"

Barry and I just look at Frank as though he'd offered us ten bob for a quickie behind the garage.

"What? …Oh is that what he wanted to tell me? …Oh well, it's not surprising is it? He and Wayne smoke like a pair of chimneys in the garage every chance they get."

"It is lung cancer then?" asks Barry.

I nod, "Yeah. Like Florence Nightingale says, it's not surprising."

I exhale loudly… "Well, we can't stand here all day, like they say, the world moves on."

"I suppose so," mumbles Barry absently.

"Well Frank, what are you going to do about this little problem?" I ask gesturing towards Sophie's customised car. "We could tow it around the back of the garage out of sight, till the insurers recover it - if you phone them now they'll probably recover it within a couple of hours – with a bit of luck, before Sleeping Beauty gets up."

"Beauty? You mean Ice Queen," Barry mouths at me, while Frank is still looking at the wreck.

I manage to stifle a laugh. "Why do you want an ice cream, you've only just got here?…

"…Where's Wayne today, is he not coming in?"

"Eh? What? Oh – Wayne? I'm not sure," Frank stutters unconcerned.

Frank glances agitatedly at Sophie's customised car, "Um, can you and Barry get the car towed behind the garage…?"

"What a good idea, why didn't I think of that?...Before Nisha comes back." I suggest.
"Eh. Oh god Nisha!" he squeals. "Yeah – oh my god I don't want her to see that as soon as she turns in the drive - I'd better phone the insurance company."

"Okay, have you got the keys, we'll need to unlock the steering lock – I hope Sophie isn't sleeping with them under her pillow," I joke.
Frank considers this possibility for several seconds before replying, "Oh I'm not sure, she might've."
"Will you have to phone your Dad for the insurance details? You could say that you want to add something to the cover," I suggest.

Frank heads off for the house, with the demeanour of a Christian heading for the lion's den. Probably composing three or four conversations; one for the insurance company, one for his dad at the office, a third for Sophie if she's up yet, and another for Nisha. I wonder if any will concur.
"I'd love to be a fly on the wall," I say to Barry.
"Oooh you are cruel - you shouldn't mock the afflicted," he chuckles.

"I'll see if I can find a rope in the garage while you back up to the patient," Barry instructs with uncharacteristic authority.
"Oooh, you're so masterful," I laugh, and head off to see if the keys are still in the Range Rover.

We attach the rope to Sophie's car and the Range Rover. While waiting for Frank to bring the keys we discover that the handbrake had not been employed at all, nor had the car been left in gear. We discover that the front wings of the car had been pushed back against the front wheels and caused them to lock; producing the skid marks. Fortunately the wings have less metal in them than a coke can, so it was easy enough to pull them away from the wheels.

"The makers weren't kidding when they describe cars as having 'crumple zones."
Barry laughs dryly. "Blimey, it's a wonder it hadn't rolled away down the slope anyway."

We turn at the sound of the front door opening to see Frank wave a set of keys at us, and then wordlessly stoop to place them on the step and then retreat.

In no time at all Sophie's customised car is out of sight behind the garage, and just to be on the safe side, we leave Frank's Range Rover facing the right way for him; pointing down the drive. The only evidence to show for Frank's ride on the dodgems, is a scattering of plastic shards from the headlights and a stream from the radiator in the middle of the car park, to the apple tree that appears to have been ravaged by a half-hearted beaver. The gleaming white scar of freshly exposed cambium layer signalling a badge of honour. If the tree could talk it would say, *You should see the other guy.* Shards of rear light, and a sprinkling of rear screen particles, form an apron around the base of this new gladiator.

"I suppose we could clear up all this glass," suggests Barry.
"Yeah – anything to delay going inside."

Twenty minutes or so later we survey the scene. "I don't think there's much more we can do – apart from maybe rub some mud into the tree's war wound," I suggest.
Barry laughs, "Now who thinks he's Florence Nightingale - Do you think it'll make it feel better?"
"No," I laugh, "…but it might make it a little less obvious…besides, I always wanted to be a *Tree Surgeon.*"

Just then the front door opens, and Frank emerges then closes the door behind him with uncharacteristic stealth. He avoids the path, but instead navigates his way silently to his car via the grass.

"I take it Sophie's still in the land of nod," I say.
"Oh hi," he whispers, "Yeah, well ya know, it seems a shame to wake her – she works really hard ya know like that."
I refrain from laughing.
"Are you okay Frank, did you strain your voice on the phone?" I ask loudly as though talking to the deaf.
"Shuush! Keep you voice down," he whispers, flapping his arms, as if beating out a fire.

"But we haven't exactly been quiet up until now Frank," I whisper, trying to keep a straight face. "In fact if she's slept through you remodelling her car, and Eric bawling obscenities, I would imagine nothing short of a bomb could wake her – in fact the way today's going we might just get one."

A raven, possibly the same one as before judging by his sense of timing, honks overhead, almost causing Frank to be the one to jettison *his* load this time.
He flinches and yelps, "Fuckin' bastard bird!"
"Shuush, you might wake Sophie," I whisper.
Barry silently convulses behind Frank.

"What did the insurance company say?" I ask.
"Eh. Oh, er no problem. They said they'll arrange to have it collected within a couple of hours."
"So you're hoping Sophie's going to sleep all day…So what did you say happened?" I ask.
"Eh? Oh, ya know, I er just told them ya know, what happened, you know - more or less."
"Hmm. More or less," I repeat, glancing at Barry, who raises his eyes in despair.
"Yeah, ya know, more or less – well it doesn't pay to tell them the truth – ya know what insurance companies are like," Frank argues.

I shake my head in disbelief, "You afraid they wouldn't have believed the truth?" I laugh dryly before adding, "I just hope you haven't involved me in it."

"Nor me," says Barry emphatically.
"But you were both witnesses," Frank squeaks in an attempt to keep his voice down.
"I don't mind being a witness, so long as you only want me to tell 'em what happened – I mean if you're not careful they'll want a police incident number - and you haven't got one," I explain.
"'S right Frank – we could all end up in the poo," agrees Barry, with the tone of a hanging judge.

Frank couldn't look less comfortable if he'd filled his pants on a hot day, and been forced to run ten miles home.
"They um, they um asked for one of those - I said I'd get them one – How do um, how do you um get one?"
Barry and I just stare at Frank unable to speak. My mind is whirling with scenario; and none of them pleasant.
Eventually I break the silence, "I think I can smell a lorry load of that poo heading this way Barry."

The familiar puking sound of Wayne's horn, signals his approach in the lane.
"Phew! Wayne stop play," I sigh with relief. "I've never been so pleased to see him or hear that van's disgusting horn," I mutter to Barry.

Chapter 22

Wayne clambers out of his battered Transit, accompanied by the tortured screams of lubricant-free door hinges. He regards us suspiciously, suspecting a reception committee; although it doesn't deter him from his ritual ball juggling, farting and belching.

"Oops, pardon me – Sorry I'm late, I had a puncture," he explains, waving a blackened hand towards his van.

"I always thought it was a stupid place for the spare wheel," I say sympathetically, "…especially as it's usually peeing with rain into the bargain, while you're scrabbling about under the back end to retrieve a wheel that's been sprayed with all the mud off these lanes for months."

Wayne produces one of his curtain opening grins, "Yeah, bloody right - at least I didn't have the rain, just the muddy wheel," he laughs, still regarding us suspiciously.

"Well um, I'd better get up to the er, office," Frank declares awkwardly.

"You want me on the patio?" asks Wayne.

Barry and I snort in unison.

"Oooh. Do you want us in any particular order?" I ask, flicking a limp wrist at him.

Wayne and Barry's laughter almost drowns out Frank's response.

"Yeah, whatever – it would make a nice change," he mutters, "…actually Wayne, could you do the mowing?" then scuttles over to his car.

Wayne's mouth twitches to respond, but I get in first.

"Do you…" Frank excludes my question with the crumph of his closing door, "…know when the bathroom suite is coming?" I ask the rear of the departing Range Rover, noticing a few shards of stowaway plastic perched on the rear bumper.

I shrug my shoulders, "Ah well, please yourself then Charles."
I theatrically consult my watch, "Ah, bait time."

"So why's he want me to do the mowin'? That's Eric's job. Is he havin' one of his check-ups today? …Waste of fuckin' money if ya ask me – the Doctors must know they're wastin' their time and money – our fuckin' money."
I look at Wayne, a ham and tomato sandwich half way to my mouth.
"What do you mean, *our money,"* I ask gesturing to include the three of us, "Don't you mean, *our money*," I say, this time only indicating Barry and I.
Wayne looks puzzled, "That's what I said, *our money.*"
"Yeah, but I assumed you meant, *our money,* as in the taxpayer's money," I say winking at Barry, whose eyes seem to twinkle to indicate that he's following my argument.
"Well yeah, 'course," he says, irritated by my pedantry.
"So when was the last time you paid any tax Wayne?" I ask seemingly innocently.
"Eh? I can't fuckin' remember."
"Have you ever paid tax?" Barry asks innocuously.
"Eh? No. Course not. No fucker pays tax if they can get away with it," he says defensively, before adding, "…Don't tell me you do?"
"Well obviously no more than I have to … But the thing is if you don't contribute towards the services, like the NHS, then you can't criticise how it's spent," I argue levelly.
"It's still a waste of fuckin' money….Eric's smoked and drunk hi'self half to death, they ain't gonna reverse the damage he's done - so why fuck about openin' him up an' 'avin' a butchers inside, shakin' their 'eads and tuttin' - and then sewin' 'im up every six fuckin' months or so."

I swallow the mouthful of sandwich that I'd managed to grab during Wayne's speech, and wash it down with a mouthful of my usual imitation coffee.

"The thing is," I say, pausing to remove a piece of bread that's moulded to the back of my top front teeth, "…the thing is, Eric maybe better smoked and pickled than the contents of your average deli', but he paid tax all his working life, well until he came here after he retired from his garage, so surely that's only like making an insurance claim; he's paid his premiums after all - That was a rather unfortunate choice of analogy after what's happened this morning," I laugh.
"Yeah, but true though," laughs Barry.

Wayne perks up, believing himself to be off the ropes, "Why what's 'appened this mornin'?" he asks, vainly running his hand along the top of a steel beam in search of an abandoned fag.
"Oh we'll come to that in a minute – You'll be glad to know your hard earned taxes aren't going to be wasted any longer…" I pause to allow Wayne to complete a sweep of another beam, before returning disgruntled, to his chair empty handed.

There didn't seem to be an easy way to say it, so, " Eric's got lung cancer, and he's got less than a year – Oh, and he said to say goodbye to you – well actually I think he said to say, 'ta-rah,' to you."

Wayne's expression goes from inquisitive, to stunned, then as he digests the news, to anger, "You bastards! Ya fuckin' bastards!…"
Barry sucks a grape through a keyhole, "Oooh, language, there's no…"
"Fuck my language! You let me slag Eric off knowing he's fuckin' dying!" he snaps.
"Well you're entitled to your opinion. Would it be different if you'd known?"
"Well no, well I…"

"You mean, you just wouldn't have aired them…I must admit - I'm inclined to agree with what you were saying about opening him up every year. I think if he's paid into the system he's entitled to be cured – I mean, sportsmen get repaired free of charge, and they're self-inflicted injuries – but they shouldn't mess about with him as though he were a guinea-pig - he deserves some dignity"

"Yeah but, I suppose they're learning something by monitoring what's going on inside him – so other patients can benefit. Anyway, I don't suppose they actually open him up, they probably just scan him, or whatever it is they do," argues Barry.

We digest this, and our bait in silence, apart from the occasional slurp of coffee and Wayne's reptilian masticating.

Our private meditation is interrupted by the sound of the front door of the house opening and gently closing; not the customary attempt at frame splitting, associated with Frank or Nisha.

"Soppy Sophie 'ere is she?" asks Wayne.

"Shit that's all we need right now," I say, glancing at Barry.

Wayne perks up like a gun dog, when his master goes to the gun cabinet, "What's the problem?"

"We'll tell you after we've got rid of Princess Sophie…" I mutter, "…or should that be Ice Queen," I add glancing at Barry.

"Charles, is Eric not here today, I can't see his van?"

That's not all you can't see.

"I'm afraid not Sophie. Um he's not well enough to come in - he's decided to retire on health grounds."

"Oh… Well that's not very convenient."

"He'd probably agree with you, he probably feels it's a mite inconvenient as well," I say trying to hide the sarcasm.

"Was there something you particularly wanted to ask him Sophie?" Barry asks.

"Well yes. I don't suppose it matters this week," she says looking around the car park and realising for the first time that her new toy has been removed from its prime position.
"I was going to tell him to wash my new car each week before he mows the lawns - but I suppose if he's not coming back it'll have to be one of you," she states with the air of an eighteenth century, Lady of the Manor addressing the maids.

I nearly choke on my chocolate biscuit, Wayne splutters bread and crisps over my legs, and Barry's eyes widen as he attempts to sink into his overalls like a submerging frogman, to avoid her attention, and risk saying something he might regret.

"Well good luck with that one," I say flatly, adding, "I can show you where the bucket and shammy are though."
"The shammy?" she says, in a tone to suggest one was being offered rough cider as an alternative to Bollinger champagne.
"Yeah, the chamois leather - you dunk it in the soapy water and wash the car with it, like you use a flannel – and the bucket, is the container with a handle, to carry…"
"Yes. I know what a bucket is Charles," she says testily, "but I haven't time to wash it myself. …Where is my car? I left it just there," she declares, pointing to an empty space.

"In the middle of the car park, in neutral and without the handbrake on – yes we've all admired it – some closer than others," I reply. "Your dad discovered a small dent in it so he's arranged for them to change it," I say flatly, trying to avoid looking at Barry.

"Oh really," she says sourly, then brightens, "…I wonder if he'll change it for a TT."
"Only if one of the T's stands for Tank," I quip.

Barry stifles a snort, while the bemused Wayne regards each of us like the only sober person at a rugby club.

"Would someone mind telling me what that was all about," demands Wayne, once the front door closes.
"I think it would be simpler if you go behind the garage and admire Frank's handiwork. Did you know Sophie was getting a new car yesterday for her birthday?"
"No, but it doesn't fuckin' surprise me," he says resentfully.
"Well Frank's modified it - obviously he's shit scared of telling the powers that be, namely Nisha, Sophie and his dad - and not necessarily in that order," I say flatly.
"I bet Alice'll piss herself when she hears," Wayne hoots.
"Yeah well Barry and I are worried about what cock and bull story he's told the insurers, as we're witnesses."

Our attention is diverted to the sound of an unfamiliar vehicle slowing, as it approaches. We watch as a metallic silver Ford Focus cruises as though intending to turn into the drive. Instead, it pauses across the end, long enough for the driver to crane his neck to look back, seemingly to check the property is the one he's looking for.

I watch the driver scan the house and the vehicles, his gaze traverses the garage where we sit in the open doorway enjoying the spring sunshine. He does a double take when he unexpectedly clocks three faces, curiously watching him. As he makes eye contact, even at nearly forty yards, I recognise a nano second of panic before he regains his composure, nods a good morning, and then pulls calmly away.

I look at Wayne and Barry in turn, who just shrug.
"Must be looking for somewhere," says Barry.
"Who cares," Wayne says over his shoulder, already nearing the corner of the garage, to gloat over Frank's attempt at producing the world's first flat-pack car.

"I suppose we'd better try and do something," says Barry, with the enthusiasm of a eunuch in a brothel. "What you gonna do?" he asks.
"Eh? Oh - apart from go home and start again? I'm not sure…You painting in the bathroom?" I reply with equal enthusiasm.
"You still thinking about Eric?"
"Amongst other things… Just something about that bloke in the car."

"Bloomin' heck Charles, one minute you're Florence Nightingale, the next your Sherlock Holmes," he laughs, "He was probably lost – looking for another house."
"So why did he spend so long checking the place over, when the name plate at the end of the drive would have told him it wasn't the house he was looking for? It's not exactly a joy to behold - an architectural orgasm – it may have a pretentious name, but you could plonk it on the average new development, and no one would bat an eyelid."

Barry digests this for a couple of seconds. "So do you think he was casing the place for a burglary?"
"No I don't think so, he's not the archetypal burglar - not that I'd know a burglar if I fell over one – I suppose he could have been one that specialises in art or antiques, but you'd imagine them to look like one of those guys on the Antiques Roadshow; blazers and chinos."

Barry laughs, saying, "You're not telling me you could see what he was wearing – you'll be telling me next what aftershave he was wearing."
"You can laugh, but I'm telling you there was something dodgy about him – He looked like a cross between a copper and a social worker, dressed for rambling, not art dealing – And I may be half deaf, but I could have sworn the car stopped around the bend, probably in that lay-by."

Barry laughs, not sure whether I'm winding him up, "Yes kemo sabi."
"Oh bugger off. Isn't there a stagecoach needs saving from Red Indians? You'll be calling your Camper, Silver next – I can imagine you at half four, I rock my chair backwards onto two legs, Hi-ho Silver away!" I mimic.

*****

I look up at the sound of Wayne's phone warbling for about the third time since he eventually got started on the patio. I watch from the kitchen window as he goes through his by now well-rehearsed sequence.

Scrabbling to his feet with remarkable alacrity, he then dashes across the newly laid setts and grabs his phone from its improvised holder, high on the trellising, where he's discovered it receives just enough signal to alert him to a potential buyer. He then jogs, like a lame badger up the field while repeating, 'Hello', into the mouthpiece until he's high enough up the slope to receive a signal, where he invariably collapses against the fence.

I shake my head, and wonder for the thousandth time, why he doesn't get fitter, and slimmer, after running up and down that field all day.

As I turn back to marking the template around the sink in front of the window, I catch sight of a movement at the top of the field. Looking back up the field, I think I must have imagined it. There are usually dozens of rabbits; perhaps one has caught my peripheral vision. But there are none. I wonder if a fox could be stalking them, it wouldn't be the first time I'd watched one from here; it's almost the perfect hide, behind this double casement window.

In the left hand of the frame I can clearly see Wayne, talking animatedly on his phone. Frequently checking the signal strength indicator on the screen, then pacing a few yards this way and then the other; desperately trying to maintain a conversation.

Perhaps it's Wayne that's scared the wildlife away. I laugh, watching him wave his arms in frustration and then jog further up the field. I suddenly remember Frank had asked him to do the mowing, I wonder if he forgot; or perhaps there's no diesel. I bet he wishes he were sat on the mower rather than running up and down the field.

Wayne struggles up a few more yards, just where it gets steeper. His body language suggests he's got a strong signal; he leans back on the fence like a boxer on his last legs. My head-shaking is cut short when a figure darts from behind one of the oak trees that patrol the top boundary, and secrets himself behind the next; nearer to Wayne. A couple of seconds later the figure darts to the next.

"Barry!"

"Yeah! Do you want me?" comes a muffled reply.

"Look at the oak trees at the top of the field," I shout, not taking my eyes off the last tree I saw the figure dive behind.

"What about them?" shouts Barry.

I wonder which glasses he's wearing, "Can you see the oak trees?"

"Yes thankyou," he says laughing, "I ain't that blind."

"Well watch the fourth one from the top left corner of the field."

After what seems several minutes, but was probably less than one, Barry shouts,

"I'm watching. What am I supposed to …Oh who's that?"

The figure had quite clearly leant out from behind the trunk, and appeared to photograph the house.

Barry's muffled voice comes through the ceiling, "I think I owe you an apology Kemo Sabe."

"You'd better get Silver out and ride up there and lasso the nosey bugger," I call back.

"You don't have to shout," he says in my ear.
"Christ," I laugh, "I didn't hear you come down," I say, keeping my eyes on the fourth tree from the left. Or was it the third?

Wayne wanders laterally across the slope, still engrossed and oblivious to our furtive friend, who darts from tree to tree keeping one tree behind Wayne; staying out of his peripheral vision.

Wayne turns to look up the slope, probably to locate the mewing buzzards that we can hear through the open backdoor, and the photographer snaps another quick one, before sliding out of sight.

Barry and I look at each other, and then up the field to confirm our thoughts.
"He's not photographing the house, he's photographing Wayne," we chorus.

"Who's photographing Wayne?" asks a squeaky voice from behind us.
"Oh hi Sophie. I think it's the paparazzi," I reply cautiously.
"Oh, it could be something to do with what mum was organising," she says openly.
"What was that then?" I ask, casually.
"I don't really know – I just heard her on the phone - after we got back from picking me up from college….I heard her telling someone the days that Wayne would be working here this week."
"Maybe your granddad needed to know, perhaps he wants Wayne to do some work up at his place," I say, doubting full well.
"No, it wasn't grandpappy - When I asked who it was, mum just said, she was organising a surprise for Wayne – Is it his birthday then?" she asks innocently.

I shrug, "I've honestly no idea. I'm not big on birthdays – I'd even forgotten yours, happy birthday for yesterday by the way."
"Thankyou," she says, almost graciously.

"Well as it's supposed to be a surprise, best not let Nisha know you've told us," I say conspiratorially.
"Okay," she says, unquestioningly, sounding more like a seven year old than a seventeen year old.

I avoid looking at Barry until I hear Sophie close the door to the living room behind her. Barry has managed surreptitiously to maintain observation of the furtive photographer, during Sophie's revelations.

"You're wasted as a chippy, sorry cabinetmaker," Barry declares, quickly correcting himself. He hasn't been the first to receive, *the difference between a butcher and a surgeon,* lecture.
"Is our happy snapper still up there?"
"Yeah, so is Wayne - Wayne's moved back over to the fence, but matey has stayed behind the one, two, three, four, five, six, seventh tree from the left," he counts off, pointing with his finger.
"Hey, impressive," I laugh.
"I'm just glad he hadna gone much farther, we only larned up to ten when I was at skoowel," he jokes
"You mean, any more trees and you'd have been stumped," I joke.
Barry raises his eyes, "Anymore jokes like that, and I'll wish that bloke up there had a rifle instead of a camera."

"I wonder if he knows we've clocked him?" I muse.
"You reckon he's the guy in the car?"
"Pretty certain – even at this distance – and I'm also pretty sure he's not a Kiss-o-gram." I say, watching Wayne ambling back downhill towards the patio, hitching his jeans. "I bet he's got a good one of his cleavage," I add.

"Are we going to tell Wayne about …Hey-up. It looks like he's pointing a ruddy great canon down here!" exclaims Barry.
"Nothing wrong with your eyes, if you can see the make of the camera at this distance," I joke.
"Bazooka then – I've never seen a camera lens that long before," chuckles Barry.

"Nor me – He'll have to watch he doesn't smack Wayne 'round the ear-ole with it."

"Don't you think we should tell Wayne?"

"I wonder if we should wait till we find out who he is from Nisha first - Smile, and I hope you've got your best teeth in," I say nodding towards the enormous lens.

"Do you mind, these are my own," he says indignantly, tugging convincingly at his top set, "Uuugh!" he spits in the sink, then looks suspiciously at his fingers for the source of something unsavoury.

"Perhaps we should tell Wayne to shave and perm his hair before tomorrow though," I say. But look at Wayne kneeling on the patio, with his head bowed towards us, "Hmm, second thoughts, I'm not sure you can perm a tennis ball."

"Perhaps he should just dye it green then," suggests Barry absently, gurning while still investigating his fingers.

Chapter 23

"Well isn't this nice," I say, looking around the kitchen table, "I can't remember the last time we all sat down to a meal together in the week," I say, topping up Alex's and my glass, with a fresh, clean tasting Pinot Grigio, under Alex's censorious gaze.
"I'm sure you've got an alcohol disorder," she comments.
"To be sure, I always drink alcohol in dis order; first da beer den da wine den da whisky," I say, in probably the worst Irish impression since the Irish decided they were going to talk with a funny accent.
Lizzie groans and raises her eyes, "Don't give up your day job dad."

"It's nice to have such adoring fans….So how did you manage to get home so early, don't tell me you've been expelled?"
Lizzie laughs, "You can't expel the Headmistress."
"Headteacher…" Alex corrects, "…we haven't been called Headmistresses… or Headmasters for years."

I can see Lizzie is annoyed at her mother's pedantic response, after all, it was only a slip of the tongue on Liz's behalf; we've had the lecture regularly since Alex got the Headship. I narrow my eyes at Liz in a warning look over the top of my wine glass, until I'm sure she's got the message, then wink imperceptibly.

"Well, anyway it makes a nice change from your cooking dad," Liz says, stifling a smirk.
"Yes very tasty," I say through a mouthful of lasagne.
"Oh for Christ sake, we're not the bloody Waltons," Alex says, "…can't you two just act normally," she adds, grinning broadly and shaking her head, bemused.

"I'll drink to that," I say, raising my glass, and taking a generous sip, despite the cooling effect it has on Alex's grin.
"Moving quickly on," I say, "…talking of drink…"
"Just for a change," quips Lizzie, but I can tell from the way Alex laughs, that she was beaten to the draw.

"Well any way, Little Eric got breathalysed over the weekend; apparently he was about three times over the limit."
"Oh blimey. Well it doesn't surprise me; he's always pissed isn't he? It's probably a good thing, before he kills someone."
"Little Eric's the bloke that does gardening for Frank right?" asks Lizzie.
"Yeah. Or rather he did, he dropped by today to resign; well he wouldn't be able to get out there without a car."
"Will he lose his licence then," asks Lizzie.
"Oh yeah…but he dropped another bombshell." I consider the most sensitive way to put it.

Alex and Lizzie sense by my tone that his bombshell is grave news; no pun intended. They both regard me expectantly.
"Apparently he's been diagnosed with cancer," I say sombrely, feeling that a bit at a time would be less shocking.
"Oh my god, that's awful," they chorus.
"Where?" asks Alex.
"In a hospital, Hereford I think."

Lizzie snorts to suppress a laugh, before joining her mother in chastising me.
"Daad! That's so not funny,"
"God you're sick," says Alex, "…you never know when to be serious."
"Well you didn't want the Waltons," I protest.
"Well I didn't want the Adams family either."

We pause to savour that image, and almost simultaneously erupt, despite feeling disrespectful. It was a long time since I'd seen Alex laugh.

"You knew what I was like when you married me."
"Yes I know, but I assumed you'd grow up," Alex sighs.
"Sorry to disappoint you Morticia - at least Eric appreciated my black humour, he said he hated people getting all emotional; he laughed so much at one point I thought it was going to finish him off…He's got it on the lungs – quite advanced apparently."

I sense that Alex would rather I gave her the sordid details without Lizzie present. She starts to clear the table.
"Do you want coffee Lurch?" she asks.
"Mmm, yes please, Morticia."
"Will you two pack it in," laughs Lizzie, adding, "…you'll be calling me Wednesday."
"It's Wednesday today, would you like me to call you Next Wednesday, instead?

"…Anyway Frank gave Eric the best leaving present ever; so original and priceless…"
"I don't suppose it'll do him much good…" says Alex.
"What was it?" asks Lizzie.
"A demonstration in customising a brand new car," I say, and then proceed to tell them in graphic detail how Frank rammed Sophie's car into the apple tree.

One minute they are both stunned in disbelief, the next nearly falling off their chairs laughing.
"So what did Nisha say about it?" asks Alex, expectantly.
"I don't know, she didn't come back at lunch time, and it was recovered late morning."

I didn't relate the events with the photographer; or my suspicions regarding Nisha's failure to show up for the rest of the day.

"So have you got school work to do?" I ask Alex after Lizzie has gone to bed.

"Well I have - but sod it – Why don't we sit and watch telly together?" she suggests.
"Steady on were not the Waltons, don't forget," I laugh.
I flick through the channels, trying in vain to find something interesting, or entertaining.

"I spoke to Mike Howarth today - you know my Chair of Governors…"
"That must have been nice."
"Be serious for once."
"Ooh, I like it when you talk serious," I say, nuzzling my face into her neck, and sliding my hand inside her blouse.
"Behave a minute…" she laughs, pulling my hand out as though we were teenagers about to be disturbed by parents, "…I can't concentrate when you do that."

I check my watch, "Okay you've got a minute – starting now," I purr. "So what was the pow-wow with Mike about?"
"I've asked for more non-contact time…"

I didn't think it was possible for us to have any less.
"…I told him I just can't get on top of the planning and writing school policies and everything else I'm expected to do, on top of my teaching commitment."
"Is it just one day non-contact at the moment?" I ask.
"Yes Mondays. But the authority often arranges meetings for Mondays, so I invariably lose my day."
"Can you not change your non-contact day?" I ask cautiously, daring to state the obvious.

"Not really, it's the only day Trish can manage, and I don't want anyone else – she's really good at science and environmental stuff – she's putting the application together for our Green Flag Award, it's a lot of work; and the kids really like her."

"So what have you asked for, and what did he say?" I ask, sensing that the boat into the tunnel of love is drifting off without us.

"I've asked for another day at least, which isn't really enough, considering there are Heads in some smaller schools who get more non-contact time than me, and a lot my size have non-teaching Heads; but I wouldn't want that - He has to put it to the governors, but he said he'd support it."

"Great, so will that mean less time on the computer here?" I ask, nuzzling back in towards her, murmuring, "Minute's up."

"Hopefully," she murmurs.

"…Would you leave me?"

"Oh do I have to?"

"No seriously, do you still love me?"

"Of course," I say, in my sincerest voice, cuddling up even closer.

"Well you never tell me anymore," she murmurs.

"We ran out of post-it-notes," I murmur, sliding my hand back to first base.

"Not down here, someone might come," she murmurs, again removing my hand.

"I'll do my best," I murmur suggestively.

"I'll hold you to that," she says struggling to her feet, and dragging me after her.

"It's a long time since I held you to it."

Chapter 24

The radio DJ has wheezed interminably in anticipation at his own joke, for miles without playing a record.
"Oh for Christ sake, you senile old sod," I snap, "…just because everyone else seems to think you're an institution, it doesn't mean they can't retire you – even institutions get pulled down and redeveloped."

I really must stop talking to myself…I press the source button, and switch over to my ipod.

I promise myself that I'll remove some of these and download some more. There are several hundred, but I'm getting a bit sick of hearing them – mind you that's probably more than the average radio play list, judging by the frequency that they repeat songs.

Marvin Gaye is bemoaning the fact that he's the last to know about his girlfriend's infidelity, I Heard It On The Grapevine. Hardly a comparison I know, but it reminds me of Sophie's, apparently innocent revelation - I can't help speculating about our phantom photographer. A couple of possibilities come to mind.

Swinging into the car park at The Grange I'm surprised to find I'm not the first this morning.
"Bloody hell Wayne. What's wrong, you shit the bed or summat?" I laugh, having found Wayne refuelling the Kubota., with a face like a smacked arse.
Wayne laughs dryly, "Nah, Frank fuckin' phoned me at 'ome - just as I was about to si' down to me tea …"
"I know, his timing is immaculate," I say, "hope you were having salad; he usually goes on for hours."

"Yeah he does usually…Anyway the cheeky fucker only rang to remind me to do the mowing today – seeing's I didn't get it done yesterday."
Did he ask you why you didn't do it yesterday?" I laugh, knowing the real answer.
Wayne laughs, "Yeah, I told 'im that I couldn't bring meself to sit on the Kubota, so soon – I told 'im, it would be like stepping into dead mens shoes – I couldn't fuckin' tell 'im I hate doin' the mowin' – I forgot all about it anyway…

"…Like I said yesterday, it were 'cos of that strange phone call just after bait, when I was looking at Sophie's car round the back- made me forget."
"Oh, I remember you saying you just forgot; you didn't say anything about a phone call," I say, intrigued.
"Nah, well I don't suppose it were that strange – Just someone asking if they could come round to the 'ouse…"
"Your house?"
"Yeah, not here – anyway, they asked if they could come round to the 'ouse…"
"They? Was it a man or a woman? …Did they say what for?"
"A woman. I just 'ssumed she wanted to buy some of me finds, that I've bin advertisin' – S' funny now you mention it, I've never 'ad a woman buyer before…

"…anyway, when I said I wasn't there, at 'ome like, she asked if I was workin' at The Grange?"
"What did you say?"
"I just said yes – Then she just said she'd try again, asked when I'd be 'ome? It were only after that I wondered how she knew that I was workin' 'ere? …That's what made me forget all about the mowing, til it were too late to get it done in time - fuck it I ain't stayin' late, 'e wouldn't pay extra."

He already pays you enough for doing sweet F.A; the mystery woman must be the only person who does think he works here.

Mysteriouser and mysteriouser, I wonder if the mystery caller is connected to the man with the enormous lens….I'm surprised Frank didn't phone me last night then, while he was in that sort of mood – mind you I'm glad he didn't.

The noise of the front door being wrenched open snaps me out of my reverie, and Sophie and Alice scoot out like scolded kittens, running with their tails between their legs. Nisha follows close on their heels, with an expression that deters any small talk; her mouth is set as though sucking the last fragment of a mint by pushing it against the back of her top teeth with her tongue.

She is again impersonating a fishing float, though today she's a red and black one.

"Hi girls. Hi Nisha, going to the gym again?" I risk.

Sophie and Alice regard me as though I must be suicidal. The perma-frost on Nisha's face thaws imperceptibly, "Oh hi Charles, got to go, we're running late, see you later."

She sees Wayne lurking in the garage, "Oh hi Wayne," she offers, before she and Sophie scoot into the Range Rover. Alice risks a wide-eyed look of mock terror, before following suit.

"What you on today?" asks Wayne, as the Range Rover sails out of the drive.

"I'm not sure to be honest, I'm getting a bit fed up of this pissing about as though I'm their bloody handyman…I'm going to look at a job on Monday which sounds quite promising; could be several months work – So if Frank doesn't pull his finger out and get this bathroom suite organised, you'll end up fitting it on your own," I say, hoping that Wayne will relay this information to Frank, and panic him into action.

Frank likes to think that he employs us, rather like an extended part of the factory workforce; he enjoys feeling in control of us. He doesn't think twice about laying us off at a moment's notice, claiming poor cash flow at the factory, with no regard for ours, or the fact we may have arranged our other work to suit him. So he hates it if we have work commitments that prevent us being at his beck and call - It's amazing what projects he dreams up sometimes just to keep us on site.

I wonder what the relationship between Wayne and Frank is like at the moment, and whether my revelation will get passed on. I wonder if Frank is aware of Nisha's conspiracy; whatever it may be.

"That should be good," says Wayne, flatly, "I wish I could pick up some other work, I'm pissed off with this fuckin' place…"
"You getting fed up with the poor phone signal, having to run up and down that field?" I joke, adding, "I thought there was loads of site work you could get at twice the rate."

"Yeah well the site work is drying up, they're laying blokes off on a lot of the sites … but I don't fancy taking over the mowing, I can see that coming – If he expects me to take a cut, I'll tell him where he can park his fuckin' Kubota.

"I wish I could do detecting full time, working on archaeological surveys; I've got a couple of weeks surveying that road widening, come by-pass outside Hereford."
"What that piece towards Stretton?" I puzzle.
"Yeah , that's it – it's part of the old Roman road."
I laugh dryly, "You're a completely different person when you're talking about detecting and archaeology – I've never heard you talk enthusiastically about bricklaying; or patio laying," I add, nodding at the unfinished patio.

Barry's immaculate Camper van cruises majestically to a halt beside Franks Range Rover. At the same time as Frank emerges from the front door.
"Morning Frank," Wayne and I chorus.

"Morning," Barry says brightly to Frank, as he slides sedately from his van.
"Oh Wayne, do you think I could er, have a word?" Frank says, inviting Wayne to follow him around the corner of the garage; managing not to sound like a question.
Barry and I shake our heads, and mouth, 'IGNORANT', in unison at Frank's retreating back; although I also add the word, 'SOD', which doesn't seem to be in Barry's vocabulary.

"Didn't hear your horn this morning," I say, as Barry struggles into his overalls.
"No, well I passed Nisha near the village so I thought I'd be safe," he laughs, then remembers a bigger hazard, "Mind you, I forgot about the possibility of meeting Frank, I'm a bit later than normal – I got held up by a convoy of tractors- Shouldn't be allowed on the road," he laughs, while casting about for eavesdroppers, "Do you reckon he's having a quiet word with Wayne about his work, or rather lack of it?"

I make an exaggerated show of also checking for eavesdroppers, "Possibly. Or they're having an affair," I say dead-pan.
"Well that would explain why he gets away with so much – or rather, so little."
"Now I know what Wayne meant when he said he had Frank over a barrel," I laugh.
Barry grimaces.
"Actually I expect Frank's just paying him. I don't know why he has to be so secretive, is it cos he's paying Wayne cash?...

"Are you in the bathroom; you must have done all you can do in there for the moment?"
Barry raises his eyes in frustration, and again casts about and lowers his voice, "Didn't he phone you last night? He phoned me and said he wanted me to repaint the sitting room, while he got you to panel the bathroom. Apparently he's seen some in a magazine

that he thinks would look good in there – he said he was going to phone you."

"I'm bloody glad he didn't; it would have spoilt our romantic evening, nudge nudge, wink wink," I attempt a Leslie Phillips impression.

"Ding dong," says Barry, "… that wasn't a bad Frankie Howerd," he laughs.

"Yours wasn't a bad Arthur Askey," I laugh.

Barry again has a quick look around to see if Frank's within earshot, seeing the coast clear, he leans towards me, conspiratorially.

"Oy no tongue," I say jerking my head back.

"Oh, I thought you liked it," he feigns pained rejection. Re-checking Frank's whereabouts, he continues in a whisper, "I could hear Nisha in the background last night – while he was on the phone…" Barry casts a glance over his shoulder.

"I vill zay zis onlee vonce," I quip, also casting about for eavesdroppers.

Barry gives a brief laugh. "She was yelling about already having one room out of action; the bathroom - She reckons he's got the brains of a shit-fly," he says, looking pointedly at me.

"A shit-fly. Are you sure? I wonder where she got that expression?" I say as if butter wouldn't melt.

"I wonder? Mind you I haven't heard you use it for ages – I couldn't believe my ears, but she definitely said, or rather screamed, that."

"That explains her mood this morning; she's probably negated the country's efforts to reduce global warming single handedly." I muse, "His timing couldn't have been better – unless he did it to distract her from the car remodelling," I add, only half joking.

"Nothing he does surprises me anymore," he says despairingly.

Frank emerges from around the side of the garage, looking a little uncomfortable.
"Feeling better Frank? How much does Wayne charge?" I solicit, knowing that Frank is more perverted than the rest of us put together; so it should appeal to his warped humour.
"Eh? What? Oh," Frank splutters, before computing what I'd implied.
"Oh he's very cheap," he laughs, "…but I suppose you get what you pay for," he grins salaciously.
"So long as it's nothing a good clinic can't cure," I suggest.
"Oh god I hope not! … I'm already in Nisha's bad books without having to explain something like that," he squeals hysterically.

Barry and I exchange furtive glances, like a couple of puppets out of Captain Pugwash. I look behind me for the men in white coats, while positioning my arms across my chest, imitating someone in a straight-jacket.
"I thought you only had to be mad to work here; not to live here," I say dryly.
Barry attempts to mask his convulsions, and tries to hold his vibrating stomach, like a silent version of, 'The Laughing Policeman'.
"With all the laughing we do here, we should all have six-packs, instead of party-fours," I suggest.
"Can you still buy those big cans; I haven't seen them for years?" asks Barry.

"After the week I've had, it wouldn't surprise me, if I ended up in The Funny Farm," Frank shrieks hysterically.
"I thought you already ran it," I mutter .
I wonder whether Frank has always pretended not to understand our humour, or whether it has taken him nearly ten years to work it out. Barry and I watch him laughing hysterically, with growing unease.

"What's the joke?" asks Wayne, standing back as though Frank may have something contagious.
"I don't know what you did to him round there; but I think he's flipped," I answer, adding, "I hope his eyes are only watering from laughter."
"Eh? I ain't no fuckin' bum bandit, marmite miner, fudge packer or whatever you wanna call it," Wayne responds indignantly.
"Rent-boy?" I suggest.
"No. I ain't one of them either!" he snaps.

Fortunately, or otherwise, Frank has regained some semblance of normality.
"Phew. I don't know what came over me then," he proclaims.
"What ya been smokin'," I joke.
"Probably stress," says Barry, sympathetically.
"Yeah, probably," I agree, "…must be why students do daft things around exam time; act like bloody infants and think it's hysterical."
"Yeah. Ya know, ya know, you wouldn't believe the pressure I've been under lately," he confides, "…work's been manic, ya know, you wouldn't believe…"

"Your right," I quip.
Undeterred, Frank continues, oblivious to Barry and Wayne's snorting,
"…you wouldn't believe the pressure at work, things are just manic at the factory, ya know like that – orders coming in left right and centre, ya know, ya know like that…I'm doing quotes, ya know like that, I'm just thinking of a number and then doubling it," he laughs nervously.
"What's new," I ask solicitously, trying to avoid the looks from Wayne and Barry.

I think I prefer the fruitcake; at least he was more plausible.

"So, you're rolling in filthy lucre then Frank," I suggest.
Sensing encircling vultures, the smug bravado evaporates from his face, and is replaced by an expression more appropriately worn by

someone anticipating being mugged; his brain flips into damage limitation mode, to discourage thoughts of rate rises.
"Eh? Oh well, ya know ya know it could be months, maybe years before they come on stream. Yeah, maybe years," he feigns frustration and disappointment.

"Anyway. Barry, can you make a start with redecorating the living room? I know Nisha's not very keen, but it's gotta be, nearly a year since it was last done…
"As long as that?"

"Yeah you wouldn't believe it was so long, ya know, ago would you Charles…We should still have loads of the paint from last time…"

"… Charles, I was thinking ya know like that…"

You mean you've seen a picture in a magazine.
"…I was thinking like that, ya know, I was thinking, what would look nice, what would look really good in the bathroom, ya know…"
"A bath?" I suggest.
"Eh? No, we're gonna have one of those. What I think would look really good, ya know, what would look really classy ya know…."

I'm gonna give up the will to live and slash my wrists in a moment. I risk sideways glances at Wayne and Barry, and judge from their suppressed hysterics that they have read my mind.
"…what would look really good in the bathroom would be panelling."
It takes me a second to realise he has actually unveiled his piece de resistance.
"Oh that's so passé!" I camp up, flapping a limp wrist at him.

Frank deflates, embarrassed, as though he's turned up at a Vicars-and-tarts party, as a tart, only to walk into a room full of genuine nuns.

"Sounds as though it could be quite effective Frank," I relent, "What exactly had you in mind?" I ask, knowing what the answer will be.
Frank immediately brightens, beaming at Barry and Wayne, as if to say, *I knew he was joking...* but then realises I'm expecting a positive decision on this.

"Eh? Oh, ya know, panelling ya know – like they have in bathrooms."
I resist raising my eyes and asking the Man upstairs for strength. I mentally count to ten …"So do you envisage it being painted or stained and polished - four feet high or up to the ceiling - actual panels or tongue and grooved match-boarding…" I pause for Frank to digest.
"Oh no. I don't want tongue and groove boarding, I want proper panels – I don't know how high," he looks panicky. "Er, you decide, you decide."

Oh Christ I'll still be here at Christmas, I groan inwardly. "Is it to go all the way round the room, or stop at the bath? Obviously it's not going in the shower," I say more for my own benefit, knowing I'm on my own now.

"Well I'll leave it with you; I know you'll do a good job," he says, turning and scuttling rapidly for the sanctuary of his car, like a mouse that's been alarmed and bolts for its hole.

*****

"I'll leave it to you. Ha, bloody ha. Whatever I do he'll want changing", I mumble to myself, as I start sketching out the bathroom, and measuring up to get the proportion of the panels right.

"You know what they say – about talking to yourself." Even from a kneeling position, I almost perform a vertical take-off.

"Christ! Where the fffflipin' 'ell did you come from? I didn't hear you come back – That was a short gym session," I say incredulously.
"Sorry, didn't mean to make you jump," Nisha laughs, "It was body pump for beginners, so no it wasn't very long; they don't want to kill us off yet."
I admire her pneumatic curves, "It's working well," I say encouragingly.

Must be a bloody big pump.

"Hope you're not wanting to use the shower," I say, indicating the empty bathroom.
"No, it's okay; I'll use the one in the girl's bathroom."

"How the heck do you get in – and out of that outfit, it looks sprayed on?" I ask, trying to avoid looking where it seemed to cut in rather uncomfortably. I've heard it called a 'camels toe' but it looks more like a slice has been taken out of a peach.
"Are you offering," she says suggestively.
"Sorry, I forgot my tyre levers," I joke, but instantly regret the choice of words given the association.
"Oy, you cheeky bugger! Are you referring to my spare tyre?" she feigns affront.

I resist the impulse to correct her use of the singular, on health grounds; my health. Instead I hastily respond, "No no, I was referring to the tightness of your outfit…

"…If you want to see something funny, take a look at Wayne," I say, indicating the Kubota streaking down the field. Nisha follows me over to the window. Despite being a bright spring day, it can get quite chilly on the mower, especially in the shade of the trees at the top and sides of the field. His heavy coat that he wears for metal detecting in the middle of windswept fields billows behind, giving him a hunchback. He's also wearing a hat with earflaps that trail in his slipstream.

"My god, what's he like?" she laughs throatily, appearing to have forgotten the foul mood she was in a couple of hours previously.
"Beer, curry and metal detecting."
"Eh, oh very funny. I mean what's he look like? …What's that he's got on his head?" she laughs, covering her mouth, but seemingly unaware that she appeared to be trembling like a two-tone jelly; though I can't imagine what flavours.
"I think it's called a Peruvian Beanie," I offer, "…the way his coat gives him a hunch like that and with those ears flapping, he looks like our Labrador going to the toilet in the middle of a hurricane."
"God Charles, you're disgusting, trust you to think of that - Couldn't you have thought of something pleasant?" Nisha groans, looking at me as though I'd trodden in the fruits of the dog's labours.
"Sorry, it was the first thing I thought of," I say, apologetically. I look back at Wayne, hoping for inspiration for a pleasant simile; more suitable for The Sound Of Music.

As Wayne hurtles uphill, he stands up on the footplate, and appears to play a frantic game of pocket-billiards.
"Always said he was a tosser," Nisha jokes, laughing throatily.
"Now who's being crude?" I admonish.
After much rummaging, Wayne produces his mobile from his trouser pocket.
"I think you owe him an apology," I suggest.

Wayne stops the Kubota, dismounts, and then hobbles across to his usual perch on the fence.
"Perhaps not," I say contritely.
"Hmm. I think I preferred him playing with himself; at least he was still managing to mow," she says despondently, chewing the inside of her mouth.

I turn away; even Wayne is a preferable sight to Nisha's impression of a prolapsed cat's bum. As I scan the field, a sudden

movement catches my attention; instinctively I know our sneaky snapper is back.
I glance at Nisha to see whether she'd seen him.
"Are you thinking of putting this place on the market?" I ask.
Nisha gives a puzzled laugh, "You must be joking- the state this place is in…" she replies, gesturing to the gutted bathroom.

"…Why do you ask?" she laughs, suspiciously; suspecting an oblique motive for the question.
"Just wondered why a photographer was taking so many pictures of the house – from so far away – I assumed he was trying to produce those typically misleading photos," I say innocently.

God I'm wasted here; I'm sure it's not these boards I should be treading.
"Really! Where? Is he out there now?" she blurts quite convincingly, following the direction of my intense stare.

A fellow thespian?
As though on cue, the photographer leans around the trunk of a tree and casually points his canon sized lens at an oblivious Wayne.
"He was here yesterday," I say nonchalantly, looking at Nisha pointedly, with eyebrows raised questioningly.

Nisha does an impression of an inverted thermometer. Her face blushes as red as her mixed race colouring will allow, more aubergine; spreading down her neck and continuing downwards below her low cut lycra.

"We'll have to start calling you Robin," I say, nodding at her colourful cleavage.
"He definitely looked like he was more interested in Wayne than the house – Do you think Wayne's famous, could it be the paparazzi?" I suggest enthusiastically.
Nisha manages a laugh, "Yeah famous for his statue impressions," she snorts.
"So, do you know anything about him?" I ask directly, "Our secretive snapper; not Wayne."

Nisha looks uncomfortable, her eyes follow imaginary gambolling rabbits out on the field; I assume she is exercising her Right of Silence. I blame too many cop shows on the telly; everyone knows their rights nowadays.

I try a different tack.

"I suppose it was bound to happen sooner or later…"

The tension in Nisha's body relaxes perceptibly while she waits for me to continue. Her eyes continue to search the field, presumably for the photographer.

"…I mean – with all this ebay selling – some of it must be of historic value as well as commercial. Then there's his creative accounting, and tax dodging…."

I suspect the surveillance is unrelated to these activities, and I take Nisha's continued silence as confirmation.

"… I can't imagine Customs or whoever, would bother with photographing him at work; they'd just visit his home for any evidence…

"…I would imagine the only people who would need photographic evidence…" I speculate, as we watch the happy snapper takes advantage of Wayne turning away from him towards the house, to dart like a wood mouse, from cover to cover behind the trees, until he gets to the lane. "… he must have got enough evidence – or got fed up waiting for him to do any work," I digress.

Nisha tenses, as though bracing herself for the thumbscrews.

"…P'raps a private detective - maybe Wayne's wife believes he's been playing away from home, after your Oscar winning performance the other day…" I suggest mischievously.

"…After all, she did leave home and go to her mother's for a couple of days."

"Really? Oh my god. Does he know it was me?"

“Well it wasn’t too difficult even for Wayne to work out, as you were the only female in the house, let alone the bathroom where he’d left his phone.”
“Oh shit… Was he really cross?”
“Fuming; he reckons it nearly cost him his marriage - He’s planning revenge; and I don’t think Wayne is capable of anything subtle.”

Nisha pales, and cogitates.

“I suppose Lenny The Lens may just be from a Benefits Agency.”

Nisha stiffens; but continues to plead The Fifth Amendment.

Chapter 25

"How did athletics go?"
Lizzie looks blank.
"You did have athletics after school, didn't you? It is Thursday isn't it?" I ask, wondering if I'd got the day wrong.
"Oh yeah – fine," she says absently.
"What's the problem?"
"Nothing."
"What's up then?"
"Nothing."
"What's wrong then?"
"NOTHING! – I'm just tired that's all," she snaps.

"You would tell me if I was getting on your nerves, wouldn't you?"
Lizzie stifles a laugh, "Dad, just shut up. Can we just get home," she says, holding her school bag tightly to her stomach.
"Period pains?" I ask, sympathetically.
"Dad!"
"What, I bet mine are worse than yours."
Lizzie suppresses a grin, "Dad, you don't have periods."
"But if men did, they'd be worse than yours – it's like man flu is far far worse than woman flu," I argue.

"I wish you did, then you wouldn't make jokes about it," she protests.

"I'm not making a joke of it, it's a natural event, it happens every month, you should be able to talk about it - I'm only trying to be sympathetic."
"Aaagh! Yes I've started my period. Happy now?"

"Delirious. It's so nice having these grown up discussions, don't you think? Just like being The Waltons," I say reversing into the driveway.
"I can't imagine the Waltons discussing period pains," Lizzie says flatly, as she clambers from the van and stomps ahead towards the front door.
"John-Boy?...
"Yes mama?...
"Do you think you could possibly bring me a tampon down from the bathroom-cabinet, honey?...
"Certainly mama. Would you like me to do you a hot water bottle as well mama?...
"Why thankyou John-Boy. You're such a swell son John-Boy," I mimic the infuriatingly sickly, thankfully obsolete, American TV characters.
"Dad! Get inside, someone'll hear you," she shrieks with laughter.

"Right, can you make a pot of tea while I start the dinner? You're mum shouldn't be late tonight – that'll be a record, two nights in a row," I say with exaggerated enthusiasm.
"Okay dad. You can stop now. Anymore references to the Waltons and I'll wrap that frying pan around your head."
"Okay – Mary Ellen," I laugh, ducking, "…By the way, this frying pan's a wok."
"Ebony, bite him!" Lizzie commands.
A bemused Ebony simply beats a tattoo against the side of her basket with her tail.

"I'm going to have a shower while that brews," Lizzie declares, clattering the lid on the pot and then ramming the cosy over it, as though finally managing to get a hat onto the head of an uncooperative child.

No sooner has Lizzie left the room than the phone rings.
"Why does it always ring at mealtimes?" I mutter irritably.

"Guess what?" says Alex, "We've had the call for Ofsted," she announces, not waiting for any daft contributions from me. "They're coming in on Monday…" Alex pauses for the implications to sink in, "So I'll be back late tonight, and I'll have to be in school all weekend," she says, sighing loudly.

At least I don't have to worry about keeping you out of the way when Slyman realises he's been set up.

"Do you need me to come in and help do anything at the weekend?" I ask, wondering what use I could possibly be. "Are you going to eat when you get back?"

"No it doesn't matter, everyone's here, someone's going down to collect takeaways from the pub later – it'll be too late to eat when I get back – Sorry – We should be okay at the weekend, everyone's coming in and you've got to take Lizzie to cricket on Sunday. Has she got hockey tomorrow?"

"You mean Saturday, yeah they're supposed to be finished until the summer league, but they've got one to play that they missed because of the bad weather back in January or February…. Oh shit! Something's burning, better go, see you later, don't worry about it you'll pass with flying colours – Bye."

I peer into the wok and study the carbon contents. Maybe that should have been, frying colours.

"Hmm, not doing much to reduce my carbon footprint – at least it was only the onions," I mutter, scraping the charcoal into the compost bin.

*****

"Can you clear away and load the dishwasher, I need to give Ebony a proper walk, she didn't get much of one earlier? – That's if I can persuade her of the health benefits of a good walk compared to scavenging the scraps of a stir fry."

"Oh do I have to, I hate loading the dishwasher?"

"No, course you don't - you can just wash it all by hand instead if you like?"
"P'raps I could get used to it," she replies, lowering the door to the washer.

After shutting the chickens in for the night, I fling open the pedestrian gate in the garden hedge to allow Ebony and I to walk the fields.
An unexpected thud is accompanied by a deep grunt, followed by lots of expletives, usually associated with The Funny Farm.

"What the bloody hell are you doing?" I demand of the figure rolling in the nettles. After several seconds of impersonating an upturned beetle he manages to roll over onto all-fours and frantically scrabble about as though looking for something. He eventually locates a camera which he briefly inspects for damage before hastily placing the strap around his neck.

The slightly dishevelled and embarrassed figure doesn't seem to know which part of his anatomy to attend to, or defend first. Alternately rubbing the rapidly growing lump above his left eye, and frantically scratching the nettle rashes spreading across the exposed hands and wrists, ankles and a spotty spare tyre that bulges over his thin black leather belt. None of this is made any easier by Ebony's persistent goosing; the liberal application of sheep muck to his attire has obviously made him quite irresistible.

"Is that the latest dance craze?" I ask brusquely, unsure whether I'd inadvertently and almost literally, stumbled upon a burglar – I'm in two minds whether I should just lay him out and call the police; but criminals seem to have more human rights than the rest of us.

"Sorry, I was looking for the footpath," he blurts unconvincingly, between his even less convincing John Travolta impression.

I eye him suspiciously. He doesn't look like the average walker. But then he could be just starting out on a new health regime. As well as being a few stones overweight, he isn't exactly dressed for walking; not in a field full of sheep muck anyway. His shoes wouldn't look out of place in the average wine bar; except for the sheep muck squidging out from under the soles. His grey flannel trousers and dog-tooth jacket aren't exactly de rigueur of even the average walker; although, again the addition of sheep muck has somewhat countrified the appearance. He doesn't look much like my idea of a burglar either – especially carrying an expensive camera.

I stand my ground. "The footpath is right over there, it goes diagonally across the field from that gate," I instruct with a wave, "...to that gate over there – quite a well-worn path; no need to crawl about at the bottom of my garden gate to find it…

"I'm going that way myself; I'll show you where there's a good clump of docks…"

"Docks?"

"Yeah, Dock leaves for your nettle rash."

I can't believe he's never heard of dock leaves for nettle-rash; maybe he automatically thought of a courtroom.

"I presume you're going that way, otherwise you'd have been on the path and just followed it to the gate just over there," I gesture to the gate out onto the road, about thirty yards away.

"Um, yeah well I might not bother now," he mutters, furtively casting about by his feet, "…I might just go back to that pub up the road and have a drink instead."

"Good idea," I encourage, "…although most of the farmers in there like to leave the smell of sheep behind when they go out for a drink," I say nodding at his newly christened clothes, "I think you'll find that the rumour about the relationship between farmers and their sheep is just one of those urban myths."

He seems to have taken on the appearance of the reluctant disco dancer who's preparing to leave the floor and swagger to the bar. His scratching has slowed to a half-hearted rubbing, and the squirming to deflect Ebony's snout resembles a child suffering a bad case of worms, with the associated infuriating and embarrassing itch.

"That's quite a lump you've got there," I observe, "…looks like you might be getting a bit of a shiner too – The joys of rambling eh."

"Yeah," he laughs nervously, still hovering

"Well don't let me keep you… Have you lost something – apart from your way?" I ask observing his furtive glances around his newly made crop-circle.

"No, no it doesn't matter," he says rather unconvincingly.

I watch him shuffle reluctantly in the direction of the gate out of the field onto the road that runs past the front of our house. I again consider phoning the police; talk about suspicious. As I take a couple of steps further into the field to keep him in sight, I feel and hear a sharp cracking sound.

I lift my foot to reveal a broken lens cap for a Nikon SLR lens.

Chapter 26

Arriving later than usual at The Funny Farm, after collecting materials for the panelling on the way in, I'm met by Barry; who appears to have been waiting in his Camper.
"Morning Barry – Where's everyone, did Frank and Nisha leave before you got here then?"
"Morning Charles -Yeah, and it doesn't look as though they've left a key," he replies, obviously disgruntled at having to wait in his van for the best part of an hour.
"If I hadn't guessed you'd be collecting materials, I'd have thought blow it; and gone home."
"Oooh , I can tell you're vexed when you use strong language," I laugh.

Barry gives a half laugh, "It's no joke sitting in the van for an hour, not for a man in my condition," he almost mouths.
I instinctively flick a glance at the source of his *condition.*
"Yeah, I can imagine," I say sympathetically.
"Have you checked the inside of the pedestrian door? They often leave the keys in there if they know I'm coming," I say, walking over to check the garage door.
"To be honest I forgot they did that; it's so long since I got here before anyone else," he replies, slightly embarrassed.

I open the door and retrieve the keys from inside the lock, "Ta-da," I trumpet.
"I must be getting old," he says sombrely.
I sense that there's more to his mood than misplaced keys; and senior moments.
"What's the matter Barry?" Then so that he didn't think I was going all soppy on him, I'm sure new-age men make him feel uncomfortable, I add in mock parental tone, "… surely you didn't

think we'd left you all on your own?" I stop short of ruffling his hair, what there is of it, or pinching his cheeks.

He laughs, not quite his usual full gusto, but it was an improvement.

"I was quite relieved when I first saw Frank and Nisha's cars gone," he laughs dryly, "…but then I realised I couldn't get in and get on …. I really wanted to get so's I could put the room back together before I leave tonight…"

"You won't have finished by tonight will you?" I ask, surprised.

"…No. But I've had me call-up papers; they want me to go in next Tuesday to have me hernia done," he declares in a tone that suggests they were actually military call-up papers.

"That's good news isn't it? That's sooner than you expected, did they have a cancellation?" I say enthusiastically.

"A cancellation prize, ya mean," he jokes. "So I wanted to leave it fairly habitable, cos I probably won't be back for a few weeks – if at all," he half jokes.

"Course you will. You're as strong as the proverbial ox," I encourage, "…and hung like the proverbial donkey," I laugh.

"Nice of you to say," he half laughs, "…but general anaesthetic isn't without risk - especially at my age," he says less than cheerily.

"Nah, you'll be fine; you'll be skipping about within a week – or two".

"That'll be a miracle then – I couldn't skip before," he laughs.

"No Wayne then," I observe, curiously.

Barry laughs, "No, we've been lucky with the weather, it'll probably make up for it in the summer."

"Oh god," I laugh, "… you giving me a taste of my own medicine?

"I wonder where he is? He did say he'd be here today, didn't he?"

"Yeah - In fact he was quite keen to get paid today; he reckons Frank didn't pay him last week – He was moaning about the fact Nisha brought your money, but not his."

"I thought that's what Frank took him behind the garage for - even more reason for him to be here today - unless of course he doesn't need it," I say thoughtfully.

"I wonder if it's got anything to do with that photographer that's been lurking about for the last couple of days," says Barry, surveying the trees at the top of the field.

"Yeah I was wondering that…hmmm.

"Anyway, best get on, *this isn't getting the bairn new shoes,* as my neighbour would say. Do you need a hand, moving furniture or anything?"

"No you're alright; I'll give you a shout if I do."

*****

I switch the screaming router off, and remove my earplugs. Thank god I can do most of the machining in the garage; I'd hate to be worrying about this racket and dust in the house.

" Mister Hall, Mister Wayne Hall?"

Startled, I turn around, and instantly recognise Lenny the Lens. He doesn't look any larger than he did nearly three hundred yards away at the top of the field; in fact he even resembles a wood mouse – without the tail obviously – He's definitely not the one I nearly laid out last night.

"Yes I'm Wayne and so's my wife," I reply in Pythonesque fashion.

He raises his eyes, for a few seconds longer than necessary, "Comedian are we? Monty Python has a lot to answer for."

"I'm only serious in my spare-time, and I don't have a lot of spare-time - apparently."

"Well can you spare five minutes of your serious time?"

"Hmm, I can see it was a waste of money having the signwriting done," I say nodding at the van, "…you've taken enough photos of Wayne, to be able to recognise him bandaged up

like a Mummy. Haven't you picked them up from the chemist, or are they too blurry?"
"Welcome to the digital age, Mr Wilson…. And no they're not blurry – sharp enough in fact to show you and the painter in the kitchen window, and you and Mrs. Knight, in the bathroom window," he says smugly, adding "Does anyone actually do any work around here?"

"Oooh can I have copies? Are we going to be in Hello Magazine, or even Homes and Gardens?" I say excitedly, casting an appraising glance at Frank's palace. "Actually, it's a bit difficult to work when you're being distracted by the antics of Secret Squirrel," I say in reply to the original question, hinting at his inept attempt at covert surveillance.
"If this is you being serious, you should be in A Home, not Homes and Gardens."
"You'd get on well with my wife," I say.

"And who might you be?" I ask, adding, "My mum warned me about talking to strange men."
"So, is Mister Hall not here today?" he asks, ignoring my question, and looking around the car park, making a show of noting Barry's VW and my Transit; as if he hadn't already noted the absence of Wayne's battered Transit when he drove in.

As he twists his body without moving his feet to take stock of the vehicles, his jacket pulls open to reveal a laminated identity badge, clipped to his waistband. His name, legible below his weasely features, which are also surprisingly recognisable for an identity badge; suggesting a recent photo.

He seems to be taking quite an interest in Barry's immaculate VW.
"Nice motor," he declares, turning back to find me apparently preoccupied with marking out timber, "…that belong to the painter?" he asks, casually.

"You haven't learnt much during two days scampering among the trees," I reply dryly.

He ignores my sarcasm.

"What's his name, I'm looking for a good painter?" he says, almost believably.

I bet you are, and anybody else you can nab I think. I reckon I've got competition for the Oscars.

"He's retired, he's just helping the Knights out as an old friend," I lie, probably just as convincingly. I just hope Barry doesn't come out of the house.

A brief glimmer, flashes through his eyes, betraying his disbelief.

"What did you say his name is?" he asks again, a little less casually this time.

"Roy Palmer," I answer casually, "What did you say yours was?" I ask, just as casually.

Roy Palmer's nonchalance immediately evaporates. His eyes widen imperceptibly as he stiffens involuntarily, and shoots me a questioning look. His jaw slackens as if about to speak. For a split second he looks as though a doctor has checked his prostate gland, without prior warning, and rather brutally with a rather large digit; and probably still wearing a chunky sovereign ring.

I endeavour to return his questioning, startled look, with one of angelic innocence, and hope it doesn't look like trapped wind.

"Roy Palmer," I confirm, adding, "… you can probably look him up - in an old Yellow Pages, under Painters and Decorators…

"Who shall I say has been looking for Wayne – and a good decorator?" I ask casually.

He forgets his mask, and continues to study me. Weighing up the chances of stumbling on someone sharing the same name; or whether I'm taking the piss. And if so, how the bloody hell do I know his name?

He regains his composure, and slowly nods his head repeatedly, endeavouring to signal that he understands the situation. Wordlessly, he turns and continues the appearance of a recent rectal examination by imitating the John Wayne walk towards his car, no doubt memorising Barry's registration.

"Good bye Mister….?" I'm tempted to say Palmer, but decide to leave him with an element of doubt.
I make pretence of returning to my work, but follow the sound of his Ford Focus retreating down the lane, before going to warn Barry.

"Bloomin heck. That's all I need - DWP did you say?"
"I think that's what it said on his badge; I didn't really get a good look at it – What is DWP?" I ask, watching Barry visibly pale and deflate.
"I don't know, but I bet they all talk to each other; it won't be long before the bloomin' tax man comes knocking on my door," he says despairingly.

"…This is all Nisha's fault, she's opened up a right can of worms trying to drop Wayne in the shit – I should never have told her about Wayne pinching that money."
"You told Nisha…"
"Yeah, I told her what you told me, after Frank and Nisha had had that blazin' row…I didn't think it was fair that we were all under suspicion – So I told her that I'd heard Frank accuse her of taking the money, and I thought she should know what you'd seen."
"I wondered why she'd never mentioned the money to me…She must have thought I was a right shit for letting her take the blame… I wonder whether she told Frank?

"Anyway I told the happy snapper you were retired and were just doing it as a favour, to an old family friend – so if you and Frank, and Nisha stick to that story, I suppose they'd have a job to prove otherwise – You're not exactly living the high life," I say trying to sound encouraging.

Barry doesn't look too convinced, but eventually laughs.
"I'd love to have seen his face when you gave him his own name."
"I'd love to be a fly on the wall when Frank finds out Nisha has got us all investigated - there won't be anyone working here at this rate; talk about ten green bottles."
"You're alright, I didn't think you were doing anything wrong – I thought you invoiced him."
"I do, but I put it down as maintenance at the factory – so maybe technically I'm aiding and abetting Frank in tax avoidance – I don't fancy being the last green bottle to accidentally fall – It won't be The Funny Farm without you guys; I'd probably end up in one if I worked here on my own.

"Anyway, I'm not so sure about me being alright, I reckon I had one spying on me at home last night – nearly laid the fucker out with the garden gate…"
"You never threw a bloomin' gate at him?"
I laugh at the image, before filling Barry in on last night's events.

Chapter 27

About a mile out of Burley I notice a car in the wing mirror gaining rapidly, as though it's anticipating overtaking on one of the few stretches available before Kenchester. I ease off to allow it to pass easily, but instead the silver grey Mondeo, settles in about a hundred yards behind.

"Shit, I bet that's a bloody unmarked cop-car."
Lizzie perks up at the prospect of something comparatively exciting, and contorts herself to view Mondeo-man.
"I thought the police cars always had two in them," she states almost disappointedly.

As I pull up at the leisure centre, I notice Mondeo-man dither, but eventually drive past us sporting an enormous pair of sunglasses, and park at the far end of the car park. I watch him in my peripheral vision, trying his camera out for range.

Is he really pointing that at me, or is he just testing for light or whatever photographers do? With his sunglasses pushed up on top of his head a beautiful black-eye is still visible at this distance, giving the impression that he has found a convenient and original holder for his lens-cap.

That's the same sneaky bastard…Who the fuck is he? I wish Ebony had used her teeth instead of her nose now. My perineum twitches at the image, and my family jewels try to hibernate.

Hmm, could be interesting; the leisure centre has a strict policy on photographers at minor's and women's matches – You never know what perves are about. Maybe I'll go and stand amongst some of the other spectators on the other side of the pitch; if he wants photos of me he'll have to take them through the girls playing.

First I'll do my civic duty by notifying the staff on reception of my suspicions.

*****

"What were the police doing with that man in the car park?" Lizzie asks excitedly.
"I've no idea; but he seemed to be getting quite stroppy," I say as if butter wouldn't melt.
"I know," she laughs, "Did you see the way they threw him into the riot van? Some of the girls were saying at half time, that the police were looking at his camera, before they took him away."

Maybe he'll have another shiner to match by the time he explains his way out of that.

"Really – perhaps if they'd concentrated on the game they might've won a little more comfortably." I say stifling a laugh at the racoon image.
"Dad, that's not fair. How could anyone concentrate with that going on?"
"True; maybe they should have halted the match."
"That's what we said – even the opposition said that."
"Unsurprisingly…Yeah it's not fair that you couldn't all watch the most exciting thing to happen in Kenchester, since a Morris dancer sprained an ankle, about twenty years ago," I say dryly.
"Ha ha," she says, trying not to laugh.
"I'll see you in the bar – I presume you're having something to eat after you've showered and changed."

I wonder how long before Slyman risks phoning – and how long before he realises he's been set up….I laugh at the image of Slyman and his couple of achers; I wonder if his ambition was to be a smallholder.

My self-satisfied grin evaporates like hail on hot tarmac - What if he and Alex have been in touch and know that I've been impersonating her… and have both gone to this hotel? …There would be no way I could have her back if she went that far.

My stomach feels as though it's dropping through the floor again, at the prospect of the repercussions; only the sudden thought of the improbability before an Ofsted prevents it plumbing full depth.

I half laugh at the memory of Mondeo-man being thrown unceremoniously into the riot-van, and the raccoon image…

It would be really funny if I knew who he was and why he's been following me… I can't see how it could be connected to Slyman - and I can't see it being the DWP that have been skulking around The Funny Farm; it's not as if I've been claiming benefits or avoiding tax…I don't earn enough to warrant this level of surveillance.

Next time our paths cross we're going to have a little chat.

Chapter 28

"Why do you keep checking your watch?"
"Maybe because I haven't learnt how to use the sun."
"Ha ha. Have you got to get back home for something?"
"Not especially, but there is a list of jobs as long as my arm – I don't know where to start first…

"…Is that definitely the last match – no more Saturdays with freezing feet?"
"What, how could you have been cold today, it was lovely and sunny?"
"It is today, but from about October to March I wish I had more Polar Bear in my genes."
Lizzie laughs at the various possible images, before suggesting, "I've never seen a Polar Bear in jeans – Anyway we couldn't afford all the fish…

"Anyway, it's only just gone two, so you've got plenty of time to get on with something once we get back."
"Why thankyou massa."
"Dad, that's racist."
"I thought it was called slavery."
"Ha ha…What time do you think mum will be home?"

I simply shrug. I'm more concerned about Slyman contacting her and finding out I know about them. I'm not exactly looking forward to that possibly life-changing confrontation.

*****

"Hi, the lawns look nice – it's amazing the difference just mowing makes to the garden."

"Hi, you're back early," I say, instinctively checking my watch, "It's still daylight, I'm surprised you recognised the house," I laugh.

Alex laughs, "I know – There's not much more to do at school, so I thought I may as well bring the paper-work home – there're a couple of reports that have to be done for the inspectors…

"Have you walked Ebony yet? I could do with a walk."

"I don't think her collar will fit you – Actually I could murder a cuppa first."

Or should that be, a couple?

"You could feed the chickens while I make a pot," I say heading indoors. I wonder if she's heard from Slyman?

While waiting for the kettle to boil I retrieve her phone from her handbag. A quick glance informs that there are several unanswered and unopened voice and text messages, as well as several missed calls. I make the tea and leave it to brew.

"Tea's brewing, I just need the loo," I shout down the garden to Alex's rear end as she collects the eggs from the nest boxes.

Ensconced on the throne I examine the text and voice messages from Slymon in chronological order. First text message timed at three-twenty-five.

"Sorry running L8 will xplain wen i arrive make yourself comfy! xx"

God I hate text language. Why can't people write properly, it doesn't take much longer.

The second text is timed at four- fifty-three.

Hmm not long ago.

"Sorry just arrived where r u? Xx"

Hmm not exactly punctual, they're well suited.

Voice message timed at four-fifty-seven.

"Hi Darling, sorry I'm late, I've had a hell of a day, I got arrested – mistaken identity but it took some explaining,

they thought I was some perve and knocked me about a bit, thought I wasn't going to get away, I've just got to the hotel, where are you? Reception said you hadn't arrived.

Arrested? It can't be the same perve, surely. Why's he bloody following me? If he's a Head how come he's got time to follow me about? Alex hardly has time to wipe her arse.

Better send him a text to keep him quite for a bit.

Sorry stuck in traffic on the Worcester ring road hopefully wont be long don't forget to pop your pills! Try not to start without me!

I quickly delete his messages and mine from the sent file, set the phone to silent and flush the loo.

I wish Blackberry would bring out a simpler phone for us oldies, perhaps call it an Elder-berry.

"Thought you must have died in there."

"Sorry to disappoint you – I've got a bit of a gippy tummy, so it probably just smells like I had; so I hope you don't need to go for a bit."

"Thanks for the warning – just as well I don't need to – I've only just poured yours, there's brewed and there's stewed," she says, offering a steaming mug and a plate with a slice of sponge cake.

"Ooh, cake. Are we celebrating?" I ask taking a welcome sip, "Ah that's good."

"Thanks. I was trying to forget about Ofsted for a couple of hours.

"A couple of hours eh?" I raise my eyebrows imperceptibly.

"God that's all you think about," she half laughs.

"That's all I'm allowed to do."

"Maybe after Ofsted… if your good," she says suggestively, patting my best friend.

"You mean if you're at least Good, preferably Excellent," I laugh.

"Ha ha, thanks for reminding me – you certainly know how to seduce a lady."

"Lady?"
"Cheeky sod," she feigns affront and punches me in the stomach
I double up feigning injury, "You certainly know how to seduce a gentleman."
"Gentleman?...

"Talking of ladies, where's Lizzie? How did she get on at hockey, did they win?"
"What is this, twenty questions?" I laugh, "…She's in her room, supposedly doing homework, but I would imagine she's asleep if she hasn't heard you come home – They won, despite the distraction, she played okay, she still lacks confidence when she plays with the ladies. Ladies?" I half laugh, "… they're rougher than the men."

In more ways than one.

"What distraction - were the men watching again?"
"Yeah some of the men's team were watching, but it wasn't that – the police arrested some perve for taking photos of the girls playing."
"Really? Do they know who it was? Did he take any of Lizzie?" she asks anxiously.
"Oh, I don't know, there's a small chance he might have, but don't worry, the police nabbed him quite soon into the game, and they'll remove all the pictures from his camera for evidence, so he won't get a chance to drool over them – or worse…"
"Charles!"
"Let's walk Ebony."

I wonder what other photos were on there, if there are surveillance type photos from the other night, will the police turn up here – especially if they also check his mobile phone records? Shit! They're bound to check his computer!

Chapter 29

I pull up to The Old Barn; such an imaginative name. I look across at the original sixteenth century timber framed farmhouse, with its eighteenth century brick façade. The original fold yard has now been gravelled, with an old cider press acting as a roundabout.

This old barn used to be covered in weather boarding, if I remember correctly. The boarding has been replaced with brick panels and several windows. It looks pretty impressive I must say, although I sometimes wonder where this obsession with wanting to live in a barn came from. All the ones I've been inside look pretty spectacular, but they lose a lot of space to passageways and stairwells.

I inspect the new impressive, substantial oak door and frame, looking for a bell. I should have known better, bloody purists, there's no such concession to the twenty first century. In the middle of the door though is a massive eighteenth century cast bronze knocker, in the form of a sea serpent; it looks like a cross between a dolphin and a carp.

I heft the weighty beast and let it drop against the strike plate. I half expect to be showered with stone tiles from the roof. The resounding echo from within suggests the place is empty. A second knock seems unnecessary; I sense rather than hear movement within.

I stare expectantly at the door for several seconds but then feel as though I've been put in the corner at primary school. I turn my back on it and think about the weekend's events. I'd managed to hide Alex's mobile again. She's beginning to think it needs tying to her wrist like a child's mitten.

Fortunately the frantic messages stopped after about half-nine on Saturday night. It's a good job Alex didn't get them - he was calling her every imaginable expletive; and even some I couldn't imagine. I managed to delete them all and place the phone where Alex couldn't fail to miraculously discover it on Sunday; but not before making sure it was still set on silent. I bet when she discovered it in the bread-bin when she went to make toast, she must have thought she really was losing the plot.

"Hello. Mister Wilson? Would you like to come round the back way?"

I turn, thinking, I'll try most things once, *but I won't do that*, to quote Meat Loaf.

At the corner of the building stands an extremely attractive young lady, of about half the average age of my clients; I would guess not much older than thirty. I manage to approach her without gawping, or tripping over my tongue, which was pretty difficult, but I think I managed not to be too obvious.

"Hello. Rachel Foxley? Charles Wilson," I say offering my hand.

"Hi, glad you could come over, come on in," she says, smiling warmly while she firmly shakes my hand. Her bluey-green eyes lock onto mine, as confidently as her handshake.

She leads the way, apologising, "Sorry about bringing you in the back way, but the front hall has some leftover sheets of plaster-board stacked in it."

"I'm used to the tradesman's entrance," I laugh, admiring the rear view, and then try to work out whether the long hair which has been made to look as though it's been casually thrown up out of the way, is naturally blonde.

We enter through an already open oak stable door, and pass through a hallway of waxed coats and Hunter wellies, and into the pseudo traditional farmhouse kitchen - complete with the smell of dog.

The source of the smell leaves his bed and makes a bee-line for my crotch. I deflect his snout casually, with a well-timed knee; and the black Labrador retreats to his bed.

Does everyone in the county own a Lab.?
Rachel puts a ring less left hand to her mouth in an apologetic gesture.
"You've done that before," she observes admiringly, as though I'd just broken a record for keepy-uppy.
"I've got a Black Lab., I know what they're like; I should put a warning notice on the gate for my customers – She's rather more persistent, than him though, and discerning," I laugh.
"Discerning?" she asks, smiling.
"Ebony only gooses women," I say.

I'll have to remember this isn't The Funny Farm. I'm also reminded that Ebony seemed quite taken with that perve the other night.
"Ebony" she repeats, "I like that."
"I'm afraid she was bought for my son Adam and he named her; if I'd had my way she'd have been called Snowy."
She laughs, "Well Barney introduces himself to everyone. Would you like a cup of coffee? Or would you prefer tea?" she asks, smiling, displaying naturally white and slightly uneven teeth.

I'd noticed her teeth when she'd smiled outside. It sort of adds to a person's character, and makes a nice change from all the cosmetic dentistry we see nowadays on so-called celebrities; their unnaturally white and uniform teeth look like dentures. It reminds me of the characterless plastic window frames that people replace traditional windows with on an old property.

"Coffee would be lovely," I reply.
"While the coffee's doing, I'll show you the chest," she suggests, while spooning coffee into a shiny-chromed retro looking contraption.

I'm beginning wonder if she's more Barbara Windsor than Sophie Dahl, I just hope I can resist the Carry On double-entendres.

Apart from the ubiquitous blue AGA, the kitchen appears to be furnished temporarily, with cheap mass produced, readily sourced items. Perhaps moving in was the priority, and then replacing with considered pieces later. Hopefully made by yours truly.

"Yes, don't look too closely at the furniture," Rachel pleads, noticing my interest. "I just wanted to be able to move in – You said you made furniture? If you've time I'd like to discuss all the things I'd like done in the house, after showing you my chest in the stable. Would that be okay?" she asks, in a tone that suggests she fears I might refuse such an offer.

"Great," I say, while resisting the impulse to admire her chest in the kitchen.

She laughs, "Wonderful. Follow me," she says with a twinkle in her eye.

I try to put thoughts of her chest out of my mind as I follow her back through the hall, which isn't too arduous, given the view. Her sprayed on jeans displaying an absence of any VPL, as Lizzie calls it. I assume she's wearing a thong, and not into going commando.

We follow the side of the house and then turn across another gravelled area at the rear of the house. It's one way of cutting down the mowing.

"Does your dog not follow you around everywhere then?" I ask, noticing that he didn't stir from his bed, and for want of something to say apart from the stock comment on the weather.

"Barney? No, not nowadays, he's just a lazy useless old so-and-so – I'm afraid he's older than he looks…he didn't even respond to your knocking."

"So is it true what they say, about people and their dogs then?" I ask smiling but wondering whether I was getting into over familiar territory.

You and your big mouth Charles, you'll get a kick in the spuds one of these days.
Rachel laughs, "Useless and lazy, or not looking their age?"

Phew!
"Well you're obviously not the former, otherwise you wouldn't have taken on this massive project," I say, gesturing towards the house, "...and you must be extremely well preserved if you're a day over twenty-one," I add, tongue in cheek.

She shakes her head and laughs, "Aren't we the flatterer, add another decade and you'd be nearer," she says, smiling, "I hope you're better at dating furniture," she laughs, withdrawing the bolt on the stable door, and pulling it open.

Ah, but I have to remove the drawers and have a good rummage first.
"Be my guest," she says flicking the light switch and gesturing inside.

One of these days I really will find I've been thinking aloud.
I approach the distinctive serpentine shape, recognisable even under the old duvet that's draped protectively over it. I carefully remove it to avoid possibly snagging any loose veneer on the corners, and walk around the chest to lay it on some hay bales at the back of the stable; admiring the quality of the mahogany veneer, and to check the condition and configuration of the backboards. Then I return to the front, via the other side, noting more damage to the opposite carved canted corner. I'm aware of her gaze following me as I come around to admire the front.

"What do you think?" she asks eagerly.
"I think you have a lovely serpentine-front chest of drawers," I say. Taking hold of one of the brass swan-neck drop handles I withdraw the top drawer, and examine the construction of the drawer linings and bottom, and inside of the drawer front for evidence of previous handles.

Rachel moves in close in order to look at the details as I do. I'm aware again of her perfume, I'd noticed it during our introductions, and feel her breath on my face as she looks over my shoulder. I resist the impulse to turn my face to hers, but I couldn't stop myself from flushing.

I straighten up, and explain the construction detail, and point out the wear to the linings, and invite her to feel the corresponding wear to the boards inside the carcase, between the drawers, that act as the drawer bearers. Returning our attention to the drawers, I point out the absence of any evidence to suggest previous handles.

"I didn't know there was so much to know about drawers," she smiles.

"There's more to drawers than just a snug fit…" I say, wishing I could control my gob "…but I won't bore you with the full lecture."

"Oh no, it's really interesting."

I give her a suspicious look.

"Seriously," she stresses, "I find it really interesting - How can you date a piece by the way it's made?"

"Well it's not an exact science, especially with furniture made in the provinces; away from the cities. Cabinetmakers and joiners didn't always keep up to date with fashions and technology; they might stick to techniques they learnt as apprentices all their working lives..."

"So they might be working for about forty years," She suggests, like an eager student, "…that's nearly half a century – as you say, not exactly precise."

"I suppose a working life in those days could easily have been half a century – they might have started their apprenticeships at fourteen, and worked until they dropped; there were no pension schemes in those days…

Not that mine is any good either; so no different two hundred and fifty years later.

"...But certain styles, and construction techniques, and even the introduction of certain woods can be quite specific – according to records; so that can provide the earliest possible date..."

"So what wood is this made from?" she asks.

"Mahogany – which started to be imported around seventeen ten...but drawer construction changed around the middle of the eighteenth century – They changed the direction of the grain in the drawer bottoms, from back to front, to left to right; like these," I say, offering the drawer in my hand for inspection.

"So why did they do that, couldn't it have just been the fashion?"

"It's all to do with understanding the properties of timber – it only shrinks across the grain - and expands, depending on humidity."

There's nothing worse than sticky drawers when it gets humid.

I laugh, "I'm glad all my customers aren't as inquisitive as you, I'd have to start charging for the lecture – Actually it makes a change to find someone that's not only interested in how much it's going to cost."

"I can see there's quite a lot to do, so I'm not expecting it to be cheap."

"Well you won't be disappointed then," I assure her.

She laughs, "Thanks – So you think it's no earlier than mid eighteenth century?"

"Yes, they also started to introduce two short drawers at the top around that time; this still has the single full width drawer."

I check the remaining drawers and bearers for wear, and assess the damage to the outside of the carcase, including the carving on the canted corners, and an unfortunate watermark, which I suspect is the result of an over watered plant.

"Have you seen enough? The coffee should be ready," Rachel says, watching me step back at last.
I replace the duvet, and we return to the kitchen.

"You said on the phone that you had someone else coming to look at it, have they been?" I ask, while Rachel pours the coffee. I can't help but notice the warmth of the kitchen beginning to reverse the effect that the chilly stable had had on her; talk about chapel hat-pegs.
She shivers as if reading my mind and crosses her arms across her chest. "Brrrr. It was surprisingly chilly in the stable, out of the sun; I hadn't realised how cold it was until we came back into the warm."
"Yes talk about brass monkeys."
She laughs, "I should have put something warmer on."

I'm glad you didn't.

More gallantly, "I hope you don't catch a cold, it's my fault for boring you with the lecture."
"Not at all, it was really interesting, you sound as though you enjoy your work," she says enthusiastically.

"Milk and sugar?"
"No thanks, just as it comes."
"How do you know it's not a reproduction?" she asks, handing me a blue mug.
"Thanks. Mmm, smells lovely…The quality of the materials, and the carving for a start," I say, "You couldn't get that quality of West Indian mahogany, or that tight oak grain in the drawer linings by the time they started making reproductions in the nineteenth and twentieth century."

"The other guy tried to tell me it was a nineteen-twenties mass-produced reproduction," She says, raising a challenging eyebrow.
"And I suppose he offered you a couple of hundred pounds as a favour," I say cynically.

"Something like that... What would you give me?"

A cinematic image of what I'd like to give her springs to mind. I reluctantly erase the image; and store it for later.

Before she notices me drooling I quickly continue, "I'm not a dealer, but I know it's more than I could afford – it's worth a few thousand – If you're seriously thinking of selling it, I'd advise against having the restoration work done, and put it into an auction as it is – You probably wouldn't recoup the cost of restoration, and you may well put off the dealers - They prefer to get the work done themselves - they're a suspicious lot; they judge everyone by their own standards," I add only half joking.

Rachel regards me with a restrained smile. After a couple of seconds she studies the contents of her mug. Finally she pushes herself off the AGA, where she's been leaning and thawing herself out, and leans on the opposite side of the island unit; specially imported from Sweden via a Far Eastern sweat shop. She studies me in silence, as though still assessing me.

"Has anyone ever told you look like Sophie Dahl?" I ask to deflect the attention.

"Thanks," she laughs coyly, flushing nicely, "I presume that's a compliment - I wish I was as tall as her though, she must be nearly six inches taller than me. Isn't she about six foot?...

"I really appreciate your honesty- about the chest…I have no intention of selling it, like I said on the phone, I inherited it from my grandmother. I'd really like it restored, if you're sure you can do it?"

"Thanks, I'd love to…" I say almost too eagerly.

She smiles broadly, "That's great. Only I wanted to find someone I could trust, and get on with – As I said, I've got a lot of other things that I'd like done, so it makes sense in some ways to find someone who can do the lot," she explains enthusiastically.

"That sounds great," I say, relishing the prospect of seeing more of her; and possibly less of Frank.

"I should have thought to have asked you to bring a portfolio, it would be interesting to see some of the furniture you've made as well as restored."
"I could bring a portfolio over when I return the chest – unless you want to see it beforehand; I suppose you wouldn't want to commit yourself to a cowboy – I could pop it over, or if you're passing…"

"My you are keen," she grins, "…that would be interesting, I could see your workshop as well…and I'd love to see what you've done to your stone house, I quite like the idea of some stonework features outside," she says enthusiastically… "Cowboy, no I don't think so, I've had enough here already to recognise one a mile off now," she says smiling reassuringly.

"I only have one reservation about working closely with you," Rachel says cryptically.
"I thought the reservations were for the Indians, not the cowboys," I quip, looking expectantly at her, inviting elaboration.
"We'll just have to see how we get on…"

*****

"Phew. That was heavier than it looks," says Rachel arching backwards with hands pressed to the small of her back…Have you got time to look around and discuss the other projects? I feel conscious of taking up your time." she asks, checking her watch, while I secure the chest of drawers to prevent it sliding around inside the van. "Crikey, it's nearly half eleven," she announces.
"Doesn't time fly…"
"When you're enjoying yourself?" she interjects, raising a quizzical eyebrow.
"Most certainly," I smile, "Sure, I've got time if you have – What's for lunch?" I joke.

What's for breakfast, I think.

"Cheeky. Actually if I showed you everything you'd be here all night," she says innocently.
I savour that thought for a second, before laughing and saying, "In that case, what's for breakfast?"

She laughs, "I assumed you'd be happily married; I think that might take some explaining to your wife."

I didn't think I was this time last week. I wonder briefly how Alex's Ofsted inspection is going; and what sort of mood she'll be in when she eventually gets home.
"I am," I say, taking advantage of her leading the way, and allowing my eyes to rove appreciatively.

No harm in looking though.
She holds the door leading from the kitchen, inviting me to pass; I tingle as I brush passed and feel myself flush.
"Well behave then," She feigns admonishment and blushes, averting the hundred-watt eyes which seem to have dimmed to forty.

"I'm not sure what to do with this area; apart from getting rid of the pile of plasterboard," Rachel says absently as we cross the front entrance hall and enter a large sitting room, or lounge.

My eye is instantly drawn to a lovely faded early eighteenth century, burr walnut bureau. Which isn't difficult as it's practically the only stick of furniture in the room, apart from a threadbare settee, an Ercol coffee table and a flat screen T.V.
"Oh lovely," I drool.
Rachel's pride is evident by the size of her grin.
"I thought you might like it – I inherited this from my grandmother as well," she explains.
"I'm beginning to feel sorry for your parents. Did they inherit anything?"

Rachel laughs, and confesses, "It belonged to my maternal grandmother – she knew my father didn't appreciate antiques, he

would've probably flogged it and bought a car; and apparently it's been in mum's family since new."
I raise my eyebrows in a, *that's what they all say* expression.
"Sorry, I didn't mean to be rude. You realise it dates back to about seventeen-twenty, and I don't mean twenty past five in the afternoon."
"Rachel laughs, "Not bad, I'm impressed - Seventeen-fifteen, if I remember correctly."
I raise my eyebrows, "Blimey. You certainly are well preserved," I say.

She laughs before explaining.
"I don't know what's happened to it, but I remember my grandmother showing me the original sales receipt, and the date stuck in my mind; probably because as a young girl I couldn't get over the age… August 15th 1715," she recites proudly.

"That's amazing … have you looked in all the secret drawers?" I ask, risking the obvious.
Rachel frowns, "What do you mean, *all the secret drawers,* I only found one – and I only looked for that because gran hinted that I might find something hidden inside, when I inherited it."
"Was there anything in that one?"
"Only a letter to me from gran – at the end she hints at there being something else, but I couldn't find anything," she says disappointedly.

"Would you like me to take a look?" I offer, eagerly.
"Oh would you?" she encourages, "Do you know where they are?" After a brief pause she laughs, and says, "Of course, drawers are your speciality…"

Well I seem to have had a lot of experience lately. I can't help thinking of Nisha's mountain of 'apple-catchers'. You could probably get about fifty thongs out of a pair of Nisha's drawers.

"So where are these secret drawers then," Rachel asks, redirecting my attention to the bureau.

"Well, there isn't a strict rule about them – it was down to the imagination and skill of the cabinet maker – but there seem to be standard ones, which I always thought defeated the object of the exercise – maybe they were designed to satisfy the average burglar, and light-fingered domestic servant; and anything of real value was secreted in a really secret drawer or cavity…

"Let's look for the traditional or obvious ones first – Oooh isthn't this excthiting," I say, attempting to imitate the lisping Violet, from the Just William series, adding, "Perhapth we'll have lashings thof ginger beer afther."

Rachel laughs before proclaiming, "Lashings eh? My mother warned me about men like you."

"Don't knock it 'til you've tried it," I say, lowering the faded burr walnut, fall-front of the bureau onto the lopers.

"…Which one did you find?"

"Sorry," she apologises, leaning passed me, "…this one," she says, opening the central door among the pigeon holes, and reaching inside to pull, what appeared to be a shaped apron at the top, forward.

"Voila!" she announces, as she withdraws the shallow drawer.

"Hardly a secret," I tease, "Is that your grandmother's letter?" I ask, indicating the small brown envelope lying in the bottom. The spidery scrawl, suggesting an elderly hand.

I raise my eyebrows quizzically, "Buster?" I read, suppressing a quizzical smile.

"It was gran's nickname for me – apparently I was a bit of a tom-boy when I was young," she explains, reddening.

Still appropriate now, I muse, resisting the urge to reappraise her outstanding features.

"So, do people call you Buster now?" I ask.

"Definitely not," she says emphatically, "You're the only person outside my family, who's even heard it."

"Your secret's safe with me …Buster".

Rachel bites her lip, "It better be…. Show me these other so called secret drawers."

"Well the obvious or usual ones are these…"

I slide the two pilasters forward that flank the central door, and remove the two slim compartments that are attached.

"Voila!" I imitate Rachel, and offer them to her. I notice that they contain paperwork.

Rachel receives them open mouthed, "I thought they were just loose mouldings, I didn't like to pull them too hard."

She carefully empties their contents onto the writing surface. I step back and survey the room affording some privacy, I feel like a shop assistant avoiding witnessing the customer's PIN number. The makeshift curtains, together with the sparse furniture give the impression of someone camping rather than living here.

I take the opportunity to examine the top of the bureau; I suspect there may have been a cabinet or bookcase. But I don't want to get distracted from secret drawer hunting.

Rachel interrupts my thoughts, "Oh look, here's the receipt, see I was right, August 15th 1715," she announces triumphantly, and offers it for my inspection.

"Pity the ink seems to have faded…Is that Robert Williams, or Williamson?" I think aloud, it's described as *a wall nut desk and cabynet,* maybe you have a distant cousin who has the other half…Does that say five pounds, six shillings and six pence?"

Rachel looks disappointed.

"…Shall we see if we can find anymore?" I suggest, laying the receipt on the other papers, adding, "That's really interesting, you should take care of that…pity he doesn't give a more detailed description; there might be another bureau cabinet somewhere."

"I'm beginning to wonder just what gran might have left me," she says flatly.

I quickly check the pigeonholes and interior drawers. We discover a small compartment behind one of the small drawers, containing a Victorian silver propelling pencil and an old porcelain inkwell.

While Rachel examines the pencil I turn my attention to the drawers below the desk. I slide the paperwork back off the fall-front into the desk interior, so I can close the desk.

"Right let's have a look in here," I say, pulling open the top drawer, between the lopers that support the fall-front.

"Hmm, what have we here?" Instead of being able to extract the drawer from the carcase, it stops about six inches short.

"Oh that drawer doesn't come out," Rachel says casually.

"Ah, but why not? I ask myself," I say, opening the second drawer down so I can feel the underside of the top drawer bearer, I continue thinking aloud, "The fall front doesn't rest on the top drawer so there has to be a reason…ah ha." My fingers locate a hole in the boards that the drawer runs on. It would look like a knot hole to the uninitiated.

"What have you found?" Rachel asks excitedly.

"Maybe nothing, just the means of extracting the drawer," I mumble into the carcase.

"Right - feel under here," I instruct.

She gropes unsuccessfully for a few seconds.

"I can't feel anything," she complains.

I laugh. I thought it was supposed to be men that were useless at finding the spot.

"Here, let me show you," I say, taking her warm hand I guide it to the centre but a couple of inches back from the front of the drawer bearer. I manipulate the fingers of her right hand until her finger finds the hole in the board.

"Right can you feel that hole?"

"Yes, I thought it was just a knot hole when I'd looked before."

"Well, if you push you finger up, you should feel something springy. Can you feel it?"

"Oh yes!"
"Well keep it pushed up, and pull the drawer forward a few inches with your other hand."
"Okay. I've done it! Wow!"

I laugh at the image, "You sound like something straight out of The Famous Five."
She blushes, "Sorry, you must think I'm a right idiot. I'm really excited, I've never taken this drawer out before, I can't wait to see what's behind it."
"Well I hope you're not disappointed. Now let's just take the drawer out."

Rachel quickly removes the drawer, and almost discards it in her haste to look into the carcase. Fortunately I manage to catch it and turn it over to examine the mechanism underneath.
"Nothing. Not a sausage!" she sighs loudly, not hiding her disappointment.

"What are you looking at there?" She asks, straightening up.
"Just looking at the mechanism for removing the drawer. Quite simple really, when you pushed you finger through that hole in the board, you flattened this strip of wood here," I push the springy piece of wood attached to the bottom of the drawer.
"If you look at the top side of the board that you put your delicate digit through," I instruct, smiling at the obviously crestfallen Rachel. I carefully put the drawer aside on the floor.

"What's the matter? Drawer construction suddenly lost its appeal?" I laugh as if withholding a secret.
She sighs, "Sorry, It's not that. It's just that… well I thought my Gran had left me something important to her…not necessarily valuable…Now it looks as though she hadn't bothered," she adds, her voice noticeably tightening. "You must think I'm a right spoilt bratt," she sniffs and looks quickly away, while wiping the side of her hand across her eyes.

I feel rather awkward. This seems to becoming a habit. Not that I'd mind performing the same tango with Rachel that I'd been forced to perform with Nisha recently.

"Hey, don't give up yet, I haven't finished," I say, ducking down to examine the vacant drawer space.

"Mmm, the drawer looks at least six inches shallower than the carcase," I muse.

"What does that mean?" Rachel says, sounding slightly more interested.

"Well it could mean … a compartment at the back…This looks promising."

I press what appear at first to be drawer stops at the back on the sides of the drawer housing. They employ the same simple strip of wood let into a shallow grave, to create the same leaf spring method that prevented the drawer from being accidentally removed.

"What have you found," She blurts excitedly, nearly head-butting me in her attempt to look into the carcase.

"Steady on Lara," I laugh.

"Sorry," she laughs. "Lara?"

"Lara Croft, the fictional female equivalent of Indiana Jones, played by Angelina Jolie."

"Hmm, first Sophie Dahl, now Angelina Jolie, have you got a thing about celebraties?"

"I wasn't aware of it… does rather give the impression of Hello magazine reader, I can assure you I only get to read it in dentist waiting rooms…

"Anyway, watch this," I instruct. I depress the right-hand block, and what was intended to look like the carcase back board, nudges forward on that side.

"Oh wow!" Rachel blurts in my ear.

Ignoring the blast of warm air around my lug-hole I repeat the operation on the opposite side. The dummy backboard springs forward; just enough to clear the retaining blocks.
"Oh wow!"
I resist commenting on the limited vocabulary, but cannot resist laughing.

I start to withdraw what now felt like a drawer, by once again inserting my finger in what appeared to be another small knot-hole. Judging by the weight it was far from empty. I had a sudden thought.
"Why don't you do the honours as it's your prize… Hopefully."
She didn't need asking twice.
"Thankyou," she said excitedly, thrusting her finger in the hole before I was barely out of her way.

Rachel withdraws a lidded box, rather than an open drawer. Out of interest I inspect the back of the vacant drawer housing. As I suspected, I could see a larger version of the leaf spring, attached to the backboards; designed to propel the box forward the moment the retaining blocks were depressed. On each side of the box, projecting beyond the back of it, is what could be described a tapered wing; presumably to depress the retaining blocks and allow the box to be returned.

The box lid was locked.

"Fuck!"
"It's a bit premature to celebrate," I say dryly, "Shouldn't we find the key first?"

Rachel had instinctively put a hand to her mouth apologetically "Oh god I'm really sorry, I never swear," she gushed.

"You must be a quick learner…I obviously bring out the best in you…

"I remember finding a secret compartment in a bureau a few years ago. It was small enough for possibly a few gold coins or important keys. That one held nothing, apart from eighteenth century cobwebs."

I pull the left loper out until it comes to a stop, and feel the side of the top drawer housing which also guides and accommodates the loper.

"Ah ha," I triumph, removing the loper.

"How did you do that?"

"A similar leaf spring as for the drawer- stops," I say, demonstrating by pressing the wooden plug.

Tapping the rear end of the loper, on its topside, I detect a cavity, concealed by a sliding cover.

Rachel leans over, her apprehension is palpable, like a cat coiled outside a mouse-hole. Her hair obscures my view and tickles my face.

I laugh, "Let the dog see the rabbit."

"Sorry," she laughs, withdrawing her head a little, explaining, "It's so exciting." "You really should get out more," I joke, while concentrating on inserting my thumbnail into the hairline joint. Once I overcome the initial inertia, I slide the cover quite freely.

"Anything?"

I proffer the empty cavity, bar the ubiquitous cobwebs, for inspection. Rachel mouths her obvious disappointment. I'm tempted by the offer.

"Never? You seem to be making up for lost time."

"Sorry," she titters.

Rachel's embarrassment suddenly switches to one of puzzlement. "How do the spiders get into a sealed compartment?"

"I've often wondered that myself; another of life's mysteries," I say, replacing the loper and turning my attention to the other.

I repeat the same procedure on the right hand side. This time, in addition to the cobwebs, the cavity contains a bunch of about half a dozen small keys.

"Oh wow! Does one fit the box?" shrieks Rachel excitedly, hardly able to contain herself.
"Only one way to find out," I say selecting one of the smallest. Sensing Rachel's apprehension, I quickly add, "Don't worry I won't open the lid, I'll leave you to do that in private."
Rachel visibly relaxes. "Thanks; you're a real gentleman."
I give her a suspicious glance, but her expression seems genuine.

I quickly determine which of the keys belongs to the box, unlike the films it's not the last one, it's only the second; turning the key back and forth to establish that it operates the latch. I lift the lid a fraction to confirm it unlocks before closing it again.

"Well I hope it's what you've been looking for, I'd better leave you to it," I say reluctantly.
"Yes, thankyou," she responds absently.
"I'll give you a ring when I've done the chest of drawers."

"Oh Charles," Rachel blurts as I near the door. "I'm so sorry. What must you think of me? I'm not thinking clearly. Thankyou so much, I would never have found it. I've been looking for ages. I don't know how to thank you.

A couple of scenarios flash through my mind: but for once I keep my big mouth shut.
"…Look. The bureau is looking rather neglected, could you take it with you and bring it back to its former glory… I'll drop this box off at your place in the next couple of days, if I may; in case it needs any TLC - and to keep them together."

"Okay," I say brightly at the prospect of an early reunion.
"I could look at your portfolio as well," she adds.
"I don't show my portfolio to just any young lady," I say coquettishly.
"Not even if I ask nicely," she laughs.

Chapter 30

"Hi. Have you had a good day?"
"S' all right."
"How was netball?"
"Oh, okay – we won."
"Well done, who were you playing, what was the score?"
"It was a tournament, I can't remember the score."
"Well can you remember who you played."
Lizzie sighs, "Um, Aylestone, St. Mary's and Kingstone I think – We beat The Cathedral in the final."
"Brilliant…" I enthuse, "… So do you go through to another tournament?"
More sighing, "We both go through to a tournament in Birmingham, I think."
"When's that?"
"I don't know…What's for dinner?"
I sigh, "I don't know," I huff, "I can't remember."
"Look dad, I'm just ty-urd – How long's dinner?"
"About two foot-six - Vehicles have tyres, you're tired; since when have you been Welsh," I correct Liz, and then imitate her, "…ty-urd."
"Ha. Ha."

Lizzie stabs a finger at the CD player, and adjusts the volume, to eliminate any more conversation. Tina Turner proclaims her lover is simply the best.

Well bully for you.

*****

"What time will mum be home?" asks Lizzie, dumping her school bags in the middle of the floor.
I look quizzically from the abandoned bags to Lizzie.
"I'll move them in a minute," she huffs…"…So what time's mum home?"
I sigh, and then huff, "I don't know."
"Daad. You're not going to keep this up all night are you? It's not funny," she laughs dryly.

"Actually, I don't know – Your guess is as good as mine at the best of times; but I dread to think what time she'll be back today."
"What's happening today?"
"Don't tell me, you've forgotten? After she's been in school all weekend? She's got Ofsted today and tomorrow?"
"So what's new - Oh god, is she going to be in a foul mood? I can't stand it."
"That depends on today's feedback – She'll either be high as a kite…"

Or I may as well leave home.
"Or?" Lizzie drags me back from my reverie.

"Or she's been arrested for choking an Ofsted inspector – Anything less than Outstanding, and your mum will probably ram the report down his or her throat, and hang his body on the school railings as a warning to other inspectors – Or drag him - or her up the wall-bars in the hall, like King Kong – Or…"
"Yes dad. I've got the picture – Mum won't be very pleased if she doesn't get a good inspection report," Lizzie says patiently, in a tone normally reserved for the mentally challenged, or hard of hearing – she probably thinks I fall into both categories.
"Not just *Good,* it has to be, *Outstanding,"* I correct.

"Whatever…I'm starving, what's for dinner?"
"I don't know – What is for dinner?"
"I can't do it; I've got homework," she protests.

"Facebook, you mean –Anyway it's shepherd's pie, so it'll probably be an hour."
"What? An hour? I'm starving," she moans.
"Well it's not easy finding shepherds nowadays; they're a dying breed," I explain.
"Perhaps they should ban shepherd's pie, if they're being over-hunted then," she says dryly before stalking off towards her room.

"Bags," I shout after her, as though dog training.
Lizzie returns and wordlessly collects her bags.

I set about peeling spuds – Oh, the celebrity lifestyle.

*****

I debate whether or not to phone Barry, and wish him good luck for his op tomorrow, I wonder whether quarter to ten is too late, and whether he'd read too much into me wishing him good luck; and worry needlessly. I also wonder whether he's had anyone following him.

The scraping at the front door lock decides the matter; Alex will expect my full attention.
The scraping and scrabbling suggests she's laden with school boxes of paperwork. I get to the door and pull it open, causing Alex to almost fall into the front room.
"Bloody hell what did you do that for?"
"Charming – just trying to be helpful – Have you eaten? How did it go?"
"I've just had a sandwich, I don't feel like eating now; it's too late," Alex sighs heavily, making me wonder if I shouldn't have had an early night, but she quickly brightens.

"Yeah, it's gone really well today – some really positive feedback so far; two Outstanding, and a Good lesson and the parent feedback forms were full of really supportive comments,"

she says enthusiastically, then laughs, “The inspector asked if we’d paid the parents.”
“Did you tell him you’d considered it, but the school budget was too tight?” I say facetiously.

Alex ignores this remark. Instead she looks at the boxes and stifles a yawn, “I need a coffee, before I start on that lot.”
“Here, I’ll make it – I was going to say, sit down for a bit, but I reckon you’d fall asleep.

“If you did get an Outstanding inspection, would that strengthen or weaken your case for more non-contact time?” I ask. Alex considers this while I measure the water and coffee into the machine.
“I see what you mean. - You mean if I can manage to get good results with the time I’ve got, then I don’t need less contact time?”
“Yeah – a less glowing report could highlight the problems of too much teaching commitment,” I say half joking.

“The lead inspector has already commented on my teaching load; he was surprised I was teaching more than two days – It’ll probably be in the report.”
“That’ll be good leverage,” I say encouragingly.
“If the governors refuse, then I’ll look for another Headship; there are several coming up at bigger schools,” Alex says indifferently.

Great! I may as well look for a monastery.

I place the coffee cups on the worktop beside her, and place my hands on her hips, “You look exhausted, don’t you think you should try and get an early night?”
“That’s all you want me for,” she says, attempting to joke.

I wouldn’t have stuck around this long if that’s all I wanted you for.
I pretend to consider her statement for a few seconds, “No it’s not – You couldn’t lend me fifty quid could you?...
“Ha ha.”

I suddenly remember Liz

"…Oh,do you think you could pop up and say goodnight to Liz, if she's still awake?"

"…Oh, how did you get on today? Did you go and see that new client?"

"Oh, not very well," I reply, turning to check on the coffee.

"Why what happened?"

"Well she was a Sophie Dahl look-alike…"

"Ooh, right up your street," Alex coos, but fails to hide her jealousy.

"Yeah, but I could tell she was only after my body- I hate women that do the chasing," I say flatly.

"Ha ha. She's welcome to you – she must be desperate - I'm surprised you didn't jump at the chance for a quickie," Alex says sourly.

"Oooh, I love it when you talk like a headmistress…" I murmur.

"…I found a secret drawer in a lovely early eighteenth century walnut bureau full of treasure…"

"What really happened?"

"Well that was after I'd examined her chest in the stable and…"

"God, you're a bloody idiot, you can never be serious; that's all you think about – I can never have a serious conversation with you," she huffs and turns for the door, "I'll see if Lizzie's still awake."

I catch sight of my reflection in the window above the worktop. I raise my eyebrows and shrugging my shoulders, "Nobody can say I'm not an honest idiot though."

Mmm she's welcome to me is she? I wonder if I should get that in writing.

Chapter 31

My thoughts return to yesterday morning - yet again. The phone rings. I instinctively consult my watch. Ten-twenty. At least it's not Frank time.
"Oh, bollocks," I still curse the interruption, not only to my thoughts, but the disruption to the work; at least I could daydream *and* assemble a chair; it's not just women who can multitask.

"Oh hi Charles – hope I'm not interrupting anything?"

Oh bollocks!

"Oh hi Frank, no it's all right..." I answer unenthusiastically, wondering whether I'd actually cursed outloud.
"...Is everything okay?"
"Eh? Well er, well er, it's not actually – That's why I thought I'd better give you a call..."
"What's the...."

"The fuckin' shit's hit the fan – The place is crawling with fuckin' Customs and Excise and Tax Inspectors..." he blurts.
"Oh shit," I say flatly, wondering what the repercussions will mean for me, and simultaneously registering Frank's lack of stammer; perhaps he should rant more often...or panic.
"Why are they there, I mean now?" I ask, suspecting I already know the answer. I think I'll play ignorant for a while.
"I reckon Wayne's fuckin' dropped me in it..."
"Why would he do that?" I ask, incredulously.
"I don't know. After all the fuckin' favours I've done him over the years...I really don't know," Frank wails.
"Are you sure it was Wayne?" I ask calmly.
"Yeah I'm bloody sure..." he pauses, as though considering whether or not he can risk incriminating himself further,
"...Wayne's the only one ya know... ya know who knew ya know... all, er..."

"Your little scams?" I prompt.
"Eh? Oh er, yeah," Frank admits.

"Don't you think he could have done it to get even?" I suggest casually.
"Eh? What d'ya mean? I haven't done anything to him …In fact Nisha and I have had some huge, ya know some really big rows over Wayne lately…"

Yeah, I do know what huge means Frank.
"…she reckons he's been taking the piss the last few months, spending all his time on the phone flogging all his fuckin' treasure…"

"He has been taking the piss as you put it, Barry and I have resented the fact that he's been doing sweet F.A. for months, while complaining about not getting what he thought he could get on the sites – *But,* we didn't drop him in it."

Apart from Barry telling Nisha that Wayne had nicked the cash – What did she do with that ammunition?
"Eh? What do you mean, drop him in it?" Frank squeaks, "I haven't dropped him in anything either – Who's dropped him in it? In what?"

"Well, I don't know for definite … but last week there was a guy from The Department for Works and Pensions, spying on Wayne; taking photos of him working…" I laugh at the thought, "he must have had the patience of a wildlife photographer," I joke, then add for Frank's benefit, "…waiting for him to do some work."

"What's the department for works and whatever, want to photograph Wayne for?"
"Works and Pensions," I half laugh, and then continue, "I know, Wayne hardly works and I should think he'd be the last to subscribe to a pension … from what I've been able to find out on the internet, they're responsible for benefit fraud – or rather, investigating it…

"…Did you know Wayne was claiming benefit Frank?" I ask bluntly.
"Eh? Oh, er, I might have, I er can't remember – He might have said something in passing."
"Easy thing to forget," I mumble.
"Eh? What?" Frank squawks.
I ignore this and continue, "Did Nisha know?"
"Eh? Know what?" Frank squawks again.

God if he keeps squawking in my ear I'll go round there and throttle him – talk about care in the community. I take a deep breath, and try again.
"Could Nisha have known Wayne was claiming benefits?" I ask calmly.
"Eh? Oh she might have done; I might have mentioned it to her – Why? … She wouldn't have shopped him." Frank replies, rather unconvincingly, as though considering the possibility.

"What benefits was he claiming?"
"Eh? Oh, er, I'm not sure…I know he claimed unemployment benefit a couple of years ago, when he didn't have any work just after Christmas – I think that was only for a couple of weeks…Surely he would've stopped claiming once work picked up though." Again Frank sounds unconvincing.
"I can't see them mounting a surveillance operation like that for an old claim, especially as small as that – What else was he claiming?"
"Eh? Oh, er, I think he tried to claim some sort of disability allowance…"

"Well Frank, all I know is that when I mentioned the photographer to Sophie, and what he seemed to be doing, she thought it must be the surprise she overheard Nisha organising for Wayne on the phone…"

I could sense Frank computing this at the other end of the line.

"… And, when I told Barry that he'd taken an interest in him as well; trying to find out what his name was he nearly shat himself…I wouldn't be surprised if you don't see Barry again," I say flatly. "I told Barry that I'd told the investigater that he was an old family friend doing some decorating for you as a favour…"
"Eh? What? A favour? He's left the living room in a right fuckin' state!" Frank shrieks.

"Maybe he thought … well maybe he knew Nisha had dropped us all in the shit - to some degree or other – actually he may have run out of time last Friday, because he couldn't get in the house - you and Nisha had left before he arrived, and I was late - collecting materials – I know he was really desperate to get all squared up before he left 'cos he's been called in for his op.; I think it's today," I offer in Barry's defence, but I know he'd done it deliberately.

Fuck Nisha, the stupid cow, had been Barry's exact words, and left everything like a frightened virgin, in the path of a marauding army, as soon as he'd heard about the DWP interest in him.

I'd been more shocked by Barry's language, than by his actions; I'd never heard anything stronger than 'bloomin' heck', from Barry in nearly ten years.

"Oh fuckin' hell," Frank shrieks in my ear. "Oh bloody hell," he groans, "Wayne must have told them everything… When they've been through the books they'll probably come and see you."

Somebody already is, but it doesn't seem right for it to be the DWP. It could only be Simple Slymon trying to get revenge if he knew it was me that set him up; the timing doesn't seem right for it to be him either.

"Thanks for the warning, I'll bake a cake," I say, wondering just how dim a view they take of aiding and abetting tax evasion. I hope it's just a slap on the back of the leg.

"So do you want me to finish the bathroom while you're in prison then," I joke, "Be a nice coming out surprise for you."
"Eh! Don't even joke about it; it could come to that," he squawks. Then as he realises the repercussions, "Christ, It could be months before you can continue with the bathroom – Christ what are we gonna do; we haven't got a bathroom? We'll have to keep sharing with the girls," he groans.
"Oh the poor girls, you'd better buy them some wellies."
"Eh?"

"Well good luck Frank."
"Eh? Oh yeah, thanks, I'll er, I'll er give you a call, er when er,…"

You've got a little less time.
I simply say, "Yeah, bye Frank."
"Yeah, bye Charles - sorry if it's messed up your plans."

I hang-up and stare vacantly at the window above the bench without actually seeing through it, while I contemplate the possible repercussions.

"Shit that's all I need…I know I wanted to spend less time at The Funny Farm, but…" I tail off at the sound of a theatrical cough. I turn to find Rachel standing in the doorway to the workshop, with a large brown leather travelling bag by her feet, and wearing a bemused expression. I grin nervously, wondering how much she had overheard, and more to the point why was she here with an overnight bag?

"I'm sorry," she eventually manages to say, "I could see you were on the phone, so I waited outside until you'd finished," she apologises.
"Well I must admit, this is an unexpected but welcome surprise; I never thought I'd hear from you again so soon," I say, a little too enthusiastically, and resisting the impulse to step forward and greet her with a kiss on the cheek, as if we were old acquaintances. Instead I quickly ask, "Is it my turn to be mother?"
"Coffee?" I ask in response to her puzzled expression.

"Well I don't want to hold you up, but if you're having one, that would be lovely," she says.
"You haven't tasted my coffee."

I experience a brief frisson as I register the same expensive perfume as yesterday, and feel her warm skin brushing my arm as I reach passed her to close the workshop door behind her.
I cough dryly, "Follow me; it's your turn for the tradesman's entrance," I say leading the way out through the back of the workshop.

Before we get to the open backdoor to the house, Ebony who has been lazing in the sun gets up to greet the owner of the unfamiliar voice.
"Brace yourself," I warn Rachel, then turn my attention to the dog, "Ebony, No!" I bark.
"Brace myself? For wh.. Ooh! – I see what you mean, you did mention her um, friendly nature, yesterday," she laughs embarrassingly, and swings the heavy bag protectively from her shoulder as though it were a riot shield, preventing a second goosing.

"I'm sorry about that - you must be the first female customer that's younger than their furniture; she's probably puzzled by the lack of lavender and talcum powder."
Rachel stifles a laugh, her eyes searching mine. I hope she's not wondering if my knowledge of geriatric crotches is empirical.

"Well put the coffee on then..." she instructs as though yesterday wasn't the first time we'd met. She places the large bag carefully on the Victorian pine kitchen table.
"…I expect you're wondering why I'm here so soon?"
"Well, like I said, I hadn't expected to see you quite so soon…not that I'm complaining," I say over my shoulder as I organise the coffee.
"I'd love to commission you for all the projects…."

Relief floods through me; I exhale loudly, “That’s brilliant… Thankyou,” I say trying to restrain my enthusiasm.

“Are you sure…only you seem a bit…”

“Oh yes, I’m really keen I could kiss you; actually it’s a bit of a life-saver a big client is having a few problems at the moment.”

Rachel’s eyebrows disappear theatrically into her hairline while she chews her bottom lip as though considering this option, before smiling, “I try not to mix business with pleasure.”

I feign disappointment, “Shame, I expect the pleasure would be all mine,” I say, returning my attention to the percolator.

“Talking of mixing business with pleasure – that was another reason for coming over,” she says brightly, gesturing toward her travel bag.

“How many more reasons did you have for coming over?” I ask, taking a couple of mugs from the cupboard, “Black, no sugar right?”

“My, you really are observant, it’s not just visible panty lines you notice,” she smirks.

That why you’ve decided to wear a thong again today? I muse, trying not to return the smirk, and wondering how she knew I’d been ogling her rear.

“Actually, I was hoping to see your portfolio as well, and to see what you’ve done to this lovely house; it does have a lovely feel to it…” she says, looking around admiringly.

I resist the double entendre with portfolio, not to mention a lovely feel.

“Could I interest you in The Grand Tour?”

Rachel considers the offer for a second with an expression that suggests she suspects I might have an ulterior motive for getting her upstairs.

“Really, I’d love to, but I don’t want to take up too much of your time today; perhaps you could show me another time if that’s okay.” Then adds rather pointedly,

"Perhaps when your wife's here… I expect she'd love to show off the house; you know what women are like. What did you say her name was?"
"I'm not sure that I did…Alex."

I don't suppose Alex can remember what the place looks like in daylight.

"Did your mum warn you about going upstairs with strange men?"
She gives a short laugh, "Something like that… I was trying to protect your reputation," she adds smiling.
"My reputation? Do I have a reputation?"
"Perhaps reputation's not the right word - I was concerned how you would explain being upstairs with a strange woman, if your wife were to walk in."

Hmm, it would have given my roving rambler some incriminating shots; depending on who he's working for. Surely it can't be Simple Slymon himself?
"Oh, I wouldn't call you strange," I laugh, wondering whether she's fishing, and thinking of several more appropriate descriptions.

"Alex goes out with the larks, and returns with the bats."
Rachel seems to digest this for a couple of seconds. "What did you say she does?"
"Head teacher; but I think she must moonlight as a long-distance lorry driver or something as well," I laugh dryly, adding, "She probably got fed up with asking me to get a proper job, so she got herself a second."
"What do you mean, a proper job? I wish I could do your job."
"That's what everyone says. *Oh how wonderful,* or, *oh that must be really interesting.*"
"Isn't it?"
"Oh I really enjoy the work- most of the time – it's just that the cash flow can be more erratic than a hermit's love life."

Or mine.

Rachel laughs at the image. “Anyway - The main reason I came over was to thank you for finding the secret compartment…”
“All part of the service.”
“Anyway, I wanted to thank you…and to show you what was in the box,” she says enthusiastically, withdrawing it from her capacious bag.

“Oh, and I thought you’d brought your overnight things,” I say disappointedly, quickly adding, “Thank god for large handbags, that must weigh a ton, it felt pretty heavy yesterday – good job you don’t need to carry much make-up,” I observe.
“Thankyou,” she blushes, “I’m stronger than I look,” she smiles.
“Not just a pretty face then.”
“Not just older than I look either,” she smirks at the reference to my poor attempt at guessing her age yesterday.

I move closer as she ceremoniously opens the rough unimposing box, designed to look like the back of the bureau carcase, and watch in awe as she unveils stunning pieces of jewellery in the Art Nouveau and Deco styles; celebrating each piece with inane, and blasphemous expletives, “Wow,” or “Oh, my god,” or simply, “Jeees.”

“What do you think?” she eventually asks, in the hushed tones, usually reserved for museums, galleries and libraries.

The contents, which filled the box to the brim, are now arranged on the kitchen table; with barely space between. My eyes wander over the sea of colour, like butterflies over a blooming flowerbed.
I’m aware of Rachel studying me as she awaits a more considered reaction.
Again, “Wow,” is all I can eventually say.

I turn to Rachel who is grinning from ear to ear, “Wow… Was all this jewellery your grandmothers?” I ask incredulously.
She simply nods.

"It's fantastic," I enthuse, "Really fantastic."

My eyes wander over the individual pieces, trying to recognise the different maker's style from what I'd only ever seen before in reference books.

"This looks like it might be by Rene Lalique," I say excitedly, pointing to a gold and enamel brooch and resisting the temptation to touch…God is this necklace by Liberty? …Oh wow, is that what they call plique-a-jour?" I ask excitedly, picking out an enamel and diamond brooch that could easily have been made by Louis Aucoc.

"…My favourite period," I add, continuing to drool over the table… "They're beautiful… Oh my god, I feel dizzy just looking at them all," I say almost hysterically, "I feel like someone's drugged me."

"I'm so glad you like them…"

"Like them? I love them, they're gorgeous," I interrupt.

"My gran knew I always loved them, I used to go to her room and just admire them; sometimes she would put them on me or let me try them on myself. She started to collect them when she was young, she loved the fact that I loved them for their beauty; I had no idea they were valuable …That's why she wanted me to have them…

"…Gran hid them from my father because he would have just sold them to pay off debts, or to buy flashy cars, or even given them to his various mistresses," Rachel says bitterly.

"Who was it that famously replied in an interview, when asked if he had ever been unfaithful to his beautiful wife, *Why eat out, when I can have prime steak at home?*"

"I don't know, I've never heard that before," Rachel laughs, and then asks, "How do you know my mother was beautiful?"

Reluctantly, I tear my eyes from the Aladdin's cave scene, "Well you had to get your looks from somewhere."

"You're such a charmer," she laughs, slowly shaking her head and blushing.

"What are you going to do with it all? I know it's admirable that you appreciate them for their aesthetics, but you can't possibly just leave them lying around your house, they're worth a fortune; you'd be heartbroken if they got stolen."
"Well I'm not going to put them in a bank vault, never to be appreciated … I can keep them in the bureau, if you show me how to put the box back in - and get it out again," she reasons.

"Trouble is Rachel, the bureau alone is a very desirable piece; there are burglars who specialise in antique furniture… If you really want to keep it in the house, then why don't I make a secret compartment, or several, for that matter, so you don't have all your eggs in one basket, so to speak?"
"Like where?"
"In a fire proof safe concealed under the flagstone floor?" I suggest. "Trouble with that is…" I say turning to face her, "…what if anything were to happen to you?"

We drool over the table in silence, savouring each exquisite piece. I risk a slapped wrist and pick them up in turn to examine and appreciate the workmanship.
"They really are beautiful," I repeat at the risk of becoming boring. A thought occurs to me; call it lateral thinking.

"Call me nosey if you like, but why did you use the past tense regarding your mother's looks? – She can't be very old; she must still be quite stunning."
Rachel drops her eyes as though focusing on the topaz and marcasite pendant in her hand, "You really don't miss much do you? …Okay *Nosey…*" she laughs dryly, and then quickly continues, "…My mother committed suicide – she got fed up with my father's affairs, and my grandparents were always having to bail them out financially," Rachel explains, lifting her eyes to me briefly.

"God… I'm so sorry, I shouldn't have asked," I say turning back to the jewellery, wondering why she didn't just leave him; but I think I could offer a few suggestions.

"Well it was nearly ten years ago – I swore I'd never get involved with a married man…."

"Oh me too," I camp.

"I wouldn't have had you down as the sort to get involved with any sort of man – in that way," she says, raising a quizzical eyebrow.

"Strictly a straight bat," I laugh dryly, hoping she doesn't bat for the other side and assume I'm homophobic.

Rachel laughs, as though remembering a humorous incident, "Nosey might be an appropriate nickname; if the claim that owners are like their dogs is to be believed," she says salaciously.

"I'm afraid I can't take the credit for teaching her that trick, if trick is the right word; it seems to have been instinct…You can call me Nosey but only if I can call you Buster?" I joke.

Rachel opens her mouth as if to protest, then smiling, says, "So long as you don't shorten it," she grins mischievously.

"No chance of that - that would be too crude," I smirk.

"And you're never that are you," Rachel says facetiously, and then breaks into a broad grin.

"Come on we'd better pack this stuff up, before I bang you on the head and run off with it - to a new life somewhere exotic," I say.

"Now there's a thought – We could leave out the banging on the head part though," she grins.

We set about carefully rewrapping each item, as though we are Hatton Garden jewellers. I try and suppress Rachel's last remark, but it puzzles me. She seems to flirt one minute and then put me in my place with references to Alex the next.

"How long has Alex been a Head Mistress?"

Is she a mind reader?

"Head Teacher…" I correct, "…apparently they haven't been called Headmasters or mistress' since the Ice-Age. She's been a Head nearly ten years – Her school's having an Ofsted inspection at the moment; last day today."
" Ooh. So how will you celebrate?" she asks with a distinct lack of enthusiasm.
"Now who's nosey," I tease, "…It depends on the report, anything less than Outstanding, and I may as well emigrate; life won't be worth living."

"Did she know you were coming over to see me yesterday?" she again enquires casually.
"Yes, she knew I was quite excited, from what you'd told me on the phone; about all the projects you had in mind- She knows how fed up I am with a particular client…"
"The one with the DWP and Inland Revenue prob…lems?" Rachel blushes.
"Yeah, that one," I say wondering what else she may have overheard.
"Sorry, I couldn't help overhearing; I should have moved further away when I realised you were on the phone," she apologises.
"Shall we swop nicknames?"
"I've said I'm sorry…" she laughs, adding, "…people would think you're a right bruiser."

Simple Slyman will when our paths cross.

We continue wrapping in silence, taking longer than we should because we can't resist appreciating each piece.

Rachel coughs nervously, "I presume Alex asked how you got on yesterday – or doesn't she take an interest in your work?"
I give a short dry laugh. I thought I was called Nosey
"Yes she did ask how I got on…" I pause to look briefly at Rachel, and then continue wrapping a diamond and enamel brooch, in the form of a couple of leaves.
"And?" Rachel encourages.

"Oh, I just told her what happened – that you're a dead-ringer for Sophie Dahl, and how I admired your lovely chest, and examined your drawers in the stables…"

Rachel almost chokes, stifling a laugh.

"… and how I discovered a secret drawer in your bureau… full of untold riches."

"Just a normal day then?" she laughs.

"I wish… Unfortunately she didn't believe me; she can't decide whether I'm Walter Mitty, or Walter Matthau…or Walt Disney."

"Mmm…Alex obviously trusts you?"

A couple of weeks ago I would have trusted Alex implicitly. I'm tempted to relay Alex's last remark.

"She knows I love her and the kids too much." I decide it's safer to give the impression of being happily married. I don't want Rachel to get scared off; I'm sure she would feel more comfortable about a working relationship if she didn't think I was trying to get into her knickers every time we met. There's no harm in imagining though.

As we pack the last of the items into the box Rachel asks, "Does Alex like to wear jewellery?"

"Oh yeah, but she's got nothing like this," I laugh at the thought, adding, "The cheapest here, if that's the right word, is worth a few thousand... Alex would probably trade me in for any one of these," I laugh.

She gives a sideways look raising her eyebrows, "Now there's a thought, pity slavery's abolished," she smirks, and then asks, "But she does appreciate, nice jewellery?"

"Oh yeah, actually, Art Deco and Nouveau are also her favourite periods when it comes to jewellery and artefacts – our tastes are pretty similar – except clothes; I draw the line at wearing hers," I say dryly.

"Oooh. Why not, don't tell me all her dresses make your bum look big?" she laughs warmly.
"What are you implying?" I say with mock indignation.
"Mmm, nothing…" she murmurs, checking out my glutes.

"I don't know why you're looking at my bum, I bet you've got more eligible blokes queuing from Clifton back through Kingsford and halfway to Hereford."
Rachel fixes me with her amazing eyes, and not for the first time I try to see the edge of a contact lens, but draw the same conclusion, that they are her natural colour.

"Because I witnessed the effect of my father's philandering, I assumed all men – and boys were like my father; I found male relationships difficult. Consequently I had all sorts of cruel nicknames towards the end of school, when most of my classmates were dropping their knickers, like autumn leaves…"
I laugh at the metaphor, "Don't tell me your nickname was Evergreen, or maybe, Holly?"
Rachel laughs dryly, "No, nothing as subtle as that…
"I can't believe I'm telling you this; I've only just met you," she almost shrieks in alarm.

It does seem like too much information.

"Well they probably look back with embarrassment now…especially when they bump into ex-school mates…
"Still, it's a shame that your father's behaviour has given you a jaundiced view of the male species…After all it's only ninety percent of males that are philanderers; that still leaves you ten percent," I joke
Rachel laughs. "And which camp are you in?"
"Oh definitely in the ten percent," I endeavour to sound sincere.

But I could easily be converted, if things don't drastically improve at home.
Rachel exaggerates a disbelieving look.

"Ah, if only I was thirty years younger," I say wistfully.

"I'm not looking for a toy-boy!" she laughs, and has to check herself mid-swipe from giving me a playful slap on the arm as though recognising the significance of her action. She flushes, and averts her gaze.

Rachel ceremoniously closes the lid of the box and locks it. After returning it to her travel bag, she turns to me, "When would you be able to return the chest of drawers; I could do with that doing sooner rather than later? I could let you have this box then – minus contents," she laughs.

"So distrusting, the young generation. Yes I noticed a distinct lack of furniture; you must be struggling for storage." I mentally consider my diary briefly, unnecessarily - thanks to Nisha. Nothing else is desperate; I could do with a rest from chairs.

“"Well, I could start it tomorrow… at great inconvenience," I grin, "'Should be able to get it back to you in a couple of weeks."

"Thanks – I'll make it worth your while," she smirks, "Cheese on toast okay?"

"I usually just have cereals for breakfast."

"I was talking about lunch," she flushes.

"Listen," Rachel commands, her tone suddenly serious, "I want to thank you for helping me find my gran's jewels…"

You can liberate my family jewels - one good turn…

"…I would never have found them without your help - I couldn't believe gran had forgotten, or changed her mind – I thought that my father had found them, but I couldn't very well confront him - not without letting him know of their existence," she says earnestly.

"So, I want to give you a little something," she says, turning to her bag and rummaging inside.

That's funny, I've been dying to give you a little something.

"Here, it's only small," she says, offering me a neatly gift-wrapped package, about six or seven inches long, "Please don't open it now, wait until I've gone… You never know, it might get you some post Ofsted Brownie points," Rachel says, leaning forward and kissing me lightly on the cheek, but then lingering just long enough for the sap to start rising.

"Thank you, it's quite unnecessary," I say awkwardly, "…trouble is, if it's good enough to earn me that amount of Brownie points from Alex, then she'll want to thank you in person."

"That would be nice." Rachel says smiling brightly, "I'd love to meet her."

I look for a hint of sarcasm, but she sounded genuinely keen. I can imagine Alex being extremely jealous of me having such a young and attractive client. The longer Rachel is just a name the more harmonious home life will be.

"Maybe, but then she would see that you actually are a stun' I mean Sophie Dahl look-alike, and wonder what else I'd done to deserve such a reward."

"As if finding these wasn't enough to earn my gratitude?" she enquires, hoisting her enormous travel bag onto her shoulder as though she were a pack mule.

"Here, let me carry that to your car."

"Why thank you, kind sir," Rachel laughs, dipping her shoulder to allow me to remove it.

"Christ, you really are stronger than you look," I groan, shouldering the bag as nonchalantly as I can, and leading the way.

I hadn't noticed the Aston Martin when she'd arrived; she'd parked in front of my van obscuring it from the workshop.

"Well you seem to have it all, don't you – the car, the house - the looks," I say, pointedly appraising her from head to toe, "…and the jewels," I groan, leaning into the boot that she's opened, inviting me to carefully place the bag inside.

"Yes, you'd think I had everything, wouldn't you?" Rachel says cryptically, watching me straighten up, and arch backwards.
"You could do with a good massage," she smiles mischievously.
"You offering?"
She briefly raises her eyebrows and inclines her head suggestively, but says,
"I think you'll find I've rewarded you enough." Then she surprises me by quickly stepping forward and kissing me on the cheek again while squeezing my forearm, then allowing her hand to slide down to mine and again briefly squeezing. "Thanks again for everything," she murmurs.
I cough awkwardly, "I could get to like working with you."

As though she were a knight lowering her visor, she then slides her designer sunglasses down from the top of her head, concealing her sparkling eyes. Opening the car door she glides gracefully behind the wheel; pivoting with knees decorously clamped together. I can't help comparing this to Nisha's undignified knicker flashing while scrabbling in and out of the Range Rover, and waving her legs like an upturned beetle.

*****

Rachel may have described the package as *something small*, but I could tell by the weight that it was definitely not a harmonica; even if the shape resembled one. This doesn't feel cheap; I'm going to have to very careful what I tell Alex. By the time she's confided in all her 'close' friends, every burglar in the county and beyond will be beating a trail to Rachel's door - and mine if I'm right about this, 'small gift'.

I think perhaps I'll wait and see if we've seen the last of Simple Slyman; I'm not going to give her a fuckin' leaving present.

While I weigh the package in my hand, I ponder what Rachel does for a living; she claimed to work from home. Whatever it is it appeared to pay well.

Chapter 32

Bloody hell, I hate gluing up chairs, especially with the old animal glue, I wish I was that Indian goddess what's-a-name the one with all those arms; especially as I'd promised Rachel that I'd start her chest-of-drawers tomorrow.

"Looks like you could do with another pair of hands."

"You're telling me…" I reply glancing over my shoulder at the doorway, registering two men in suits.

Bloody hell not now.

"…Sorry, I didn't hear you pull up - Be with you in a minute, I can't stop once I start gluing-up," I apologise.

"It's okay, I can see that," says the nearer and smaller of the two, as he edges into the workshop.

"You need to be Vishnu, that Indian Goddess, the one with two pairs of arms," says the second, momentarily blocking the light from the doorway as he follows his mate in.

Smart arse.

I glance uncomfortably at the pair of them, in between grabbing sash-cramps and getting them tightened before the hot animal-glue chills and congeals.

Why is there always someone watching when things aren't going smoothly. At least it stops me swearing.

"Here, let me help," offers the second, reaching forward and holding the softening blocks in place to avoid the cramps bruising the chair frame.

"Thanks," I laugh, "Shouldn't it be the other way around?" I ask glancing at the puzzled faces, before grabbing the last cramp.

"Shouldn't I be assisting you with your enquiries?"

"We that obvious?"

"Not normally, but I've been expecting you, or at least someone, since Saturday," I say, again noting the exchange of puzzled expressions, and suddenly wondering whether they're tax inspectors.

"Thanks for your help," I say, switching the glue-pot off. "Shall we start again, I'm DI Jones, and this is my colleague, DCI Smith..."

"Smith and Jones? Is this the point when I ask for I.D?"

They oblige by imitating a couple of TV cops. The slickness of their badge flashing reminding me of the dexterity of Wayne's phone answering. They could easily have been showing me their rail cards, for the amount of time I was allowed to study them.

"Do you mind telling us who you are, and why you've been expecting us since Saturday?"

I'm tempted to ask them what their success rate is, considering the van on the drive has my name on it, but realise that I could be an employee.

"I'm Charles Wilson, the person who notified the Leisure Centre staff about the perve photographing the girls playing hockey on Saturday."

Smith and Jones exchange blank looks yet again.

"I'm afraid we don't know anything about that, we're from Warwick, making enquiries about a mister Gatley – Simon Gatley. Is Alex Wilson your wife, is she at home?" asks Jones.

I laugh dryly, and make a show of looking at the sky, "You're joking it's still daylight – Actually..." I say brightening, "...it's the last day of her Ofsted, so she could be home at a reasonable hour – So it could be commiserations or ..." I rub my hands and do my best Sid James impression, "...celebrations."

Smith and Jones raise their eyes to one another.

"You should be on the telly," says Jones dryly.

"I tried that once."

"Oh, what happened?" he asks.

"I fell down the back."
Again two pairs of raised eyes. "I'm not surprised your wife prefers her school…"

I thought they were going to say, 'prefers other men'.

"We really need to have a word with your wife…"

That makes two, or should that be three of us.

"…Have you any idea what time she'll be home?"
"Your guess is as good as mine – What's it about?"

"Perhaps you could tell us what you know about Mr Gatley?"
"I've a feeling he might be the same bloke – Don't tell me he's got himself arrested over there as well?"
"I think you'd better start at the beginning," sighs Jones, sliding a hand over his stubbly head.
"Fancy a cuppa, it's a long story? If I'd known you were coming I'd have baked a cake."

I wonder what Slyman has been arrested for this time, and what do they already know about our cyber-space correspondence?

*****

"So," Jones breaks what seems an interminable silence, "You're saying that it was you, and not your wife that's been emailing and texting this Slymon, I mean Simon Gatley, because you thought they were having an affair?"
"Yes, but I've since been looking at her messages to him and I don't think they were – Alex's emails to him would suggest more of a professional relationship; not an amorous one – and the phone texts were non-existent; she's too untidy to delete – I came to the conclusion that he was the one with an unhealthy infatuation with Alex."

"I must admit, prior to the emails from the Hotmail account, I'd be inclined to agree with you."

So how come you don't know about his arrest in Kenchester earlier in the day if you've been trawling through all his text messages? I wonder whether I'm supposed to keep asking what Slymon's supposed to have done, like they do on the telly.

"So…" Jones once again breaks another silence, during which they'd both regarded me while impersonating a couple of ruminating cows. "…what do you know about viagra and champagne?"

"Nothing, I don't need the former and I can't afford the latter."

"You seem to request Sly… sorry mister Gatley provide a rather expensive champagne; that would suggest someone who knows their onions."

I stifle a laugh at the choice of metaphore.

"So to speak," mutters Jones, obviously concerned that he's losing control of the situation.

"It's amazing how educational Aunty Google is, and I wanted to hurt his pocket; hence the expensive hotel and theatre tickets as well."

"So why did you recommend the viagra? In fact your email recommended he take two."

I feel like I'm in front of the Headmaster, feeling rather hot and uncomfortable; the childish prank never seems so funny afterwards.

"I just thought it would be funny – the thought of him er, ready and raring to go, so to speak – and Alex doesn't show, it'd be like putting a jockey on a thoroughbred but not letting him take it out of the stable …" I give an embarrassed laugh, "…I er thought it would be funny, ya know the thought of him wanking himself to death."

The last remark causes Smith and Jones to simultaneously shed their air of apathy, and assume the air of a pair of Springer Spaniels.

"…So to speak," I hastily echo Jones, and laugh at the thought of it being taken seriously, before noting their stony-faced scrutiny.

"Shit! He hasn't?"

"He has…" announces Jones flatly, observing my reaction. I'm aware of Smith doing likewise in my peripheral vision.

"…he was found dead on Sunday morning by the hotel chambermaid…

"By as in alongside as opposed to on-top of?"

Smith and Jones both splutter like a pair of horses rattling their lips before regaining their severe composure.

"No, as in the room-service found him when delivering a champagne breakfast… wearing nothing but a a pair of socks and a determined expression, and still gripping a sore, but now deflated member – surrounded by a mountain of tissues, an empty expensive champagne bottle, a packet of viagra - minus two, and a mobile phone showing over a dozen calls to your wife's phone."

"Oooh shit."

Socks? I bet he tucks his shirt in his underpants as well…or did.

"What we haven't worked out yet, is how he managed to get a couple of black-eyes."

I shrug to indicate ignorance, "Perhaps his hand kept slipping off."

Chapter 33

"Blimey Charles, can't ever remember seein' ya in 'ere this time a day before."
"Y'alright Eric? I can't ever remember the last time you managed a sentence without effin," I laugh.
"It's workin' at that effin Grange that makes ya effin swear," he cackles.

I hope Eric isn't going to give one of his porn-star performances; if he spoilt my well-deserved pint I might have another death to explain.
"You're right, I can't remember being in here this early, but after the afternoon I've had I needed a quick pint of Butty, before picking Liz up from the school-bus."

"Mike, 'nother two pints a Butty over 'ere mate."
"There ya go. Don't usually see you in here this early Charles," Mike says, reverentially placing two pints on the towel in front of me, "I hope Eric here isn't getting you into bad habits," he adds plonking two whiskey chasers alongside - doubles at that.
"Hang on, I ain't here for a session, I just came for a quick one before picking Liz up off the late bus.
"That's okay, I'll just have to 'ave one before as well as after then," cackles Eric, palming one of the tumblers in his leathery paw and tipping the contents down his upturned throat.

"Ya gonna put the The Swan on the market then Mike?" Before Mike can turn back from the till with Eric's change, Eric thwacks me on my upper-arm with the back of his bony mitt.
"Eh, you know something I don't Charles?"
"No, I just assumed with all the trade Eric gives you, you must be able to retire by now," I laugh.

"Bring ya pint over 'ere…" says Eric leading the way to the bay window, "…I ain't said nuthin' t' anyone else, only 'bout

losing me licence," he mutters once he's ensconced in the window seat.
"Sorry about that I should have thought - you don't want your shares in Wye Valley Brewery falling through the floor – Actually I was wondering why I didn't seen your car outside – Don't tell me you've actually walked?"
"Don't be daft, the missus drops me off, and then picks me up about eleven."

I instinctively but unnecessarily check my watch, I've got a good idea of the time as I'd reckoned I'd got time for a quick one before Liz gets into Kingsford at half-six.
"Christ, what time does she drop you off then?"
"Oh I'd only just got 'ere before ya, usually she drops me off at six, but she's got bingo in Kenchester, so she dropped me on the way past about half-five …Not for much longer though," he adds after a couple of sips of Butty.
"Is it progressing quicker than they first thought then?"
"Eh?" Eric regards me blankly for a couple of seconds, "Oh no not that," he says, dramatically lowering his voice to a conspiratorial whisper, "No they're closing the bingo hall soon," he cackles at the confusion.

I have to admire the way the pair of them have just carried on with their lives as usual. I wonder whether they actually have any affection for each other.

"I've had an offer for me registration, for more than the car's worth," he grins, giving the impression of an old leather boot with badly drawn teeth below a couple of the eyelets.
"Well that should fund the whiskey and fags, for a few months." I half laugh.
"Yeah," he laughs absently.

"So what was the matter wi' ya day then?" Eric asks, after we have supped, silently considering Eric's short future.

I had hoped The Black Swan was going to be empty, so I could think over my interview with Starsky and Hutch; talk about poker-faced. At least they seemed satisfied with my version of events, and said they wouldn't need to speak to Alex. I suppose they had to be satisfied as they'd apparently seen all the emails that Slyman had sent her, and the ones to and from the Hotmail account I'd set up, as well as the texts and voice messages. Christ nothing's private…Jones informed me that Slyman had a couple of files on his computer containing not only apparently covert pictures of Alex, but also of me…

…I didn't volunteer the incident with the garden gate; I didn't fancy assault being added to my growing list of crimes. Jones concluded that Slyman must have been trying to capture compromising images of me with which to undermine Alex's fidelity.

I had to laugh though. They left with the air of a couple of undertakers. But as soon as they thought they were out of sight in the safety of their car, they collapsed into hysterics; Smith miming a distinctive hand gesture and smacking himself in the face a couple of times. The funniest part was their reaction when they realised I was watching, rather bemused from the front window.

"Oh nothing really…" I lied, "… the whole of last week has been a bit of a pantomime up at the fu… up at Frank's."

"Oh ah, what's been goin' on up there then?" Eric brightens.

"Where do I start…Apparently nearly two-thousand quid's missing from Frank's dressing table drawer, and he's accused Nisha of taking it to give herself a make-over. Course she's denying it so it puts us all in the frame - as they say on the telly. My monies on Wayne, but there's no proof…

"You okay Eric? Only you don't look your usual healthy shade of grey, if you don't mind me saying. In fact I don't think I've ever seen you with such a rosy glow."

Eric's face does indeed look as embarrassed as it's possible for a living corpse to look. He drops his gaze to study his pint.
"It were me," he mumbles.
As though just fully registering what I'd actually said, "I never 'ad that much! In fact, I never really 'ad any of it," he implores, as though I was judge and jury.

"Honest. Wayne 'ad told me 'bout the money in the drawer like, 'e reckoned there were about two-grand. So I thought I'd drop 'im in the shit by moving 'bout arf of it, sos it would look like it's bin nicked and Wayne would probly get the blame. I was really pissed off with 'im doing fuck-all all day and getting paid 'bout three times as much as me… then reckonin' 'e could get twice as much on the bleedin' sites… I thought 'e can fuck off onto a fuckin site then – see 'ow 'e gets on 'avin' ta work for a bleedin' change…"

"I know there's no one else in here Eric, but could you just mind your language," calls a rather alarmed Mike from behind the bar.
"Sorry Mike, I was getting carried away."
"You will be if you keep getting worked up like that. I'm beginning to think that it's Charles who's the bad influence; to think I was worried about him a few minutes ago," he laughs dryly, and we both join in.

"So what made you so sure Wayne would be suspected? After all I was the one who actually spotted it and pointed it out to Wayne."
I take a couple of long draughts from my neglected pint.
"Well I thought you was above suspicion like, you and Nisha bein'…"
"Me and Nisha being what?" I choke.
"Don't get me wrong, I didn't mean ya was… ya know, but ya know what I mean… ya seem ta ya know…"
I raise my eye-brows quizzically.

"Eric have you turned into Frank? Ya know ya know."
"Well ya know what I mean, you and Nisha seem ta get on really well…"
"Well Frank even suspects Nisha…"
"Bloody 'ell, I never meant ta get everyone into trouble – It were on the spur of the moment; I never really 'ad time ta think it through. I'm really sorry."

Eric has returned to his old colour of pastry that's been mauled by grubby hands.

"Where did you move it to? Perhaps you could let Nisha or Frank know, maybe explain what you did, I'm sure they'd be quite understanding given that you weren't the only one pissed off with Wayne."
"Ya reckon?" he responds a little more brightly. "I stuffed it behind that welsh-dresser or whatever it's called in the living-room."
"Really? Well Barry shifted that into the middle of the room to decorate…"

I wonder if he thought that was his golden handshake.

"That reminds me, Wayne's also been followed by some bloke with a camera with a whacking great lens – I've had some pillock following me with a camera as well…"
"Not you as well? They was only supposed ta…"
"Follow Wayne?" I ask solicitously, recognising a dropped bollock when I hear it.
Eric looks sheepishly into his half empty pot for several seconds.
"Yeah," he finally croaks.

I absorb this information for a few seconds.

"I suppose I should thank you – thanks to you I'm having an indefinite holiday from The Funny Farm; in fact we all are."
"The Funny Farm…" echoes Eric, cackling, "…that sounds about right for that place…What d'ya mean everyone? What's 'appened? I were only tryin' t'elp, I thought it were all wrong everyone else

workin' while all Wayne done was spend all day up the bloody field on 'is bloody phone floggin' 'is detectin' finds– 'cept when it were bait time."

"Well the Department of Works and Pensions, who I presume you're responsible for, put the wind up Barry, so he hightailed it home like a rat up a drainpipe – Wayne thought Frank had dropped him in it, so he returned the favour by informing Her Majesty's Missionaries about his scams, so yesterday they were crawling all over Frank's office."

"Fuckin' 'ell, I don't know what t' say, I'm really sorry, I was only tryin' t' elp…"

"Was it supposed to be your leaving present?"

And I don't just mean from The Funny Farm.

"Yeah," he says with a half-hearted nod.

"What puzzles me is Princess Sophie claims that she overheard her mum planning a surprise for Wayne – I wonder if it had anything to do with Wayne's mystery caller?"

And who had the other grand?

Chapter 34

"How long do think mum'll be?"
"About five foot-seven."
"Ha – Ha. Why did I know you were going to say that? What time do you think mum will be home?" Lizzie carefully rephrases.
"No idea, it's anybody's guess at the best of times. I don't know what's involved after an Ofsted. I don't know whether they are debriefed and told the result, or have to wait for a report... We may as well carry on with getting dinner ready – Was there anything particular you wanted her for? Can I help or am I only the taxi-driver?"
"Ha ha – You know you're not just the taxi-driver, you're the best..."
"Taxi-driver?"
"No way, you're not the best taxi driver, you're the cheapest," she laughs... "Actually you're the best daddy in the world," she says dramatically.
"Ha. Ha. We're not The Waltons don't forget, what do you want?"
"Dinner, I'm starving."
"Well you can do some homework while I'm making it."
"I take it all back."

*****

"Shall I lay a place for mum?"
I glance at the clock, "Twenty past seven. Yeah why not, she can't be much longer."
"Maybe five foot eight?" she smirks, "You asked for it."
"I thought your generation was all metricated."
"No, Church of England," she laughs.
"I've obviously got a lot to answer for...

"Hey-up, stand by your beds - don't forget, if it's anything less than Outstanding don't barricade your bedroom door before I've got in as well."

The sounds of keys being scrabbled around the front door are soon followed by the customary slam of door and then thud of boxes being deposited on flagstone. Lizzie and I cling to one another in mock fear.

"What are you two doing?" Alex laughs.

"Well?" we croak nervously.

A broad smile almost slices her face in half, "They've given us Outstanding overall!" she shrieks, punching the air.

Liz and I whoop and simultaneously hug Alex.

"That's brilliant, but I didn't know you wore overalls."

"God, you're a bloody pratt – But I love you," she laughs, before, gently planting a kiss.

"I love it when we're the Waltons – Liz you can go and fetch all that food out of your room now, we won't need to hide up there for the next couple of weeks."

Liz laughs, then gives her mum another big hug saying, "We knew you'd do it mum... Can we eat now I'm starving?"

"Well as we're celebrating, we'd better open a bottle…"

"You seem to find something to celebrate every day," Alex laughs dryly.

"I just have a positive outlook."

"That why you always moan when the bottle's empty?"

"Oh you've noticed as well?"

"I was only joking mum."

I consider the news about Slyman, but decide that it can wait; maybe I'll wait for the jungle drums to spread the news. I'd be surprised if the old Headteacher network isn't already on overdrive informing everyone he's had a heart-attack; even if they don't know the lurid details.

Not for the first time, I wonder how his poor wife and son are. I wonder how much the police told her.

After the table has been cleared and loaded into the dish-washer, and while Alex sorts out the coffee I pop into the office and retrieve Rachel's unopened present from my desk.
"Do you remember me telling you about that new client over at Clifton?"
"Well I remember you making your usual stupid remarks when I asked you about her."
"What stupid remarks?"
"Well you said she was a Sophie Dahl look-a-like, and you found some treasure in a bureau."
"So what was stupid about that?

"Anyway she came over today to thank me for finding her family jewels…"
"Huh, don't tell me, she helped you find yours?"
"Mum, don't be so disgusting."
"Yeah you can be so crude," I mock.
"So how did this Sophie Dahl actually thank you; and I don't want to hear your fantasies?"

"Well her name's Rachel Foxley, and she thought this might fulfil one of yours," I say withdrawing the slim package from my pocket, and placing it on the table-mat in front of her, "I haven't seen it, but I'm assuming it might be from the box I found."
"Is this another one of your elaborate jokes?"
"Just shut up and open it mum," Lizzie blurts, unable to conceal her excitement.
"We sound more like the Waltons every day; it's so heart-warming."

Alex weighs the package in her hand and studies it, "This better not be a joke; a bloody Mars bar or…"

"Mum just open it will you," Lizzie demands, leaving her seat to lean over her mum's shoulder.
Alex tugs both ends of the dark blue ribbon and it slithers undone. The ivory wrapping paper has only the minimal selloptape, allowing Alex to easily expose the old faded green leather jewellery case.
"Oh, that's a lovely old case," Alex purrs, stroking it.
"Come on mum, open it, the suspense is…

"Wow!…Are those real diamonds - and Sapphires?"
Alex and I stare in disbelief for several seconds at what appears to be an Art deco bracelet. The overhead spotlight shining directly onto it, causing the jewels to shimmer. The inside of the lid bears the name of the well-known Bond Street dealer.
"Bloody hell it's from Asprey's – It looks like it's the original box that was made for it."
"Oh my god it's gorgeous," Alex shrieks with excitement.

She tentatively lifts it from its silky nest and drapes it over her wrist, and admires it, "Wow, it really is beautiful…Thankyou," she says, leaning forward to plant a long lingering kiss.
"Well I wish I could take the credit, but like I said, it's a thankyou present from Rachel; it looks like she's put a note," I say nodding at the discarded wrapping-paper, "…Do you want to read it?"
"Can I have a look at the bracelet while you're doing that?"
"Yes, but be careful, don't drop it – and don't even think about asking to borrow it," Alex laughs, handing the glittering jewels to Liz.

I refrain from mentioning the fact that it's probably worth more than I earn in a year…or two. If they knew that it would be all over Facebook before the night was out.

Alex picks up and carefully unfolds the note as though it were an ancient and fragile manuscript. I read over her shoulder.

Dear Charles, this bracelet is a huge thankyou for finding my grandmother's jewellery; I would never have found them without your help and experience. From what you told me I think your wife will like and appreciate this 1920's French platinum line bracelet.

I'm sure you have a pretty good idea of its value and therefore the value of the whole collection, so you will understand the need for discretion; neither of us would welcome unwanted visitors.

I can't wait for you to finish giving my chest some TLC. I could tell by the way you handled it in the stable that it was in good hands. Not to mention the bureau.

Once again, I thank you, and look forward to meeting your wife.

Best Wishes

Rachel x

I nearly choke on the mischievous reference to her chest, and hope Alex is too misty eyed over the bracelet to notice. I should have known better.

"Oh yes, so you're giving her chest some tender loving care are you?"

I wish it was more of, a lick and a promise, as my mother used to say about her brood's cursory bedtime ablutions. I consider offering to give Alex's chest some TLC, but catch Liz's censorious gaze and refrain.

"Well you have to be prepared to give a complete service in this competitive market."

"I bet you wouldn't give any of your coffin-dodgers that service," she laughs, taking the bracelet from Lizzie and fitting it onto her own wrist, operating the delicate clasp as though it were the thousandth time and not the first...Obviously to the manor born.

I watch the pair of them examining and admiring it; cooing like a couple of doves. I notice Alex's face as though for the first time. I can't remember when she last looked this relaxed and stress-free. She could still give Sophie Dahl a run for her money.

Made in the USA
Charleston, SC
21 November 2013